ALL HE WANTS

ALL HE WANTS

C. C. GIBBS

FOREVER

NEW YORK   BOSTON

Copyright © 2013 by Susan Johnson
Excerpt from *All He Needs* copyright © 2013 by Susan Johnson
All rights reserved. In accordance with the U.S. Copyright Act of 1976, the scanning, uploading, and electronic sharing of any part of this book without the permission of the publisher is unlawful piracy and theft of the author's intellectual property. If you would like to use material from the book (other than for review purposes), prior written permission must be obtained by contacting the publisher at permissions@hbgusa.com. Thank you for your support of the author's rights.

Forever
Hachette Book Group
237 Park Avenue
New York, NY 10017

www.HachetteBookGroup.com

Printed in the United States of America

RRD-C

First Edition: July 2013
10 9 8 7 6 5 4 3 2 1

Forever is an imprint of Grand Central Publishing.
The Forever name and logo are trademarks of Hachette Book Group, Inc.

The Hachette Speakers Bureau provides a wide range of authors for speaking events. To find out more, go to www.hachettespeakersbureau.com or call (866) 376-6591.

The publisher is not responsible for websites (or their content) that are not owned by the publisher.

Library of Congress Cataloging-in-Publication Data

Gibbs, C. C.
  All he wants / C.C. Gibbs.
    pages cm
  Summary: "In the vein of Fifty Shades of Grey, the first in an erotic trilogy from bestselling author C.C. Gibbs!"—Provided by publisher
  ISBN 978-1-4555-2832-5 (trade pbk.)—ISBN 978-1-4555-2831-8 (ebook)
  I. Title.
  PS3607.I2254A55 2013
  813'.6—dc23
                                                      2013004651

ALL HE WANTS

ONE

She'd done her research like she always did before an interview. So she knew about him. Thirty-two, Stanford graduate, adventure traveler, and a more or less self-made billionaire who'd stopped counting zeros long ago. Quirky, too, but then so many in the start-up world were. Maybe even a little more than quirky since the death of his wife. But those rumors were confined to obscure blogs in cyberspace and were impossible to confirm.

Not that she cared about the man's private quirks. She was here because his company had recruited her at MIT and working for Knight Enterprises, *the* most innovative venture-capital company in the world, would be a dream come true.

Arriving last night from the East Coast, she'd expected to meet with one of Dominic Knight's lieutenants at corporate headquarters in Santa Cruz. But an early-morning e-mail had sent new instructions. And here she was on a quiet tree-lined residential street in Palo Alto.

The cab driver came to a stop and pointed. "That's it."

She looked out the window, mentally flipped through her Art I memories, and decided it was one of Greene and Greene's rare, turn-of-the-century homes. The structure was surrounded by a beautiful, hundred-year-old Japanese-style landscape specific to the building design. It was an unusual venue for an interview, but no explanation had been given for the site change. Although with the possibility of being offered her dream job, who was she to question the reasons?

She stood for a moment on the sidewalk as the cab drove away, surveying the small redwood building. On her junior year J-term, she'd stayed in a mountain village in Japan, in a temple inn much like this. It was supposed to have been a long weekend but, so enchanted by the quiet isolation, she'd stayed a week. Strange that a street so near a major metropolitan area was this tranquil; she glanced around, unsure for a moment whether she was dreaming, her memories were so intense.

Then a lawnmower powered up somewhere behind her. She shook off her reverie and moved with an easy stride toward the entrance to 630 Indigo Way.

A reception desk had been placed in the center of the foyer and a secretary, who'd been reading, set down her book and looked up. She could have been some teenager taking a day off from school: ponytail, jeans, waist-skimming T-shirt, and flip-flops. The girl bore a startling resemblance to the photos of Dominic Knight. Although, according to his bio, he didn't have children.

Interesting.

The young girl smiled. "You must be Dominic's four o'clock. He's not here yet, but he told me to tell you to go on in." She waved in the general direction of a hallway and went back to her book.

Dominic, not Mr. Knight. Even more interesting. As if it mattered, she reminded herself and gently cleared her throat to get the girl's attention. "Actually, I have an appointment with Max Roche. I'm Katherine Hart."

Kate stood there for a moment, an awkward pause stretching between them while the girl apparently read to the end of a sentence before glancing up. "I think it's Dominic you're seeing. Lemme check." Shoving a pencil in the book to hold her page, she clicked a computer mouse, the screen on a sleek monitor came to life, and she briefly scanned it. "Nope, not Max. Dominic." She pointed again. "Down the hall, last door. I'm supposed to ask you if you want coffee." Then she smiled and went back to her reading.

You didn't have to be a mind reader to know coffee wasn't an option, so Kate followed the suggested route. The hallway was lit by clerestory windows, the lustrous light illuminating a photo gallery of sailing vessels; some large, some less so, all glorious action shots of sleek racing yachts, sails aloft, running with the wind. She stopped for a moment and leaned in close to a photo of two racing yachts. Both were full-rigged, one boat heeling so hard to starboard that waves nearly skimmed its rails. And dangling inches above the water, one hand on the rail, the other reeling in a line, drenched with sea spray, was the CEO of Knight Enterprises, younger, thoroughly wet, a wide, exultant smile on his handsome face.

"That was a World Cup race off New Zealand. Sorry to keep you waiting. It was unavoidable."

The deep, rich voice was at ear level. Jerking upright, she swung around, gasped, breathed, *Holy shit*, then flushed. Dominic Knight in all his dark, sensual beauty was standing there, up close and personal, his quick raking glance so casually assessing she should take offense, not feel a shocking rush of pleasure. She almost gasped at the jolt, but caught herself in time because salivating in front of Dominic Knight would be super embarrassing *and* useless. He did models, aristocratic babes, high-end call girls. Researching his personal life had been like reading *Entertainment Weekly*.

Oh God, he still hadn't moved. Was he testing her sense of personal space? Was this some kind of psychological power thing? If it was, he was winning because his tall, powerful body, sleek in a navy pinstripe bespoke suit, was *way* too close, *way* too personal. Her heart was pounding, she was having trouble focusing her thoughts, the speech synapses from her brain to her mouth were misfiring, and unless she got herself under control, she was going to blow this interview. *Breathe in, breathe out.* Now say something normal. "The...weather's...great...out...here." Breathless and sputtering. Shit.

His faint smile widened.

Arrogant bastard. But having finally regained her wits, she didn't voice her thoughts.

His gaze amused, as if breathless women were the norm in his life, he blandly said, "I agree. Did you have an uneventful flight?"

Before she could answer, his cell phone rang.

He glanced at the display, frowned, and grunted, "Go on in. I have to take this."

Flustered by her response to a man who was even hotter in person than in his photos, feeling more like a thirteen-year-old Justin Bieber fan than a magna cum laude graduate of MIT, she lectured her uninvited inner adolescent as she walked toward his office. *Seriously. What was that all about? Haven't you seen a handsome man before? Get a grip. Better yet, go away.*

The hand-carved door at the end of the hall was slightly ajar; Dominic Knight conducted business casually. How reassuring. She wasn't fond of rules and protocol. Pushing the door open, she entered a low-ceilinged room with such spectacular views of the gardens that all thoughts of her embarrassing meeting with Knight Enterprises' CEO vanished.

Dropping her canvas messenger bag on a chair, she walked to the nearest window wall and surveyed the garden that reminded her of some of the royal gardens she'd seen in Japan: immaculately raked gravel, swirled in traditional wave patterns; large, rainbow-colored koi visible in the clear, limpid water of a nearby pond; artfully arranged boulders; ancient, perfectly pruned yews and pines. A small, arched bridge in brilliant red served as a picturesque focal point in the distance. The garden was a museum-quality work of art, carefully nurtured and maintained. Dominic Knight had an eye for beauty.

"I'll personally nail you to the wall if you screw me on this! You don't say no to me! Nobody says no to me! Now do your fucking job!"

She flinched at the audible fury in Dominic Knight's voice. Each word was implacable, taut with rage, the tone unexpectedly dredging up long-suppressed memories. Jesus, she'd not thought of any of that in years. Her gut tightened like it had as a child and she thought, *This job isn't going to work out. Explosive people are bad karma for me.*

She had plenty of other companies wooing her. She could pick and choose. Retrieving her messenger bag from the chair, she was almost to the door when he walked in.

"Forgive me again. I seem to be repeatedly apologizing before we've even met." But he was still distracted. He'd come to a stop, run a hand through his dark hair, his gaze unfocused.

"That's all right." She slung her bag over her shoulder. "This isn't going to work out anyway."

He looked startled. Then a second later he looked down, his gaze narrowed, fixed on her. "Nonsense. Your assignments are abroad. I won't be there. It should work out just fine." At least he didn't pretend to be confused. He seemed to know why she had reservations about taking this job. Or maybe he just didn't care. "I'm told you're the best and that's what I need."

"Our needs are incompatible." She kept her voice calm with effort, as he towered over her, his sexual charisma practically sending off heat waves, his commanding air intimidating—both seriously affecting her pulse rate.

"Tell me what you need—er"—he paused—"I'm not sure I've been told your name."

"It doesn't matter."

He looked at her as if she'd sprouted another head, then sighed. "Look, could we start over? I'm Dominic Knight. You're"—his dark brows rose in query, a touch of humor in his gaze.

"This isn't funny, Mr. Knight."

"I could call someone and get your name."

"To what purpose, pray tell?" she said, staring him in the eye with her best hard-as-nails look.

He smiled. "Really, *pray tell*? Channeling Jane Austen?" His sigh this time was barely audible. "As to what purpose," he repeated, softly mocking, "why not to our mutual satisfaction?" His voice went down a notch. "Now, tell me your name."

His deep, velvety tone melted through her body, turning on everything that could be turned on, *again*. Jeez, who would have thought using your vibrator before an interview was a requirement?

"I'm assuming you have a name," he prompted, a small smile stirring the corners of his mouth.

Asshole. Was he toying with her? Or did a mouth-watering CEO with a killer body figure every woman would roll over for him if he smiled? Her mouth firmed. "If you must know, my name is Katherine Hart. Spelled H,A,R,T."

His gaze was cool, as was his voice. "Perfect. Thank you."

"Miss Hart to you." She glanced at the door.

He noticed, ignored it. "As you wish, Miss Hart." He loosened his honey colored tie, undid his collar button. "It's been a long day." He flexed his broad shoulders with a Zen-like grace, exhaled slowly, visibly decompressed. "I've had to listen to too many long-winded people in too many boring meetings. Have you ever noticed that those who do the least complain the most and those who know the least talk the most?" He held her gaze, almost smiled. "Now what can I do to change your mind?"

How could that sudden Zen-like calm be so hot? Or maybe tall, dark, and handsome was rocking her world because she was an adrenaline junky—a prime requirement in her line of work—and just looking at all that magnificent maleness was juicing her. "Nothing really," she quickly said, needing to get away, and it wasn't just bad karma. Men didn't shake her world like this. Or at least they never had. "I just changed my mind." She took a step to her right to go around him.

He moved left and checked her progress. "Change it back."

He was like a solid wall of machismo blocking her way. She tried to keep her voice from trembling. "I can't...Sorry."

He recognized the small flutter in her voice, debated responding, decided against it. "Let's keep this simple," he brusquely said. "I need you in Amsterdam. So don't tell me no."

Jesus, that was either intimidating or damn intimidating. "Please move," she croaked.

"In a second," he said with a flicker of a smile, feeling that this difficult young lady may have finally gotten the message. "Tell me what it's going to take to get you on board. Name your price if that's the stumbling block. Max says you're beyond gifted even for a high flyer, and I need you in Amsterdam. This is important."

"To you."

"Yes. That's the point. You can't say you don't want to work for Knight Enterprises. Everyone does."

"Not everyone."

That small startle reflex again. He really wasn't used to dissent.

"Look, I'm sorry if I said something to offend you." Although there wasn't a hint of apology in his tone. In fact, his annoyance was plain. He ran a hand quickly over his face, as though to wipe away the betraying emotion. "The ball's in your court, Miss Hart."

"What if I said I want to leave?"

The pause was so lengthy, a small moment of panic washed over her before she reminded herself it was the twenty-first century.

A winter chill colored the blue of his eyes. "Do I frighten you?"

"No." She wouldn't give him the satisfaction.

He tipped his head slightly and smiled in the most disarmingly ruthless way. "Good. Then if you'll sit down"—he indicated a chair—"we can discuss my problem, your skill set, and how we might cooperate."

Deciding the chances of her fighting her way out of this office were slight to nil, she sat. "You really don't take no for an answer, do you?"

"I'm afraid not." He dropped into a large black leather chair behind his desk. "It's not unique to a man in my position."

A salient argument, but not one she chose to value. "You're putting me in an awkward position, forcing this issue."

"On the contrary, you've put me in an awkward position. I'm offering you an excellent job. Max mentioned some of our issues in his e-mails. The dark market is making inroads in some of our outlier firms. It has to be stopped. Obviously you were intrigued or you wouldn't be here. Why not accept?"

"Personality clash. I heard you in the hallway."

"Perhaps you don't understand the company's organizational structure," he said with exquisite restraint. "I doubt we'll meet again."

"I disagree. As I understand it, Knight Enterprises' organizational structure is one of authoritarian leadership. You're hands on. You demand absolute compliance from subordinates."

His mouth tightened. "You've done your homework."

"I always do. And I have several other job offers, Mr. Knight. With the worldwide level of corruption, forensic accounting is in great demand." She smiled, sure of her prima donna status in her field at least. "Yours isn't the only company losing money to the dark market."

Her cheeky smile lit up her eyes and he looked at her for the first time as if she were more than just an obstacle in his path. She didn't know how to dress, but then the clothes of the young IT set weren't couture or colorful. Neutral tones went with their left brain functions. But her hair was a riot of red curls and her eyes were a potent green. Strange word. Bright green, he corrected himself. And beneath the drab army green jacket and slacks, he could see hints of a lithe, supple body that went well with her wide-eyed innocent beauty.

His lashes drifted downward an infinitesimal distance.

Hmmm. He hadn't considered that before, too intent on talking her around to his point of view. Not an easy task with Miss Hart. She wasn't docile. Or accommodating.

A provocative thought.

But he was a businessman first; there was time enough for other things once Miss Hart had done her job. Since he'd lost Julia, he was indifferent to women for anything other than sex, and that was available anywhere. Miss Hart's sexual function was immaterial.

What *was* material lay in Bucharest and, according to Max, Miss Hart was the answer to their problem. "Perhaps we could come to a compromise," he said, determined as always to prevail. "You could join us as a contractor. After you finish this Amsterdam job, you can walk. You're a December graduate. Most of the major firms won't start recruiting for another few weeks. You'd still be in the game."

"I'd have to turn down my current offers."

"I'd be happy to make some calls and get some brief deferments for you. I know everyone in this business."

Nobody says no to me, indeed. How much did she want to piss off one of the most powerful men in the world? "You're persistent." She gave him a polite smile.

"So I've been told. Do you have family?" He preferred employees with a casual attachment to family. They were more likely to work the long hours demanded of them.

"You can't ask that," she flatly said.

His smile was mocking. "Are you going to sue me?"

"I won't have to if I'm not working for you."

His jaw clenched. "You can be a real bitch. Sue me for that too if you want. Now, could we stop playing games? I won't ask you any personal questions, other than will you accept my job offer?" Leaning back in his chair, he unbuttoned his suit coat, shot his cuffs, waited for her reply.

She couldn't help but notice his hard flat stomach under his white custom shirt. And the fact that he didn't wear cuff links. She liked that. She'd always viewed cuff links as pretentious. *Only an observation*, the little voice inside her head pointed out innocently. *No one's trying to persuade you of anything.*

His gaze narrowed. "What?"

"Nothing." Then Kate pointed. "You don't wear cuff links. Is that allowed when you're a CEO?"

A shrug, a bland, blue stare. "Everything's allowed when you're me. My company is privately held."

Her spine stiffened. As she opened her mouth to speak, he stopped her with a lifted finger, picked up his phone, and hit a button. "I'm calling Max. He's scheduled to fly out at seven. He'll fill you in on all the details en route. As will Werner in our Amsterdam office. Now, in the nicest possible way, I'd like to invite you to work for us. Just the one assignment in Amsterdam. Yes or no, Miss Hart? I'm done fucking around. Just a minute, Max." He held her gaze.

"You're a control freak," she muttered.

"Is that a yes?"

Silence.

"Two weeks, a month, that's it. Money's no object. Come now, say yes." He smiled, a beautiful, charming, practiced smile.

Why did it seem that his smile was offering her the entire world and all its pleasures? *Clearly, a lunatic thought.*

"Very well," he softly said into the lengthening silence, his blue gaze grave. "Give me two weeks of your time. I won't ask for more."

A pause, a last small grimace, a barely discernible nod.

His instant smile could have melted the entire polar ice cap in under a minute. "Welcome aboard, Miss Hart. I look forward to working with you." He grinned. "At a distance, of course."

He was way too smooth and way too beautiful and way

too familiar with getting his way. But, deep down, irra-
tionally, she wanted the job more than anything. And she
knew better than to fall under his spell. Screwing the CEO
was never wise.

As if, anyway.

Besides, the word *bondage* had come up on one of the
murkier blog sites in Europe. Whether it was true or not, a
man that rich and powerful?

Anything was possible.

TWO

Dominic walked her out to the foyer, where Max was waiting. He introduced them, made a few gracious remarks about Miss Hart joining the firm as a contractor, said, "Thank you, Max, thank you, Miss Hart, good journey," and walked away. The fact that Max was there waiting for her would have pissed her off if she'd been given the time to properly register her resentment before being whisked off in a limo by Dominic Knight's vice president, aide-de-camp, and all-around chargé d'affaires.

That Max was ex-MI6 was immediately apparent from the top of his blond brush cut to the tips of his desert-booted toes. His British upper-class accent was both calming and intimidating. "May I say how pleased we are to have you with Knight Enterprises," he said as he settled into the seat beside her. "Nick was intent on hiring you."

"I got that impression," she said drily.

He laughed. "You'll get used to it. Everyone does or they're gone."

"That was pretty clear too."

Max merely shrugged. "I don't think he even realizes. He sees it as efficiency."

She stared him down for a second. "Don't say, 'Get used to it,' or I'll strangle you."

He laughed. "I wouldn't dare."

She sniffed. "I don't need this job, you know."

"I do know. We have a serious issue in Amsterdam, Miss Hart, so take it from me personally, we're grateful for your help. Your reputation precedes you. No one quite matches your skill set in cyber forensics." He gave her an avuncular smile. "We've taken the liberty of collecting your luggage from your hotel. It's already at the airfield. I have some papers for you to sign on the plane. Nothing out of the ordinary," he said at the sudden skepticism in her gaze. "Just the usual forms for our contractors. Pam, my personal assistant, will run you through the process. Then I'll give you an idea of what you're up against. We've been trying to sort out this mess for a while, without luck. You're the talent we need. As for Dominic, rest easy, Miss Hart, you'll find it simple enough to work for him. He's interested in results and I'm sure you won't have any problem delivering. You'll have carte blanche on this project. We're trying to avoid a PR disaster. This plant is supposed to be state of the art in terms of employee health and safety. It's a pilot project for green technology and community involvement in an area of the Balkans that has high unemployment. And now morale is low, production is down, the parts aren't up to standard, workers are beginning to complain. It's only a matter of time until stories about the working conditions hit the news media. So"—he flipped his hand in her direction—"you're going to make Dominic happy and solve the mess."

Making Dominic happy was probably every woman's dream. "Someone's skimming off the top, I presume," she said instead.

"A considerable amount. At the expense of not just the employees' working conditions, but the reputation of our firm."

"Hmmm."

He smiled. "Sound like fun?"

She nodded. "I like to solve puzzles, especially complicated ones like this."

"Good. You'll have security. I don't know if Dominic told you. There's a level of criminal involvement whenever large sums of money are at stake."

Wide-eyed, she whispered, "Security?"

"It's just a precaution. Amsterdam is a long way from Bucharest. Don't worry."

"Oh crap."

Max grinned. "Charge him more."

She gave him a sideways look. "Will that bullet-proof me?"

"I'll bullet-proof you. Promise."

His quiet certainty reassured her. And Amsterdam *was* a long way from Bucharest. "Thanks. I'm a small-town girl. Bodyguards aren't in my repertoire."

"You won't even notice."

Late that night, actually in the wee hours of the morning, when everyone was sleeping in their bedrooms on the company 747, a knock on the door woke Max.

"Phone call, sir, in the lounge," one of the stewards announced.

Slipping into his robe, Max entered the lounge, took a seat in a leather easy chair, and picked up the call.

"Sorry to wake you," Dominic said.

"What the hell time is it back there?"

"I'm not sure. I can't see a clock. The reason I called is to tell you that I'll be in Amsterdam Saturday."

"What for?" The Amsterdam office was small, just a satellite, of little consequence to the company's bottom line.

"I'm on my way to Hong Kong. Thought I'd stop by."

It was triple the distance going through Europe. "She'll do fine," Max said. "She'll do better if you don't fuck with her head."

"I've been telling myself that."

"And you're coming anyway. She won't like it."

"You surprise me, Max. After all these years, I'd hoped you'd understand me better."

"She's not the starry-eyed type."

"I noticed."

"You may not get what you want."

"Of course I will. I always do."

"She might quit. Then our problem here doesn't get solved."

"I'll see that she doesn't quit. Now go back to sleep. I'll see you in four days."

Max swore as he set down the phone. Dominic could be a cold bastard. Or just reverting to type after his wife's death. Dominic's CFO, Roscoe Kern, had explained everything when Max had first come on board Knight Enterprises. While Dominic had become a friend in the five years they'd worked together, he was an emotionally detached person, largely indifferent to everything but his business. He might have tempered his need for control during his marriage, but it was back in full force now. In fact, his obsessive need to control was even worse than before, according to Roscoe, who'd been with Dominic from the beginning of his ascent to being one of the wealthiest men in the world.

Heaving himself out of the chair, Max grimaced.

He'd be earning his bloody pay in Amsterdam.

It was cool with a light rain when the plane landed in Amsterdam, the wind off the ocean bracing. Not that January weather was an issue inside a luxurious Mercedes. Nor was it noticeable in the short walk between the car and the entrance to a palatial town house in the old city center.

They were greeted by a discreetly dressed majordomo: simple black suit, sleek hair, welcoming smile. Kate was to be installed in an apartment in the eighteenth-century structure that had been restored to its original magnificence by Knight Enterprises seven years ago.

After Max conducted her on a swift tour of the richly decorated main floor reception rooms used for company functions, he escorted her to an apartment on the fourth floor and left her with a breezy, "I'll send someone for you tomorrow. Take the rest of the day off."

The door had no more than shut on him when a woman's voice said in accented English, "Would you like something to eat?"

Kate spun around.

A large, heavyset woman with short, fair hair, neatly dressed in a white blouse, blue skirt, and sensible shoes, stood ten feet away. "I'm the housekeeper, Mrs. Van Kessel. Lunch is ready if you'd like."

A housekeeper? Crap. Having a stranger around was

going to be weird. But since she was always hungry, Kate smiled politely. "Thank you, lunch would be nice."

She was shown into an exuberantly rococo room, with pink marble pilasters, gilded everything, and floor-to-ceiling windows overlooking the canal. A small table, set for one, had been placed next to one of the windows. A vase of coral-colored tulips provided a splash of color on the sparkling white linen cloth, and Kate had no more than seated herself on a rosewood chair upholstered in pale yellow satin than Mrs. Van Kessel appeared with the first course.

Over lunch, Kate found herself silently exclaiming, *Wow*, at the fine china, the heavy, ornate silver, the superb food that looked like a picture in a magazine, the unobtrusive service, the choice of wines. Was she in a dream or what?

She had repeated that question exactly to her grandmother on the phone after she'd locked herself in her bedroom.

"Nana, you should see my bedroom here," Kate said with breathless wonder. "It looks like something out of that *Marie Antoinette* movie I love."

"Now, sweetheart, you've worked hard to get where you are," her grandmother unflappably said. "Enjoy it."

Nothing ever fazed Nana. "Okay, I will. But you're going to get daily reports on this little bit of heaven I've fallen into." She'd already texted her grandmother from San Francisco, apprising her of her departure for Amsterdam.

"Send me pictures. I'll show them at my bridge club."

"And piss off Jan Vogel, who's always bragging about her grandson the doctor."

"Don't you know it," Nana said with a smile in her voice. "Now tell me about this new job of yours."

Kate explained the task before her, careful not to divulge anything that might blow back on Knight Enterprises. If PR was an issue, the less said the better. But when her grandmother asked about her new employer, she offered an even more edited version. It seemed everyone in the world, including those in the bush of northern Minnesota, knew of Dominic Knight.

"He seems nice." The Minnesota term encompassed a wide range of possibilities, not all positive depending on the tone—hers at the moment scrupulously neutral for her grandmother. "Smart, of course, articulate, you know I didn't really see him for very long. If I see him again, I'll let you know. How's Leon?" Leon was the Great Dane Nana had rescued from the pound. "Is your new fence working out better than the old one?" Leon had leaped that one in less than five seconds.

"You bet. Jerry from Lampert's says it'll still be standing when only the cockroaches are left. Leon checked it out and decided it wasn't worth jumping. Make sure you eat well, now. I know how hard you work. Such long hours, dear. I don't know what the world's coming to."

"You should talk. After school you were always coaching something." Her grandmother was the grade school principal in their small town and also coached girls' basketball and softball.

"That was different. I was out and about, moving around. You're hunched over a computer hours at a time. Really, dear, promise me you'll get some exercise."

"Yes, Nana." *Right after I put a nail through my forehead.* "You know, I might go out for a walk now. See the town." *Might* was a polite word.

"Remember, take pictures on your cell. The Anne Frank House, the Rijksmuseum, the Van Gogh Museum, all the canals of course. What have I forgotten?"

"I'll send you a book, Nana. The pictures will be better." And it would save her a lot of walking.

"No, I need them on my cell phone. Jan will have a fit when I show them to her."

Kate silently groaned. There was no way out of it. The bridge club had been in existence for fifty years and every week, Nana and Jan Vogel had been at it—in that small-town, passive-aggressive butter-wouldn't-melt-in-your-mouth smiley way. "Okay, Nana, but in a day or so. I've got jet lag." A white lie wasn't really a lie. "I'll call you tomorrow."

The next morning, Kate was introduced to everyone at Knight Enterprises' Amsterdam branch. The office was housed in another chic town house, this one with a view of the sea. Her office on the top floor had even a more glorious view of the water, not that she'd be gazing out the windows much. She was itching to get started.

Werner, the office manager, explained what they'd tried, where they'd failed, what they were hoping she could accomplish. He was a tall, young man, very blond and Dutch looking, nerdy, bright, and clearly frustrated by their lack of progress. "If you need anything," he said, standing in the doorway on his way out, "let me know. Anything at all."

She smiled, pointed at her espresso and water bottle.

"I'm good for now, thanks." Then she booted up her top-of-the-line Alienware laptop, feeling like she always did at the beginning of a search. Exhilarated. Focused. A predator on the make.

She took two breaks the first day, one for lunch, one for supper, then worked till midnight. On her way home, she thought she might have seen her bodyguard, but wasn't sure. Max was right.

She was back at the office by seven, hot on the trail of a bank in Latvia where the money was being sent. Today she was hoping to find the final destination of the money and the names on the accounts. Probably the Ukraine, she guessed, where there was no extradition treaty with the United States. But she was side-tracked into the Israeli e-mail service Safe-mail, where any sender's IP address was blocked, and after six relentless hours of knocking on server doors and bumping into impenetrable security systems, she finally found an entry point. She was on her way after that, the familiar feeling of invincibility infusing her senses, adrenaline rushing to her brain, her keystrokes speeding up until her fingers were flying over the keys, independent of coherent thought. This was the magic, the guilty thrill that motivated every hacker and every person who took risks, the vibe, the passion, the rapture that science had documented as the so-called happiness hormone.

As she worked, time and place evaporated, the world narrowed to a keyboard and monitor screen, to colors and numbers, her pulse rate running high like an athlete in a marathon. She had the key, her target was in her sights, she was closing in.

And then, finally.

Yes! Yes, yes, *yes*! There it was!

Singapore. A bank name. A bank account number. A customer name.

She fell back in her chair and shut her eyes, exhausted, drained, chilled to the bone. Noticing her surroundings for the first time in hours, she glanced at the clock. Three o'clock. She glanced out the window. Dark.

She ran a printout of the information, cautious about e-mailing it to Werner when the criminal enterprise in Bucharest, including the plant manager, had access to the company servers. She left a cryptic text message on Werner's phone, describing the location of the printout—inside the Italian dictionary on her office shelf. Then she found her coat, walked the few blocks home, and found the door to the town house opening as she climbed up the small flight of stairs.

"A late night, Miss Hart," a man she didn't know politely said. "Would you like some refreshments sent up?"

She shook her head, tried to smile, found herself unequal to the task, and managed to whisper, "No thank you."

Three minutes later, fully clothed, she crashed on the puffed-white-satin-covered Marie Antoinette bed and slept through the entire next day.

THREE

A musky scent insinuated itself into her consciousness first. Moments later a deep familiar voice breached the remote margins of her brain—an echo of the voice in her passion-filled dream—and she softly moaned.

Dominic recognized the sound and smiled. His new employee, lying facedown on the bed in her gray nylon quilted coat, wasn't all about double entry accounting. A pleasant thought, perhaps even the reason he'd taken the long way to Hong Kong. But a dangerous one as well. And at the moment, he hadn't decided what to do about her yet.

He'd have to decide by morning. The Gulfstream was scheduled for takeoff at ten. Which was just as well. In his experience, deadlines were a spur to action.

Like now.

He was here to rouse Miss Hart. Unable to wake her, Mrs. Van Kessel had asked for his help. Bending down, he repeated, "Wake up, Miss Hart. Wake up."

A petulant groan.

He lightly touched her flushed cheek with the pad of his index finger. "People are waiting for you, Miss Hart."

Touch, smell, and sound sluggishly converged, brewed and blended, intensifying her lush dream that had her lying naked on Dominic Knight's desktop in Palo Alto. Her legs were wrapped around his waist, his soft voice urging her toward orgasm, her whispered response a feverish, racing litany of yeses. His blue-eyed gaze was heated, close, hers half-shut to absorb the spectacular, high-pressure sensations as his hips moved in a slow thrust and withdrawal, touching her deeply there and there and oh, oh, oh...

She whimpered as her orgasm began peaking—the irrepressibly feverish sound suddenly shocking her awake with a jolt. *Ohmygod!* With a startled squeal, she wrenched herself up from the torrid depths of her dream. *Someone was here! Where was she?* Scrambling to roll over, she became ensnared in the folds of her coat and frantically thrashed about until strong arms lifted her and gently deposited her on her back. "There, that's better," said the voice from her dream.

She flushed with embarrassment, keeping her eyes tightly closed in hopes that this cringe-inducing moment would pass. That Dominic Knight wouldn't notice her hair and everything else was a mess, that she'd probably drooled all over the pillow. Mostly, she just prayed that he'd leave.

"Coward," he said, a note of amusement in his voice. "Open your eyes."

Seriously, were prayers ever answered? She opened her eyes by slow degrees, the brilliant green catching the light at the last. "What are you doing here?"

He noticed she didn't say, *Get out,* and was strangely pleased—a heresy he chose to ignore. "I came up because Mrs. Van Kessel wasn't able to wake you. She was afraid you were comatose. You've slept for almost seventeen hours, Miss Hart." She looked like a rosy-cheeked child just come awake, her hair a tumble of curls, her eyes still half-lidded. "How do you feel?"

A loaded question considering her recent dream; any number of answers streaked through her brain. None of them appropriate. So she opted for simplicity. "Fine, good. Did you just get into town?"

A casual question, as if they were friends. Apparently Miss Hart *could* be docile after all. "I arrived a few hours ago."

She flicked a finger in his direction. "A power suit. I like it." He looked good in gray, but then he looked good in anything.

"I'll relay your compliment to my tailor," he said with a lazy smile. "By the way, congratulations. I'm impressed with your work, Miss Hart."

"I'm pleased you're impressed, Mr. Knight." With her brain fully functioning now, she knew better than to be tempted by that killer smile. "I'll be sure to add your comment to my résumé."

"I'd be happy to write you a letter of recommendation." He played the game better than she. Ten years and forty companies better.

"Thank you. Now if you'll excuse me, I should get out of these clothes from yesterday."

A small silence fell.

He didn't say what he was thinking because he was helping her undress in his mind.

Nor did she—her thoughts less decisive but gratuitously sexual nonetheless, with her recent dream still vivid in her mind and the living, breathing Mr. Beautiful from that dream quietly staring at her...

"One of the women from the office brought over a few things for you. They're in the wardrobe." At her raised brows, he added, "You're the guest of honor at a dinner downstairs." He glanced at the bedside clock. "In one hour."

Her eyes opened wide. "God no! I couldn't!"

"It's informal. Wear your own clothes if you prefer."

She scowled. "Is there something wrong with my clothes?"

"Of course not. Greta just thought you might like something new. She's in our advertising department here and—"

"She thought I looked dowdy?"

"No, not at all." Her temper was intriguing. He rarely experienced opposition in his life, and it seemed Miss Hart scarcely uttered a compliant word—unless she was half asleep. "Greta just thought you might enjoy wearing some of her original designs," he explained. "She has her own small boutique that's often written up in fashion magazines here. She works a flexible schedule for us and, as a favor to me, I asked her to pick out a few of them for you."

I'll bet she works a flexible schedule—in your bed. "I don't want them," she crisply said. This blatant offer of designer clothes came with an unmistakable quid pro quo: he gave her an expensive gift, she gave him sex. Jeez. Talk about a supercasual transaction. Like buying a slice of pizza when you're hungry. Greta might not mind being a piece of pizza but she did.

"Certainly. I apologize. It was meant as a benign gesture." He stepped away from the bed. "Why don't we say an hour and a half? That should give you time. Werner and a few others on the staff want to sing your praises."

She was still sputtering her dissent as he walked out and shut the door behind him. She'd never before considered the term *puppet master* as applicable to anyone she knew. No more. The man was a total control freak. A crying shame he was so damned desirable though. It made that quid pro quo thing a little more dicey in terms of personal autonomy versus personal pleasure. Left her libido quibbling with her better judgment. Thank God she was almost out of here. *Before it was too late, her little niggling voice pointed out.* No, she shot back, *because* her normal, everyday life didn't have men like Domenic Knight trying to tell her what to do.

Speaking of normal, she really needed a bath. Seventeen hours of sweating in her coat was grossing her out. Oh, crap. She reeked to high heaven and he'd smelled her. Way to go, girl, she muttered.

Rolling off the bed, she was unbuttoning her coat when the sound of running bath water reached her ears. It was seriously freaky having someone know exactly when to draw your bath. Like having spies in the woodwork.

But minutes later, when she was lounging in a bubble bath in a tub large enough for a water polo team, with soothing music playing from hidden speakers, towels warming on a heated towel rack, and her choice of pricey shampoos and handmade soaps within reach, freaky morphed into a big-time plus. As did the gorgeous white silk robe hanging on a hook by the tub awaiting her pampered body.

Knight Enterprises certainly couldn't be faulted in its attentions to its employees, she decided. What she chose to ignore was the fact that no other employee was housed in this mansion.

While Kate bathed, Dominic showered in his third-floor apartment. He was currently in a damned fine mood, for several reasons: Miss Hart's swift action on the Bucharest issue for one. In addition to the PR problem, he'd been losing a helluva lot of money, and while he didn't need it, he *was* in business to make a profit. And she'd definitely been having a passionate dream from the tone of her breathy little yeses, which made the reason he was here more intriguing by the minute.

A half hour later, he was about to leave his apartment when he noticed his French cuffs. Whether it was a sixth sense or instinct, he appreciated the mental prompt. Returning to his dressing room, he stripped off his suit coat and tie, unclasped his cuff links, took off his shirt, and replaced it with one that had button cuffs. Retying his tie, then slipping into his suit coat, he gave a quick glance in the mirror as if his appearance mattered tonight. He softly exhaled. Relax.

Tonight was no different from any other night.

It was just a company dinner. How many of those did he attend each year? Too many, he grumbled. But contrary to logic and perhaps sanity, he found himself seeking out Greta as the office staff began to arrive.

"Would you do me a favor?" he asked, and without waiting for an answer, detailed what he needed.

As drinks were being served downstairs, Kate was contemplating an array of designer clothes in her wardrobe. That they were in her size was either creepy or brilliant—she hadn't quite decided. But she'd been standing there for quite a while. Indecisive. Wracked with doubt. Caught between the devil and the deep blue sea in terms of ethical conduct.

Because an absolutely over-the-top little black cocktail dress was whispering to her baser instincts.

She really should resist its lure.

Or should she?

She pursed her lips.

Now that her assignment was finished—in record time, she proudly reflected—she could *walk*. That had been Dominic Knight's offer. She was on her own again, independent, with no ties, no employer, no responsibilities. So, technically, she was free to sleep with the hotter than hot, studly CEO of Knight Enterprises. Put on the dress, take up his offer, and enjoy...

Or not. It was still an ill-advised move for her. That sort of gossip could affect her future employment. But *if* she did give into her fuck-me temptation, she'd do it on her own terms. Not because Dominic Knight casually bought her body with a wardrobe that probably cost more than most people made in a year—or ten.

His arrogance in assuming she was for sale drove her crazy. Obviously she wasn't, but maybe she would be if she indulged in one of his guilty pleasure gift dresses? She touched the rich, silky black fabric, admired the elegant lines of the dress, ran her finger down the V-neck that was discreet, yet tastefully sexy. Damn—so what would it be— self-respect, boundaries or no boundaries, the pursuit of extraordinary possibilities, or...

Another moment of indecision, another sigh. Oh, what the hell, wearing the dress didn't necessarily mean she'd sleep with him. She had all evening to decide.

Then she noticed the shoes in the bottom of the wardrobe. Ohmygod. Black, fuck-me shoes with sparkly stuff on the toes.

Jeez, could any woman turn down shoes like that?

But as she lifted the dress from the wardrobe, her complacency gave way to a hissed expletive. Along with a few more pithy observations on self-willed men. A magnificent string of pearls was looped around the pink satin hanger, and no way they came from Walmart.

Was expensive jewelry a deal breaker?

If she accepted this entire outrageously pricey *gift*, would she regret it later? Or could she consider this outfit a bonus? Would that make her less of a...She sighed. Even with a massive rationalization, there was no way around the fact that she'd be one of Dominic Knight's rentable-for-an-evening females.

She really needed her roommate, Meg, here to talk her through this sexual dilemma. She quickly calculated the time back in Montana, where Meg was interning for a semester on a dinosaur dig. Noon. Could she answer her phone at work?

First ring. "How's the dig going?" she politely asked, because she didn't know where Meg was and she had sex questions to ask.

"It's winter here. I'm just doing cataloging. I told you."

Kate knew about as much about dinosaurs as Meg knew about accounting. "Sorry, I forgot. Are you alone?"

"Sorta. Are you? I was hoping you'd be in bed with a handsome billionaire by now." Kate had texted the basics about her job before she left. Billionaires in bed had not been mentioned. But Meg had an active sex life and an even more active imagination.

"Jeez, if you're not alone, don't use my name."

"Just a new friend of mine. Don't worry." Meg giggled, whispered, "Food *first*."

"Are you in *bed* with someone?"

"Yeah, but I can talk. Pepperoni okay? And a Coke," she said off the phone. "There, I'm back on. He's ordering us lunch."

"He? You don't know his name?"

"I met him last night in the cutest bar. All Westerny, although everything is out here. I think his name is—I'm not sure. We haven't exchanged that much information yet. But otherwise, he's real full disclosure, if you know what I mean. Really just great. He's a student I think, and I know he rides horses. So how's Amsterdam? And I'm just teasing about the billionaire. Have you met anyone interesting otherwise? One of these days you're going to actually meet a man you want to jump. And not someone like Andrew or Michael, who are half-ass friends you just did to be nice."

"Can I talk now?" Kate was bursting to reveal her news and she was afraid Meg would go off on a tangent like she often did about Kate's failure to understand that sex was purely entertainment.

"Sorry. Just a minute. What's your name?" Meg quietly asked, then said in a normal tone, "Kate meet Luke. Luke says hi. And he doesn't care about our conversation because he's—Hey, hey... not yet—I'm on the phone."

"Never mind," Kate said because she wasn't going to discuss her sex problem with some guy listening in. "I'll catch you later. Have—"

"Oh, ohhh, God..."

The phone went dead and Kate's question was more or less answered.

Go for it.

She picked up the dress again.

As if she needed further encouragement, the door suddenly opened and a tall, slender, platinum-blond beauty walked in. "Let me help you with that," she said matter-of-factly. "I'm Greta. The dress is structured," she added, taking it from Kate and slipping it off the hanger. "You don't need a bra. Or panties. It's fully lined." Then she stood there waiting for Kate to take off her robe.

After a small pause, during which Greta's brows lifted faintly, Kate timidly smiled and discarded her robe. The cool blonde slipped the dress over her head, zipped up the back, smoothed the silk over Kate's hips, said nice things about Kate's breasts, and spoke so casually about the evening ahead, those waiting downstairs, and her design firm that Kate stopped being embarrassed.

"Dominic's wife helped me start my business," she explained. "Here, let me clasp those pearls for you. Julia and I became great friends." She slid the pearls around Kate's neck. "So Dominic likes seeing my clothes out in the world."

There was no sane reason to be so pleased at the revelation that Dominic Knight's wife had been a friend of Greta's. It didn't necessarily negate the possibility that he and Greta had become more than friends later. But she couldn't help it. It made her happy.

When it shouldn't matter.

When living in la-la land was for fantasy fans.

When she was going home tomorrow.

"I'll put your hair up."

Jerked back to reality, Kate tried to stop her; she didn't like pins in her hair. But she might as well have saved her breath. Had everyone at Knight Enterprises drunk the same don't-fuck-with-me Kool-Aid, she wondered as Greta managed to tame her curls into a semblance of sophistication.

Au contraire, she discovered, once she joined the gathering downstairs.

As she was greeted by a round of applause, handed a glass of champagne, and congratulated by each of the staff in turn, she couldn't help but notice the degree of deference Dominic Knight commanded. The Sun King had nothing on Knight Enterprises' CEO when it came to basking in the adulatory glow of his subjects.

Not that he couldn't be charming. Dominic Knight could have bottled his charm and sold it for millions. As she chatted with everyone, she covertly watched him work the room; a smile here, a handclasp there, a compliment that elicited a pleased reaction, a brief conversation before he politely moved on. The man was smooth.

She waited for him to reach her. While not terribly experienced, she wasn't a naive virgin; she recognized his leisurely, indirect advance. As Knight Enterprises' CEO approached, the colleague to whom she was speaking melted away, like some courtier making way for the king.

"The dress suits you," he said as he stopped before her. "Thank you for wearing it." His cool gaze slowly surveyed her from head to foot, then traveled back again to her smile. "I like those shoes too."

"They do make a statement."

"Indeed."

How does he do it? A single coolly uttered word like that and she felt like throwing herself at him and promising him anything. Luckily she was sober. "I tried to resist the clothes, but as you see." She gave a little flick of her wrist up her body.

"I'm glad you didn't. I thought you'd do Greta's clothes justice." He smiled. "You certainly do. I'm sure she's pleased."

That cool voice again, different this time—distant. He was impossible to read. Bemused at times, amused other times, and now this sudden remoteness. "You must give her a lot of business."

A puzzled look. "Why would I?"

"So you don't usually—"

"I see where you're going. No, I don't." He started to say something, changed his mind, smiled instead. "At the risk of pissing you off, I just thought you'd look better in that than your army drab slacks."

Embarrassment flushed her cheeks. "So I'm a special welfare case."

"Let's just say you're special all around."

With that, a different kind of heat flooded her senses. She looked up what seemed a great distance even in her heels and met what was definitely not a family values smile. "Are you hitting on me?"

"I'm giving you a compliment."

But his voice was soft, his gaze on the wicked side of sexy, and she felt a sudden quiver where she was most susceptible after months of no sex.

A carillon sound of church bells suddenly flowed through the room. Dominic's jaw clenched, a rare flashback gripped his senses. He and Julia had gone to services at the church around the corner from time to time, especially in the evening like this. As a Native American, she had an intrinsic spirituality that he lacked—along with any number of other good qualities that had eluded him.

Kate saw the muscles flicker across his jaw, watched him visibly gather himself, hoped it wasn't something she'd said or done. She didn't know where to look, what to say, a dozen inane comments raced through her mind—all unusable unless she wanted to sound like some ditsy airhead. She was busy checking out the fake diamonds on the toes of her shoes when he took her hand.

"Come on." He was scowling faintly. "I'll have dinner served."

She should have said something tactful and gracious, or smiled the right way to lighten the mood. Instead, she botched everything by turning too fast and stumbling on her high spiky heels.

She muffled a squeal and for a fraction of a second worried about where to grab Dominic Knight, CEO, to keep from falling. Then her boobs hit the unyielding wall of muscled chest and she clumsily snatched two handfuls of suit coat, while he smoothly caught her upper arms and steadied her against the long, hard length of his body. A *POW!!!* word balloon exploded in Kate's head on impact, every sexually specific nerve from head to toe ramped up for business, and she inadvertently moaned.

He inhaled sharply, his libido responding to the provocative sound, to the full-body press, to her nipples stiffening against his chest, her thigh jammed against his dick, the scent of her punching his pheromones. For a brief moment he seriously thought about dragging her upstairs and banging her until neither one of them could move. The moment quickly passed. He rarely acted on impulse.

Carefully easing her away from his body, he smiled faintly as a collective exhalation wafted around the room and the rapt moment of breathless expectation gave way to the hum of conversation. His voice was mild when he spoke, his smile touched with levity. "I hope we didn't bruise anything."

Yours or mine, she almost said, the imprint of his sizable dick stamped on her thigh. But she could do casual as well as he could with everyone still watching them in veiled glances. "No, not at all. My apologies. Stiletto heels aren't my usual footwear."

He glanced down, then up, his smile more personal this time. "They look good on you. But you'd better hold on to my arm, Miss Hart. It's a long way to the dining room. We wouldn't want you to fall."

Actually, it was *way* too long for her skittish senses because his lean hip brushed against her body with each step, his large hand covering hers as she clung to his arm—"Just to be safe," he'd said—was sending tingles to places she'd rather not receive them considering the company and venue. And his dark, magnetic beauty this close was doing disastrous things to her breathing. *You absolutely will not pant, damn it. Do not fall to pieces under the eyes of twenty Knight Enterprises employees.*

Oh God, he'd come to a stop in the doorway to the dining room and was looking at her, apparently waiting for an answer. "Daydreaming," she said. "Sorry."

"I was just saying you could see the oldest merchant house in Amsterdam out that window"—he nodded—"if you'd like. We're helping with the restoration funding."

"I would," she said, to be polite.

He looked amused. "No you wouldn't."

She grimaced. "Was I that obvious?"

"Don't worry about it. I like to restore buildings." He smiled. "Most people aren't any more fascinated with the idea than you are. Let's find our chairs."

The room was enormous, embellished in rococo abandon with every costly architectural flourish. Gilded panels in dove gray, mirrored alcoves to display fine sculpture and reflect the light, Versailles parquet flooring favored by palace architects throughout Europe, a ceiling mural of mythological subjects amusing themselves by playing at love—a subject much admired in the amoral culture of the eighteenth century.

Now, pristinely restored, the reception room used for royal levees in an earlier time served a more prosaic purpose. The table set for twenty was dwarfed by the space. A row of wineglasses sparkled at each place setting, splendid bouquets of spring flowers and white tulips marched down the center of the table, and the china and silver gleamed under the light of glittering crystal chandeliers.

Dominic led her to a chair, then sat to her left at the head of the table. As the others found their places with the help of handwritten name cards slipped into gilded frames, he chatted casually with her about the usual trivialities: the weather, the traffic, the more interesting sights in Amsterdam. Inconsequential small talk that matched his bland expression. He had no intention of seducing Miss Hart under twenty rapt gazes.

Especially since the toasts began the moment everyone was seated, a certain unrestrained foolishness was predictable and he didn't want it directed at him. One toast followed another, each as effusive, or more effusive, much of the praise directed at Kate. Each time she blushed, took a sip of her champagne, and blushed some more. Really, this custom was not for the shy or retiring, she decided. Although, Nana would have loved it. She drank her vodka straight.

But hours later, with the level of inebriation high and the meal coming to an end, someone sang out, "Time to initiate Miss Hart!"

The chant was taken up by everyone except Dominic in a playful, rousing chorus.

At Kate's questioning glance, Dominic leaned close so he could be heard above the clamor. "Feel free to say no. It's a silly ritual. And as you can see, no one mentions it until they're roaring drunk."

"Mentions what?"

"A tour of Amsterdam's red light district." He lifted one brow. "It can be a shock."

"Oh, I see," she said on a choked breath. "I think I'm too sober to—er—enjoy or ah—be comfortable—"

"I agree." He stood to gain everyone's attention. "Miss Hart is going to politely decline." Then he sat down.

"No, no, no, no!" Wild dissent in English and Dutch. Loud, then very loud.

Greta smiled at Kate across the table. "It's an experience

you might find interesting," she said, raising her voice above the crowd. "We'll protect you," she added with a wink.

Kate turned red.

Dominic smiled at Kate. "Ignore them. We're the only sober ones."

She'd wondered at his moderate drinking at dinner. He'd not indulged much. "I'm afraid I'm slightly out of my depth when it comes to red light districts. That's what comes from being raised in a small town, although I'm sure there are small-town people who are sophisticated—sorry, I'm babbling on. Anyway, everyone's been quite wonderful tonight." She smiled. "Thank you."

"It's for me to thank you for your expertise." He looked up with a grimace as someone began banging the table and chanting to leave. "Lord, they're bloody loud," he said with a sigh.

But their drunken colleagues wouldn't be deterred no matter how many times Kate politely refused or Dominic scowled. They wouldn't take no for an answer. Kate was reminded of college, when her friends would pile into her apartment, three sheets to the wind, and drag her off to the pub when she was trying to study. She rarely won those battles either.

Dominic could have put an end to it. Why he didn't was unclear. Max asked him as much as they followed the crowd in its exuberant passage down Amsterdam's red light district.

Dominic flashed him a wry glance. "If I knew I'd tell you."

"This is pretty hardcore for her."

"We don't know that."

"I do. I vetted her. Small-town girl, studied hard, didn't play much, made it to the big time because she was smart."

"What do you mean 'didn't play much'?"

"Does it matter?"

"I find it does."

"Jesus, Nick, are you regressing?"

"Depends what you mean by regressing."

"I mean, arsehole, are you looking for a semi-virgin?"

Dominic laughed. "There's no such thing."

"She's damn close, that's all I'm saying."

"Are you her defender?"

"You didn't answer my question."

"I don't have to." Max was protecting Miss Hart from the big bad wolf; it surprised him. "Look," Dominic said a moment later. "I'm not in the market for either a unicorn or a semi-virgin because they don't exist. She knows what she's doing."

"I'm not so sure. But she's really a nice kid, Nick. Don't fuck with her."

"Even if she says yes?"

"I'd like to say even then, but I suppose she has a mind of her own. She's just not in your league, Nick. So cut her some slack."

While the state of Kate's love life was being discussed, Kate and Greta were walking arm in arm down a brightly lit lane, busy with foot traffic. A tour guide ahead of them was leading a group of Asian couples through the area, keeping up a steady discourse for her curious audience. Groups of college kids with backpacks were everywhere, sitting on the curbs, strolling down the street, buying weed from hustlers.

Some sailors were arguing in front of what looked to be a brothel, ordinary tourists of every age and stripe wandered up and down the warren of small alleys leading off the main thoroughfare. Three- and four-story buildings lined the narrow streets and in large, neon-lit windows, women of every age, size, and description were on display. Some were clothed, others were nude, and no matter where they were from, Sweden to Angola to Holland, their services were all for sale.

Kate found the open display of women as merchandise visually shocking at first. But no one seemed to notice and she reminded herself that cultural mores differed from country to country. She understood as well that the sex trade was government-supervised, lucrative, and regulated by the police. Several policemen had been stationed at the entrance to the area as affirmation of their authority. All Kate could think was that she was a long, long way from home.

And clearly too sober.

Not that her sobriety was of any concern to her companions, who suddenly veered to the right and surged in a wave toward a bright red door in a building that bore neither a lighted window, a sign, nor a number.

Max quickly moved ahead to outdistance the young man in the lead as he shoved open the red door. Walking up to a well-dressed man stationed behind a desk in the large foyer, Max spoke to him briefly. The concierge/receptionist/bouncer looked more like a stockbroker than a guard, Kate thought as she and Greta entered the building. The black marble foyer looked more like an Italian palazzo than a nightclub, and the huge vase of flowers perfuming the air must have cost a small fortune.

As Max finished speaking, the elegantly dressed man glanced over everyone's head and nodded at Dominic, who stood in the back. Then the man waved them through black leather-padded doors that were thrown open by two uniformed employees. And they entered a room with subdued lighting, posh decor, affluent patrons, and spectacularly naked women.

A beautiful woman, nude except for a navel ring, beckoned an equally nude coat check girl to take their coats. Then she escorted them to two large black velvet banquettes set against a mirrored wall. As everyone found seats, the hostess raised a manicured finger and signaled another equally dazzling, unclad woman.

After ordering several bottles of Cristal, Max exchanged a few words with their server. As the woman left, he sat back and gave a brief nod to Dominic.

Greta, Kate, Max, Dominic, Werner, and his wife sat in one banquette, the other held the noisier half of the dinner party. Dominic and Max were the last to take their seats, and whether by chance or design, Dominic sat beside Kate.

It was an intimate venue with an unobtrusive bar to one side, six banquettes lining the walls, and four marble-topped tables fronting a small stage. The clientele was well-dressed and cosmopolitan, the conversation hushed. Even the rowdy members of the Knight party had instinctively quieted.

A small stage, framed in gilded pilasters and rich azure silk draperies, reminded Kate of Marie Antoinette's little theater at Versailles. Sofia Coppola's movie clearly had left its mark on her. The stage set represented a richly furnished Victorian sitting room: a table set for tea, a crimson brocade chaise, a spinet and a leather padded bench, sumptuous carpets, and two lace-curtained windows stage right, draped in royal blue silk.

The black velvet banquette was soft as down, the atmosphere restful, the noise level muffled. If the servers weren't nude and if a man and woman in period costume hadn't walked onto the stage just then, Kate would have thought she was drinking champagne in someone's living room.

But as the little play began to unfold, she realized she was about to witness an erotic Victorian tableau.

The couple began having tea, the man, as host, explaining to the young woman that his sister had sent her regrets at the last minute. "I sent a message to your home, but too late I'm afraid."

"Oh, dear." The pretty blonde, dressed in white ruffled muslin, made a little O with her mouth. "I really shouldn't stay."

"Come, Liza, we've been friends for years. Let me pour you a sip of sherry. It's from Papa's cellar."

"I shouldn't." She flushed a rosy pink.

And so it went, the couple drinking more sherry than tea, the young lady becoming more comfortable and talkative, the man, full of compliments and small courtesies. The acting was really quite good, enough so that Kate was drawn into the scene despite her reservations. She wasn't alone in her interest. The audience was captivated.

"I have to marry Lord Richmond, you know," the actress

suddenly blurted out, her eyes welling up. "And I hate him. He's old and ugly."

"And cruel."

She clapped her hands to her cheeks. "Oh, no, don't say that! You can't mean it?"

"I wish it weren't true," he grimly said. "But it is. Everyone knows."

Her tears began to flow. "So I'm to be...sold off...for Richmond's fortune," she sobbed. "Oh, Ned, what am I going to do?" she wailed. "Help me!"

A theatrical silence fell. You could have heard a pin drop.

His expression solemn, he reached across the table and gave her his handkerchief. "You know what he's paying for."

She looked down. "I know."

"If you weren't a virgin..."

"He wouldn't want me." She looked up, her eyes bright with hope. "How clever you are, Ned!" Then her face fell. "But the contracts have all been signed. And Mama's already counting her money."

"Then I'm not sure what he'll do."

She jumped from her chair and began pacing the room, her agitation plain. "The world is cruel when I can be sold off like so much chattel. It's not fair!" She suddenly spun around, her nostrils flaring. "I won't go docilely like a lamb to the slaughter. I won't! You hear!" She brooded for a moment, then hotly declared, "Fie on Richmond and his grubby money! I shall give *you* my maidenhead, darling Ned."

The young man looked startled. He wasn't the callous seducer generally portrayed in Victorian tales. "You have to be sure," he quietly said.

"Yes, yes, yes, yes! And darling," she gaily declared, "I've been wanting to kiss you forever!"

He still looked grave. "This is more than kisses."

She waltzed over to him, patently joyful, and held out her hands. "I know that. This will be my sweet revenge on them all."

Rising from his chair, the handsome young man took her hands in his, raised them to his mouth, brushed her fingers with his lips, and the sweetest of seductions commenced: both actors young and beautiful, their slow undressing—he helping her and she him—a languid, tantalizing production accomplished with deft showmanship. Once they were nude, he caressed her shapely form in all the ways meant to arouse, kissing her mouth, her neck, her showy breasts, her virgin cleft. When she was flushed all warm and pink, Ned eased her back onto the chaise, slid between her legs, and with an expertise admired at least by the females in the audience, brought little Liza to a rapturous orgasm.

It was clear that the actors had been cast in their roles for reasons over and above their acting skills. Ned was all magnificent male, handsome, virile, and in terms of performance art, his erection was truly star quality. For her part, Lady Liza was stunning, voluptuous as Venus, and clearly of a passionate nature.

After the initial consummation, Ned was lying on the chaise, cradling Liza in his arms when in lieu of the usual pillow talk, she casually said, "Abby tells me you have whips."

He glanced down. "Does she now?"

Liza lifted her gaze to him and smiled. "She says she likes what you do with them."

"You're not Abby Childers."

Liza suddenly sat up, a little pout on her lips. "I *might* like it."

"No."

"That's not very nice." A spoiled young lady acting spoiled.

"Come, darling," he said with a sigh. "Abby Childers likes to be tortured."

A wide-eyed look. "Tortured?"

"There, you see, you don't want that."

She nibbled on her bottom lip for a moment. "You could just whip me a *little*."

He softly sighed. "If I do, is this conversation over?"

"Yes, yes, of course."

"Very well." He pointed. "In that drawer over there. Bring me one of the whips."

She leaped up and a moment later was back. "Will this one do?" She held out a red leather quirt from which hung three knotted strands of black braided silk.

"That one's fine. It won't leave marks."

She half-turned and glanced back at the bureau.

"Don't even think about it," he muttered, "or I'll send you home. It's not a competition." Reaching out, he took the whip from her, rose from the chaise, and helped her lean over the chaise so she was facedown over the curved back. Then he tied her hands to the wooden legs, raising her pink bottom into a perfect target.

"I intend to make this unpleasant." He lifted his arm. "I don't want you to ask me to do this again. You're not Abby Childers." He brought the whip down with a crack.

A gasp went up in the crowd as the lash struck the lady's plump flesh.

Another when she cried out. Then another and another as the young man wielded his whip and the lady shrieked and moaned. Ignoring her cries, he smacked her soft rump, the insides of her thighs, the pink pouty lips of her sex— those blows in particular eliciting little frenzied screams that soon morphed into frantic whimpers.

Was she really in pain? Kate wondered. Would he stop if she was?

Kate forced herself not to openly gasp, but it was impossible to stem her feverish reaction to the lady's punishment. She was wildly aroused, desire coiling deep in her core, spreading outward in hard, forceful waves, spiking through her senses, making her edgy, making her skin tingle.

Her gaze on the actor's huge, upthrust erection, she imagined it deep inside her, could almost feel it slide in and out, wanted it, needed it. *Or perhaps someone else's*, the little voice inside her head whispered as Dominic Knight's recognizable scent filled her nostrils. His physical presence beside her was like an irresistible force, like a hot brand on her consciousness. Primal male, oppressive, blatantly arousing.

Lord, she'd had too much champagne if she was fantasying about having sex with him even with people around. Stop! Stop! Stop!

But he was only inches away, his hard, muscled thigh warm against hers, his brute strength even more potent in the darkness, and she was so crazily turned on, she was trembling inside. Clenching her thighs against the raw ache throbbing deep inside, she wished it hadn't been so long since she'd had sex, frantically prayed that the play would soon be over, tried not to look at the lewd scene onstage.

But the pretty blonde tied to the chaise was panting loudly now, the man moving into position behind her and, sexually mesmerized, Kate waited, breath held, for the stark moment of penetration. Seconds later, Ned swung his hips forward, his enormous erection disappeared from sight, and a widespread moan rose from the audience.

Since the couple was positioned so everyone could see his huge dick sliding in and out—over and over and over again—the ensuing performance provoked a low, rhythmic murmur of commentary and approval. As if in response, the man's erection lengthened, swelled to gigantic proportions, and the actress's cries intensified—whether in pleasure or pain was uncertain.

Kate was squirming now. *She should have worn panties, she was ruining her dress*, she thought in one of those housekeeping moments quite separate from the tumult in her brain. Could she escape?

Not unless Dominic Knight moved.

Fuck, she was trapped. *No, no, no, wrong word. Don't even think it.*

Seated beside Kate, his arm on the top of the banquette, Dominic had been watching her, not the play; he'd seen the tableau before. So he was aware of her increasing discomfort. Aware as well of her volatile passions. Miss Hart was a hot little thing. Impatient, too. His nostrils flared slightly at the thought.

He wanted to take her to one of the private rooms

and fuck her till morning, his libido loudly seconding the motion. Her job was finished; why not? Although he'd have to decide quickly. She was at a point where his intervention was required or she was going to come right here in front of everyone.

Sliding out of the banquette, he stood and held out his hand. "I'm taking Miss Hart home," he said to no one in particular. "It's getting late."

Desperate to escape, Kate grabbed his hand as if he were her life line in a storm.

He ignored her feverish gasp as their fingers touched, ignored his surging dick, pulled her to her feet, and quietly said, "Let's get your coat." He deliberately caught her by her shoulder as he guided her from the room, needing to touch her.

She tried to pull away.

He tightened his grip. "It's dark," he said, his breath warm against her ear. "We don't want you to stumble."

He was too close, his body heat like flame to her senses, his voice in her ear melting through her like original sin. Oh God, could she withstand the relentless tremors driving her to orgasm? She had to, had to, *had to*! But all she could think of was the scene onstage, all she wanted was Dominic Knight doing to her what the actor had been doing to the actress. She whimpered, a tiny, suffocated sound.

A room, he thought, shoving the padded leather door open.

Definitely.

But the moment they entered the foyer, she broke away and ran.

He smiled. There was something to be said for a game of pursuit. She wouldn't go far without her coat and even an assertive woman like Miss Hart might think twice before traveling alone in the reveling crowds outside.

Quickly collecting her coat, he dipped his head to the concierge as he passed his desk; the man spoke in rapid Dutch and Dominic grinned. Then a servant opened the door for him, and a moment later, he was out on the street.

She was standing to the right of the door, shivering, warily eyeing a crowd of young men coming her way. He stepped between the raucous group and her and held out her coat. "You're cold," he said.

"I wish," she whispered, turning to slide her arms into the sleeves.

"I'm sorry," he said, pulling her coat up on her shoulders, turning her back to face him. "That's a lot to take in. Or rather too much to take in." He softly exhaled. "Sorry, poor choice of words. Would you like me to call my car?"

She drew in a shuddering breath, desire still raw, all-consuming, unsated and beating at her brain. "No, no... thank you. Does the office...staff do this...often?" she stammered, trying to appear calm. Like him.

"I'm not sure. I could ask Max."

"No—don't." She noticed the young men gave him wide berth and wondered if he'd said something she hadn't heard. "It really...doesn't...matter."

Such trembling innocence was the ultimate temptation. "We're only a few blocks from the house. You don't mind walking then?"

"No, no...I'd prefer walking. It was hot in there."

He suppressed a smile. "You'll cool off now. It's cold tonight."

He hadn't worn a coat, but seemed immune to the temperature and to her carnal agitation. He carried most of the conversation on the way back, but then he spent his life being sociable to people he wouldn't bring home to dinner. Not that Miss Hart fell into that category. She might look real fine across the table from him on occasion.

On occasion being the operative phrase.

But by the time they entered the town house, he'd sorted out all his uncertainties. Miss Hart was too innocent to exploit.

When they reached her apartment, he opened the door for her, then stepped back. "Thanks for your help with the Bucharest problem. Max will have you flown home tomorrow. I enjoyed your company this evening." He turned to go.

"Wait." A small frantic explosion of sound.

He turned back, his brows faintly raised.

"I know I shouldn't ask," she said in a breathy rush. "You probably have women hitting on you all the time, but I'd kick myself later if I left without kissing—"

He moved in a blur, inhaled the word *you* as his mouth captured hers, felt a sudden, unnatural exhilaration, an impatience he hadn't felt in years. He heard her small whimper as his tongue skimmed hers, her eagerness exciting him. He shoved her coat down her arms with a sweep of his hands, had her bottom in his grip before her coat hit the floor, and, hauling her hard against his body, kissed her with a barely suppressed hunger.

She kissed him back with a rough urgency that surprised him.

It wasn't a semi-virgin's kiss.

But then Miss Hart had a no-holds-barred personality he was guessing might go with no-holds-barred sex. "Thank you," he whispered, moving one hand upward to rest in the small of her back. "I was trying to behave."

"Don't."

Her voice was a shimmering hum on his lips; he could even taste her smile. "Then we both thank you," he murmured, his erection surging higher at such welcome news. "Can you feel that?" He moved his hips in a leisurely back-and-forth motion, offering graphic evidence of his capacity to please.

"Clear down to my toes," she said with a small heated sigh, his massive erection thick and stiff against her belly. "And everywhere in between," she purred, curling her arms around his neck, melting against him, every muscle below her waist quivering wildly in anticipation.

"Now I felt *that*," he whispered.

"You couldn't!"

"I did. Like this." Repeating his perfectly targeted slow and easy rhythm, he forced her closer, his fingers splayed on her lower back. Then he flexed his hips.

The fierce jolt of pleasure spiked through her body like an electric charge, her senses taut and needy after hours of waiting for him, for this, for satisfaction. Breathless, panting, she rubbed against him, asking for more.

He glanced up, took note of Mrs. Van Kessel's absence. Not that he expected to see her standing there. He paid for her discretion. But they needed a bed. Miss Hart was on a short fuse.

"I need to come. *Right* now!"

Her hot, throaty demand interrupted his internal debate. It also gave him pause; he didn't take orders. On the other hand, he'd flown a helluva long way to do just that. He smiled. "Your place or mine?"

Perhaps it was the phrase *your place or mine* that brought her treacherous little inner voice to life. Or the smooth assurance in his tone. Or the fact that he knew he could have any woman he wanted. *Don't be stupid. This means nothing to him.* And in a terrifying flash of sanity she saw herself as he saw her: another casual conquest, another woman to be forgotten, a woman who paid him back in the usual way for gifts received.

"Stop! Stop!" Shoving hard against his chest, she broke his grip and lurched backward. "I can't," she gasped. "I'm sorry." Maybe she was too proud—or foolish…she didn't know which, but suddenly she didn't want to be another of Dominic Knight's faceless fucks.

Dragging air into his lungs, desperately trying to restrain himself, Dominic stared at her in stunned disbelief. Female resistance didn't exist in his world. A strained moment passed, followed by another, the air crackling with his frustration and outrage. Then his rancor gave way to common sense and after a moment more, he slowly exhaled. Miss Hart was the least likely woman to be playing games. He should have known better. She was a novice and the fact that she did what she did was indication of what fucking a novice entailed. A lot of work and no payoff. Lesson learned. "It's probably just as well," he mildly said, his face expressionless. Bending smoothly, he scooped up her coat from the floor and moved forward to wrap it around her shoulders.

Less capable of impassivity, her body hopelessly immune to logic, Kate's breathing turned ragged as he leaned in close.

Dominic was finely attuned to female arousal. Considering his vices, it was a valuable asset. He could have changed Miss Hart's mind.

"Good night, Miss Hart," he said instead. "Pleasant dreams."

But he stood there for a moment after she shut the door, a ghost of a smile on his face.

Christ, who knew he had scruples?

FOUR

I f he *had* scruples, they'd disappeared by morning.

When Kate walked into the dining room, shortly after eight, she came to a sudden stop. "What are you doing here?"

Dominic was seated at the small table by the window, eating. "I own this house," he pleasantly said, setting down his fork. "Would you care to join me?"

"Don't you have your own apartment?"

"I do. Did you sleep well?"

"No, as a matter of fact."

"Neither did I. It must be the weather." And he began eating again.

She could turn around and leave or she could join him and have some of the delicious-smelling breakfast spread out on the table.

It wasn't a difficult decision. She was hungry.

Dominic rose as she approached and, moving around the table, pulled out her chair. Once she sat, he returned to his seat. "Coffee or tea?" He indicated two pots on the table.

"Coffee please."

He poured her a cup, then said, "If you'd like something other than what's on the table, I'll call Mrs. Van Kessel and you can tell her."

"That's not necessary."

"Would you like me to serve you?"

"God no!"

He laughed. "Feel free to express yourself."

Then he went back to his Dutch paper. She surveyed all the delicious options on the table and ultimately made herself her favorite sandwich. Piling crisp bacon on a piece of white toast, she substituted the Green Goddess dressing next to the cold salmon for her usual mayonnaise, placed another piece of toast on top of the bacon, smashed it down, and happily took a bite just as he lifted his gaze from the paper. "My favorite," she said through a mouthful of sandwich because he was squinting slightly as though seeing a bacon sandwich for the first time. Then she went back to savoring the fabulous flavors. Really, the bacon was first rate, the toast almost as good as Nana's homemade bread, and she was hungry. Although, she was almost always hungry. Like her mother, Nana had explained; Kate had always liked the connection. From that point on, only the sound of turning pages and silverware was audible in the ornate, posh chamber. Since her breakfast companion seemed oblivious to her presence for the most part, she took the opportunity to contemplate God's gift to women for the last time.

He was casually dressed in black sweats, moccasins, and a black, long-sleeved Armani T-shirt that revealed his broad-shouldered musculature in all its glory. He apparently hadn't shaved yet because black stubble shadowed his jaw. His long dark lashes shaded his eyes as he read, but occasionally when he looked up to turn a page, the blue of his eyes made her dizzy with their saturated color.

He caught her staring once and smiled, then went back to his reading while her face turned cherry red. She vowed to keep her gaze on her plate after that and mostly succeeded, although his stark beauty was so alluring, she found herself sneaking an occasional glance.

She wouldn't be seeing him again. She was allowed.

When she finished her third sandwich, she set her plate aside and cleared her throat.

He looked over the top of his paper and lifted a brow.

She flushed under his cool, blue gaze. If he wanted to act as though nothing had happened last night, she was more than willing. "I just wanted to say thank you for everything, Mr. Knight," she said, forcing herself to speak in a neutral tone. "I enjoyed working on the project." She began to shove back her chair.

"Just a minute, Miss Hart." He set the paper aside.

There was something in his voice that made her nervous, and when she looked up, her eyes held a hint of disquiet. "Yes?"

"Don't look so frightened. It's nothing alarming. It's just that our plans have changed. I need you in Singapore. The bank manager is proving more difficult than I anticipated. And as you know, you still have eight days on your contract."

"You said I could walk when I finished the project."

"But I just told you the Singapore bank isn't cooperating. So you're not finished yet."

"What if I say no?"

He smiled. "I suppose I could sue you."

"Do I have a choice?"

"We all have choices, Miss Hart. Yours has to do with the contract you signed."

"So I don't have a choice," she said in measured tones.

"I wouldn't necessarily say that."

"What *would* you say?"

"First, I'd say you should have read the contract. Then I'd say you can't afford to fight a lawsuit. Nor would it be sensible when I need you for only eight more days at the most."

"That's it? Eight days?"

"Yes."

"Just for the record, I'd prefer not going." Mostly her libido would prefer it because it was going to be under some real strain if she had to be close to the man who'd played a starring role in last night's X-rated dreams.

"I understand." Dominic rose from his chair. "The car will be downstairs in twenty minutes. Wear something comfortable. It's a long flight. And you should think about eating something other than bacon sandwiches for breakfast. Some fruit perhaps."

As he walked away, Kate forced herself to count to ten. *She'd eat what she damn well pleased. And the car's downstairs, wear something comfortable? Jesus, did he ever quit? She didn't remember signing up for someone to manage her life!* If Mrs. Van Kessel hadn't come in just then, she would have sworn in frustration.

"Are you done, Miss?"

She managed a polite smile. "Yes, thank you. It was excellent."

"I've sent your luggage down. Mr. Knight had something

delivered for you to wear on the plane. It's in the wardrobe. May I wish you a pleasant journey."

Restraining her spiking temper, Kate smiled at the housekeeper. "Thank you. And thank you for taking such good care of me." She waited until the housekeeper was gone before she gave vent to a few pithy curse words. *Something to wear on the plane?* Christ, who the *hell* did he think he was?

Her lord and master?

FIVE

The Mercedes was parked outside the town house, the driver and Max in the front seat, Dominic in back. Max half-turned in his seat. "You—waiting for a woman?" He grinned. "Is the rapture near?"

Dominic glanced up from the report he was reading. "Cute." Then he smiled. "Although a different kind of rapture *is* possible."

"Maybe not. I don't see her sitting here."

"She's just fucking with me. It's not a problem."

"Since when?" Dominic didn't wait for anyone.

A sardonic look. "You writing a book?"

"Not yet, maybe later."

"You could try." His employees all signed nondisclosure agreements. Dominic sighed, averse to discussions of his private life. "Jake, go in and hurry her along. Tell her we have a flight on hold."

As the driver left the car, Max slid his arm along the back of the seat, turned his head, and lifted one brow. "Were you satisfied with the toned-down version of the play last night? Kees wanted me to ask you."

A faint eye roll. "They did what they could. It was fine. She recovered outside." Dominic smiled. "She wondered if you go there often."

"And what did you say? That unlike you, I'm a happily

married man and don't know everyone there by their first
name?"

"I didn't say anything. As for being happily married,
consider yourself fortunate. By the way," he briskly added,
"did you tell Liv you'll be back in Hong Kong soon?"

Max nodded. Dominic's change of subject was typical
whenever marriage was mentioned, his wife's death still an
unhealed wound. "It's been too long this time. Almost three
weeks."

"We shouldn't be in Singapore more than a day, two at
the most." The naked pain locked away once again, Dominic spoke with a cool urbanity.

"What about Miss Hart? Will she go on to Hong Kong
with us?"

"I haven't decided yet. And don't look at me like that. I
don't need another conscience. I have one somewhere."

"You should find it."

"If we're comparing roads to hell, you were a fellow
traveler not too long ago," Dominic said with heavy sarcasm. "How old is Conall now?"

Max raised his hands in surrender. "You're right. I'm done
being pious." He grinned. "Conall's going to be one next
week."

"Then we'd better see that you're back in Hong Kong
by then. Shit." Sliding up from his lounging pose, Dominic contemplated his driver as he exited the house, looking
grim. "Looks like Jake struck out. It's up to you, Max. I'd go
but it would only make things worse."

"You could leave her here."

"I actually need Miss Hart in Singapore. The bank's being uncooperative."

"Werner could bring the decoding."

"He's not my type."

Max gave him a dubious glance. "I didn't know you had one."

"If I wanted to argue, I could argue with Miss Hart. I won't hurt her. Is that better?" Dominic spoke with a level of politeness that was demonstrably strained.

Jake slid into the driver's seat. "Sorry, boss."

"Never mind. Max is going to talk Miss Hart down from the barricades, aren't you, Max?" Then even the pretext of politeness disappeared from Dominic's voice. "Carry her out if you have to."

Max shot him a sardonic look. "What about the neighbors?"

"Fuck the neighbors."

That was pretty clear. "It might take a while."

"Fine," Dominic grunted. "Go do your magic."

As personal agent for Dominic Knight the past five years, Max's diplomatic and persuasive skills were honed to a fine pitch. Fifteen minutes later, when he and Kate walked out of the house, Kate was not only smiling, she was wearing the jade green cashmere sweats and hoodie Dominic had purchased for her.

A perfect color with her hair, Dominic thought, pleased on any number of levels—personally, professionally, aesthetically. Miss Hart looked stunning—and happy.

As she entered the car, her smile faded.

Not that Dominic's pleasure was in any way quashed now that he had what he wanted. "I'm pleased you could join us, Miss Hart." Gracious, cordial, he was on his best behavior.

She looked at him squinty eyed. "I wish I could say the same."

His smile was bland. "Nevertheless, you should find Singapore interesting. Did Max mention we have a house there? One of the original trading stations. There're only a few left."

"I told her." Max spoke over his shoulder as the car pulled away from the curb. "I'm taking Miss Hart on a tour of the town tomorrow."

"Don't forget to show her the Pigeonhole." Dominic flicked a glance at Kate. "A popular coffeehouse for techies. You'll like it." Then he leaned over, held her gaze, and grinned. "It's only eight days, Miss Hart. Surely you won't pout the entire time."

"I might." But she couldn't entirely repress her smile with that boyish grin so close. And let's face it, all the glorious rest of him, too, was cranking up her body into overdrive. It was like living in a hurricane, her emotions swirling every which way, alternately pissed and not pissed depending on her wayward desires or Dominic Knight's insolence.

He sat back. "There, that's better. Did you let your grandmother know where you were going?"

Her surprise showed. The heat in her eyes did too.

"We wouldn't want Nana to worry," he said smoothly, liking the heat.

"How do you know about Nana?" *What else did he know? Hopefully, he wasn't a mind reader.*

"Tell her, Max, how you vet our prospective employees. How your intelligence contacts get you anything you need."

"Tell her yourself," Max muttered, busy texting.

"I get no respect," Dominic said with mock chagrin. "The short version, Miss Hart, is that you did your homework before your interview and we did ours. I've never lived in a small town. Is small-town living as idyllic as the movies suggest?"

"Do you really care?"

"When it comes to you, I do."

"Why?"

"Curiosity, I suppose."

"Then you must tell me about growing up in San Francisco." She gave him a brittle smile. "Just curiosity."

"Christ, you're prickly."

"Look, I know there's no privacy left in the world, but I don't have to like it. No more than I have to like being forced to accommodate you when I thought I was done. Couldn't Werner do this?"

Dominic saw Max's shoulder twitch and almost told her the truth just to see her reaction. He tamped down the impulse and spoke a half truth instead. "You're more familiar with the methodology. And I'm sure Max told you, you'll be well paid for this extra task."

"Everything's *not* about money."

"I find it generally is." She reminded him of some intrepid heroine, like Joan of Arc. But then, as now, there were always men who felt the need to chastise women like that.

"You must know the wrong people," she muttered, his bland coercion annoying.

"That's probably true. In the case of the Bucharest plant,

I certainly do know the wrong people. As soon as the Singapore bank cooperates, we'll replace the management in Bucharest. But until the bank releases my money—which is your job, Miss Hart—to explain the transfers you found... the situation's in limbo." He nodded faintly. "You see how indispensable you are."

Her eyes lit up. "So I have leverage?"

"It depends what you mean by leverage."

"I mean my skills."

"What sort of skills exactly?" he drawled. She was easy to tease; she always rose to the bait.

A high-voltage glare, glittering with affront. "I'd *love* to sue your ass."

He smiled. "Get in line, Miss Hart." Then the message ping when off on his phone. He glanced at the caller name, said, "Excuse me," pulled up the message, and began keying in what turned out to be a lengthy reply.

By the time he'd finished, the Mercedes was passing through the gates of a small airfield. Finishing up, Dominic slipped his phone into the pocket of his black leather jacket. "Offer our apologies to the pilots, Max." He reached for the door handle as the car slowed. "There are movies on the plane, Miss Hart, if you're interested," he said, glancing at her. "And books and magazines."

Before the driver came to a complete stop, Dominic had leaped from the car and was striding toward the private jet, his phone to his ear. Max helped Kate out of the car and escorted her to the plane. She heard Dominic swear, then swear some more before he ran up the ramp stairs and disappeared inside the Gulfstream.

Max showed her to a seat. "Ask the steward for anything you need." Then he disappeared into what looked like an office. She caught a glimpse of Dominic pacing inside before the door closed.

An attentive steward, middle-aged, with an air of efficiency, was hovering at her elbow. "Mr. Knight asks that you forgive his absence. Some urgent business came up. May I get you something? Food, a drink, something to read? If you'd like to rest later, the second door on the left"—he pointed behind her—"has a bed."

And so her journey to Singapore began. Two super-competent, polite stewards were devoted to her comfort while Dominic and Max remained closeted. She ate, she drank, she watched a current movie, then another, leafed through a dozen magazines. They stopped once to refuel, and she glanced out the window, but didn't recognize her surroundings. She was told they were in Kazakhstan. She was offered champagne with dinner and soon, the lure of the bed became irresistible.

She rose from her seat and moved toward the door indicated earlier. "We land in an hour and a half, miss," the steward explained.

"I'll just lie down till then. What time is it in Amsterdam?"

"Ten p.m."

She shouldn't have been so tired. It wasn't late. But she'd not gotten much sleep last night thanks to her sexual dreams starring Dominic Knight. She'd come three times before she fully woke this morning, which was both good and bad. Good because she was less likely to embarrass herself by openly drooling in his presence and bad because the memories were a continuous loop in her mind. In lush color, with sound effects and Dominic Knight in all his visual glory doing her on every piece of furniture in her apartment. The hardest part, even in her dream, was not making a sound so Mrs. Van Kessel wouldn't come running at her screams. Although come to think of it, the house-keeper wouldn't dare interrupt Dominic's amusements.

Her luggage had been brought into the bedroom, her suitcase lay open on a stand next to a teakwood dresser that held a compartmented vanity case of expensive per-fumes along with a pearl-handled brush and comb set. The bed was covered in a gorgeous blue quilt in what had to be Thai silk, a sizable bathroom was provisioned with luxury toiletries, a bookshelf was well-stocked with reading mate-rials, and the carpet underfoot was soft as silk. If she hadn't worried that the plane would go down if she texted Nana, she would have sent her grandmother a detailed descrip-tion of the lifestyle of the rich and famous.

As landing time approached, Dominic eased open the bed-room door and glanced in on his temporary employee, the modern Joan of Arc. She was rolled up in the quilt, only her wild copper curls and a portion of her face visible above the swaddling silk. Her skin was slightly flushed in sleep, her angelic profile incredibly childlike.

Christ, he'd be ten kinds of stupid to mess with her.

Softly shutting the door, he slowly exhaled. He shouldn't even be thinking about dragging her into his wayward world of carnal games. He should give her a free pass. Or maybe just give her the illusion of a free pass. Cold-blooded manipulation or decency? What would it be?

It was only a debate in the abstract.

He wanted her and nothing in his life had ever seemed so simple.

"Don't," a voice behind him warned.

"I'm still thinking about it," Dominic said, perjuring himself without a qualm as he turned to face Max.

"Stop thinking about it. Let her go home after Singapore."

Dominic's face went blank. "Thanks for the advice. What time's our appointment at the bank?"

SIX

The plane landed on an airfield that largely serviced private planes. Closer to the city in terms of drive time than the commercial hub, it saved twenty minutes of commuting for busy executives.

At five thirty a.m. the temperature was already eighty-three degrees, the humid air stifling as they exited the plane. A faint pink glow low on the horizon signaled sunrise and another day of sweltering heat.

Still half asleep, Kate followed the men down the ramp to the tarmac, where another sleek, black Mercedes awaited them. Public transportation wasn't a consideration for people like Dominic Knight, she grumpily thought, lack of sleep adding to her resentment or perhaps pique at her employer's casual acceptance of his exalted lifestyle. On the other hand, she decided with a yawn, she wasn't about to look a gift horse in the mouth. Climbing into the backseat of the air-conditioned car while the men talked to some uniformed official, she curled up in a corner and promptly went back to sleep.

When Dominic entered the car, he took one look at Kate and cautioned the driver, "No race driving today, Chu. The lady's sleeping."

"No problem, boss. You won't even know we're moving."

The driver was as good as his word, smoothly navigating the early-morning traffic like a jockey guiding his mount through a jostling pack in the homestretch. While Chu and Max exchanged local gossip, Dominic had an undisturbed opportunity to study his sleeping passenger. She looked young—or younger than she was—he corrected himself; at twenty-two her age wasn't an issue as much as her innocence. Although she was neither young nor *completely* innocent according to Max.

But Miss Hart was so far outside his sophisticated world and his usual taste in women that he felt as though patterns he'd followed his entire life were being rewired in his brain.

Or maybe he was just willing to suspend disbelief.

Or he was being rash.

Or stupid.

Whatever. It didn't matter. She pleased him.

It was as simple as that.

He found her delicacy a serious turn-on, her fine-boned slenderness perversely virginal. As were her discreet curves that you didn't notice at first and when you did you couldn't stop looking.

He tried not to stare. He tried not to think of how soft her skin would feel if he touched her. He tried not to imagine her sleeping in his bed or not sleeping, doing other things to him, for him, *accommodating* him with her delectable body and defiant mind because he could make her do anything he wanted.

He even briefly considered taking Max's advice, being virtuous and sending her home. But even before the idea had fully formed, he'd dismissed it because she stirred some raw emotion in him, unleashed a sense of *feeling* again that took him by surprise.

It was over and above lust, something that distinguished her from other women—like an explosion of color in a brown and gray world caught your attention. That captivated the hell out of him. Jesus—captivated? *What the fuck?*

He grimaced, looked away, felt a sudden guilt as though he were cheating on Julia. He softly swore, called himself every kind of fool, then deliberately asked Max a question and ignored Miss Hart for the remainder of the drive. Fun and games were fine. Anything else wasn't.

When they reached the house, Dominic jumped from the car, then waited for Max to step out. "I'd appreciate it if you'll see Miss Hart to her room. Tell her someone will wake her at twelve thirty. Breakfast is at one. We leave at one forty-five." A quick glance to see that Kate still slept. "Also, if you could talk her into wearing something of Greta's for the meeting at the bank, I'd be grateful enough to order wheels up for Hong Kong as soon as we're done at the bank."

"Deal."

Dominic grinned. "I wish I had your charm."

"You've got charm enough if you're in the mood, but what can I say," Max quipped. "She likes me."

Dominic's eyelids dropped a fraction. "Just so long as she doesn't like you too much."

A flash of a grin. "What would you do if she did?"

"The polite answer or the truth?"

"Don't bother," Max drawled. "I'm years past intimidation."

"I'm serious."

"Good. Glad to hear it. That means you give a damn. It's been a while since you have."

*   *   *

When Kate walked into the sunny breakfast room shortly after one, both men seated at the table came to their feet.

Dominic smiled. "I hope you were able to sleep, Miss Hart."

"I did. The house is amazingly quiet."

Dominic pulled out a chair for her. "The gardens blunt the noise of the city."

"They're fantastic," she said, setting her laptop on the table. "It's a tropical paradise outside, the color and variety of flowers, the heady scents. I've seen the kind of birds you have here only in the zoo."

"We're fortunate to have the acreage so close to the city center." As she sat, he pushed her chair in. "Tell her, Max, how we constantly have to fight off developers."

While Kate was served, the discussion turned on the history of the old trading station constructed in the traditional style with large overhanging roofs, open-air porches, bedrooms with garden views, and a central courtyard protected by tall, sturdy, iron-strapped gates. She learned that Singapore had been a major port for the colony when it was English, still served that purpose for the independent city state, and the trading station had come into Dominic's hands nine years ago when the former owner had gone back to England.

Two white-coated, unobtrusive servants saw that everyone had what they needed. Dominic had already eaten. He drank coffee while Kate and Max had their breakfasts. It was a cozy gathering in an exotic venue, the sensation of having every whim quietly satisfied by soft-spoken servants as close to a fantasy world as Kate could imagine.

How easily one could be seduced by such luxury. How easily one could be enticed by a man like Dominic Knight, who offered that luxury with a kind of casual disregard. Not that his looks alone wouldn't guarantee him legions of women at his beck and call. Including those in that unforgettable blog she wished she'd never seen.

"Ready?"

Jolted from her musing, she managed a quick smile. "Yes, of course. Thank you for breakfast."

"You managed without bacon," Dominic said, his voice amused.

"Because you managed not to have it served."

"You could have had it if you'd asked."

"Then I will next time."

He liked it that she alluded to a future breakfast. "If you ever want something, Miss Hart, just ask. I'm more than willing to oblige."

"Please. You're the least obliging man I know."

"I could change."

She snorted.

Max decided it was time to retreat. He had no intention of getting in the middle of whatever game Dominic was playing.

As the door closed on Max and the servants, Dominic said, "I could change, Miss Hart. You never know. Anything's possible. And thank you for wearing the suit for the meeting." Greta's teal blue suit, simply cut, was a masterpiece of tailoring. "Your clothes reflect on me."

"Surely you're not an unknown here."

"But you are."

"*My* problem is that these clothes of yours reflect on *me*," she coolly pointed out. "So whatever you want me to be, I prefer being myself."

"You don't know what I want."

"I can guess. Particularly after the show in Amsterdam. And this." She flipped open the top of her laptop, tapped the keyboard a few times, looked up. "There. See for yourself."

As he rose from his chair and walked over, a video began playing featuring a nude Dominic Knight with a braided riding crop in his hand—a long-haired, younger, superlean Dominic Knight with sleek, corded muscles and the loose-limbed grace of a large jungle cat. Even in the unprofessional video one could see the hint of menace in the spring-coiled twitch of his hand holding the crop. Four women were either tied or handcuffed to various padded sex apparatus, some dressed in kinky lingerie, others masked, one with her mouth muzzled with a rubber ball fastened around her head. He leisurely made the rounds with his riding crop. This was not a man overcome by passion. The room was large, black velvet on the walls, mirrors everywhere, crystal chandeliers lighting the scene. It was an elegantly appointed establishment. And none of the women looked unhappy. Apparently the end result was worth it, although there were no full frontal views of Dominic. There was one brief glimpse of his engorged penis that she'd stopped on the video more times than she should have, and it was obvious that the blonde he was fucking was genuinely enjoying herself—that look on her face couldn't have been staged.

Dominic watched the video for a few seconds, then leaned over and clicked it off. "That must be one I didn't shut down. Just joking. Really, it's a joke. I've never seen that before." He flicked a finger at the laptop. "Are there more?"

"It's the only one I found."

"That's a relief. Do you want an explanation?"

"Not really."

"Good, because I don't want to give one. As for you thinking I want you to be something other than you are, you're wrong." He drew in a small breath. "If you must know, I find you refreshing."

"I can see why, after those pictures." She shut down her laptop.

"I could say that was a long time ago. I could say someone Photoshopped that video."

"You don't have to say anything. I'll be going home soon."

"It might be seven more days," he said.

"I can count." Time enough to argue about her *walking* once the meeting was over.

He smiled. "I know you can." He held out his hand. "Come, Miss Hart, let's go see those bankers and you can show them how well you count."

The bank building was thirty stories high, the director's office on the top floor a visual exercise in opulence. On display was a collection of gold Shakyamuni Buddhas in various poses and sizes, as well as lighted shelves with hundreds of delicate, antique Chinese porcelains in soft, pastel shades.

As they entered the room, two middle-aged men of consequence came to greet them. Dominic, along with his attorney and Kate, exchanged bows and the requisite courtesies, along with several minutes of polite conversation before they were seated in cream leather chairs arranged around a large malachite coffee table.

Tea was served by a beautiful young woman in a black couture dress, and Kate understood why her suit mattered. The woman left. More polite conversation ensued per Asian protocol.

Finally, Dominic's attorney, Mr. Lee, addressed the issue at hand, his tone meticulously respectful. The two bankers presented their arguments. Then, negotiations began. Kate walked the bankers through the byzantine money trail in minute detail, explaining each incremental step in the process. It was perfectly clear where the money had come from and equally clear where the money now resided—name, dates, account number, total sum.

As she sat back, the conversation suddenly shifted from English. The tone changed as well, the bankers now visibly hostile in voice, expression, body language. Mr. Lee's response was equally contentious and the debate escalated in heat and bitterness.

Kate stole a glance at Dominic, lounging beside her in his chair. His expression was closed, his body motionless in a dark gray, shadow-striped, double-breasted Savile Row suit. He'd worn a white shirt with the more formal French cuffs for the occasion, his cuff links burnished gold Roman coins, a pale gray tie, gracefully knotted, completed the quiet image of wealth. Of power. Considering the rising noise levels, he was incredibly restrained, perhaps even relaxed as he apparently followed the conversation.

As Kate watched the drama unfolding, Mr. Lee's face turned grim, the bankers' voices became shrill. One of the bankers unleashed a barrage of harsh invective, then both men began to rise from their chairs.

Dominic finally moved. Lifting one finger to forestall them, he leaned forward and spoke softly in the same language as the principals, his voice entirely without inflection. Before he'd uttered more than three words, the men dropped back into their chairs, and by the time he'd finished speaking the bankers' faces were ashen.

Dominic came to his feet and this time he spoke in English. "I want my money within ten minutes. I hope we understand each other."

He nodded at Kate, who was scrambling to put her laptop in the black leather bag she'd been given at the house. "We're done here, Miss Hart. Mr. Lee will deal with the rest."

As they left the office, Kate noticed that the receptionists appeared apprehensive; they must have been listening. Dominic smiled at them, made some remark in a different dialect, then escorted Kate to the private elevator.

"Fuckers," he said under his breath, punching the down button. He slowly exhaled. "Sorry." He turned to Kate. "I try not to lose my temper, but I wasn't about to turn over twenty million to those crooks. By the way, you were superb, Miss Hart. Your explanation was crystal clear. Here, give me that. It's heavy."

She handed over the laptop bag. "Would they really have kept your money?"

"Damn right they would have if they'd had the balls."

"Did you threaten them? It looked like you did."

He hesitated briefly, then said, "Perhaps a little. I could have dragged it through the courts, but"—he shrugged—"a foreign city-state with a virtual dictatorship...the results are uncertain. Ah, finally." He held the elevator door for her, followed her in, and hit the lobby button. "That presentation of yours deserves a bonus, Miss Hart," he said, changing the subject. "Send your bill to Max."

"You're paying me enough already."

He shot her a look. "Miss Hart," he said quietly, "if someone offers you carte blanche, don't ever say no."

"I will if I want."

He laughed. "Lord, you're a breath of fresh air. Do you know you're the first person I've ever met who's turned down money? We have to celebrate miracles like that. What do you say to a night on the town in Hong Kong? Say yes. I'm in a bloody fine mood after saving my twenty mil. Come, Miss Hart, a simple yes." The doors opened onto the bustling lobby. He grinned at her. "You still owe me seven and a half days," he said. "You don't have a choice."

As she began to say maybe she did have a choice if he actually got his twenty million, that her assignment would be over—he grabbed her hand, hauled her out of the elevator, through the lobby, and out onto the pavement, where his car was waiting. "If you're going to make a scene," he said, opening the back door, "do it in the car. It's not that I'd be embarrassed," he added, politely shoving her in, "but you might be if I start screaming back." He slammed the door shut, set her bag on the floor. "The airport, Chu. Call

Max. Tell him to meet us there." Then he turned back to Kate and grinned. "Okay, I'm ready. Scream away."

Now was her chance to make her point about going back home. "I'd *like* to see Hong Kong," she heard herself say. She had no explanation; she wasn't even looking for one. She just felt happy saying it.

"You would?"

She enjoyed his startle reflex. It made him human. "Why wouldn't I?"

It took him a moment to answer, her sudden agreement unnerving.

She smiled. "Do you think I want something? You do, don't you?"

"The thought crossed my mind. Forgive me if I'm wrong."

"I do want something."

His gaze went shuttered. "Tell me what it is," he coolly said.

"A night on the town. It sounds like fun."

Flint-eyed scrutiny. "That's it?"

"Jesus. You'd think I'd asked for your firstborn. Does everyone always want something from you?"

"Mostly." He blew out a breath. "Yeah, a lot of them do."

"I don't." *Well, maybe a little something. Just maybe.*

His smile slowly unfurled. "In that case, consider it a date, Miss Hart. It's a three-and-a-half-hour flight. We should be there for dinner."

A date! She had to stop herself from verbally freaking out. "Dinner sounds lovely," she said, proud that she'd been able to keep her voice even. In contrast, her brain was practically exploding, she was thinking so many things at the same time. First the classic Cinderella dream that every young girl brought with her into adulthood regardless of the sheer futility of such a scenario. But really, Dominic Knight was as much Prince Charming as any fantasy could contrive. Then, after jettisoning the Cinderella myth, she focused on the word *date*, like some starstruck teenager. That at least was a marginal reality and she intended to relish every minute of the evening because she would be the envy of every woman who had eyes to see. And after the soft-focus lens on romance gave way to a more stark reality, she ran through possible fantasies of a more lurid sexual nature. At which point she abruptly punted and returned to the more pleasing romantic images filling her mind.

But Kate wasn't the only one pleased.

Dominic started making plans.

SEVEN

Two cars were waiting for them at the airport. Max politely took his leave of Kate, offered her good wishes for her future, told Dominic he'd talk to him next week, then loped toward a waiting car and jumped in.

"He's impatient to get home," Dominic explained as the car sped away.

"I don't suppose he gets home often with your schedule."

"We have a deal. It's every two weeks—mostly—this time it stretched to three, so he's in a hurry to see his family. Here's our car." He guided her to another shiny black sedan.

Max has a family? After the evening in Amsterdam, Kate wondered what kind of family. Was he was married or did the Roche family live here? If he had a wife, was she Chinese? Not that it was any of her business. Really, it wasn't. "Is Max married?" The words escaped before she could censure her brain, so there was no further point in being discreet. "He doesn't look like he'd be married. He looks like he should be carrying an AK-47."

Dominic gave her a blank stare for half a heartbeat. Then he said, "Max is married. He has a young son. Anything else?"

"Sorry. It's just that I've never seen anyone who looks so much like a mercenary."

"Actually, Max is a physicist."

Her eyes widened. "Like a physicist who defuses suit-case bombs? Or builds them or trades in nuclear secrets?"

Dominic smiled faintly. "You have a vivid imagination, Miss Hart." Always an asset for what he had in mind tonight. Although she'd seemed sexually demanding in Amsterdam. He'd have to tame that impulse. As for Max's MI6 history, eva-sion was best. "The work Max does for me is quite ordinary. No nuclear secrets, just business. His wife is also English," he added, in an effort to establish Max's unremarkable bona fides. "Max and Liv are both from expat families. His son, Conall, will be one this week. That's about it."

Their driver had the car door open. Dominic waited for Kate to get in, then followed her into the backseat.

"I was just curious after—well…that night in Amster-dam," Kate said. "He seemed to know everyone at that club."

Curious indeed. "The Ritz-Carlton, Dan." He settled back in the seat and smiled at Kate. "If you're asking whether Max is happily married, he is. He adores his wife and son. Hollywood couldn't do it any better."

"Oh." Surprise turned into a smile. "That's great. I like Hollywood happy endings."

"I thought you might."

"You say it like there's something wrong with happily ever after."

"On the contrary, if only it were true the world would be a better place."

"Cynic."

"Welcome to my reality."

"That's what comes from making too much money. The thrill is gone."

He laughed. "You know that, do you?"

"Call it a calculated guess."

"In any case, Miss Hart, tonight we're going to forget about reality and making money. We're just going to have fun."

She lifted her brows. "Do you know how to have fun?"

An easy smile. "You tell me tomorrow."

They'd landed at the old airport on Kowloon, so it was a relatively short drive to the Ritz-Carlton, where they were whisked up to the 117th floor with such exaggerated courtesy by the hotel manager that Kate understood Dominic Knight's financial status was well known. On reaching the club level, the small, trim man and Dominic spoke briefly in Cantonese before the manager pivoted back to the elevators and Dominic turned to Kate. "Let me show you to your room." He indicated the direction with a nod. "If it's convenient," he said, moving down the wide corridor, "I'll pick you up for dinner at eight. Hong Kong is all about food. Some say there's shopping and finance too but"—a quick smile—"mostly it's food. We'll start with drinks at the China Club." He stopped at a set of double doors. "If you need anything, ask your butler."

"Butler?" There was a word that had never before entered her life.

"They come with the suites."

Do you come with the suite? Unbidden, the words leaped to mind, her libidinous little voice chiming in without a moment's hesitation, *You can make it happen, girl! Female power rules!*

Dominic broke into her chewed-lip moment of silence. "I'm really hungry. Does eight give you enough time to dress?"

Was he talking in code or was she listening in code? Hungry? Hungry for what? "Ah—er"—she looked up—"I mean yes, yes...eight's fine."

"Good. Eight it is." As if inured to stammering women, he reached past her, opened her door, then turned and strolled away.

Christ, how gauche was that? And how freaking gorgeous is he, she thought, watching him stride down the corridor, all grace and beauty and worldly polish. She guessed those bound women he was whipping in that blog didn't really mind it when Dominic Knight was doing the whipping because they'd get him afterward. And Kate knew just how much of him there was to get after the much-watched image on the video. Although he was big everywhere—tall, buff with muscle like some Greek god or NFL player—*Jesus, stop already!* There was a butler probably ten feet away, which meant climaxing on the spot was seriously uncool.

Taking a deep steadying breath, she entered the suite and sure enough—there was a butler standing at attention in the middle of a very large room filled with couches, chairs, and *real* artwork. Christ, keep it together. Although she was sorely tempted to ask, *May I take a picture of you to send to my grandmother?* because Nana would go bonkers on seeing a real live butler. Unfortunately, that would be double gauche. So she smiled instead and dismissed him with as much I-do-this-all-the-time panache as she could conjure up from her memories of Masterpiece Theatre.

Like in Amsterdam, however, the rewards of having

a servant were immediately apparent. Her bath had been drawn, Greta's clothes had been hung up—not that she was surprised to see them after two days in the company of a man who considered himself master of all he surveyed. A great number of spanking new suitcases were neatly stowed away in the wall of closets and an open bottle of champagne on ice was waiting for her on the ledge of the bathtub. A bathtub with a 117-story view of Hong Kong. Like first class all the way! Nana was getting a picture of that texted right away, regardless that it was probably three in the morning back home or the next day or whatever. Seconds later, the photo was winging its way around the globe and moments after that, Kate was immersed in hot suds, sipping a glass of champagne and reveling in an incredible sense of well-being.

While it was tempting to empty the bottle of champagne, the lure of an evening with Dominic Knight required a clear mind. She wanted to remember this night on the town. Every second, every heartbeat, every word and smile and tilt of his gorgeous head. How he ate and drank, *what* he ate and drank, the entire fantastic imagery of her date with—let's face it—the handsomest man on the planet.

And she didn't often indulge in over-the-top superlatives like that.

Dominic Knight was definitely an exception.

After her second glass of champagne, she bathed, toweled off, then went to survey her neatly hung designer wardrobe. She could, of course, wear her own clothes. She probably *should* wear her own clothes. *Or*—she could wear that floaty chiffon number that was enticing her like the veritable apple in Paradise. Let's see—her own slacks and a blouse or that dream dress. It wasn't even close. Did Dominic Knight know women or what?

To soothe her conscience or feminist principles, she told herself she was just borrowing the dress for the night. Using the dress on loan didn't make her one of those women in the video. She wasn't like them. But at the end of the day, if she wanted to sleep with Dominic Knight, why shouldn't she? Oh jeez, what if she asked and he said no because she'd blown him off in Amsterdam? How embarrassing would that be? Maybe she'd better not ask.

She was seriously dithering about sleeping with Dominic Knight mostly because of two things: the video, of course, and the spillover in terms of the absolutism that constituted so much of his personality.

She almost felt like flipping a coin.

Then again, when it came to wanting what she wanted, that left too much to chance.

So with Greta's dress enticing her, along with the promise of a night on the town in Hong Kong with the most beautiful man in the world, it didn't take long to put her insecurities to rest. If she felt out of her depth at some point in the evening, she'd do what she did last time. Just say no. There was no way she was backing out of this once-in-a-lifetime opportunity, because seriously, it was a *once-in-a-lifetime* opportunity.

And Meg would never let her forget it if she passed up sex with Dominic Knight.

There. Done. Case closed.

Sliding the chiffon dress off the hanger, she slipped it

over her head and let the silky fabric swish down her body. Gazing at her image in a floor-length mirror, one of Whistler's paintings of a gauzily dressed female sprang to mind. The flowered print, the sheer fabric, the pale, cream background was—with the exception of its short length—very much like those dresses in a Whistler painting. Although the tomato-red ribbon at the waist was a vivid touch of creative whimsy on Greta's part. After tying the silk taffeta into a floppy bow, she briefly admired her handiwork before considering shoes. Naturally, there were silk, sling-back heels in tomato red. You could see how Dominic Knight could manage every detail of a global empire.

For a fleeting second, she wondered if this fantasy would evaporate at the stroke of midnight. Would Dominic Knight disappear in a puff of smoke and she'd discover that this was all just a dream?

A clock on the dresser suddenly chimed, reminding her that she actually was at the Ritz-Carlton, Hong Kong. And, she noted, checking the time, she still had a half hour to do some exploring of the club floor. A date with Dominic Knight was a memorable occasion; she wanted all the little details etched on her memory.

Five minutes later, her tour complete, she discovered that with the exception of the concierge and bartender, she was alone. Stopping before a beautiful young Asian woman behind the concierge's desk, Kate smiled. "The view's absolutely stunning up here. You must hear that a lot."

"I do. But it is stunning, I agree. We have the distinction of being the world's highest hotel." She arched her perfect, black brows. "May I help you with anything?"

"No, I was just looking around. Is it always so quiet this time of night?"

"Not always. It depends on the guests in residence." The concierge smiled politely. "Would you like a drink? Po makes a lovely Earl Grey martini rimmed with sugar and salt and infused with orange. He says it's a perfect way to regain focus. Come," she added, rising from her chair. "Let me introduce you to Po."

A few minutes later, Kate was seated at the bar, sipping one of the most delicious martinis she'd ever tasted. Not that she was a connoisseur with her drinking. Her experience was primarily limited to college haunts and pitchers of beer, but she was definitely broadening her horizons in a really satisfying way.

Po, the young bartender, brought over a plate of exquisite hors d'oeuvres, an embroidered linen napkin, and a finger bowl. She was impressed and told him so.

"The Ritz-Carlton prides itself on its service." He smiled. "Enjoy."

It turned out that he was a native of Hong Kong and when Kate began asking questions, he recounted some of the history of the city, described the major tourist sites, and acquainted her with the best restaurants on the islands, as well as pointing out some of the tamer nighttime attractions. He also knew the more licentious establishments, too, places Dominic patronized. But he purposefully kept his mouth shut about all of that.

Every bartender in the city augmented their salary by selling information to the tabloids because gossip, along with money and food, fueled Hong Kong. Naturally, Po was curious why a rich *gweilo* like Dominic Knight had chosen to stay at the Ritz-Carlton with this pretty young lady who wasn't a *working girl*. The billionaire had a home on the Peak. Why hadn't he taken her there?

"Have you known Mr. Knight long?" Po casually inquired.

Kate shook her head. "I'm just working on a project for him. Was," she added with a smile. "I'll be going home soon." To his polite query, she explained where home was, described northern Minnesota in broad strokes, and finished her drink only to find another being slid toward her. "I shouldn't. We're going out to dinner."

"I made it weak."

"What time is it?" A question looking for an excuse. Maybe it was the drink or the two glasses of champagne or the fact that the privileged set knew how to relax, but it was truly like sitting in the clouds up here—calm, peaceful, the lights of the city twinkling and sparkling across the harbor.

"Seven fifty. Emmie will tell him you're here. Have you seen the Peak yet?" The bartender was curious whether this young lady knew about Dominic's house. "It's one of the most high-end real-estate areas on earth. In fact, the most expensive residential site in the world sold last week for two hundred thirty-one million dollars."

"No, I haven't. It sounds posh."

She didn't know. "There's no restrictions on who buys here," Po explained. "Hong Kong is the freest market in the world. We have lots of foreigners like Mr. Knight buying property here."

She stared at him for a moment, unable to keep the surprise out of her voice. "He has a place here?"

The bartender shrugged.

"And you're wondering why he's staying here?" It was her turn to shrug. "Sorry, I don't know. Or, for that matter, care. Now why don't *you* tell *me* something. Why is it so quiet up here? Where are the other guests?"

"There aren't any." *And the ones that had been here had been herded out at Mr. Knight's request.* "You didn't hear it from me."

She lifted one brow. "Or you won't get a tip?"

"I already got one." *And he expected more, since Mr. Knight had reserved the floor for a week.*

"Wow. Do you see many people like him here?"

"Some. This is the financial center of Asia."

"There you are," a familiar voice said. "I'll have one of those, too." Dominic pointed at Kate's glass as he slid onto the barstool next to her. "This view is on a lot of bucket lists," he remarked, running his hands over his wet hair and flicking it behind his ears.

"I can see why," Kate replied, determined to come across as casual as he did. "It's breathtaking."

"I could say the same about you," he said with a smile, his gaze raking her from head to toe. "And I like the dress too."

"You don't look too bad yourself." A vast understatement for a man who could silence a room with his stark beauty.

She began to wonder if he didn't wear cologne, if that musky fragrance was his own personal animal scent. "Do you wear cologne?" she blurted out.

Even the bartender turned around at the weirdness in her voice.

"I mean," she quickly said, trying to do calm and collected, "it seems familiar. Or is it one of those personal fragrances distilled for you?"

Dominic smiled. "It must be the shampoo. I don't wear cologne."

"Oh," she said, because her mind was blank with the exception of the words *animal scent*, which she had no intention of discussing. And rather than stammer on under that amused gaze, she picked up her drink and drank it down.

The bartender began to move; Dominic gave him a look that stopped him. "You better pace yourself, Miss Hart," Dominic said, pleasantly. "Or you won't remember dinner."

"I never get drunk."

"A shame," he said.

She looked up at his tone.

He smiled. "I thought we were going to have fun tonight."

Ohmygod, could she freeze this moment in time? The sinful look in his eyes, the heart-stopping smile on his gorgeous mouth, that little lift of his brows that was hotter than hell.

But before she could answer, before whatever she was about to say appeared in the gossip columns tomorrow, Dominic turned to the bartender. "Would you call down and see if our car is here?"

As the man walked away, Dominic leaned in close and whispered, "I am so fucking hard."

She looked down; his erection was huge, the fly of his trousers strained to the max. Her breath caught, her body opened in undisguised welcome, and she was about to impulsively blurt out, "Let's skip dinner."

But he spoke first. "So don't get too close, Miss Hart. We have reservations. And I'm hungry."

Wide-eyed, she whispered, "Can you just stop everything like that?"

He held her gaze. "I can do anything, Miss Hart." His voice took on a raspy edge. "I'll show you later." Then he tossed a few bills on the bar for Po, stood, and with complete nonchalance as though his voice hadn't just been rough with desire, flicked his hand toward the elevators. "Shall we? The car's waiting."

He described the restaurant and its reputation as they walked to the elevator, the conversation one-sided, with Kate trying to suppress her all-consuming desire. She was still trembling slightly when the elevator began its descent.

He stood across from her, humming softly. He glanced at her. "I'm in the mood for steak. What about you?"

"Don't talk to me," she breathed, trying to get a grip on her frenzied nerves, her hands clenched into fists at her sides.

"Think of something else. You'll relax."

"We aren't all automatons," she said with a little sniff.

"I know. That's one of the things I like about you. Your spontaneity."

She shot him a harried look. "While your worldview is pure logic."

"Maybe you could reform me." He smiled as the elevator doors opened. "Would you like to try?" He held out his hand.

"I can't think of a more hopeless project. And I'm not touching you."

His hand dropped. "You first, Miss Hart." He held open

the door for her and, as she passed by, gave her a sunny smile. "Maybe you could look on me as one of those puzzles you like to solve. Max says you like the complicated ones."

"I don't see myself in a therapist's role," she said over her shoulder.

He caught up to her in two strides, swung in front of her, came to a stop, and took a quick step back so she didn't run into him. "What role were you considering?" he lazily asked, his gaze resting for a moment on the neckline of her dress.

"I thought you were hungry."

"It can wait. I'm curious. Do you like to play games?"

"I don't know. Do you?"

"That's what I do. You haven't played before? Would you like to?"

There was a splintering silence while she debated how to answer and he debated what he'd do if she answered one way or the other.

"You're the kind of man who might leave scars," she said a moment later, her voice deliberate, as though clarifying her position not just to him but to herself. "But you're also the kind of man who might end up leaving a tattoo on my sex life that I'll enjoy looking at later. Something between hearts and flowers and your blood type inked into my psyche. You hit me that hard. So give me a little time. It's complicated."

"Complicated is better. More intense." Then he smiled almost shyly, although it was still a lion's smile. "Maybe I'll give you a rose tattoo. Something dewy fresh like you."

"Maybe you won't give me anything. I still haven't made up my mind. I'm not sure I'm looking for trouble."

He laughed. "And I'm trouble. Fair enough, Miss Hart. I won't argue about that." He dipped his head, so their eyes were level. "I like your honesty. Take your time. I won't rush you."

"You couldn't anyway."

He lifted his head and smiled. "I'm sure you're right," he politely said, not about to discuss what he could do or could not do. "Now let's get out of here."

EIGHT

After they exited the hotel, Dominic abruptly stopped and gazed at Kate with a slight frown. "You're going to be cold." The air had a bite to it, the wind off the harbor chilly; Hong Kong in January required a jacket. "Come, we'll get you in the car."

Once Kate was seated, Dominic leaned in. "I'll be right back." He shut the door and sprinted back inside the hotel. Minutes later, he returned, a white cashmere shawl draped over his arm. "She said white goes with everything." He tossed the shawl to Kate as he entered the car. "I should have thought of it before." He signaled the driver and the car pulled away from the hotel entrance.

"No, you shouldn't have. Here." She held out the shawl. "I keep saying no, and you keep ignoring me."

"I don't like hearing no," he said, like it was the most reasonable statement in the world. "And why should you be cold tonight? It doesn't make sense."

His gaze was dead serious. "I suppose." She let her hand drop. "Still."

"Still, nothing." He gave her a nod. "Put it on. It cost a few bucks. Don't make a federal case out of it."

"I'm still trying to deal with these clothes," she said, plucking at her skirt. "What it says about me."

"You're taking this too seriously. There's nothing to deal

with. Wear them or don't wear them, give them away. I'm sure some charity will take them."

"You gotta be kidding."

"Not in the least. If they make you unhappy, don't wear them. Although," he said, his gaze sliding down her body, "you look beautiful in every one of Greta's designs. So if I get a vote, keep them. Now put this on." He took the shawl from her lap, said, "Sit up," wrapped it around her shoulders, and dropped back against the seat with a grin. "Why don't we wait until we're really drunk before we fight. It'll be more interesting."

"Or maybe it'll just be more violent."

A wicked smile. "Now I'm really hopeful."

Oh Lord, that sexy smile and treacherous murmur zeroed in on her like a heat-seeking missile, detonated, and sucked the air from the car, from the universe. She tried not to let him hear her gasp, tried not to squirm—and failed miserably.

"You okay?"

Another one of those I'll-take-you-to-the-moon smiles, damn him. He knew exactly what he was doing to her and probably to every other woman who came within his sexual force field. "I'm good," she choked, forcing herself to think about glaciers or lake ice or snow.

"If you need anything, let me know."

The low, husky tenor of his voice was like silk on her skin. "Nothing right now, thanks," she firmly said. Call her bitchy or maybe competitive, but she didn't want to be so fucking *available*. He had it too easy with women. "And we're not done talking about these clothes," she added, wanting to change the subject, curb her libido. "You can't always have your own way."

"I know how to compromise," he said mildly, having watched with admiration as she'd brought herself under control. She wasn't the only one who liked complicated puzzles. She might be naive, but she had a self-confident willfulness that intrigued him.

Kate snorted. "Remember, I just saw you in action in Singapore."

"They were stealing my money. Why should I compromise?"

"The question is—do you ever compromise?"

He tipped his head faintly in her direction. "Are we still talking about the clothes?"

"No. We're talking about you rolling over anyone who gets in your way."

He grinned. "May I roll over you? Later? Right now, I'm starved."

She gave him a jaundiced look. "Such smug arrogance. Do women like that?"

"Women like me, Miss Hart, because I have a helluva lot of money. Ah, here we are." He unfurled from his lounging pose.

The car came to a stop near a quay where a sleek cruiser was moored. They were shown into a warm cabin, where a steward offered them drinks. Kate shook her head, Dominic said, "A single malt," and soon they were speeding across the harbor to Hong Kong Island, where another car was waiting.

They were driven to the China Club, a members-only

oasis taking up the top three floors of the old Bank of China building in Hong Kong's Central District. "We'll cab to Cépage from here," Dominic explained to the driver. "Meet us there."

The club interior was colonial 1930s Shanghai teahouse decor with elegant ceiling fans, rotary phones, Art Deco architectural touches, an extensive art collection, and a dress code. Informal here meant a suit and tie.

Since the handover of the territory from the British to the Chinese in 1997, fewer white men were members. But Dominic was ushered in with his usual deference because he *was* a member and even if he hadn't been, men like Dominic Knight were always welcome everywhere. Even without a tie.

An attendant showed them into the small, cozy library, empty of guests.

"Would you prefer champagne or drinks?" Dominic asked as he ushered Kate to a fawn-colored leather club chair. "The cellar is excellent here."

A small, irresolute pause. "You decide."

Dominic gave her a teasing look as he dropped into an adjacent chair. "Feeling out of your element, Miss Hart?"

"Am I not allowed?" she testily retorted.

"Ah—that's better. Compliance doesn't suit you."

"I didn't think you even knew the word."

He grinned. "It depends on how it's being used."

She shot a quick look at the waiting attendant.

"They don't listen," Dominic said.

"Of course they do, and if they're lucky, they get paid for the information they put on the Internet. I believe you already figure largely on one of those sites."

"Not anymore."

A spiking glance. "You shut it down?"

"I didn't personally, but someone in my organization did."

"Maybe I shouldn't drink at all or I might be on You-Tube tomorrow."

"The site you referred to was shut down with a good deal of money as an inducement. *Along with a threat.* So rest easy, you won't be on YouTube. I promise."

"That was really you? It wasn't Photoshopped?"

"No."

"No, it wasn't you or no it wasn't Photoshopped?"

He smiled faintly. "No, it wasn't Photoshopped."

"Obviously, that doesn't bother you?"

"No, but since it bothered you, I had it taken down."

"You didn't have to do that for me."

"I got the impression I should. If you want to know something about what you saw, just ask." He glanced at the young man standing at attention. "A Krug Clos d'Ambonnay '96 and two plates of tea-soaked shrimp. There now," he said as the attendant walked away. "What do you want to know?"

"Where was it?"

"Paris."

"Why so many women?"

"For the usual reasons, variety, self-indulgence, lack of restraint—"

"I saw plenty of restraint."

He shrugged. "That's part of the game. Excess is an escape for me, a defense against old ghosts and what seems at times a soulless reality—present company excepted, of course," he said with a small smile. "I like to feel something rather than nothing and that's why I do what you saw in that video." His eyes went blank for a moment and his nostrils flared, as though he were struck by some internal image, then he shrugged again in such obvious dismissal that his shuttered gaze came as no surprise. "Vanilla sex works for some people. I need more. Sorry if I've frightened you. You shouldn't have asked."

"I wouldn't like any of that—stuff that hurts," Kate said, wanting to make her position clear.

"You don't know," he said casually. "You might."

"Now you *are* frightening me." Half breathless, she pressed into the chair back as though putting distance between herself and danger.

"Then let's not talk about it." His voice was tempered, like his gaze; he could have been discussing the weather. "Let's just enjoy a night on the town. And seriously, don't worry about YouTube. You won't be on it."

His level of indifference was amazing. He didn't care that he was übernotorious for probably more than that single video. And he talked about kink without inhibition; she could have been asking him whether he liked puppies or kittens. He obviously considered it unexceptional. But just to be clear, she confirmed her position. "I'm not interested in superkinky sex."

He smiled. "Does that mean you're interested in something less than superkinky?"

"Maybe. I told you I don't know yet."

He suddenly laughed. "Actually, I don't either. I go crazy

for a while wanting you, then talk myself out of it, then go crazy again. Christ, now I've offended you. It's not a question of your appeal, Miss Hart. You're tempting as hell. I've been equivocating because we might be from two different universes, galaxies...whatever—and I'm not so sure you can deal with it."

She immediately took offense, even though they were clearly on the same page. An unreasonable reaction that had nothing to do with logic, and everything to do with having a man say no to you before you could say no to him.

"Look," he said softly, leaning forward slightly. "Don't be pissed. It has nothing to do with you. It's me."

She gave him a pouty look. "That's the classic line when you're blowing off someone."

"I don't do classic lines, Miss Hart," he said, thinking her pouty look was really fucking hot. "I'm just trying to be honest. Ah—here's our champagne and shrimp." He smiled at her, then at the server, waited while their glasses were filled, said, "That will be all," and raised his glass to Kate. "To a memorable evening." His smile was so sexy it had to be illegal. "Drink up, Miss Hart. We're not going to think too hard. We're just going to have fun."

She exhaled, felt her tension ease. She was within touching distance of God's gift to women, warmed through and through by that sexy smile and honestly—like him, she wasn't entirely sure what she wanted to do. Although right now, it wasn't out of the question that she could come to orgasm just by looking at him.

Dominic was casually dressed in a black T-shirt, a sepia and black small houndstooth check sport coat, black slacks,

and sepia suede lace-up shoes, his dark silken hair gleaming in the subdued lighting, curling slightly at his nape, his
high cheekbones and fine straight nose the gold standard
for classic beauty. His brilliant blue gaze was pure temptation because he was smiling at her like she was the only
woman in the world. Even if it was in play, that smile-
across-the-room moment took her breath away.

"Hey." Soft, low, almost a whisper.

She slowly smiled. "Hey back."

"Enjoying yourself?"

She wanted to get up and hug him she felt so good. "Yeah,"
she said instead. "I'm checking this moment off my bucket list."

"Maybe I can give you some more moments later," he
drawled.

Conscious of the deliberate mood shift, she flirted back.
"Maybe I'll let you."

"*Let* me?" An infinitesimal edge had entered his voice.

"Do you have a problem with that?"

His gaze was suddenly cool. "You'll know if I do."

Kate dragged in a shaky breath, her carnal nerves
twitching big-time, like they'd been jolted by a power surge.
"Don't," she whispered.

"It's really complicated, isn't it?" he softly said.

"Seriously fucked up," she said as softly, wondering
what was wrong with her that she responded to his authority with such instant lust.

His brows settled into a slight frown. "I haven't done
this virginal dance before, if it matters."

"And I've never been turned on just looking at someone," she said in the same grudging tone.

He suddenly laughed. "We're going to have to lighten things up."

"Easy for you to say when you can turn off your sex drive like a spigot. I can't do that." She shifted slightly in her chair as the heated pleasure waves rippling inside her punched it up a notch as though to emphasize her point.

Dominic noticed, covertly glanced at his watch. Christ, it was only eight forty-five. And selfishly, he was damned hungry. "Lesson number one, Miss Hart. Think of something else. Or let me help you. We don't have to discuss this now if you'd rather not but it just occurred to me that I haven't heard from Roscoe whether we had the twenty million wired to our account. Care to lay odds on whether we won that little game or not? I'll give you two to one the transfer's been made."

"I'd be stupid to take that bet after seeing what you did to those guys."

"How about odds on who drinks more tonight?"

"Again, not a reasonable bet. We *could* guess each other's favorite ice cream."

He grinned. "Seriously, ice cream? That's gotta be a woman's question. It's always chocolate, isn't it? Don't look at me like that, the only woman I know who eats ice cream is my sister. Okay?"

"Okay. Then who's ahead on points in the NBA?"

"Now I'm impressed. The Heat."

"Only by six points."

"Now I'm *really* impressed."

"Thanks," she softly said. "You did good."

"See how easy it is." He grinned. "Watch and learn, babe."

But he liked that she was so adaptable. Swift to arouse, she could be pacified just as quickly, her mind and body extremely sensitive to stimuli.

How gratifying.

He was deeply obliged to Max for having found Miss Hart. Quite separate from her whiz kid capabilities in forensic accounting, her company made the world less gray.

Champagne seemed appropriate to the occasion.

After their drinks, they cabbed to the recently designated "best restaurant in Hong Kong." Cépage was the Hong Kong affiliate of the highly rated Les Amis restaurant in Singapore. The decor was sleek and modern, from the paneled red-wine cellar to the teak dining room with burgundy velvet armchairs to the rooftop gardens where cigar smokers could retire after dinner. The menu was cosmopolitan, all the best cuisine of Asia and Europe drafted into seasonal roles. The wine list included the pricey '96 Krug Clos.

They started with a carpaccio of Hokkaido scallop, citrus fruit, and lemon balm, topped with a little sea salt, moved on to the Tayouran egg confit, with truffled oxtail gelée, ibérico ham, and croutons. Then to a Chin Chow classic, spectacularly moist goose meat—an extra serving for Dominic—with a soy sauce fueled by ginger and anise. Along with a simple steak frites on the side for Dominic while Kate finished her goose.

Not that she picked at her food, Dominic noted. She ate everything with relish. He liked a woman with an appetite.

Dominic Knight ate enough for three men, Kate thought. How did he stay so buff? Sex probably, damn him; as if she had the right to be pissed.

Two bottles of champagne later—the majority downed
by Dominic—they finished their meal with a sour kumquat
ice cream on a nutty cookie base and, leaning back in his
chair, Dominic motioned for the check. "Unless you'd like
coffee."

"God no, and lose this nice buzz?"

He grinned. "You're always frank, Miss Hart."

"In contrast to everyone else you meet?"

"Yes." He peeled off several large bills from the folded
money in his pocket, dropped them on the table, and
looked up at Kate with a smile. "Thank you for your company, Miss Hart. I enjoyed myself."

"Thank *you*. The food was delicious." The company
was more delicious, but she wasn't quite drunk enough to
say so.

Minutes later, they were standing on the sidewalk outside the restaurant, the electric excitement of the city swirling around them, the pavement a crush of people.

"Would you like to go dancing?" Dominic offered.

"I'm not sure I can move after all that food." Kate looked
up at him. "You'd have to carry me around the dance floor."

He smiled. "I could do that."

"You're different," she abruptly said, giving him a
searching look.

"I am?"

"Normal, happy."

"Probably drunk. You haven't seen me drunk before."

"Are you drunk?"

"Not really." He tapped his thigh. "Hollow leg. It's a real
advantage at a Chinese business dinner where there's a

toast every five minutes. Or in Moscow, where vodka's consumed like water." His brows flickered up and down briefly. "I never sign the wrong contract."

"I'll bet others do."

"Sometimes." He grinned. "Have I gotten you drunk enough to sign the wrong contract?"

"I come from a town with ten bars on the two blocks of Main Street. What do you think?"

"Maybe we should do shooters."

"Are you *trying* to get me drunk?"

He raised an eyebrow. "Could be."

"For?"

"For you to make a move on me. I've been trying to behave."

"And I'm trying not to make a move on a man who's got so many notches in his belt, I'd fade into oblivion a second afterward."

A quick smile. "After what?"

"I'm not going to say it."

"Should I?"

She looked around at the stream of humanity swirling past them.

"No one cares," he said. "We're just an impediment in their way. So let me be clear. I want to sleep with you, Miss Hart, despite your earlier indecision and mine. I've wanted to since the first day I met you. Maybe you could take pity on me before you leave. I promise to be gentle, if that helps."

She didn't say he was the last man on earth who was a candidate for a pity fuck. She said, "Why me?"

"I don't know," he said. "Maybe it's because you're so smart." He grinned. "Or smart-alecky. Or maybe you remind me that wild, urgent feeling still exists in the world and even someone like me can feel hope. Now tell me to shut the fuck up. Seriously."

She smiled. "So you're not all badass and ripped edges and cutthroat after all."

"Don't get your hopes up," he said gently. "I'm ninety percent irrevocably damaged."

"Maybe I don't think so."

"And maybe that's part of your disobedient personality," he said, more softly than necessary, his long lashes partially hiding his eyes. "You haven't learned to agree with me yet."

"That's probably not going to happen," she warned.

He looked at her with a slightly wry smile, his gaze thoughtful. "Sure, kill all my dreams." The sharp rise of his cheekbone twitched, his smile widened.

And she suddenly saw him through a raw, unfiltered lens—he looked bulletproof, self-sufficient, not damaged, broad-shouldered enough to hold the world on his shoulders, unadulterated male of such obvious beauty, she said without thinking, "I'll bet women never say no to you."

His lashes dropped slightly. "It's a mercenary world, Miss Hart."

"Please. They don't all want your money." She knew better. Money or not, he wouldn't lack women in his life.

"Let's just say, it's a trade-off. I want something, they want something."

"So I should ask for something. Is that what you're saying?"

His smile was breathtaking. Moving into her space, he slid a finger under her chin and gently lifted her face so the blue of his eyes glittered in the neon lights. "Name it, Miss Hart."

She caught her breath. He meant it. "Anything?"

Ignoring the crowd, he slid his free hand down her back, pulled her into his body, bent his head until his mouth was hovering a hairsbreadth from hers. "Anything at all," he whispered.

She could feel his erection hard against her stomach and her response was instant. And it had nothing to do with any monetary quid pro quo. "How gentle is gentle?" The website video was still vivid in her memory.

Her question was swallowed up in the noise of the street.

He turned his head so his ear brushed her mouth and when she repeated what she'd said, he swept her up in his arms and said loud enough to be heard above the tumult, "It's up to you."

She grinned. "No orders? I don't believe it."

"I have my moments."

"When you want sex."

"When I want sex with you."

The virtual traffic gridlock aside, his car was waiting at the curb near the restaurant and despite Kate's protest, Dominic slid into the backseat, still carrying her. "It doesn't matter," he murmured, settling her on his lap. "You don't know anyone here."

"But everyone knows you."

"Are you kidding? In this crush?" He dropped a quick

kiss on her nose, then spoke to the driver. "We're going back to the Ritz. Try not to run over anyone."

The driver understood, and leaning on the horn, he slowly forced his way through the stalled traffic, until they finally broke free two blocks from the harbor.

"God, you feel good in my arms like this." Dominic said, husky and low. "There's something about you..." His voice trailed off. Full disclosure was always a mistake.

"There's something about you, too, and I can feel it"— Kate wiggled her bottom—"in all its impressive glory."

"Are you saying we impress you, Miss Hart?" Back on safe ground, his voice was teasing.

"Do fish swim?"

He laughed. "Clearly, a romantic."

"I doubt you want a romantic."

"True. Still," he said with a grin, "I'd hate to think you want me only for my impressive size."

"Sorry," she murmured, with a playful flutter of her lashes. "But I'm only in the market for stud services tonight."

When in the past, he would have been grateful for such a reply, he suddenly felt otherwise. "Maybe I can change your mind." His smile was impudent. "I can be very persuasive."

"I'm sure you can. But Nana didn't raise any dumb kids, so your persuasion might not work."

"We'll have to see, won't we?" he asked, arching his hips upward and pleasing them both.

She shut her eyes and softly moaned, the hard length of his erection pressed into her bottom firing up every sexual receptor in her body.

"Did you like that?" he whispered. "Would you like to

feel me inside you? Deep, deep inside? Open your eyes, Miss Hart." His voice suddenly took on a hard edge. "Look at me."

Her lashes slowly lifted, her gaze moody. "I don't respond well to that tone of voice."

"Maybe this time you should." A slow smile formed on his lips. "Because I have what you need."

Her nostrils flared, a hot green flame lit her eyes. "I don't *need* you. I have a vibrator."

"I know."

"Jesus," she hissed, trying to shove him away. "Have you ever heard of privacy?"

His grip tightened. "Don't make a scene," he said quietly. "We're here now—at the docks."

She glanced out the window, saw a man suddenly materialize at the car door. Dragging in a breath, she reminded herself that she was in Asia with a man she barely knew who could make grown men quail. Dominic's people were everywhere and until she reached the hotel, she was subject to his authority. The hotel staff would be less beholden to him. "I'm fine," she calmly said. "I won't make a scene. But I'd like to walk if you don't mind."

He looked at her askance for a moment, surprised at her sudden docility. Then he dipped his head. "Suit yourself." When the door opened a second later, he lifted her from his lap, set her on her feet outside, joined her a moment later, and led her to the launch. Neither spoke as the boat accelerated away from the dock at high speed. Pouring himself another single malt, Dominic left the cabin without a word and soon after, Kate heard his voice up on deck.

He came down for her as they approached Kowloon,

and after docking, escorted her to a waiting car. The trip to the hotel passed in a cool silence.

She didn't exactly flounce into the Ritz-Carlton, although it was clear to anyone looking that Mr. Knight's female companion was unhappy. His expression, in contrast, was placid. To the hotel staff, however, the state of Mr. Knight's disposition had sizable financial consequences.

The night manager came running up as they crossed the lobby. Bowing like any practiced courtier, he breathlessly inquired whether he could be of service to Dominic.

"Thank you, no." Dominic smiled politely. "Although, if you'd see that we're not disturbed until morning, I'd appreciate it. Miss Hart is tired."

The man shot a glance at Kate's stubbornly set jaw, understood that it was safer to defer to Mr. Knight's request than not, and crisply said, "As you wish, sir."

If you only knew what I wished. "I *will* need coffee at eight tomorrow morning though," Dominic said mildly.

"Yes, sir."

The manager held open the elevator door for Kate and Dominic, and the moment the doors shut, he called up to the club level. "Both of you get down here," he snapped to the concierge. "Mr. Knight doesn't want to be disturbed tonight."

NINE

So much for help from the staff, Kate thought, as the elevator carried them upward. The manager had practically kissed Dominic's ring. Which meant she was on her own and her only true security lay in a locked and chained door.

When the elevator came to a stop and the doors opened, thanks to an evening's worth of champagne, a fuming temper, and a sense of self-preservation, Kate shot out like a sprinter from the blocks. *Don't you fucking dare follow me,* she muttered under her breath as she stalked away without a backward glance.

Had she looked back, she would have seen Dominic Knight contemplating her hasty retreat with a faint smile.

The moment she entered her suite, she slammed the door, turned the lock, and jammed in the chain.

Oh Christ. Was the butler still here? She spun around. No. Thank God. She exhaled in relief. Dominic could say all he wanted about people not listening, but they did. And as far as she was concerned, it was only a question of when they'd spill the beans, not if. But then she probably read more *National Enquirer* articles than he did.

Tossing aside the shawl, she kicked off her shoes and moved across the softly lit living room, past the artfully arranged fruit and cheese tray on the coffee table set next to the bottle of champagne on ice, and grinned. *Fuck you,*

Dominic Knight. Everything doesn't always go your way, does it? Untying the bow at her waist, she entered the spacious bedroom with the million-dollar view, unzipped the back of her dress, and let it slide from her shoulders. Pausing long enough to step out of the puddled silk on the carpet, she slid her thumbs under the elastic of her panties, paused again so they could slither down her legs, and with a slightly inebriated skip and a jump, left them discarded on the floor. Two steps more and she dropped onto the bed already turned down by unseen hands.

The mattress was soft as down, the sheets some outrageous thread count and smooth as silk, the pile of pillows a minor distraction until she tossed all but one on the floor and curled up under the wisteria-colored king-size quilt covering the king-size bed. If someone was watching—and someone was—they would have marveled at how quickly she moved from wakefulness to sleep.

Five seconds. Dominic smiled, dropped his watch hand, and gently shut the door to the suite next door. Had he been a prideful man, her indifference would have been humbling. As it was, it left him with plenty of time to decide what he wanted to do. Or, more precisely, how he wanted to do it.

With Miss Hart sleeping, he took the opportunity to check his e-mail because urgent mail was a constant in his life. Someone, somewhere, always needed an answer. An hour later, the most pressing messages had been addressed, and stripping off his clothes, he put on a T-shirt and pajama pants. Moving through the silent corridors, he walked into the bar, filled a glass with ice, and poured himself a rye.

Alone in the room that boasted one of the best views in the world, he slowly drank his rye and contemplated the dazzling splendor of Hong Kong, all blazing neon and sparkling lights against the darkness.

Unfortunately, the splendid view took second place to his thoughts. Miss Hart had looked exactly as he'd pictured her in his imagination. Slender, lithesome, great tits, and legs that went on forever. Her skin had been unusually pale in the moonlit room—the word *immaculate* had suddenly taken on a presence. Along with all the perverse connotations having to do with that notion. As if purity itself was a challenge. Christ, he needed a little restraint here. Miss Hart wasn't bought and paid for. It had been a long time since he'd approached a woman who wasn't aware of her role and function. He'd have to make sure he didn't scare the hell out of Miss Hart. With that in mind, he poured himself another rye and enjoyed the view and a rare moment of solitude.

After he finished the drink, he reached over the bar and set the glass in the sink. He might have staff and employees in almost constant attendance but he was capable of taking care of himself. In fact, there were times he preferred it.

Like now.

Sliding from the bar stool, he stood motionless.

This occasion felt very different and it wasn't just because there was no money involved. On the other hand, he'd never once seriously questioned his intentions toward Miss Hart. Or at least not since Amsterdam. So...

He slipped the key card from his pocket.

*   *   *

A half hour later, Kate rolled over, squinted against the moonlight for a second, then suddenly sat bolt upright. "How the hell did you get in here?" she gasped. She suddenly felt vulnerable, alone on this hotel floor with a man who had no limits, was accountable to no one, who bought anyone and anything without constraint.

Dominic reached out, picked up the key card from a nearby table, raised it slightly, and tipped it in the direction of an adjoining door. "These suites all run together."

"I suppose you're next door," she said tartly, taking the offensive. *Never show fear,* Gramps had always said. *It takes away your advantage.* "I should have known."

She was perfectly comfortable sitting nude before him. It gave him momentary pause. He would have expected a quick covering up. On the other hand, Miss Hart's sumptuous breasts gilded by moonlight made it easy to dismiss his reservations. "Actually, I'm three suites away." He smiled faintly. "Although, not at the moment."

"No kidding. Do you want something?"

"Not necessarily. I couldn't sleep."

"So you decided to be a voyeur."

He shrugged. "I don't know what I decided." As he'd watched her sleeping, he'd begun to wonder if he was doing the right thing again. Which was why he hadn't wakened her.

"Why don't I tell you."

His brows rose.

"You're not reinventing the wheel, Mr. Knight."

"Dominic."

"Mr. Knight," she coolly repeated. "Look, you're a big-time plutocrat. I'm a nobody. You've been thinking you might fuck me before I leave, then send me on my way. You've apparently decided. And here you are."

"So you've been in this situation before?"

"Answer me. Am I right?"

"Maybe. I don't know. Now you answer."

"You're the first big wheel to invade my bedroom. How's that?"

"What about some other room? Have you done it with some big shot in some other room? Your professors maybe?"

"Jesus, are you my guardian?"

"I could be."

"No you couldn't," she hissed. "You don't have enough money."

"Of course I do."

"Let me rephrase that. You don't have enough money to be *my* guardian or warden or whatever the fuck turns you on."

"Do I have enough for one night of your time?"

"No."

"No?" Cool, impudent, assured.

"Definitely no," she said, oversweet and smiling. "I'm so sorry," she bitchily added. *Arrogant prick.* She was feeling more assured. Unless he was going to physically force himself on her, and he didn't seem to fit that role lounging in his chair, conversing with her in that unheated tone, she was safe.

His dark brows settled into a frown. "Yet you don't mind sitting there like that." He flicked a finger at her nude torso.

"I didn't know modesty was a requirement." Flip and snide.

"It isn't. I'm just surprised," he calmly noted, having checked his momentary resentment that she may or may not have sat casually nude like that before.

"After seeing that video, I'm surprised anything can surprise you."

"Not much can," he said, ignoring her provocation. "You, however, are the exception. Why don't you put on a robe, Miss Hart, and come talk to me. I promise to behave." He indicated the chair beside his with a small wave.

"And if I don't?"

"Feel free to go back to sleep."

"And you?"

He softly sighed. "I may not behave enough to leave."

"So I'm supposed to sleep with you sitting there watching me?"

"You could. Or you could come and talk to me. Would you like a snack? I can have the kitchen send up something."

"They're probably sleeping."

"Then they'll get up. Would you like something?"

You on a platter for starters. Christ, where did that come from? She dragged in a steadying breath, beat back her irresponsible libido, told herself Dominic Knight was too dangerous no matter how powerful his allure. "No...no—really, I'm fine."

He noticed her small hesitation, her resolute little breath, the slight tremble in her voice when she spoke. "Not hungry?" he softly queried, understanding the game was fully in play now.

"Not for that. There, that must please you," she said with

a grimace. "Your record is unblemished. Every woman in the world wants you." *And why wouldn't they,* her troublesome, headstrong, overly confident little voice murmured. *When he's gorgeous and sexy as hell lounging there, his T-shirt molded to his muscled body, the tie on his pajama bottoms just a tug away from displaying world-class cock.*

"I thought maybe *you* didn't," he said quietly.

"You thought wrong. But I'm going home without, shall we say, getting to know you better. Sorry."

"I'd like to change your mind."

That calm, quiet voice again—like nothing fazed him. "I'd like a lot of things," she said brusquely, not capable of his equanimity. "Most of them I won't get."

"I can give you whatever you want."

"You don't understand. I don't want to be number two thousand twenty and counting in your world of kinky sex."

"Ah."

"Exactly. There must be a cast of thousands anxious for the role. You don't need me."

"You're unusual, Miss Hart."

She smiled. "I like to think so."

"I can keep you for six more days, you know. I could say I'm not sure the Singapore bank has performed yet."

"I suppose. But the question is, why would you?"

He grinned. "To get my money's worth. Come, Miss Hart. Keep me company. I can't sleep for wanting you. Talk to me at least. That can't hurt."

"I don't trust you."

"Or yourself?"

"Yes. Happy now?"

"Not yet. I could be. But that's up to you. Where's your robe?"

"Wherever your butler put it."

"He's not my butler, he's your butler."

"No, he's not. You paid for him like you pay for everything else."

"But not you."

"No, I mean, yes, not me."

He laughed and came to his feet. "I'll find your robe. Then I'll take you to the bar, where you can enjoy the world's best view and my charming company. That should be safe enough."

"If only," she muttered.

"I heard that," he said over his shoulder as he moved toward a bank of louvered doors. "My heart did a little flip-flop."

"Please."

"Word of God."

"Jesus, you'll say anything for a fuck."

Dragging her robe from a hanger, he threw it across the room. "I'm not going to look, because you're probably right. I might do anything for a fuck."

"Finally," she said, rising from the bed and slipping her arms through the sleeves. "A little truthiness."

He chuckled. "I gather you watch Colbert. We could probably find him somewhere on the Net if you want."

"Don't bother." What she wanted wasn't on the Net, anyway. He was ten feet away, the murderously handsome, bad-boy version of sex personified. And much too dangerous to her future if she were being sensible. She finished tying the belt on the robe, and said in a tone somewhere between politesse and a mild warning, "You can look now."

Totally ignoring the warning-off part, Dominic turned and smiled. "Very nice. Although everything about you is nice. And restful."

"I'm not sure that's a compliment."

"Believe me, it is. I lead a hectic life." He held out his hand. "Let's see if there's something to eat at the bar. I'm hungry."

"You just ate."

"Two hours ago." He wiggled his fingers. "Afraid?"

She moved toward him. "Should I be?"

"No." As her fingers slid through his, he called on whatever reserves of willpower he possessed. "I promise."

TEN

He played bartender, pouring her a glass of champagne and himself another rye. Then he rummaged through the three small refrigerators under the bar and came up with cheese, cold cuts, olives. Placing them on the marble bar top, he gave a wave toward the lounge. "I'm going to find some crackers."

He came back with nuts, crackers, pickled peaches and lychees, and madeleines, as well as two boxes of chocolates, one French and one local, and dumped the foodstuffs on the bar. "You have to be a little hungry," he said, beginning to rip open boxes.

"Twist my arm," she said with a grin and pointed. "Push those chocolates my way."

"How about a madeleine with your champagne?" He slid the two boxes over.

Soon he had all the tins, bottles, and boxes opened, he'd found some silverware, plates, a pile of those embroidered napkins, and he'd poured them both another drink. "Am I resourceful or what?" he said with a grin, lifting his glass to her.

"If I were dropped into some jungle clearing in the middle of nowhere, you'd certainly be the right man to have along." She smiled over the mocha truffle she was about to put in her mouth. "I didn't even know I was hungry."

"After seeing you eat at dinner, I thought you might be," he said, busy arranging a line of crackers on a bar towel. "You have a good appetite."

"Is that an insult?"

A swift glance from under his lashes. "God, no, don't glare."

"I'm not glaring."

"Fuck if you're not." He set down the cracker box. "So you like to eat. It's a good thing. Different, that's all. Most women pretend they don't eat." Picking up a package of sliced cheese, he began putting one on each cracker.

"The women *you* know."

He wasn't going there, not even close. "You're right. It's a narrow segment, I agree. Cheese? No? Did you try the lychee nuts?" He eased the bottle closer to her.

"Are you changing the subject?"

"That was my intent. Do you always take a bite out of every chocolate first?"

She smiled. "So you're not going to talk about the women who pretend not to eat?"

Dominic's turn to smile. "Nope. Sure you don't want a cracker?"

"And pressing you would be useless."

"Very." He spooned a dollop of pâté atop the cheese on the first cracker. "Tell me about the chocolates?"

She lifted one brow. "Maybe I don't want to."

A twitch of a smile, quickly suppressed. "Do you squabble with everyone, or just me?"

"I'm pleased you find me so entertaining," she said with a sniff.

"Then we're both pleased." Another quick glance up through his lashes.

She dragged in a sharp breath, his fleeting glance explicitly carnal, his voice like velvet on her skin.

"What?" He smiled lazily.

"Nothing," she whispered. She drew in a deep breath of restraint and the full swell of her breasts, only thinly veiled by the white silk of her robe, rose in two perfect round fuck-me spheres.

Dominic slid the spoon back into the pâté jar. Those ripe tits nearly bursting through the delicate silk would give a monk a hard-on and he was far from abstemious. Food was no longer a top priority. Although Miss Hart's tremulous approach to sex had to be dealt with gently. And patiently. "I'm assuming you don't like creams," he casually said, indicating the half-eaten chocolates in the box with a wave.

"How polite you are. Do you actually want an answer?"

"I do. I'm curious." He dipped his head in the direction of the ravaged chocolates. "I've never seen that before." He picked up a cheese and pâté cracker. Since he wasn't going to rush Miss Hart, he had time to eat.

"Nothing so uncouth, you mean."

He grinned. "No. It reminds me of some three-year-old in the jam jar." He popped the cracker in his mouth.

"You know about three-year-olds?" *Christ, she shouldn't have asked.* "Sorry," she quickly said.

He finished chewing and swallowed. "My sister has"— he counted on his fingers briefly—"six children." He smiled. "I've seen my share of little three-year-old hellions." He stabbed a finger at the box. "So?"

"So—I don't like creams," she said, flustered that she'd embarrassed herself by suggesting he might have children. *Although he hadn't actually answered, had he? Rich men like him could have children they discreetly supported so long as the mother was content with the financial arrangement.* "Checking out the flavors saves me calories," she went on under his cool-eyed gaze. "And I don't bite every chocolate like that unless they're mine—or in this case, yours."

The word *bite* and *yours* caused a predictable jolt to his libido, but he was long past youthful impetuosity. "You don't have to worry about calories."

"Thank you. Nor do you." There. Better. Unruffled.

"I work too hard. I have to eat a lot just to keep my weight stable."

She tried not to look at the results of his eating regimen, but his T-shirted torso was only a bar width away, and his powerful arms were even closer as he spooned more pâté on top of a cheese-covered cracker and slid it in his mouth. "One more drink and then I'd better stop," she said in lieu of all the other possibilities racing through her brain. The ones having to do with unbridled sex and Dominic Knight.

He understood body language better than most. It was a requisite in his line of work. Miss Hart was restless. Since he didn't want her to bolt, he moved back, leaned against the counter under the liquor bottles, and brought up the subject of her Bucharest success, his tone temperate, the topic intentionally banal. He wanted to put her at ease and purposely asked questions about her methodology for breaking through firewalls. She visibly relaxed as she answered, eventually started on the second box of chocolates, found several she liked, and ate them with the same appreciation he'd noticed at dinner. Definitely a woman of appetites.

Over the course of the next half hour he managed to curb himself and his desire for her. And if she hadn't said out of the blue, "Tell me something. The fact that I'm leaving soon accounts for your interest in me, right?" the night might have proved uneventful.

He paused with his refilled glass halfway to his mouth, his expression guarded. "Honestly?"

"Is that a problem?"

He set his glass down, met her gaze straight on. "No. And yes, the timeline's a factor."

"Ha! I knew it!"

Her little jiggle of elation made him smile. "You like to be right?"

"Don't you?"

He shrugged. "I'm flexible."

"Like in Singapore?"

"I *can* be flexible."

"For the right incentive."

But there was a teasing note in her voice now and her green gaze was bright with triumph or flirtation. Or champagne. He'd have to find out which, or whether it even mattered anymore. "What do you have in mind?" he drawled, thinking he'd like to kiss her rosy cheek first, taste that soft, sweet freshness. "I'm open to any incentive, large or small."

The word *large* scorched through her brain, sent a flame-hot rush of desire into every susceptible crevice in her body, triggered a small gasp she wasn't able to contain.

He didn't move, he didn't so much as blink, and when

he spoke, his voice was no more than a whisper. "Is there something I might do for you perhaps?" Champagne nearly sloshed over the rim of her glass and, moving quickly, he lifted it from her trembling hand and set it aside. "All you have to do is ask."

"I don't want to." Gathering herself, she leaned back in her chair to put some distance between herself and temptation, braced her hands palm down on the bar to steady her nerves, and tried to breathe normally. Then she lifted her cat-eyed, restless gaze. "If you must know, it's too humiliating to be just another mindless fuck."

"Christ, that's not what you are. Look." He hesitated, his feelings so far from what passed for normal lately he was entering new territory. "I don't—" He stopped again, not sure whether honesty was beneficial or if it was safer to lie. He'd never actually been truthful to all the temporary women in his life. "I can guarantee you wouldn't be"— another pause—"that," he finished, rather than repeat her blunt phrase. "The fact is—I didn't want to send you home after Amsterdam. I have no idea why. Werner could have handled Singapore for me." Faced with the new, baffling dilemma of his fascination with this young woman, recognizing that what he had to offer wasn't in her best interests, in fact, might be ruinous for her, he reluctantly made a decision. "On second thought"—he exhaled heavily—"this"— he did a back-and-forth motion with his index finger—"you and me isn't a good idea. Not for you anyway." He took a breath, reached for his glass. "We'd better call it a night." Raising his glass to his mouth, he poured the liquor down his throat, then shot her a look as he set the glass down.

"Go before I change my mind." Grabbing the bottle, he refilled his glass and lifted his chin toward the door. "Go."

"I don't want to," Kate quietly said. "Not really. Unless you want me to." She couldn't tell if he did or not; this was not a man bent on seduction. He might even be inherently decent, which surprised her. She'd seen him domineering, arrogant, even tyrannical, but not like this. Not Dominic Knight being virtuous.

With a soft oath, he set the bottle down. One of them should be practical; he thought he had been. *Now what?* A rhetorical question quickly dismissed. "I hope you know what you're doing," he said, thinking how unbelievably sexy she looked biting down hard on the inside of her lip. "Because I'm not sure I do."

"I think so."

"You'd better be sure." His voice was gruff.

She took another deep breath that lit up his retinas, smashed his moral compass, and set the evening in motion even before she said, "I'm sure. I find you irresistible."

A small sigh. He appreciated the irony. He couldn't remember when he'd last said no to sex. Another sigh, deeper this time, because what he was about to say was sobering. "I feel the same way about you."

His quiet declaration made her heart flip. "You don't have to say that."

An easy smile. "It's a compliment. Say thank you."

"Thank you. And now if you don't mind."

"You're impatient."

"It's been a while."

He wanted to ask how long, but stopped himself

because it didn't matter. Instead, he walked around the end of the bar, came to a halt beside her, lifted her off her bar stool, seated her on the end of the bar facing him, and moved between her legs. Smoothly untying her robe, he slipped it off her shoulders and let it fall down her arms. "Very showy," he whispered, running his palms over her large breasts, gently stroking the soft, yielding flesh.

Leaning forward, he kissed her rosy cheek and felt such surprising pleasure, he kissed her again—on her lips.

As his mouth lifted from hers, she blushed, looked down, then slowly raised her gaze to his. Innocence waiting to be fucked, he pleasantly thought. *And his*, he decided with the proprietary instincts of a modern princeling. He traced the pale curvature of her breasts with his fingertips. "You shouldn't hide these," he said softly. "We'll get you some clothes you can wear for me…in private." Capturing her nipples between his thumbs and forefingers, he gently squeezed. "Something to show these off," he said, husky and low, watching the peaks swell with the increasing pressure.

She groaned as the ravishing sensations flowed downward, curled hot in the pit of her stomach, instantly liquefied her body as though she welcomed his casual coercion, as if she were utterly shameless, as if his touch, no matter how willful, inflamed her lust. Squirming on the marble bar top, she whimpered, "Please, please…oh Lord—"

"Easy." His voice was low, silken, placating. "We have all night."

She wanted to say, *I can't wait all night*, but her brain was consumed with frenzied lust, not speech, her senses in tumult, the ache between her legs relentless. His grip on her nipples was firm, hard, insistent, his fingers strangely rough, as if he worked with his hands—*Oh God*—with ropes and whips. A terrifying sense of powerlessness ran up her spine at the thought of Dominic Knight with a whip and she shivered.

"Hey, hey…slow down," he whispered, letting his fingers slip from her nipples. "Relax."

His lips brushed hers, his kiss soothing, the warmth of his mouth lingering on hers with such gentleness, she could feel the wildness inside her ease. "How do you do it?" she whispered.

Another benevolent little kiss. "It's better if you don't move too fast."

"And you can make it last?" Her body was purring in wait mode.

His smile was close, heated. "We'll try." Then he slid his palms under her breasts and raised his hands slightly. "How does this feel?"

"Like I want you inside me."

He grinned. "You're rushing me, babe." He adjusted the weight of her breasts in his palms. "Maybe I don't feel like doing that right now. Maybe I want you to wait." He spread his long, slender fingers, gently squeezed her soft flesh.

She swallowed hard as a heated surge streaked downward from her breasts and a ripple of unbearable longing flared inside her. "What if I can't wait?"

He looked up. "You have to."

A resentful flash in her eyes. "Excuse me?"

"I'm the one with the dick and you're the one who

wants it," he said gently. "It's not complicated. Now look. We're going to go—just a little higher? Like that? More? A little more? Jesus," he breathed, his gaze on her large breasts shoved up into towering mounds. "I'm going to have to fuck these huge tits."

Even as she gasped at the discomfort, her body treacherously welcomed Dominic Knight's coercion in a hot liquid rush of desire. She moaned, shifted slightly on the cool marble bar top, clenched her thighs against her stark craving.

Not yet, he selfishly thought. "Too high?" But he didn't lower his hands; he pushed her breasts higher.

She cried out in shock or distress or something else entirely.

That something else was too enticing to ignore. She didn't mind a little pain. "No more waiting for you, Miss Hart?" he said pleasantly.

"I'd rather not."

Clipped or randy, he wasn't sure. "So you need a little help?" But he was already slipping a finger into her slick cleft. "Umm, there we are." His fingertips tenderly touched her hypersensitive clit. "Nice." He squeezed delicately, looked up; his voice softened. "Did we get that right?"

She softly moaned as a riptide began rising inside, her cheeks flushed.

"Here—lean back." He helped her shift her weight back on her hands. "Give me a little room." He slid his finger past her clit, deeper, but not too deep, teasing her. "Better now?"

She pressed into his finger, moved her hips, lifted her big-eyed gaze to his.

"Wound up tight, babe?"

"Please...I mean it, please..."

A flicker of a smile. "You need to come down, don't you?" His hand brushed her cheek, slid down to her breast, cupped it gently, found her nipple, and squeezed. Her small gasp warmed his cheek as he bent to add another finger to her silky heat. Pushing gently, he slid the second finger alongside the first, thrust both in slowly, lingered on her tingling G-spot, her swollen clit, looked up as she softly sighed. Then he settled into a slow, rhythmic, in and out stroke, taking his time, watching her.

Gently rocking against his fingers, eyes shut against the building bliss, Kate finally gave in to her on-again, off-again burning hot craving for Dominic Knight. She didn't care anymore about kinkiness or control freak issues. He could be Bluebeard for all she cared, so long as he didn't stop doing what he was doing. He was worlds better than any vibrator and a universe better than any of her former fumbling sexual partners. Really, with them the phrase *Lie back and think of England* was totally appropriate. But with Dominic, she groaned in a little musical exhalation of heavenly rapture. His selfless attentions to her G-spot were awesome.

"You like that?"

She could hear the smile in his voice, the satisfaction, and on some perversely primal level it gave her pleasure to satisfy him. Not that the quid pro quo wasn't unbelievable. Breathtaking. Seriously worth the wait.

Unhurried, focused, he massaged her clit, around and around, slowly, gently, perfectly on target, then stroked her G-spot with equal thoughtfulness, watching her from under his lashes, waiting for her to catch that perfect wave.

Her body suddenly went still, her breath caught.

"Look at me or I'll stop."

She heard his soft growl through a red-hot, preorgasmic haze. Then the exquisite pressure on her clit disappeared. A fraction of a second passed before the significance of the two actions registered in her fevered brain and another second before her eyelids flew up.

She met Dominic's smile.

"Good girl. I want you to look at me when you come. Can you do that?"

"Do I have a choice?" A tight-lipped hiss.

Another smile, fainter. "I'll take that as a yes."

He waited briefly, saw she was in no position to argue, and resumed his gentle stroking.

She saw the flicker of amusement in his gaze, but she was beyond resistance, needing what he could give her, already feeling the sumptuous pleasure rekindle inside her. Her greedy clit quivered in delight, the throbbing between her legs matched the racing of her heart. Forced to meet his hard, blue gaze, she yielded to his authority and to the rising frenzy of an imminent orgasm.

"I want you to understand who's in charge of your climax the next few days," he said coolly. "So there're no misunderstandings."

While a teeny, tiny part of her brain was telling him to fuck off, the rest of her mind was lit up like a Christmas tree, every pleasure center blazing bright with feel-good color, and right now, she was willing to promise him anything. "Got it," she whispered, then gasped, "Oh God!" and began to tremble.

"Don't shut your eyes."

The sharp command coupled with a tap on her clit made her wince.

Made her take notice.

Dominic recognized the effort it took for her to raise her lashes, decided it was time to end this little game. "Just so we're clear. I'm going to be fucking you all night, Miss Hart. If you please me, we'll make some decisions after that on how to make further use of your skills. We'll have a job evaluation in the morning, so do your best."

She felt the first orgasmic ripples surge as she thought of Dominic Knight, cool-eyed and all business in that navy blue pinstripe suit evaluating her sexual competence in the morning. Sucking in her breath, she felt the next powerful wave slam through her body and nervously glanced up at Dominic.

"You have my permission, Miss Hart," he said gently, his fingers buried deep inside her. "You may come now."

As if her body was his to command, as though she had no will, as though she was a slave to raging lust, she uttered a breathless sob and instantly climaxed. For stark moments, the world disappeared, her senses overwhelmed by orgasmic spasms so intense she felt as though she'd been swallowed up in a tidal wave.

Literally gasping, still half dazed, she broke through the surface of illusion, jerked back to reality by a mouth on her nipple. "No, no, don't!" Swinging her hand up, she tried to push Dominic away, every nerve still shell-shocked.

He brushed her hand down, held her gaze, lifted his brows fractionally—his message clear. Then he bent his head.

She went rigid, not quite sure whether she was fearful or pissed.

Looking up just before his mouth touched her nipple, he grinned. "Come on, Miss Hart. Another orgasm can't be that bad."

She sniffed. "How would you know?"

"All in good time," he murmured and bent his head.

But he was supergentle, his tongue soothing her nipple with little tender butterfly licks, his fingertips resting quiescent on her clit, the pressure feather light. Her spine eased, then her constraint, and short moments later, she surrendered to lush sensation, squirmed against the rising heat coursing through her body, uttered a small sigh as Dominic drew the taut peak into his mouth and nibbled lightly. Just nips at first, then little bites, and as her breathing began to change, he clasped the tender tip between his teeth and exerted enough force to leave marks.

Her shocked cry quickly altered to a low throaty groan as hot pleasure nullified the sting.

"Don't move." His strong fingers sank into the soft, pliant flesh of her breast, held her prisoner as he drew her entire jewel-hard nipple into his mouth and began to suck. Hard, deliberately hard, sharply, punishingly, ignoring her whimpers—a predator taking what he wanted by force.

Her protest died in her throat—a casualty of a hot, spiking lust that left her speechless and disturbed. She shouldn't be responding to such flagrant force. *Or such flagrant sensation*, a little voice pointed out. Then she heard him whisper, "You're really wet, Miss Hart. Does that mean you like me?" And she felt her face turn hot.

Even while mortified at her willing response, each authoritative bite of her nipple intensified the decadent, riveting sensations. "Damn you," she panted in blanket grievance against his authority and her breathless need. Then she sat up, shoved her fingers through his dark, silken hair, dragged his head closer, arched her back, and strained against the unspeakable ecstasy.

Forceful and firm, ungentle and methodic, he first sucked the nipple in his mouth at length, then transferred his expertise to the other breast. His fingers also fully engaged.

Priming her for the night ahead.

She no longer felt the full impact of his brutal assault on her nipples. She felt only a volatile, white-hot lust: analgesic, incandescent, melting away reason and intellect, preference or choice.

As her breathing escalated, Dominic jerked his head from her grasp and leaned back slightly. "Ready, Miss Hart?"

No longer moored in reality, she didn't hear him. Her eyes were half closed, her swollen nipples were throbbing in time with her heartbeat, and skittish preorgasmic flutters were beginning to spin out of control.

He smiled. Was six days enough to fully explore his new employee's hot-blooded passions? Should he change his plans, bring her along? He frowned. That meant moving outside his comfort zone. Not that he wouldn't be well compensated. Sex on demand didn't look like it would be a problem for Miss Hart.

A soft whimper interrupted his musing.

Recapturing her nipple in his mouth, he gripped the soft,

elastic tissue with his teeth, grasped her other nipple with his free hand, and eased his head and hand back by slow degrees until both nipples were stretched and distended. Intensified his focus on her G-spot as well for surefire results.

Whimpering in a ragged little cadence, Kate no longer knew if it was pleasure or pain bombarding her brain, the raw sensations overwhelmed by a raging hysteria. Whether it was torment or bliss she was feeling, the result was drenching her sex, stealing her reason, shattering her nerve endings, driving her with churning force toward orgasm.

"Oh God," she panted. "Oh God, oh God, oh—"

Her explosive scream shattered the stillness, an all-encompassing, soul-stirring ecstasy invaded her soul. *I never knew, I never knew, I never knew it could be this unbelievably good*...And she willingly gave herself up to the awesome, can-you-die-from-such-acute-pleasure orgasm that streamed, gushed, poured through her body for so long she ran out of breath to scream.

And was reduced at the end to a purr of contentment.

Then silence.

When she finally opened her eyes, she whispered, "I love the whole, entire, indescribably *glorious* world..."

Easing his fingers from her body, Dominic stood upright and smiled. "A dynamite orgasm will do that for you."

"You really *are* good," she breathed.

"You're really easy to please," he pleasantly said. "There's more when you've recovered."

She languorously stretched, smiled. "Because you haven't come."

"No. I was thinking of you." His blue gaze was benevolent, his voice mild. "You're a natural. We're going to get along."

"Did you think we wouldn't?" How could we not after *that*, she naively thought.

He shrugged. "You never know. Although," he said with a warm smile, "I'm looking forward to the night."

Maybe it was the look in his eyes rather than his words that caused her alarm. "I may not last a *whole* night," she said nervously.

"I don't think we have to worry about that." He reached out, ran his fingertip leisurely across the underside of one breast, his gaze assessing. "I've noticed you never wear a bra. You should," he said as if they'd been discussing her wardrobe rather than a night of sex.

"I don't like bras."

He knew she didn't, like he knew everything else about her now that he'd actually read Max's brief. "Nevertheless, we'll remedy that."

She frowned. "Just a damned minute."

"Is it a problem?"

"Of course it's a problem."

"We'll have to work out something then."

"I've seen your working out *something*," she muttered. "For your information, I'm not easily intimidated."

He laughed. "I'm sure you're not. Still, you'll look gorgeous in a bra." He cupped her breasts. "These are stunning." They were high, firm, ripe, and round; she didn't *need* a bra. That wasn't the point. "Maybe blue lace or black—what do you think? Perhaps virginal white."

She slapped his hands away.

Or she slapped at his hands and he humored her by complying.

"We'll just get a few bras to show off your great tits," he blandly said, as if they were discussing choices on a dinner menu. As if she hadn't just told him no. "You won't need panties," he added as though they'd already agreed on his agenda. He lightly brushed his knuckles over her silky pubic hair. "I want you available for fucking. How does that sound? Do you think you'd like to give me unrestricted access to your hot little body—in one of my offices perhaps, or maybe in a private room at the China Club, or up against a wall somewhere with people walking by ten feet away? Does that interest you?"

She'd clenched her fists on the bar top three sentences ago, he noticed. She was astonishingly easy to arouse; a little nymphet at his beck and call. And fully consenting. He'd given her a chance to leave.

Contemplating her hot, sexually charged green gaze, the flush of arousal pinking her face, he decided, defiance aside, Miss Hart was primed again. "I can keep you for six more days," he said, his voice exquisitely soft. "You're not going to sue me. We both know that, don't we?" He waited for her reply, a faint smile on his lips. "Don't we?" he pressed when she didn't respond. "Answer me."

How did he do it? Make her instantly desperate for sex by simply ordering her about as if he had the right. She bit her lip to keep from squirming, to still the sordid pulsing between her legs, to damp her unreasonable craving for the beautiful, audacious, troublesome, demanding Dominic Knight.

"You're going to have to learn to speak when spoken to,

Miss Hart. It's only common courtesy. Tell me you understand you still have six days to fulfill on your contract."

"Don't do this," she sullenly said.

"And your duties weren't definitely described as I recall,"
he said, as if she hadn't spoken. "Isn't that right?"

She scowled. "Damn you," she muttered, hating that he
had this power over her. Not that her aversion altered the
fact that she was wired, wildly horny, as if she'd not just
come short minutes ago, her body already taut with expectation and her curse was breathy with need.

He noticed, but his voice was bland when he spoke.
"Such a quick temper. We'll have to work on that. You'll be
less touchy once you've come a few more times."

*He couldn't possibly know the extent of her arousal,
could he?*

"I can smell your hot pussy," he murmured, as though
reading her mind. "So tell me you understand."

She reluctantly nodded, weak with longing, damn him;
willing to do anything he wanted right now if it meant he'd
satisfy her cravings.

"That's a good girl." His cool gaze traveled down her
body, then up again. "Time to play again?"

She was having trouble concentrating with lust swamp-
ing her senses.

"You really are impatient," he said, smiling faintly. He
lightly tapped her cheek with his finger to gain her attention. "You haven't been listening. Aside from our little
encounter a few minutes ago, when did you last have sex?"

She half opened her mouth to say *Screw you*, but after
one look at his cool gaze, she changed her mind.

"Very smart," he murmured. "Now answer me."

She scowled. "Stop it."

"It's a simple question."

"I don't remember."

"Think." He slid the backs of his fingers up her inner thighs, smiled at her flinch, at the small muffled sound she uttered as he reached the soft, sensitive hollow where her legs met her hips. "How long ago did you have sex?" His knuckles came to rest against the soft folds of her sex and he gently rubbed. "Exactly."

She dragged in a sharp breath, the pressure of his fingers riveting, every nerve in her body screaming for more. "Three months ago," she said on a suffocated breath.

"And who was the lucky man?"

"Jesus Christ," she irritably said.

"Only if you were hallucinating," he sardonically returned.

She gave him a mutinous look. "Are you enjoying yourself?"

"Not completely." He smiled faintly. "But I have expectations."

Twisting his wrists slightly, he slid his thumbs, palm deep, into her silken cleft. "A name."

She shuddered as his thumbs circled her pulsing tissue, up and down, around, the delicate contact masterful; teasing, testing, indulgent, überskilled. It would be stupid to succumb to anger when she was feeling insatiable.

"Andrew Knolls, you fucking control freak," she snapped. So she wasn't a complete model of restraint.

He had an agenda too; he had no intention of losing his temper. "Was he good?"

"Not bad. Is this a competition?"

He laughed. "If it is, the bar isn't set too high."

She glanced down at his prominent erection lifting the dark silk of his pajamas. "What do I have to do to get that?"

His lashes dropped fractionally. "You probably shouldn't phrase your question exactly that way."

"Would you please fuck me soon?" she crisply said. "Clear enough?"

"Crystal," he murmured, his thumbs smoothly massaging her ripe, pouty flesh. "Showtime?"

"Yes, please, and I say that with all due deference considering your prickly mood."

"Or yours."

Her nostrils flared. "If you say so."

He smiled. "Ah—compliance at last."

Her temper spiked but she didn't respond to his jibe because his fingers were making her frantic and the ache of longing deep inside her was so powerful she felt as though the pressure might split her apart. She must have been fantasizing about Dominic Knight way too much or maybe her sex life had been lacking of late. Regardless, he was the solution. "Since you're nonchalant about this and I'm not, would you mind if I came again first?" she said in a tumble of words before she lost her nerve.

He suppressed his smile at her breathless candor. "No problem. Here or in the bedroom?"

"Here is fine. You scared everyone away anyway. No one will hear me scream."

He grinned, slipped his thumbs upward to her clit and gently pressed. "You *do* know how to scream."

It took her a moment to catch her breath and a moment more before the sexual jolt subsided and she found her voice. "I hope it's not a deal breaker."

"The way I'm feeling right now," he said, abruptly withdrawing his thumbs, stripping off his T-shirt with one swift jerk, "the world coming to an end wouldn't be a deal breaker." Pulling open the tie on his pajama pants, he let them slide to the floor.

She gasped. Really, she couldn't help it. He—*it*—was magnificent. Astonishing. The wild drumbeat of arousal reached crescendo pitch, she melted inside, and whispered, "Ohmygod." Reaching down between her legs where he and his glorious cock were standing tall, she ran her fingertips over the swollen head of his towering erection. Stroked the sleek, turgid flesh, circled the flaring flange once, twice, before he stopped her, gently cuffing her wrist with his thumb and middle finger. "If you want me to entertain you first," he murmured, "we'd better take a pass on this."

"You're sure you don't mind me being selfish?"

"Not at all."

"Oh, good," she said with relief, "because—look." She held out her trembling hands.

It was the most erotic gesture he'd seen in a very long time and for a moment he didn't know whether to be delighted or apprehensive. But he didn't think about it long because he was here for entirely selfish reasons.

"Give me your hands." He spoke gently; she was clearly on the brink. Taking her hands, he placed them on his shoulders. "Hang on now. Legs too." Wrapping her legs around his waist, he slipped his palms under her bottom, lifted her off the bar, shifting his hold so he was supporting her thighs with his forearms, and moved toward the window walls.

The head of his erection was nudging her cleft as he walked toward the windows, each easy stride deepening his penetration, the pressure on her G-spot increasingly intense. "I can't wait! *Hurry!*"

He abruptly halted. "Don't give me orders," he gruffly said.

She dragged in a breath because his thick cock was lodged snugly against that most tender, swollen bundle of nerves and the sweet pleasure was beginning to peak. "I'm sorry, I didn't mean it. Just—please..."

Readjusting his grip, he eased the pressure on her G-spot because he refused to take orders and he needed to make that clear. "We need some ground rules."

"How did you do that?" she asked breathlessly. Even her clit had stopped pulsing.

"What?"

She flicked a glance downward. "That miracle switcheroo. My brain is functioning again."

He smiled. "Lots of practice." Then his smile faded. "We have to talk."

"Oh God, you're going to stop because I pissed you off."

"Maybe, maybe not. It depends. Why didn't you leave when I gave you the chance?"

"Because you're hot in every way that matters. You can't say you don't know that. Every woman who gets this close to you must feel the same way." Another of those downward glances. "And if you think you can talk me into leaving when you're halfway inside me and I'm dying for another orgasm"—she gave him a hopeful look, a really sweet smile. "Could we stop talking now? I promise to listen later—truly I will."

He stared at her for a moment, as if she'd just landed from Mars and he wasn't sure if she was friend or foe. Then he slowly exhaled. "What the hell am I going to do with you?"

"For starters, don't put me down yet if you don't mind," she quickly said, feeling as though things might be going her way. "I'm kinda in a fuzzy limbo right now. And second, I'm hoping for another orgasm ASAP—again, only if you don't mind."

He laughed and she felt it in a nice little buzz that stroked her libido just the tiniest bit. "How about I promise not to ever, *ever* give you an order."

"It's not just that." He paused long enough to make her nervous before he continued in a carefully modulated tone that you'd use to tell someone that their puppy died. "Look," he said with a long-suffering sigh. "I can do vanilla sex. I just don't know how *long* I can do it. And at that point, I'm not sure I can trust myself with—" He stopped.

"Someone like me."

"Yes. I have control issues. You know that."

"And you've been doing the should I, shouldn't I, ever since—"

"Palo Alto. And I don't even believe in the word *virtue* for all the obvious reasons, but I've been trying. You're really young, and inexperienced, but, unfortunately, you're also irresistible. And I'm used to taking what I want."

"If it helps, you're preaching to the choir. You're sizzling hot in a thousand different ways not even counting your extravagant lifestyle and"—she grinned—"I want you *bad*. Not to mention, you can stay hard"—she wiggled her hips—"apparently forever."

"Not forever." His brows flickered in amusement. "Only until you've had enough."

"Ummm—I like the sound of that. Aren't your arms getting tired?"

He smiled. "You don't weigh much."

"Jeez, how sweet is that? Not that you don't have your weird side, but maybe we all do. Did I mention I have my own AK-47 that my gramps bought for me on my sixteenth birthday?"

"No, you didn't." He looked amused. "Should I be worried?"

"Uh-uh, I like you." Her smile was part sweet and part flirty. "So, do you want to go for it? Beyond vanilla sex fun and games. For six days starting tomorrow?"

"My rules." He picked up without missing a beat.

She gave him a narrow-eyed look. "If you push me too hard, I push back."

"Agreed."

"And you'll be my path to sexual enlightenment?"

"We'll give it a shot," he said with a smile, feeling as though a path to enlightenment of another kind may have opened up for him. One with a very pretty guide currently warming his cock. "Rules now or tomorrow?"

"Let's start slow with vanilla sex tonight. Tomorrow I'll sign anything—just kidding. I've learned my lesson about signing your contracts."

"I'm glad you're staying." His smile was warm as a summer day. "I thought I might have scared you off."

"I don't scare easily—especially when I want something. We're not so different there. But where you want to control things, I operate purely on instinct. In my kind of work you never know what's coming up, where you're going, what's behind the next portal. The great unknown is my adrenaline rush, my happiness hormone, the guilty thrill, the feeling of invincibility. Don't get me wrong. If I see a cliff up ahead, I stop. But otherwise..." She smiled. "So how about it? Are we cool with this sex thing?"

"Definitely. Would you like to come a few times now?"

"I thought you'd never ask."

"Come on, babe, let me show you a good time," he said, moving toward the windows once again. "I've been thinking about doing this since our drinks at the bar. What better addition to a bucket list than to climax while looking out over one of the best views in the world? How does that sound?"

"Anything with the word *climax* in it is on my bucket list."

He carried her to the corner of the room where the glass window walls met, so they both could take in the view, even with her back against one of the windows. "Which direction do you want?"

"I want the one where your dick hits my G-spot. I have a real preference for G-spot orgasms."

He grinned. "Apparently the view is secondary."

She smiled back. "Maybe later."

"In a hurry?"

"Always. It's part of my adrenaline rush personality."

"Gotcha." *He'd have to see about changing that, but not tonight.* She wanted vanilla, she'd get vanilla. He positioned her so her back was against the east window with the better view, shifted his hands slightly to tilt her hips at the right angle, and smiled at her. "Ready?"

"Yesterday," she whispered back, arching up to kiss his chin, then his mouth as he lowered his head to accommodate her. "God, you're polite," she breathed against his mouth.

"Try this for polite." And he slowly forced his way deeper into her hot, slick, gloriously snug sex.

Holding his shoulders, she leaned forward, ran her tongue along his collarbone, in some primal act of acquiescence, and sighed with pleasure as he filled her by slow degrees.

"Just a warning," he whispered, as he slid deeper into her melting heat, "I'm going to fuck you for the next six days, everywhere and every possible way...all day, every day."

She was panting in little breathy gasps and so slippery wet he felt only pressure, not friction, and when he was finally completely submerged, he thought with deep appreciation, *Christ, she's tight.*

At that exact second, as if they'd both been gauging the proper balance between sensation and distance, he grunted in satisfaction, and her wild orgasmic scream exploded. The pealing cry echoed through the high-ceilinged room and left a ringing in Dominic's ears that he recognized as approval for a job well done.

She was still convulsing when Dominic splayed his fingers wider for greater purchase and forced himself a small distance deeper.

"No, no, don't!" she gasped.

"Hush," he whispered, dipping his head, kissing her cheek. "You'll like it."

As if on cue, a second wave of raw ecstasy overwhelmed her, spread a lethal flood of agonizing pleasure through her body, bathed her senses in a glittering rapture so dazzling it brought tears to her eyes.

"Good?" He looked pleased. "Try this."

Still cushioned in a sumptuous cloud of sensual delight, she was only half aware of the low, husky whisper. And before she could register the full impact of the comment, Dominic moved delicately against her favorite sweet spot and with a sharp cry, she climaxed violently again.

"More?"

The voice seemed to come from another universe. Distant, unintelligible, shot through with cool, blue light.

"Would you like to come again?"

She heard him clearly that time, but still trembling from aftershocks, she could only shake her head.

"Sure?" Engulfed in her silken heat, he was colossally horny, the feel of her around his cock, against his body, under his hands—unbelievably fine. Maybe he could be sure for both of them. "How about just a little more?" Sliding his hands under her bottom, he slowly raised her up his hard length, then down again, gently, gently, in deference to her numerous orgasms.

She softly groaned.

The familiar heated sound brought a smile to his lips.

"Again?" He lifted her effortlessly; she was small, light, and dripping wet around his dick. Always a good sign. He lowered her with slightly less deference this time.

And her small cry warmed his chest.

He was even more gratified moments later when she slid her arms around his neck and began to match his rhythm, he up, she down, slowly, slowly, amplifying, heightening the frenzy. Very quickly, their breathing accelerated, feeling took precedence over reason, the world narrowed to a slow, undulatory slick flesh-to-flesh seesaw of exquisite sensation. When her high, panting scream exploded, he half smiled. It never took long.

Deciding Miss Hart had been suitably gratified, he finally indulged himself. Plunging deeper, he shut his eyes against the sudden, intense, improbable shock of impact and wondered for a moment if he was going to come instantly like some sixteen-year-old kid fucking for the first time. *Christ!* Panting, he managed to restrain himself for a moment because he wouldn't allow himself to be so undisciplined. But self-willed or not, he could no longer stop the orgasmic surge building inside him and his climax broke in a teeth-clenched, mind-blowing, seemingly endless seminal flood that filled the lovely Miss Hart. And seriously shook his composure.

He could always, *always* wait.

And mind-blowing was not, and never had been, part of his vocabulary.

Not even when it came to money.

And never with sex.

Fuck.

Exactly the point.

He forced his mind to go blank. There was time enough for introspection once he was done with the hotter-than-hot Miss Hart in six and a half days.

Carrying her over to a sofa because his arms were finally beginning to cramp, he lowered himself to the bright red cushions without dislodging his still rampant cock from the sweetest pussy in Hong Kong—and that was saying a lot. Her head was on his shoulder, her nude form collapsed against his chest. Such lurid vulnerability was a prime aphrodisiac. The clever, competent, smart-alecky Miss Hart had given herself up to him with complete abandon.

As she rested in his arms, he lightly stroked her tousled curls. "Do you need anything?" he softly murmured, feeling strangely content. "Food, a drink, music—a band?"

She slowly lifted her head from his shoulder, gradually sat up, shifted ever so slightly to fully absorb his indefatigable cock, and smiled. "What if I said yes to a band?"

"I'd get one up here." He gently flexed his hips. "Do you want one?"

A short pause ensued before her eyes opened again. "You're impossibly arrogant, you know," she said pettishly because he'd probably moved like that in a woman a thousand times before.

"And you're impossibly sexy," he said, ignoring her petulance. He ran a fingertip over her lush bottom lip, then touched it to his mouth. "Just tell me what you want and it's yours."

"Keep making me feel this good, and I might just stay. How about that?" She immediately felt his body stiffen.

"Or did you mean something else?" she asked with teasing innocence.

"Don't forget," he threatened, "I know how to use a whip."

"But I get to say no. That's part of the push back."

"We'll see about that."

"Hey, you agreed."

He smiled faintly. "Maybe you'll ask for it. You never know."

"I won't!"

"Fine. Don't move."

"What will you do if I move?"

"Nothing, but if you do what you're told, I'll make you feel good."

"I feel good already."

"I'll make you feel better." He tumbled her back on the couch, followed her down, spread her legs, dipped his head, and offered her another version of vanilla sex.

His mouth was just as good as his dick at getting her off. He was masterful, his tongue capable of reaching her G-spot and keeping her hovering just short of orgasm for an indefinite period of time. When her body was literally strumming and humming with bliss and she was so jacked up she could come in under two seconds if he'd let her, she began to seriously think about staying longer than six days. But talk of staying was apparently taboo. He'd gone completely rigid when she mentioned it.

So she was polite and didn't bring up the subject again and he was polite about vanilla sex and it turned out to be a night of really incredible sex and multiple orgasms all around.

Long before morning, Dominic had begun adjusting his schedule.

He briefly questioned his sanity, but then she whispered, "Are you awake?" and glancing down at the wide-eyed, pink-cheeked woman in his arms, he smiled. "You're going to wear me out."

"I'm sorry."

"No, you're not."

"Well, maybe just a little."

He rolled over her and settled between her legs in one smooth motion. "You're lucky I like you," he said with a grin.

"Do you really?"

He hesitated a fraction of a second.

But her eyes were huge with entreaty.

He knew what she wanted to hear.

"Yes, really," he whispered.

He might have even meant it.

ELEVEN

Shortly before seven, when they were both lying sprawled on their backs breathing hard after another explosive climax, Dominic turned his head and said quickly before he changed his mind, "I have a home here."

Kate shot him a sideways glance and winked. "I already know that. You're not the only one who has sources of information. I even know all your bank account numbers."

As if. But he smiled. "And I know yours."

She catapulted up into a seated position and scowled faintly. "You can't."

"There's no privacy in the world, babe."

"There better be."

"I'm not going to take any of your money if that's what you're worried about."

"No, that's not what I'm worried about," she grumbled. "You're just too damned invasive."

"Sometimes you don't care," he drawled. "You certainly didn't last night."

"Very funny. Now I'm going to have to change my bank account."

"Don't bother. Max can find anything."

"Jeez! Do you mind? I have a life of my own."

He found the thought distasteful and that bothered him. Since when did he care about the particulars of any woman's life? "Consider it forgotten," he said smoothly. "It was just on Max's brief. I'll toss it," he lied. "Are we good now?"

"I suppose," she muttered. "It's mostly your money in there anyway. I had three hundred dollars in my account before Max paid me."

"If we're done arguing, I mentioned my house for a reason. I was wondering if you'd care to spend our play date there instead?"

"Why?"

"It's nicer than a hotel."

"You hadn't thought of that before?"

"No."

She smiled. "I'll bet you did."

"You'd lose. I didn't." *He never took women to his house, women he screwed at least.*

"So has something changed between us?" A question only a woman would ask.

"It must have." An answer only a man would give. A therapist might know what had changed and why but he didn't. He just knew he didn't want this to stop. "So, do you want to go? The house has great views."

"Better than these?" She waved at the windows.

Not better than his view of the high swell of her milky-white breasts. He smiled. "Definitely."

"Wow! Better? I can't believe it!"

"Word of God." Her artlessness always amazed him. He had never met someone like her before.

She bit her bottom lip. "Are there going to be people around?"

"No one you know. Don't worry."

"That's not what I meant."

"I only have staff there. They're loyal and discreet. Better?"

"I suppose in a way it's better. There are tons of people in the hotel who might see us."

"Only if we venture off this floor. But I'd prefer my house."

"Why?"

"I don't stay in hotels much."

"Still, I don't know. It seems well—too"—she was going to say "personal" but that was a joke after what they shared last night. "A hotel might be better," she equivocated. "You know—like neutral ground." She couldn't say she didn't want to get to know him too well because he was Mr. Gorgeous with a world-class dick and he could be really, really nice. And she wasn't made of stone.

Dominic was trying to figure out what the hell she meant. Not that he was going to ask her to bare her soul, because he always avoided those kinds of conversations with women—actually with anyone. "I don't know why we need neutral ground," he said finally, choosing his words as carefully as she had.

"I didn't mean that, so much as…oh hell—I don't know what I meant." She wrinkled her nose and looked like she was five.

God, she was cute, and he'd never considered the word part of his vocabulary before. Which just went to show how crazy she made him. She looked up as the silence lengthened. "Are you mad at me?"

"No. Thinking."

"I don't like to be this—unstrung." She exhaled with a grimace. "I'm kinda of freaking out here."

"Same here, but look, I don't want to overanalyze this. I want you with me. I want you at my house."

She wrinkled her nose in another little bunny twitch. "After last night I probably should just say thank you and not argue about where or when," she said in a very small voice. "Because...you made me feel...well—I never knew I could feel that way. Like I was going to die if I didn't have—"

"What you want. I know." He smiled. "I can give you that."

"That's the good part," she said, with a twitch of a smile. "About those rules, though." She looked at him from under her lashes. "There are things I won't do."

"Then we won't do them," he said with painstaking calm, surprised at how much he wanted this, not sure what he'd do if she refused. "You'll like my house." His tone was deliberately casual. "It's a Victorian monstrosity, but as they say, charming. It even has a turret."

"A turret?" Her eyes lit up with delight. "Why didn't you say so?"

A lift of his brows. "Because?"

"Every little girl wants a room in a turret."

He smiled. "Interesting."

"You're a man," she said, her smile full of sass now. "What would you know about turrets?"

"Why don't we have drinks up there, watch the ships go by?"

His voice was sweet temptation, his gaze brazenly provocative. She could feel the flush rising on her cheeks.

"We could sleep up there if you like. I'll have a bed brought up." *Or whatever it takes.*

A short silence.

Then a boat horn trumpeted far below, the sound muted by 117 stories.

"Compromise?"

"Certainly." *A superb negotiator, he knew better than to refuse.*

"If I'm uncomfortable, we'll leave."

He liked how she said, *We.* He liked even more that her compromise didn't involve reneging on the six days. "Agreed," he said affably.

"Very well." She took a small breath. "I'm good."

He didn't say, *I would have taken you there no matter what.* He said instead, with exquisite courtesy and a winning smile, "Thank you."

As if she actually could have said no, she silently admitted, when Dominic Knight dispensed pleasure beyond the limits of any measure known to man. And not just sexual pleasure—the full gamut of creature comforts and joy.

"They're bringing up coffee at eight, along with some other food I ordered. Do you want anything?" He had what he wanted; he was willing to indulge her every whim. He smiled. "Bacon sandwiches perhaps?"

"Bacon sandwiches sound *wonderful*. I'm starved. You worked me like a field hand last night." With all the vexing issues of wanting someone too much dismissed, she stretched lazily like a cat in the sun, satisfied and content.

Don't touch, he warned himself, as she sensuously arched her back and her large, luxurious breasts rose in flagrant display. *Not yet.* "We could argue about who worked whom harder," he said with a smile. "But I enjoyed myself, Miss Hart. I just want you to know."

"Thank you, Mr. Knight," she said, lowering her lashes coyly in play. "I thoroughly enjoyed myself as well."

He chuckled. "Very tempting, Miss Hart. Virtuous maids are in short supply."

She gave him a seductive little glance. "Please be gentle, sir."

He dragged in a breath, slowly blew it out, reined in his libido. "We'll have to wait on this game. Unfortunately, I have too many calls to make, too many messages to retrieve. And," he added with a grin, "if you don't mind my mentioning it, you *could* use a shower."

"It's not my fault," she said with an answering grin. "You're the one who came in me all night."

"With great delight I'll have you know." Giving in to temptation, he rolled on his side, slid his hand between her legs, slipped two fingers up her sleek cleft. "Ummm.. nice and wet." He shut his eyes, called on every shred of willpower he possessed, then rolled away with a grudging sigh. "You have an incredibly tempting pussy, Miss Hart. But I've probably forty e-mails by now that need answering. So duty calls." Throwing his legs over the side of the bed, he grabbed his phone from the bedside table and came to his feet. "Let's say breakfast in my suite at eight." He started to walk away. "It's the corner one down the hall."

"Would you care to join me in the shower?" She wanted him every minute, every second. It was awesome and terrifying.

He turned and glanced up from scrolling down his messages. "Next time." His voice was distracted, his gaze returning to his phone. "Damn it. I thought I dealt with that yesterday. If you'll excuse me." And he strode away, indifferent to his nudity, the phone to his ear.

He called his driver next and made plans to have them driven to the launch. "I'll call you back when I know the exact time."

After that, he spent fifteen minutes dealing with the most pressing of his messages.

Then he called the concierge for a number and at seven twenty he made one of the calls he needed to make before they left the hotel.

"I apologize, Mrs. Hawthorne, for ringing you at home so early in the morning, but I have a rather urgent request. I'm Dominic Knight. If you could accommodate me, I'd be most grateful."

It came as no surprise when he heard a warm, cultivated English accent say, "How may I help you?" Money always talked.

"I understand your shop is the best in the territory," he said pleasantly. "And I need your help. I have a guest staying at my house and I'd like to supplement her wardrobe. Let's see." He glanced down at the open folder on the dining room table. "She's five-five, a hundred ten pounds—that's about...what, fifty kilos—and—ah—here it is...she's an American size eight or nine. Does that help? She has very large breasts by the way, so bring whatever you have in those sizes."

"I'm not quite sure what you want. Could you be more

precise?" Her male clients were generally unaware of anything other than that they wanted something black and risqué.

"Whatever women wear under their clothes, Mrs. Hawthorne. You'd know that better than I."

"A full selection of lingerie, then?" That was unusual.

"Yes, and some nightwear too. Robes, pajamas with buttons. Bring whatever you have in your shop. I'll buy it all. And come alone. I don't want any gossip."

He didn't ask about price, but price probably wasn't an issue to someone who said, *I'll buy it all.* "When would you like me there?" Mrs. Hawthorne inquired. No one in Hong Kong had to ask where Dominic Knight lived. He owned the original governor's mansion on the Peak.

"Say ten thirty? Is that time enough for you to collect the things we need?"

We. If her livelihood didn't depend on complete discretion, that word would have been broadcast around Hong Kong within the hour. Dominic Knight was notorious not only for his wealth and the latitude of his vice, but for his disinterest in normal female relationships since his wife's death. "I'll be there at ten thirty." *Anxious to meet this paragon of womanhood who had wrought such a major upheaval.*

"Thank you," he said crisply, and punched in another number.

A number that rang and rang and rang. Frowning, he dropped the phone on the table, picked up the folder, and strode toward the main bathroom in the four-thousand-square-foot suite. Twenty minutes later, showered, shaved, and dressed, he was on the phone again. This time the call was answered and a man he'd dealt with many times before wished him a good morning in Mandarin.

Dominic replied in the same language, and apologized for calling so early. He politely inquired about the man's family, expressed interest when the man told him of his son's imminent graduation from UCLA, offered help with a position if the boy wanted to stay in the States, and gave him Max's number. With the amenities dispatched, he quickly dictated a list of items he wanted. "I need them delivered immediately," he said. "Can you get someone out early this morning? Good. Excellent. No, not the garden retreat. Send everything to my house. Yes, that's right—my *house*."

Dominic turned and saw Kate standing in the doorway. "Ah, you're finished." Abruptly ending his call with his thumb, he smiled at her. "You look lovely, but then you always do"—his brows flickered—"dressed or undressed. Is that Greta's? I like the color." Kate wore a simple, long-sleeved, wool dress in a pale shade of lilac.

"Who else's would it be?"

"I like the buttons down the front. Handy."

"I thought you might like that."

He smiled. "Do I detect a more accommodating stance on your wardrobe this morning?"

"I'm not completely averse to being obliging."

"I like the sound of the word *obliging*."

"I wasn't *unobliging* last night, was I?"

"No, you were quite, shall we say, amenable. I expect your breasts are tender this morning."

"Perhaps a little. My nipples particularly. But this dress is lined in silk so it's not so *very* uncomfortable."

"I'm sorry. I should apologize."

"Don't. I could have said no."

And if she had, I would have stopped. "Just to be clear, you can always say no. It's only a game."

She smiled. "A very pleasurable one—awesome, in fact. Like everything about you." She made a small moue. "I was hoping you wouldn't be dressed yet." He wore dark slacks and a dove-gray V-neck sweater, the sleeves pushed up, his wet hair slicked back. He was barefoot.

"I'm afraid we have to leave right after breakfast." He'd rearranged his schedule to allow him six days with Miss Hart and he had some pressing business matters to wind down this morning. "I wish we didn't. But I'll make it up to you, I promise."

"When?"

What a charming little fretful pout. His cock twitched in recognition of Miss Hart's insatiable appetite for sex. A quick glance at his watch; there should be time before Mrs. Hawthorne arrived. "Say in two hours?"

"Thank you," she said, smiling shyly.

He smiled an altogether different smile. "My pleasure."

"Thank you again. I seem to be addicted—to constant orgasms, to the phenomenal bliss." Another smile. "I blame you."

"I willingly take responsibility. And I'm more than happy to take care of your every desire."

That simple promise simply stated shouldn't make her

body open in welcome but it did. Instantly. As if he'd flicked a switch and every shameless nerve breathlessly responded. She could feel the flutter of arousal in the pit of her stomach, the damp, melting heat, the small ache of longing.

He gave her a knowing half smile. "Are you getting wet?"

She nodded, embarrassed and flustered. Not sure how to answer.

He crooked his index finger. "Come. I can see your nipples swelling from here." His voice took on a cool briskness. "Come, Miss Hart. *Now.*"

"Be nice," she whispered, struggling to maintain some independence against his rough authority.

"Oblige me, Miss Hart," he said gently, in response to her small rebellion, "and I'll unbutton that nice row of buttons on your dress and suck on your nipples. Would you like that?"

With a satisfied smile, he watched her capitulate. And a few moments later, when she came to a stop before him, his voice was hushed. "Very obedient. I like that." He slid his fingers down the row of jeweled buttons on the bodice of her dress. "But then you want sex again, don't you?" He glanced at his watch. "Not even an hour since you came last. We're going to have to teach you some restraint."

"Don't," she whispered.

"Don't what?"

"Do this to me. Play this game with me."

Something in her voice gained his attention, her earnestness perhaps or maybe the wistfulness. Both rare in his world. He sighed softly. "I don't mean to be difficult," he said, when in fact he had been, "but we have very little time. Our breakfast will be here in ten minutes."

"Postpone breakfast. Please, Dominic?"

She'd not used his Christian name before. It startled him. Disarmed him. "If I do," he said, a smile beginning to warm his eyes, "you owe me."

"Yes, yes." She dipped her head. "Anything."

His cock surged at the possibilities. But his tight schedule didn't allow him to act on impulse. "I can't postpone breakfast," he said, his voice subdued. "I have a dozen calls to make, people waiting to hear from me." *Before I disappear for six days.* "But I don't have to open the door right away. How would that be?" He slid his finger under her chin and lifted her gaze to his. "Would that do?"

No, she wanted to say. But not yet lost to all reason, she nodded.

Competent and perhaps more familiar with expeditious sex than most, he rapidly unbuttoned her bodice and gently cupped her breasts in his hands. "A quick orgasm to take the edge off?" With her eyes shut and her breathing rapid, he didn't wait for an answer. Bending his head, he drew a nipple into his mouth.

She gasped, went rigid.

"Should I stop?" he asked, raising his head. "I should," he said, after taking one look at her.

"No, no, don't." She met his gaze, exhaled slowly. "I'm fine."

"We should wait until there's more time, other options."

"Please, no, it doesn't hurt that much."

Softly swearing, he swiftly moved to plan B, shoving her skirt up with his left hand. *No panties. A pleasant surprise.* His cock immediately took notice. A very short internal debate occupied his thoughts before he dismissed impractical considerations. They were pressed for time. His satisfaction would have to wait...

Sliding his right hand between her legs, he slipped two fingers up her hot, slick sex with a technical flair that focused on her G-spot and heard a different kind of gasp. A good one. At which point, capable of working blindly, he let her skirt drop, deftly located the holy grail with his left index finger, and knew this wouldn't take long. Her engorged clit was hard as a baseball bat.

As a matter of fact, Miss Hart probably would have broken the Guinness World Record for orgasms if one existed. He barely had time to slide in another finger before she climaxed like some wind-up sex doll. Seriously, she was going to kill him before the six days were over. Although fucking to death wasn't a bad way to go.

When her tremors ceased along with her soft moans, he withdrew his fingers and grabbed two napkins from the table—one to wipe his fingers, the other to put between her legs. Then he lifted her in his arms and carried her, soothed and satisfied, to the table. Depositing her gently in a chair, he brushed her cheek with a kiss before seating himself to her right at the head of the table.

Lounging back in his chair, he put his fingers to his nose, softly inhaled, and smiled. Jasmine soap and Miss Hart's fragrant scent redolent of horniness and lust. Pouring himself a glass of water from a bottle on the table, he dipped his fingers in it, wiped them with a napkin, and fondly regarded the flushed, oversexed beauty who was going to amuse him for the next six days. He expected she'd give him a great deal of pleasure—once he'd cleared the press of events from his calendar. One of which was getting out of here. He glanced at his watch. "Five minutes before breakfast, Miss Hart," he softly warned.

Eyes shut, her head thrown back, she nodded.

Her dress was still unbuttoned, her full breasts attractively framed by lilac wool, her soft, pale flesh a lush counterpoint to the pastel fabric, the amethyst buttons a glittering flourish to the succulent display. He'd have to thank Greta again for so quickly assembling a wardrobe. And Miss Hart for so picturesquely showcasing Greta's designs. He was tempted to take a photo but neither he nor Miss Hart could afford such carelessness. A shame. She was definitely a tantalizing sight.

A brisk knock on the door curtailed his scrutiny.

"Button up, Miss Hart," he said briskly, coming to his feet. "The servers are here. I don't want them ogling my tits," he added only half in jest.

He was suddenly looking into snappish green eyes.

"They're *my* tits."

He smiled. "We'll have to see about that. Five minutes ago, you promised me anything. Those might be on my list." His eyes took on a quixotic, edgy look for a moment. "Button up," he said curtly, disturbed on so many levels by Miss Hart's capacity to fuck up his life and schedule. Then he walked away.

Kate's fingers were shaking as she buttoned the front of her dress and it wasn't from fear.

A moment later, Dominic opened the suite door and stepped aside to let in three servers pushing large silver-domed carts. "Put everything on the table," he said in a colloquial Chinese, his accent pure Hong Kong. "We'll manage after that. The lady's not feeling well, so if you'd work quickly, I'd appreciate it."

Following them in, he stood like a stern sentry at the back of Kate's chair while they laid out the food. Then accompanying them back to the door, he tipped them generously and returned to the table. Taking his seat, he reached for the coffeepot, nodded at Kate's buttons, and smiled. "Thank you. Very modest." He picked up the chased silver coffeepot. "Coffee, right? Black?"

"Yes, please. You intimidated those men."

"I doubt it. I just told them I was in a hurry." He poured them both a cup of coffee, slid Kate's toward her, added milk and sugar to his, and waved at the array of food. "Bacon sandwiches, as ordered, Miss Hart. And the fruit in Asia is excellent."

"I don't need instructions. I eat fruit."

"Good." He passed the plate of sandwiches to Kate. "Did you take your pill?"

She set down the plate. "I beg your pardon?"

"Your birth control pill." He was piling herbed scrambled eggs on his plate. "Did you take it? It's a simple question."

"You're overstepping. That's my simple answer. It's none of your business."

"Actually, it is at the moment." He set down the platter of eggs and reached for a colorful aspic of salmon that could have passed for artwork.

"I see. Would you like to take charge of them for me? Is that one of your countless rules and directives? Would you like to know when I take a pill for a headache, too, or what kind of shampoo I use in the shower or whether I put my shoes on left foot or right foot first?"

His hand momentarily arrested midair, he calmly waited for her to finish. "You forgot to take it I gather." Dropping his hand, he drew the plate of salmon closer.

"I might have taken it."

"Then we wouldn't be having this conversation." He shot her a look. "I came in you a dozen times last night. It might be a good idea not to skip one." He sliced off a portion of salmon with a fish fork.

"A good idea for you, you mean," she muttered.

The fish fork hit the platter with a clang and he turned to her, his expression incredulous. "You're not actually telling me you want a child, are you?"

"No."

He softly exhaled, bit back the vulgarity on his tongue, and kept his voice level. "Then I don't see why we're fighting. I want you to take it, you want to take it. Simple."

"I just don't like orders."

"No shit." He gave her a vicious look. "Keep it up, Miss Hart, and you might get the spanking you deserve."

"Promises, promises," she purred, derisive and mocking.

She could practically see the switch click on in his brain.

"I didn't mean it," she quickly said. "I didn't. Don't even think it."

"Then don't tempt me." He stood so abruptly she flinched.

"Relax. I haven't spanked a woman in a long time. I'm just going to get your birth control pills."

"You don't know where they are."

"I'll find them," he said flatly. "Eat your breakfast."

He came back five minutes later with the case in hand. Returning to his seat, he opened the container, took out a pill, handed it to her, and slipped the plastic pod into his trouser pocket.

"I didn't say you could do that."

"Trust me. I'm more responsible." He jabbed his finger at the pill in her hand. "Take it."

"That sounds like an *or else.*"

"You're catching on, Miss Hart. Now take the fucking pill."

There were fights you could win and those you couldn't. She took the pill.

"Thank you. I appreciate your understanding."

His voice was well mannered and gracious, his smile couldn't be improved on for boyish charm, and then he softly added, "I don't want you anxious about anything afterward, that's all."

"You're right." *He was, of course. And truthfully, she* had *forgotten.* "I shouldn't be so temperamental," she murmured. "But I'm having trouble with all your orders."

He wasn't about to plunge into another argument about how she responded to his orders last night with a wild intensity that was pure anarchy and incredibly beautiful. How she knocked him for a loop and fucked with his head in ways he'd never felt before. Instead, he cleared his throat, a muscle at the back of his jaw jumped, then he spoke in a voice that was quiet and cool. "I know my shortcomings. As you've mentioned, being a control freak is one of them. Why don't I try to be better? Would that help?"

Jesus, he could melt her heart with that polished charm. She wasn't foolish enough to accept it completely at face value. But it was nice of him to try. "I'll be less confrontational as well. Nana always said I should mind my manners. As you see, I haven't listened very well."

"It's one of your many charms. Don't worry about it. I can hold my own in a fight."

She rolled her eyes. "The understatement of the century. I'll never forget those two grown men collapsing in their chairs in Singapore."

"Speaking of Nana, have you called your grandmother lately?" he asked, preferring some other subject, grateful to be beyond personal issues he'd rather not think about.

"I already texted her this morning."

"You should talk to her." He checked his watch. "It's two o'clock her time."

"And say what? I'm sleeping with the boss? I'd rather not."

"Tell her you're busy working. Tell her you went for dinner with some business colleagues in Hong Kong. Tell her you have a nice view from your hotel room." He lifted one brow. "Do you want me to write it down? You haven't talked to her for two days."

"How do you know?"

Since he didn't want to start a fight, he said, "Just a guess."

Kate sighed. "Fine, I'll call her."

"There, that wasn't so hard."

"Jesus, you can be troublesome."

"Speaking of troublesome, I recall a young lady who had to come even though we were really pressed for time."

She threw her hands up. "You win." She grinned. "And

I thank you from the bottom of my heart for coming to my assistance."

His smile was genuine this time, all roguish grace and charm. "Anytime, Miss Hart. We're here to please. Now be a good girl and eat your breakfast because we have to be at the house by ten thirty. I have an appointment." There was no point in telling her with whom. Time enough for that at ten twenty-nine, when she had less opportunity to throw a tantrum.

TWELVE

Ten-foot-high ornate wrought-iron gates with the original escutcheons still in place slowly rolled open as their car approached and what could only be called an estate was unveiled. Manicured lawns left and right, the occasional border garden, ancient trees lining the drive, in the distance a huge Victorian mansion in gray stone.

Kate's eyes were wide. "Wow. I'm impressed." The mansion stood at the end of a long drive, three stories of bays, wings, loggias, miles of windows, and, as advertised, a soaring turret complete with a crenellated battlement.

"It's typical Victorian overkill," Dominic said of the eclectic mishmash of architectural styles. "But I like it." He could have been saying, hold the mayo, so unaffected was his tone.

"Palo Alto and this. You don't like modern, do you?"

"I prefer a house with a past. It reminds me of all those who lived before me. That life's short. And overweening hubris is for fools." He turned to her with a smile. "So that makes me pretty conservative when it comes to business decisions."

She snorted. "Like your space rocket? Your pet project takes up five pages in the Knight Enterprises' prospectus."

He shrugged. "Someone has to pay for exploration. And the financial rewards come eventually." He gave her a teasing look. "You've heard of Columbus?"

"And your rocket's just as dicey a gamble."

"Perhaps. Or a gamble I might win. Are you interested in rockets?"

"I should say yes with that gleam of excitement in your eyes, but I know next to nothing about rockets."

Her honesty always surprised him. Most women would have feigned interest. "If you like I could run through the fundamentals for you sometime."

"You'd have to keep it simple."

"You're too modest. Anyone who can infiltrate impenetrable firewalls can grasp some simple laws of physics. Maybe over drinks some night in the turret room?"

My God, he could be sweet. How easy it would be to fall under his spell and forget who and what he was. "That sounds very nice," she said, determined not to lose sight of the ruthless man behind the cultivated grace.

He was about to question the coolness in her voice when he caught sight of the car parked outside the main door and the hairs on the back of his neck began to rise. It was too early for Mrs. Hawthorne. And there were very few people who felt free to use his home, none of whom he cared to see right now.

But he politely helped Kate from the car a few moments later and ushered her up the stairs, preparing himself for whatever trouble lay inside. As they approached the entrance door, Kate stopped short and exclaimed, "What a beautiful stained-glass window!"

Hers wasn't an unusual reaction. "I'm told it's one of Rossetti's few. His wife, Elizabeth Siddal, I believe."

The door suddenly opened and a young, brawny man

in a black suit stood on the threshold. "Good morning, Nick."

"Morning, Leo." Grateful that Kate was studying the stained-glass window and standing slightly apart, Dominic quietly asked, "Who's here?"

Leo took a step closer and lowered his voice. "Your mother."

Dominic groaned. "When did she come?"

"A week ago."

A subtle alleviation of his frown. "Then she's leaving soon."

"Tomorrow."

"The car's waiting to take her shopping, I suppose. Oh Christ," Dominic muttered as he saw his mother come down the grand staircase. "Have her out of here by ten," he said under his breath. "I don't care how you do it, just do it. I have a visitor coming at ten thirty." He nodded toward a pile of packages on the console table. "From Cheun?" At his major domo's affirmative nod, he crisply added, "Send those to the Garden House and make sure the place is cleaned." He gave Leo a telling look. "I mean sanitized. And I want flowers," he quickly added before his gaze veered to one of the major liabilities in his life closing in on him. "Hello, Mother," he said in a conversational tone. "What a surprise."

"You should answer your phone."

"I'm sorry, I thought I did. I don't remember you mentioning anything about Hong Kong."

"You never listen to me, dear. You're just like your father. Who's your little friend?"

Kate had spun around at the word *mother*, gone pale, and found herself literally shocked speechless. A petite, trim blonde in pink Chanel, nipped and tucked to not look a day over forty, was staring at her with a derisive half-smile.

"She's a colleague, Mother." Dominic put out his hand and drew Kate forward. "Mother, may I introduce Miss Hart. She just saved Knight Enterprises twenty million dollars. We're extremely grateful for her expertise."

"How clever of you, Miss Hart. I can see you've impressed my son. Is that one of Greta's?" A huge diamond caught the light as she flicked a manicured finger toward Kate.

"No, Mother. Miss Hart is from the Midwest. As is her wardrobe, I believe," he blandly added.

"Will we be seeing you at dinner, Miss Hart?" The question was expressed with soft artifice, as if to say, *colleague indeed.*

"Unfortunately, no," Dominic interposed, fencing with his mother a familiar sport. "We're leaving Hong Kong this afternoon. We just stopped by for some papers Max sent over. Miss Hart is going to decipher all the numbers for me. She's one of the best forensic accountants we have."

"Commendable, I'm sure," Letitia Knight murmured coolly. "We'll do lunch then. Twoish. I'll be back from shopping by then. Talk to your chef, will you? Something French I think. You said Max is here?"

"Yes, he's visiting his family."

"I don't know why you can't meet some nice young woman like Max's wife, Olivia. British, upper class, her family has been in government in Hong Kong for centuries."

"Not anymore, Mother," Dominic drily noted.

"Nonetheless, the point is you should find yourself a wife from a *good* family this time."

A muscle twitched along Dominic's jaw. "I'm not look-ing for a wife."

"That's what you said last time and look what hap-pened."

"That's enough, Mother." His voice was pure ice.

"Remember your manners, dear. What will Miss Hart think?"

Dominic's nostrils flared. "If you'll excuse us, Mother. We have work to do."

"Until two then." Her smile was model perfect and just as artificial.

Looking grim, Dominic nodded and touched Kate's arm. "This way, Miss Hart," he said politely. "My office is in back."

As they moved away down the long corridor, Kate wanted to say, *I'm sorry*, or better yet, take him in her arms and com-fort him. No wonder he was hard as nails. He'd had to have been to survive a mother like that. "You don't have to speak for me," she said. "I could have answered your mother."

He shot her a look. "What's the point? She'd just ask you another question."

"Maybe she's really interested in your friends."

"Is that what you are?" he said with a wicked grin. "My friend?"

"I could have been."

"No you couldn't have. Not with my mother. You saw her look at you—calculating how rude she could be. Best to let me deal with her."

He suddenly went silent and she vowed not to bring up his mother again. It wasn't a topic that brought a smile to his face. Nor was she going to ask any questions about his wife after that curt conversation between mother and son. Even though she'd really, really like to. But just because she'd had sex with Dominic Knight didn't make them tell-me-your-deepest-feelings friends. In fact, it didn't make them friends at all.

She was available, that's all. Dominic's favorite kind of woman.

So she remained silent on their passage down a long hallway brightly carpeted in a red oriental rug, past dozens of gold-framed seascapes lining the cream brocade walls that reminded her of the yachting photos in the Palo Alto office. Obviously, he had a passion for the sea.

When they reached the end of the hall, Dominic opened a heavy oak door, waved her in, shut the door behind him, and locked it. "Don't be alarmed. I just don't want"—he blew out a breath—"any company."

"Are there really papers from Max?"

It took him a moment to respond. "No—I had to say something. We'll go somewhere else after lunch. Please, sit down. I could have coffee brought in if you'd like," he said, his courtesy automatic despite his air of distraction.

"I'm fine. I'll just enjoy the view," she said, moving toward a bank of French doors that offered another spectacular ocean vista. The house was on a headland with sweeping sight lines.

A hushed silence descended.

Her back to the huge room, she heard him drop into one of the leather chairs in a silken whoosh of air, heard his soft sigh and a muted expletive.

"I apologize for my mother," he said into the stillness. "And knowing her, I'll apologize again after lunch."

Kate turned and smiled faintly. "I don't think she likes me."

"Don't worry about it. I don't think she likes me either." He grimaced, then rose from his chair and strode toward a liquor table behind his desk. "Would you like a drink?" he said over his shoulder.

"It's a little early for me."

His laugh was acrid. "It's never too early when you're dealing with my mother."

"Do we have to do lunch?"

He turned to face her, a bottle in one hand, a glass in the other. "We only have to last an hour. I'll have Leo come in with some emergency. I try not to openly war with my mother. Long story. I won't bore you with the details." He held up the bottle. "Sure?"

She grinned. "It might not be wise. You know how mouthy I can be. I wouldn't want to shock your mother."

A little dip of his head, a sideways glance. "I might pay to see that."

"Don't tempt me. You've never seen Nana in action. I've learned from a pro."

His laugh this time was warm with humor. "You're a cheeky little thing. Come." He set down the bottle. "I'll show you my first editions."

"Are you trying to seduce me? Etchings, first editions?"

He lifted his glass to her and gave her a look that fired up all her erogenous zones. "Sorry. Not until she leaves."

But his mother left late for her shopping, almost too late. Generally nerveless, Dominic was restive. With an apology to Kate, he booted up his computer and redirected his focus on his e-mails, dealing exclusively with those that didn't require more than a yes or no answer. With his thoughts in tumult, he needed a simple task. Glancing at his watch, he realized Mrs. Hawthorne would arrive soon and he sighed. The prospect of his mother meeting Mrs. Hawthorne was unnerving. Since his mother was familiar with every expensive shop in Hong Kong, the fiction of Miss Hart as a business colleague would be exposed. And he didn't wish to damage Miss Hart's reputation. He felt responsible for her.

A knock on the door and Leo's announcement, "She's gone," brought a smile to Dominic's face. He called out his thanks, then glanced at the clock. Ten twenty. Just under the wire.

Moving from behind his desk, he walked toward Kate, who was seated by the windows, engrossed in one of his first editions.

Looking up at the soft creak of leather as he'd come to his feet, she watched him cross the room with lithe, athletic grace and thought him too beautiful for his own good. Or more to the point, for hers. He was stunningly handsome and blatantly male: hard, lean, disturbingly powerful in every sense of the word, physically, professionally, sexually—his virility like a living force. *May the force be with you* wasn't just a line from a movie when it came to Dominic Knight's unrestrained libido. He was like a fucking machine that never wound down. Oh God, she was starting to get wet just thinking about last night.

"I have a request," he said, stopping before her.

She smiled. "I think I have the same one."

He shook his head. "It's something else."

His voice was restrained, his gaze too cool. "That sounds ominous."

"No, not at all." A very faint smile. "It's just a small challenge."

"If it's about your mother, I won't embarrass you. I'll behave."

"No, it has nothing to do with my mother. She's a problem, but nothing to concern us."

His voice was softly dismissive when he spoke of his mother, the same tone he'd used in Singapore before he scared the shit out of those men. *And glory, hallelujah, he's said us. So how bad could it be?* "Well, tell me about this request. I'm listening."

He softly exhaled. "Promise to hear me out before you get all indignant."

She groaned, the ache between her legs gaining strength. "Don't say you're not going to keep your promise. You said two hours and—"

"God, no. Of course I'll keep my promise. But first I want you to do something for me."

Her gaze narrowed. "I don't want to be whipped."

"Christ, I wish you'd never seen that website."

"Don't forget, I saw the Amsterdam show too."

"That wasn't *my* idea." He glanced at his wristwatch and, pressed for time, hoped he was choosing the right words. "What I'm asking of you is perfectly innocuous."

"Then why all the buildup?"

A roll of his eyes. "Because you fly off the handle over nothing."

"Your nothing and my nothing are usually different," she replied with a lift of her brows. "So what's this *innocuous* request?"

It took him a fraction of a second to answer, a surprise for a man who could strong-arm an opponent without a qualm. "First, I'd really like you to do this for me. And second, it's nothing out of the ordinary. I have someone coming over with some lingerie for you."

She groaned. "Really? Is this one of your stupid rules?"

"No. But Mrs. Hawthorne comes highly recommended. You might like some of her lingerie. And if you do this for me, I'll do something for you in return. Just tell me what you want." He held up a finger. "So long as it doesn't interfere with our six days."

"You're crazy."

A roguish smile. "Define crazy."

"All this dressing-me-up stuff," she muttered. "I wonder what a therapist would say about that?"

"Maybe he"—Dominic smiled—"or *she* would tell you to relax. It's just a gift."

"A really expensive one," she grumbled.

"Not for me."

"So this is like a pack of gum for you."

"Pretty much."

She slid down in her chair, looked up at him, then said, "It's not some weird lingerie, is it?"

"No, it's perfectly normal lingerie. Tell me what you want, to do this for me. I have vast resources at my disposal. There isn't much I can't give you."

"Jesus, you don't have to buy me. In fact, the whole notion pisses me off. What the hell's wrong with you?"

"My detractors have a long list. My mother does too, although I'm less inclined to give credence to hers. Look, I'm sorry if I offended you."

"That's a really sweet smile. Does it always work?"

He laughed. "Barring a couple family members, yes, always."

"For your information it still does. But I don't need gifts to stay here. Clear?"

"Yes, ma'am," he murmured. "Perfectly clear. Does that mean you'll stay if I give you something?" he said with a twitch of a smile.

A sulky scowl. "You never give up, do you?"

"Not usually, no."

"And I'm locked in here," she said, her scowl deepening.

"You're not and you know it." He gestured behind him. "The key's in the door."

"So I could leave."

"Of course." A slow drawl, an easy smile. "So long as you go back to the hotel. Six days, Miss Hart. They're not going away."

"Oh fine, then." Her sulky look gave way to a speculative squint as she weighed her options. Perhaps the most pleasing option was standing before her in all his scorching sexiness. That his trouser fly was at eye level and it was clear he preferred his dick on the left may have affected her decision. "You're sure now, that it's average, everyday lingerie."

His smile could have brought a corpse back to life. "I'm sure," he said, all cool and composed.

She sighed, then sighed again. "Oh God...you're so annoying." *And don't forget kick-ass hot*, her could-we-please-get-laid little voice pointed out.

"It shouldn't take long," Dominic offered, gracious and conciliatory. "A half hour I'd guess."

"You're not going to be there, are you? Because that would be *fucking* embarrassing."

"I won't be there. Tell me what you want in order to do this for me. I insist."

She grimaced. "Don't say *insist*."

"I apologize. I would be *grateful* if you told me what you wanted."

She suddenly grinned. "Goddamn, are you kissing my ass?"

"Don't push your luck, Miss Hart."

But he looked amused—and handsome as sin and so awesomely sexy standing there that maybe pushing her luck would be a whole lot of fun. Her belly did a little flutter of anticipation just thinking about it. "Okay, give me a ride on one of those fantastic Chinese junks and we're even," she said, refusing to ask for *things*.

"Done. I have one. We'll go for a sail tonight. That's not enough though. Ask for something else." In his world, everything had a large price tag.

She gave him a look from under her lashes. "You understand I came here for sex?"

"Absolutely. There's no question in my mind."

"Okay, then. A ride on your boat and sex."

This wasn't the time to explain the difference between his full-rigged, beautifully restored nineteenth-century sailing vessel and a boat. Nor was it worth further argument about degrees of gift-giving. "You have yourself a deal, Miss Hart," he said warmly. Leaning forward, he took the book from her lap, set it on a nearby table, and pulled her to her feet. "I'll show you my dressing room."

THIRTEEN

By the time he returned downstairs, Mrs. Hawthorne had been ushered into the green sitting room, her car had been emptied of boxes, and she was having a cup of tea.

"Thank you for coming on such short notice," Dominic said, as he walked into the large reception room with sweeping views of the harbor. The formal furniture was original to the house, gilded, brocaded, some fine eighteenth-century pieces. Dominic had brought in a decorator to temper the ceremonial pomp and Mrs. Hawthorne was seated on one of the more comfortable sofas. "Leo tells me everything was unloaded. The boxes are being taken upstairs. You didn't have any trouble finding the place?"

"No. None at all."

"I'm Dominic Knight," he said, taking a seat opposite her. He smiled at the well-dressed, slender woman of indeterminate age. "Call me Dominic, please."

"Elizabeth, then," she said with an answering smile, surprised to find him so young and informally dressed. He didn't conform to the image of a wealthy oligarch in his sweater and slacks, although the clothes were expensive, as were his custom glove-leather shoes. His dark hair was slightly long and in disarray, as though he'd recently run his hands through it. And he was much more startlingly handsome in person than in his photographs—his bone structure was superb. The kind of arrestingly beautiful man that in her younger days would have generated thoughts of a gratifying afternoon of sex in some discreet hotel room.

He leaned forward slightly, curtailing her illicit thoughts.

"I wanted to speak to you first," he said, resting his elbows on the oatmeal-colored linen of the chair arms, his voice courteous and soft-spoken. "The lady you will be fitting is...ah"—he briefly opened his palms in a considering gesture—"let's say, independent in nature. So I wanted to warn you that a certain amount of tact might be required." He dipped his head faintly. "I apologize in advance."

"You needn't concern yourself, Mr. Knight." She found it difficult to address him casually despite his suggestion. "Tact is a requisite in my business. You might even say the essence of my business."

She may or may not have smiled, he wasn't certain. Her mouth barely moved. But then she added, "Telling a woman who's thirty pounds overweight that she might like to consider a sturdier undergarment requires a great deal of tact."

His smile was instant, like a ray of sunshine. "Thank you. I'm relieved. My friend and I had a minor disagreement about—the suitability of this situation, event, occasion—whatever best describes it. She was concerned that some of the—er—garments might be...I believe her word was *weird*. I assured her they should be perfectly normal lingerie. I hope that's the case."

"Yes, of course. My stock is of the finest quality, most of it handmade, some one-of-a-kind. I'm sure she'll be pleased."

He came to his feet. "We can only hope. If you *should* need my help," he said, his tone deliberately bland, "I'll be next door in my study. It's the first door on your left as you leave the bedroom."

In the course of their journey up the broad staircase and down the hushed upper hall, Dominic conversed pleasantly about local matters, asking Mrs. Hawthorne about Hong Kong's massive rebuilding projects, whether she found the increased traffic congestion a deterrent to her business, if she was often called from her shop for fittings.

She found him very American, casual in speech and manner, cordial and friendly, unlike most men of great fortune when dealing with a small business owner. She wondered what this woman found to resent in such an attractive man.

Dominic stopped at the door to his bedroom.

"The dressing room is to your left as you enter. Just go on in. She's expecting you."

Mrs. Hawthorne walked through the door he opened for her, heard it shut behind her, and surveyed the large bedroom filled with light from six large windows. A huge four-poster bed with a canopy and bed curtains in gunpowder green silk was placed opposite the windows; the views from the bed must be spectacular. An arrangement of chairs and a sofa upholstered in brick-red faille fronted a fireplace with a magnificent cast brass surround. The walls were papered in hand-painted scenes from the Victorian period, the artistry delicate enough to suggest a woman's hand. The carpet was new, her feet sank into the plush pile, the colorful pattern from the Asian steppes. A number of Victorian narrative paintings, beautifully framed, hung on the walls.

The room was exquisite. An example of everything that

money could buy if one had a good eye and superior taste. Could the same be said of the woman waiting for her? Dominic Knight had clearly been solicitous of the lady's mood—whatever the price of her company. Mrs. Hawthorne took a small breath as she approached the designated door, not sure what kind of female she'd find in the dressing room.

A spoiled aristocrat, a temperamental cinema star, a high-priced prostitute with attitude? Someone else's wife?

But when she opened the dressing room door, she came to an abrupt halt, her eyes wide.

The figure before her was a startling facsimile, albeit a modern one, of the French print she had in her shop. The little Irish courtesan could have been this young lady's twin. Perhaps it was the rolled arm daybed on which she was sprawled, or the cut velvet upholstery in the same shade of serpentine. Or the pose—facedown, rosy cheeked, her legs spread wide on the pillow bolsters. In this case the lady was clothed, although her skirt was hitched up so her pale, slender legs were on full display. And the face had the same nubile beauty, her tangle of red curls only adding to the remarkable likeness. She cleared her throat—whether consciously or unconsciously—and the portrait came to life. Slowly, languorously, the figure rolled over with a soft groan and a flutter of her lashes, revealing a voluptuous body. The lingerie she'd brought would complement such a lush form, Mrs. Hawthorne reflected, provided the lady was amenable.

Although Dominic Knight's *If you should need my help* comment gave the impression the lady would be found amenable one way or another.

Mrs. Hawthorne smiled. "Good morning. I understand you might like to try on some lingerie."

Still drowsy, Kate quietly sighed. "I suppose he said that."

"I could come back later if you like?" Having been warned of the lady's reluctance, she was all deference and courtesy.

"No—no, that's not necessary." Kate shoved herself up into a seated position against the sofa arm, surveyed her visitor through her lashes. "Come in. I already promised I'd do this." She smiled. "So please stay."

Mrs. Hawthorne decided this young couple might have the franchise on dazzling smiles. Or perhaps it was nothing more than their youth and beauty that dazzled. "Why don't I unpack some of the boxes while you're waking up?" she said with a meticulous courtesy.

"He must have told you I'd be grumpy?" Kate waved her hand in a little nullifying gesture. "It has nothing to do with you, it's him. He has his way too often. My name's Kate," she pleasantly added. "I'm sorry Dominic dragged you out so early."

"I'm Elizabeth Hawthorne. And it's not a problem."

Kate flicked her fingers at three large boxes. "That's a lot of lingerie."

"Mr. Knight didn't know what you'd like."

Kate snorted. "I told him I wouldn't need anything but he ignored me. He's very charming, isn't he?"

"Yes, he is."

"Does he do this often?"

"I don't know. He's not a client."

A startled green gaze. "He isn't?"

"Not of my shop."

"You own the shop?"

That small surprise again; the young American—her accent unmistakable—didn't know him well. "Yes, the shop is mine."

"And this is important enough to get you here at ten thirty in the morning?"

"*He's* important enough."

Another small sigh. "I've noticed that. Do you have to deal with many people like him?"

"Some. This is a wealthy city. What would you like to try on first?"

"A robe so I can go back to sleep." Kate smiled faintly. "Just kidding. You decide."

"Why don't we begin with the basics? That way I can get an idea of sizes and it won't be necessary to try on everything."

"Perfect. Then this shouldn't take long."

"We'll go as quickly as we can, my dear."

As Kate discarded her dress, Mrs. Hawthorne selected several items from the boxes and laid them out on a large table in the center of the room.

The young woman was naked beneath her dress, Mrs. Hawthorne noted. She wasn't shy about standing nude in the center of the dressing room. In that respect, at least, she and Dominic Knight must be compatible.

"I hope this doesn't take long," Kate murmured drowsily. "I'm tired."

It wasn't difficult to imagine what had caused the young

woman's fatigue. Rumor had it, Dominic Knight's interest in women was anywhere between eccentric and deviant, depending on the informant or source. "We'll try to hurry things along, my dear."

The fitting went as well as could be expected with a client who was clearly uninterested in any of the lingerie and half asleep. Mrs. Hawthorne fitted two bras, both gorgeous if she did say so herself, two pairs of lace panties, one garter belt, a bustier, and one pair of silk pajamas. It was enough for her to know what sizes Dominic Knight's companion required. As a favor to herself, she fitted a last garment: her pet designer's pièce de résistance bustier in gold lamé, beribboned and beruffled like some delicious confection. It was so absolutely stunning on the bored young lady's shapely form, she could no longer remain silent. "If you don't want to do this, my dear, why are you doing it? An observation only. Most women who have men buying them expensive things are generally pleased."

Kate's lashes lifted. "Really?"

"All of them, to be perfectly honest. My lingerie is very costly. And quite unique. For instance, this is real gold lace," she added, adjusting the ruffle that showcased Kate's breasts with a little flick of her fingers.

Kate ran her hand down the gleaming lamé reducing her waist size by inches and adding them to her boobs. "How much is this?"

"I haven't decided. Let's just say you have to be well off to afford it."

"And he's buying all this, too?" She waved at the pile on the dressing room table.

And all of the things still in the boxes. "Mr. Knight wanted a full selection for you."

Kate's cheeks flushed scarlet.

"There's nothing to be embarrassed about, my dear. Mr. Knight was very respectful."

"I suppose that means he pays you to be discreet."

"On the contrary, my business is based on discretion. No one pays me for that. Many men and women have reasons for wanting confidentiality. You're quite safe in every way."

As if to contradict that sweeping statement, the dressing room door suddenly opened and Dominic stood in the doorway. "Excuse me. Not quite finished I see."

He stepped into the room, closed the door behind him, and surveyed Kate slowly, from head to toe, then back again, his gaze coming to rest on her ripe breasts mounded high above a wide swath of ruffled gold lace.

As the silence lengthened, Kate's cheeks turned flame red. "Do you want something?" she said tartly.

He looked up. "We have to dress for lunch. You wanted me to remind you." His voice was neutral, his gaze was not. It was shameless in its intent.

"This is the last item, Mr. Knight," Mrs. Hawthorne quickly interposed into the crackling silence. "Then we're done."

"I hope you found some things you liked." His voice was ultra soft. "That"—he half lifted his hand in Kate's direction—"certainly is...ah...attractive."

As Kate opened her mouth to reply, he said politely, "Just a minute," and turned to Mrs. Hawthorne. "I'm afraid we've run out of time. Just leave everything. Leo is waiting downstairs to pay you. Tell him which you prefer—cash or check." His smile couldn't have been improved on by God himself. "We can't thank you enough for all your help, Mrs. Hawthorne." He swung back to Kate, slowly surveyed her, his gaze glittering with undisguised lust. "Isn't that so?" he added, his voice edgy and low.

The shopkeeper suppressed a gasp. "Dominic!" Kate hissed, shooting a nervous glance at Mrs. Hawthorne, who was clearly shocked.

He didn't respond.

She panicked. She could see the *National Enquirer* headline now.

Then he slowly exhaled, leaned in close. "Don't move," he said, under his breath, whip-sharp and taut.

She bristled at his tone. "What if I do?"

"I'll have to punish you." Another small breath brought his erection under control and, turning to Mrs. Hawthorne, he said calmly, "Let me show you the way downstairs. It's easy to get lost up here."

FOURTEEN

As the door closed on Dominic and Mrs. Hawthorne, Kate let out a deep breath. Was she foolish to stay? Was this particular game more than she could handle? If push came to shove, could she prevail against someone like Dominic Knight? Although, on the plus side, he offered pleasure beyond her wildest imagination and she'd always had more self-confidence than she needed; maybe she should consider Dominic Knight as just another challenge.

Liabilities aside, though, one thing was certain. He was a sex dream come true.

As if to underline that undeniable truth, or perhaps put an end to her debate, the door opened and Dominic walked in.

"That was quick."

"And you didn't move." He leaned back against the door, his face impassive. "Would you like a reward?"

"Depends on what it is."

"Perhaps I wasn't plain enough. I'm going to fuck you."

"So no punishment?"

His lazy smile was unrepentant. "Your choice."

"Great choices," she murmured, a touch of mockery in her voice.

"Misbehave and there'll be no choice," he said, moving away from the door and toward her.

"I haven't agreed to any of your rules just yet. I have choices."

"I haven't agreed either," he said quietly, stopping before her. "So there aren't any rules."

He suddenly seemed too close, too large, intimidating. She took a step back. "Don't look at me like that," she said breathlessly.

"It's just so damned tempting to spank you when you're dressed like a—like that," he said in a soft rasp, his gaze flame hot.

The video flashed before her eyes, spooked her.... "Don't touch me!"

He closed the small distance between them in one long stride, grabbed her hands, shoved them behind her back, and dragged her body into his. "Don't touch me?" he growled. "When you're wearing that fuck-me number?"

"It's *your* fuck-me number," she snapped, staring him straight in the eye, her temper spiking at warp speed when he pushed this hard. "I didn't ask for it. I'm fine with vanilla sex. Especially with your mother around."

The transformation was instant, the bucket-of-cold-water metaphor entirely apt. He even gave his head a shake as though coming up for air.

"You've got fucking nerve," he said with a hint of a smile. "I'll give you that." But he didn't move, his grip still harsh, his body still crushed against hers.

"So I've been told."

He remembered saying that to her at their first meeting. His brows lifted faintly. "Are you mocking me, Miss Hart?"

"No, I'm pushing back. I said I would."

He gave her a considering gaze for a brief moment, then said quietly, "We'll see how that works out." He brought her arms around to her sides, smiled. "My mother won't be around long, Miss Hart. You're going to have to get more creative."

"There's always no."

He laughed softly. "That should tax my self-restraint."

"Or your integrity."

He didn't immediately respond. "You talk a lot," he finally said.

"About things you don't want to talk about."

"That I never think about."

"Because women never say no to you?"

He hesitated, then blew out a breath, and said, "Right."

He had small chinks in his armor, like now, when he would have preferred not answering and did. And meeting his mother this morning had been revealing, as was his easy rapport with Max. His kindness in offering her orgasmic pleasure first and often was unselfish too. "Should I stop talking?" she asked, wanting to please him when he had that small furrow in his brow, wanting to please him almost always.

He gave her a heart-stopping smile. "Maybe for now. There's not much time before lunch."

"Oh," she whispered, his words, his beautiful smile, sending all of her newly addicted senses into full-out operational mode.

He smiled. "You like that?"

She took a calming breath. "Just a little. How do you do it?" She glanced at his crotch, smiled. "Silly question."

"You do it to me, babe. Twenty-four/seven." He slid his fingers over her bound waist, down the taut line of her stomach under the boning, took a small breath before returning his hands to her waist and squeezing slightly. "And this ultimate bondage is just frosting on the cake. I wanted to eat you alive when I saw you in this."

"No kidding. Mrs. Hawthorne practically passed out."

"This gold lamé thing is really hot, you're hot," he murmured, as if she'd not spoken. He raised his hands and passed his palms over the soft silken swell of her breasts with breath-held delicacy. "*These* are fucking hot."

"Hey, watch it, that lace is real gold," Kate whispered.

"Perfect. It goes with your real tits," he murmured, his fingers gliding over her pliant flesh, his focus starkly unambiguous.

"She wouldn't tell me the price." Kate caught her breath as Dominic slipped a finger down her cleavage, then two.

"It doesn't matter. I can afford it." Scooping the heavy weight of one breast from the half scallop of fabric supporting it, he bent his head and stopped her from talking. His mouth was deliberately feather light on her bruised nipples, the warmth of his lips no more than a whisper on her flesh.

As she uttered one of those low, languorous moans that he'd learned last night unlocked her pussy, he reached behind her and ripped open the covered hooks with a wrenching twist of his wrist, letting the costly garment fall to the floor. Lifting his mouth, he swept her up in his arms. Compelled by a savage need he neither liked nor understood, he swiftly kicked the door open, walked into his bedroom, and moved toward the bed. Although the still-functioning portion of his brain blamed his blind impulses on the get-your-rocks-off bustier.

"Now," he said on a suffocated breath, "I'm going first." He tossed her on the bed, pulled off her panties, unzipped his slacks with a jerk of his hand, crawled on top of her, shoes and all—a first for a man of enormous self-control. "Keep up if you can." He guided his rampant erection to her sex. "We'll play"—intent on positioning his cock precisely on her pouty cleft, his voice trailed off—"after..."

A second later a low, throaty groan rumbled deep in his chest as he plunged so deep inside her that she momentarily reeled at the sweet agony, then softly moaned as unalloyed ecstasy flooded her senses. "Christ," he whispered, as the staggering jolt to the head of his dick vibrating wildly up his spine, spiking through his brain, had him momentarily seeing stars. Dragging in a harsh breath, he waited for the stars to recede, then, impatient to duplicate the raw sensation, he pulled her clenched fingers from his shoulders, moved her arms to her sides, circled her wrists with his fingers, and held her still. Flexing his legs, he withdrew, tightened his glutes, and plunged back in, the force of it moving her a grudging inch up the silk comforter.

To that inflexible point of no return.

She gasped, open-mouthed at the prodigal shock, then gasped again at the flame-hot explosion of raw, soul-stirring rapture that left her shaking.

He grunted as his rigid cock met the ultimate resistance: an unspeakable thrill washed over him in hot waves, the scent of her filled his nostrils, her little moans of pleasure as she writhed beneath him made him harder and longer and thicker.

His concentration narrowed to the finite pressure on his dick as he slowly withdrew. Plunging in deeply again, he shut his eyes against the wild delirium ravaging his senses. "Damn it, I should send you home," he muttered, disturbed by his ungovernable craving for this woman he barely knew.

"You should," she whispered, arching her body up to meet his next savage thrust, feeling him move and swell inside her.

"Jesus Christ." His voice was rough, breathless.

Correctly interpreting his expletive, she licked his throat. "Good. Because I'm not finished with"—she gasped as the force of his next downstroke propelled her farther up the bed and urgent, trembling, as desperate as he to feel the inexplicable, addictive pleasure, she tightened her vaginal muscles—to hold him, possess him, to preserve the gluttonous bliss. And for the first time, she truly understood the corrupting power of desire—the ache, the need, the wanting that never stopped, the breathless, fatal longing.

A shame Dominic Knight was the most emotionally unavailable man on the planet.

Driven by his own thin-skinned surliness, blaming *her* for amping him up, for inciting such manic compulsion, Dominic selfishly pursued his climax. He was a millisecond from orgasm when her explosive scream shattered his eardrums and he didn't know whether to be annoyed that she came first or amused at his own naïveté in thinking she couldn't keep up. Since his libido was currently focused on riding the orgasmic wave, however, speculation gave way to fiery sensation and he quickly caught up, matched her rhythm, and spilled a white-hot river of semen into her shuddering body.

"Nice," he whispered in her ear afterward.

She smiled up at him, her gaze still pleasure hazed. "Anytime...get undressed."

"Is that an order?" His voice was a low rasp, his breath warm on her cheek.

"Definitely," she purred.

He glanced at the clock—a man once again in control. "An hour, then we have to wash up and dress before we face the battlefield of lunch."

She grinned. "I expect you to save me."

He smiled back. "I consider it my duty."

"I'll do something for you then."

"I'm sure you will. I know you will."

"Ummm—that voice of authority. It turns me on."

"Everything turns you on."

"Everything about you."

"Better yet," he drawled. Postorgasmic, he viewed Miss Hart's impact on his life more charitably. She was unnecessary, even slightly high maintenance when it came to soothing her quick temper. But she was straight-out irresistible and the state of the universe was less raw when she was around.

"Undress now. I want to feel you."

"Yes, ma'am." He kissed her smiling mouth, whispered, "Two minutes," and slid off the bed.

She watched him like an infatuated lover watches the man she loves, although she knew better. But he was so fine, so beautiful, so glorious in every way, she allowed herself the fantasy. It was only six days. How could it hurt?

He kicked off his shoes, bent to strip off his socks, then

straightened up and turned to blow her a kiss. "I'm a lucky man." His smile was affectionate. "You look perfect lying on my bed. I think I'll have to keep you."

"Maybe I'll let you."

"We'll work something out," he said from under the sweater he was pulling over his head. He dropped his sweater to the floor and unbuckled his belt. "Tell me what you want first or I'll figure out something." His slacks fell to the carpet; he stepped out of them and slid his boxers down his lean hips. "I'm taking orders, Miss Hart," he said with a grin, standing nude a foot from the bed.

"You know more than I do. Surprise me." Lord, he was impressive; male perfection—tall, broad-shouldered, lean, with steel-hard muscles that were honed by some major exercise. He had to work out to have a six-pack and pecs like that. His cock had regular workouts, too, she suspected. Not that she was complaining, seeing how she was the current recipient of that strong, agile, indefatigable erection. The man had stamina. "I need your awesome dick. Pronto. Add that to my order."

He was moving toward his bathroom. "Haven't you ever heard of foreplay?" he said over his shoulder.

"If it makes me feel as good as an orgasm, I'm interested. Otherwise, not so much."

"Ah—a novice to be schooled." His voice echoed from the white marble bathroom, the sound of running water in the background.

"You make it sound really salacious."

"It is. You'll like it." He reappeared, carrying some towels and a wet washcloth.

A moment later the silk comforter was on the floor, the towels were at the foot of the bed, and he was wiping away the residue of his semen from between her legs.

"You make a very nice houseboy," she purred, his washing up gentle and invasive and seriously turning her on.

He looked up and smiled. "I can be nicer. How's that feel?"

"Really, really good."

He glanced up. "Are you always so easily aroused?" He didn't mean for his voice to be edgy. "Sorry," he said quickly, grinning. "Just asking."

"I'm not—or haven't been until now. You get the gold star."

"In that case, I'll have to see that I perform up to the required standards."

"I'm sure that won't be a problem for you." It was her turn to quash her displeasure. "And I mean that most sincerely," she added with a smile.

He grinned. "It's amazing what an orgasm can do for one's serenity, isn't it?"

She nodded, her gaze amused. "I think I found inner peace."

"Same here, babe. At least temporarily. Now let's see what I can do to make you glimpse nirvana again." He lobbed the wet washcloth through the bathroom door and, turning back, eased her into the center of the bed. Spreading her legs with a gentle brush of his palms, he lay down, lifted one of her legs on his shoulder to give himself enough room, then settled on his stomach between her legs. He looked up and smiled. "Something simple first. Foreplay 101." He slid his finger up her cleft, softly touched her clit at the top of his stroke, felt her leg on his shoulder relax, and following his finger with his mouth, licked a path up and down her soft, pink flesh.

She softly exhaled, flexed her hips faintly, and sucked in her breath as he gently nipped at her. He was fastidious in his attentions, licking, sucking, concentrating more and more on her clit, bringing her up to a frantic panting, then easing the tension by moving on to less sensitive areas. He kissed her inner thighs, moving downward to her calves, ankles, feet, his lips smooth, warm, tantalizing.

And when she whimpered in overt demand, he glanced at her. He was kneeling, her foot resting on his thigh, his thumbs massaging the sole of her foot to exquisite effect. "Patience. It only gets better." His thumbs were centered on the curve of her heel where the pressure points for her pelvis lay.

"I don't want to wait," she fretfully murmured.

"You have to. Feel this?"

She softly groaned.

"And this?" Her pelvis came up as he pressed his thumb into her heel. "See, you liked that." Raising his other hand, he placed a palm on her mons and forced her back down, the tips of his fingers strategically placed over her G-spot.

He played nice for a very long time; his repertoire beyond fucking was extensive. And when he finally let her climax— purely with massage—she came in a long, drawn-out progression of screaming orgasms that pleased them both.

Dropping into a sprawl beside the breathless woman in his bed, Dominic kissed the corners of Kate's mouth, her throat, her eyelids, as she lay with her eyes shut, basking in the glow. "After lunch, we'll go somewhere quiet, no people, just us."

She smiled and uttered a soft purr of assent.

Resting on one elbow, he ran his finger down her arm, then up again in a gentle rhythm, his touch whisper soft, and watched her fall asleep before his eyes. Like a child, he thought with a smile. Although in all else, she was lush, bewitching temptation. The kind of woman that brought men to their knees. He grinned. Later—when their privacy was assured.

Rolling off the bed, he bent and lightly kissed her cheek.

He didn't believe in magic, but if he did, he would have found her magical. A sweet escape from the cynicism of his life.

Although a glance at the clock brought reality back with a vengeance.

One fifty.

Miss Hart wasn't used to being up all night. He'd let her sleep for a half hour or so, then come up and get her. Covering his sleeping beauty with a blanket, he quickly dressed and went downstairs to have lunch with his mother.

It helped that his psyche was cushioned by a warm euphoria after an hour in bed with Miss Hart.

He could handle anything now—even his mother.

FIFTEEN

Really, Dominic, must you?" his mother snapped as he walked into the dining room. "You reek of sex."

"You're mistaken, Mother. Like you are so often about my life," he said, taking his seat at the head of the table, waving a servant over to fill his wineglass. "Did you have a pleasant time shopping? I see you bought a few things." The hall was filled with boxes.

"I suppose that woman won't face me now."

"Miss Hart is not *that woman*. She happens to be on a conference call. She'll be down as soon as it's over. As you know, Mother, if not for Miss Hart, the manager at our factory in Romania would have stolen twenty million from me. So kindly put your suspicions aside. Everyone isn't focused on sex." He nodded at the servant. "Leave the bottle and bring another."

"You figure often enough in the tabloids, the headlines are often risqué as I recall."

"The tabloids are entertainment, not news. I hope you don't spend too much time reading them." He smiled at the young man serving his soup. "It smells good, Zhu." *Shrimp bisque; that should be French enough.*

His mother barely touched her food, as usual, moving it around her bowl or on her plate in the manner of ladies who lunch. As if he wouldn't notice she didn't swallow anything. Not that he cared. He ate everything in sight. Sex always made him hungry. When he was served the steak and fries he'd asked for in addition to the quiche his chef had prepared for lunch, his mother snidely said, "You should watch your calories, Dominic. If you eat that much at every meal, you'll soon be as fat as your father."

Dominic looked up, several fries in hand. "My problem isn't gaining weight, Mother, but losing it. I live a physically active life." He shoved the fries into his mouth.

She sniffed. "Your father favored those same activities. His fourth wife is going to end up being his nursemaid."

"Who cares? Let the man be, Mother. You've been divorced for twenty-five years. How can it possibly matter what he does? And consider, he's still paying you alimony. I wouldn't bitch."

"Must you be vulgar?"

He sighed softly. "Sorry, Mother. Tell me what you bought today. Antiques I assume. Any new jewelry?"

Shopping was Letitia Knight's raison d'être. It was always a congenial topic—one of the few they had in common other than that of his sister and her children. Melanie's husband was off limits; Matt didn't quite come up to his mother's standards. So Dominic listened politely to a detailed account of his mother's shopping expedition, added a comment here and there to show interest, and fortunately heard her when she asked him about the China Club. He was able to reply to her question, which wasn't always the case when his mother was holding forth on a shopping monologue.

As dessert was being served—crème brûlée or chocolate mousse—Dominic pushed his chair back and came to his feet. "Let me check on Miss Hart. Perhaps I can bring the conference call to an end so you'll have a chance to visit with her before we leave." He didn't want any disparaging rumors spread by his mother; Katherine didn't deserve the notoriety. "Zhu, coffee for us," he said to the young man standing at attention behind his chair. "And tell An, Miss Hart may want to eat as well. Excuse me, Mother. I'll be right back."

He took the stairs at a run, speedily traversed the upstairs corridor, and quietly let himself into his bedroom. Pausing inside the door, he briefly debated the necessity of waking his houseguest. He had to, of course. Knowing his mother, if he didn't squelch her suspicions he might as well put up a billboard proclaiming to the world that he was fucking Miss Hart. His mother was a notorious gossip.

Collecting Miss Hart's dress and shoes from his dressing room, he gently kissed her awake. "Lunch, I'm afraid," he murmured.

She groaned.

"We have to go down or she'll come up."

Kate instantly sat up, tried to open her eyes, didn't succeed.

"Just sit there, I'll dress you," he said. Pulling away the blanket, he dragged in a breath of restraint at her sumptuous nudity. He was like a horny teenager around her. "Hold out your arms," he said gently.

Still half asleep, she automatically obeyed and he dressed her like one would a dozing child, sliding first one arm into her dress, then the other, tugging the soft fabric over her plump breasts, buttoning the amethyst buttons with dispatch. "Feet," he murmured and she dutifully raised them. Slipping on her black leather heels, he lifted her from the bed, placed her on her feet, said, "Don't move," and straightened the dress over her hips and legs. A quick glance to see that the buttons were all shut. "Wake up, Katherine," he said, deliberately brisk. "Do it and I'll fuck you in an hour."

He smiled as her eyes snapped open. But the lambent heat in the incandescent green of her eyes wiped the smile from his face, punched him in the gut. And he rapidly ran through possible options for avoiding lunch.

All hopeless, of course. They had to make an appearance.

"I'll make it under an hour. Did you hear me?" Her eyes were almost shut again.

"Yes, yes, under an hour. Thank you."

At least she was semiconscious—he smiled—and polite. "You don't have to answer any of my mother's questions. If you don't, I will. Got it?"

She nodded, gave her head a shake, and finally looked up to meet his gaze. "Save me. You promised."

"I will, don't worry. Wait—I forgot your hair." Grabbing his hairbrush from the dresser, he smoothed out her tangles, pronounced her perfect, tossed the brush on the bed, and took her hand. "Now, listen..."

As they moved out of the room, down the corridor and stairs, he filled her in on her fictional conference call, gave her a few names and a topic she could discuss if necessary. "You needn't go into any detail. You can say it's all confidential. *I'll* say it's confidential. I'll cover for you if you get flustered."

"Why am I doing this?"

"So my mother doesn't make your presence here into a scandal. I don't want your reputation compromised."

She shot him an amused look. "Is this the nineteenth century?"

"The twenty-first century is just as bad, believe me. I'm just being cautious."

"Except for renting the entire top floor of the Ritz-Carlton."

"They were paid to protect my privacy."

"Are you sure?" She thought of the bartender.

"If they don't, I'll sue their ass off. Here we are. Smile. This won't last long." He pushed the dining room door open and propelled her in with a hand at her back. "I dragged Miss Hart away from the phone, Mother. The Stonehall Group had enough of her time today." He turned to Kate, his expression bland, his voice urbane. "Could I have some food brought up for you, Miss Hart? I'm afraid we're on coffee and dessert."

"Dessert will be fine, Mr. Knight." She looked up at him with impeccable innocence. "I had an excellent breakfast, more than ample."

He suppressed his smile at her allusion to breakfast, escorted her to a chair, spoke briefly to Zhu, took his seat, and glanced up as the servant left the room. "Zhu will get your dessert, Miss Hart. Tell Mother about your initial interview with Max at MIT. We have Max to thank for recruiting Miss Hart, Mother." His gaze swiveled back to Kate. "I believe you said you thought he was a spy."

"I'm totally embarrassed about that." Kate smiled demurely. She had a real flair for drama. He should have known she was a quick study when it came to sex. "I had to explain to Miss Hart that Max was actually a physicist."

"He looks like someone from MI6," Kate said, wide-eyed and slightly breathless. "He could have come directly from central casting."

"Max's family is English gentry, ancient and titled." Letitia's voice was condescending, as if someone like Kate required a tutorial on class rank. "His family and estate go back to William the Conqueror. Sussex, I believe. Isn't that so, Dominic? You've been there often enough." Letitia Knight offered her son a glossy smile before addressing Kate again. "I'm trying to make Dominic understand that a wife from such a refined background would be useful in his business. He needs to find some nice young lady from a *good* family."

Why not just use a hammer, Mother? "I'm not sure a wife's antecedents count for much in my world," Dominic said coolly. "Deal making's about money, not class rank."

"You couldn't be more wrong, my dear," Letitia said with the complacency of her narrow worldview. "Good breeding is *always* important."

"Why don't I check out *Burke's Peerage* and see who's available? Any special age group I should consider—child-bearing age I suppose. That's another of your requirements, isn't it, Mother? That I procreate."

"Mock me if you wish, Dominic," Letitia said with a sniff that fluttered her thin nostrils, "but pedigree still matters and you're not getting any younger. You'd do well to consider both. Your father had money, but it was through *my* family that he gained entrée into the right clubs and met notable and distinguished people. An aristocratic wife could be very helpful to you."

"You're right, Mother." There was no point in arguing. His father could have bought his way into any of those clubs with or without his mother's family. As for children, his parents weren't exactly models of parenthood. The word *shallow* was coined for his mother and, while Charles Knight was a successful financial trader, Dominic found his father's cavalier view of ethics and legalities objectionable. Not to mention his father's serial marriages to increasingly younger women, and the fact that his father hadn't spoken to him more than ten times in as many years.

"Tell me about *your* family background, Miss Hart," Letitia said coolly, her gaze razor sharp. "Dominic mentioned you were from the Midwest."

"My family is quite ordinary, Mrs. Knight. My parents died young and I was raised by my maternal grandparents in a small town near the Canadian border. My grandfather owned a canoe outfitter. My grandmother was the grade school principal. That's about it."

A small silence ensued because Letitia Knight had no idea what a canoe outfitter was, nor a small town, and the word *ordinary* was to be ignored at all costs.

"Miss Hart's grandmother is interested in infusing liquors." Dominic broke the silence, offering up the information just to see the expression on his mother's face.

Letitia Knight's lips pursed like she'd sucked a lemon.

Kate's mouth dropped open in surprise.

Dominic smiled at Kate. "Max's brief, Miss Hart. Personally, I find your grandmother's hobby interesting. We recently bought two small firms that infuse liquors—one in Northern California, one in Oregon. Their products are exceptional. Does your grandmother have a favorite flavor?"

Stunned, Kate's mind was blank.

"Blueberry perhaps?" Dominic prompted. "I understand they grow wild in Minnesota."

"Yes," Kate shakily replied, wishing she could disappear into the floor.

Dominic looked up as Zhu returned, followed by Leo. "Leo—I'm not sure I want to know why you're interrupting us," Dominic remarked with counterfeit affront.

"Sorry, sir." Leo leaned down to whisper in Dominic's ear.

Dominic nodded, spoke quietly for a moment, nodded again, then said, "Thank you, Leo. Have a car brought up." Dominic glanced down the table at his mother. "There's always some emergency, Mother. We're going to have to leave Hong Kong earlier than expected." He offered Kate a polite smile. "I'm sorry, Miss Hart. We'll find you something to eat on the plane." He pushed back his chair and came to his feet. "Leo will take care of you, Mother. It was nice to see you again."

With escape in sight, Kate was on her feet a second later. "It was a pleasure to meet you, Mrs. Knight."

"Yes, I'm sure," Letitia dismissively murmured, then waved a finger at Zhu. "More coffee."

Dominic was already walking away from the table.

Kate didn't precisely run after him, but as near to it as courtesy allowed.

As they moved down the corridor to the entrance hall, Kate asked, "Are we really leaving?"

"Not Hong Kong, just this house."

"I left my messenger bag upstairs."

"It should be in the car."

"What if it isn't? I'll check."

"Leo's efficient. Don't worry."

It amazed her how smoothly his life advanced, every wish and whim anticipated, every concern attended to by a staff of minions, every expectation satisfied. It was a different world, rarefied, insulated, impervious to the variety, hiccups, and irksome snags that gave life its flavor. Although he wasn't a man to be pitied. He lived an enviable life.

On reaching the door, Dominic said, "Thank you, Leo. I owe you."

"Not a problem. Have a pleasant holiday."

"We're good?" A cryptic look passed between the two men.

"Everything's fine, Nick."

Dominic smiled. "Perhaps we'll come for dinner one night."

"An would enjoy the opportunity to cook for you and Miss Hart."

"We'll see. I'll call you." Dominic dipped his head.

Leo nodded at the houseboy standing at the door and the door was opened.

"There, that wasn't too bad, was it?" Dominic took Kate's hand and moved through the open doorway.

"It could have been worse."

"I wouldn't have let it get worse. I don't want you unhappy."

She smiled up at him as they walked down the stairs. "Lucky me."

"I'm the fortunate one. Watch your step." They reached the car, the back door held open by another staff member.

Dominic followed her in, pointed out her canvas bag on the seat, saw that the privacy glass was up as ordered, and the moment the door shut and the car moved off, he unzipped his slacks and reached out for her. "We both need a reward for surviving lunch." Lifting Kate onto his lap, he quickly swung her around to straddle his thighs, brushed her skirt out of the way with a brisk sweep of his hand, raised her just enough to deftly align himself. Once the tip of his cock was nuzzling her sex, he eased her down his erection with a low, grateful sigh.

Blissfully impaled, Kate wrapped her arms around his neck, rubbed her cheek against his, and whispered, "How do you always know what I want?"

"Because you always want the same thing."

There was a smile in his voice.

She lifted her gaze and wiggled her hips. "Complaining?"

"Uh-uh. I'm happy."

"Me too." Deep down, uncomplicated happy.

Her simple reply was like an antidote to loneliness, when

Dominic had never thought of himself as lonely. "Good," he said, because he didn't want to look at the collective bargaining that had become his life. The frantic pace, the emptiness. Instead, he held her by the waist, raised her up his rigid length and pressed her back down, slowly, leisurely, so they both felt the silken friction register in every obsessed, devoutly expectant nerve ending clear down to their toes.

He didn't rush. The drive would take twenty minutes, maybe more with traffic. He saw to it that Kate didn't rush either, although that took all his considerable skill to keep her from climaxing. And when he finally let her come, when he did as well in a razzle-dazzle turbulence that matched her wild scream, when she lifted her head from his shoulder and smiled at him moments later, he felt as though life had given him a present.

"I don't know how I'm going to be able to screw another man without feeling deprived. Damn you—and damn this world-class equipment"—she moved her hips on his barely diminished erection. "It's going to be hard to duplicate."

"Don't forget these." He held up his hands and flexed his fingers.

"And this." She ran the pad of her finger across his smiling mouth.

"We have a full arsenal of equipment, babe." His smile widened. "You need us."

"Such smugness practically screams for payback."

His brows rose. "And you can do that?"

"Maybe," she purred. "Have you ever seen those naughty librarian commercials?"

"I haven't." He grinned. "But I have a feeling I wish I had."

"You have a lot of late fees, mister," Kate recited in a low, breathy, luridly sexy tone. "Maybe someone should teach you to return your library books on time."

Dominic laughed, the blue of his eyes filled with delight. "Anytime you want to play, Miss Hart, count me in."

"See, that's the problem," she grumbled. "I'm going to miss all that. Maybe I could stop by once a month and we could spend a day in bed fucking."

Or other places, fucking. "You might have yourself a deal," he said softly, his brain rapidly ticking through the logistics necessary to make it happen. "Call me and I'll send a plane for you. In the meantime though, don't go. Stay. Work for me." He had a brief moment of panic as he heard himself vocalize what would have been unheard of three days ago. On the other hand, he wanted what he wanted—for now. "You should have taken my job offer from the beginning."

She squirmed a little so she could feel the full extent of his swelling cock. "The fringe benefits *are* awesome."

"You could be my ADC, work closely with me—very closely," he said, smiling faintly. "Max could go home every week instead of every two weeks. You could fill in."

"Tempting, Mr. Knight. Especially if you promise to fill me in return."

"With pleasure, Miss Hart."

"Only for fun," she said softly, knowing she'd have her heart broken in the end.

"I'm serious."

"We'll talk about it." She had six more days; she wasn't going to ruin them fighting.

"Agreed." He knew better than to argue now. But he intended to keep Miss Hart—at least temporarily. "If you want to come again before we get there," he said smoothly. "We have time."

SIXTEEN

Dominic's Garden House was near the Happy Valley Racecourse and the Emperor Hotel, both useful in terms of entertainment. The track was open from September to June, the Emperor Hotel was open 365 days a year, which meant there was always sex for sale. And conveniently near the hotel was the residence Dominic had purchased three years ago and that functioned on occasion as his fuck pad.

At the moment though, he wasn't interested in either public venue. He had his entertainment, and horse racing was the last thing on his mind.

The car entered the property through electronic gates, although nothing as pretentious as the gates for his house on the Peak. The drive was abbreviated as well, although the gardens were superb—a jungle of foliage that made the house, when it appeared, a surprise.

The red structure had been built as a summer house in the late eighteenth century, the design an idiosyncratic amalgam of Chinese and Portuguese elements. With the original Portuguese trading port of Macao a short sail from Hong Kong, there was evidence that the first owner had used the house as a private retreat—for personal entertainment. Much like the present owner.

Dominic had had the summer house converted to a

year-round home, upgrading the plumbing and electricity, adding heat and air-conditioning, replacing windows with more environmentally suitable glass, insulating the walls, bringing in a decorator to re-create some of the original ambiance, including a room that resembled a tai chi studio.

The Garden House hadn't been his first choice. He would have preferred entertaining Miss Hart at his house. But his mother's presence had required the change in plans.

As the car came to a stop, Dominic spoke through the intercom to the driver. "We need two robes, Liang, and some towels," he said in Cantonese. "Toss them on the front seat. Then you can take one of the other cars in the garage back to the house. We'll manage here on our own."

The driver's door opened a moment later.

"He's getting us robes," Dominic translated, lifting Kate and placing her on the seat beside him. "Relax," he said to the sudden apprehension in her eyes. "No one cares what we do. This is Hong Kong."

"And you're rich."

He smiled. "That too."

They waited in the luxury Benz, concealed from the world behind smoked glass windows. Dominic related some of the history of the house, spoke of his remodeling, talked about inconsequential things to soothe her nerves. Miss Hart wasn't used to ignoring the world. He'd had a lot of practice.

In a few minutes, the driver's door opened and closed. Shortly after, Dominic hit a switch and the privacy glass slid away. Rolling up from his seat, he leaned over into the front of the car and grabbed the robes and towels.

"Here you go. We'll leave our clothes in the car."

Kate looked like a deer in the headlights. "You told him we needed towels?"

"You need to calm down. I have people who take care of me. They're happy to do the same for you. It's nothing personal. It's their job." He tossed her a towel. "Do you want help with that?"

"No!" Her cheeks turned red. "Don't look."

He laughed. "Tell me what I haven't seen."

"I don't *care*. Just don't look."

He turned his head because it was a silly argument, not worth pursuing. And when she said, "Here," he looked back, took the towel, and dropped it on the floor. Pulling his sweater over his head, he let it fall on top of the towel.

"You're just leaving those there?"

"Someone will deal with it."

"None of this embarrasses you? Not even a little?"

He was taking off his shoes and glanced up. "Uh-uh. My staff is well paid; they couldn't care less." He lifted one brow. "Want me to unbutton?"

She sighed and slid a jeweled button free.

"No one will say anything to you. I promise." He pulled off his socks. "You're going to like my bed," he said, changing the subject. "It's antique, 1793 I've been told, and enormous."

"Don't tell me why. I don't want to know."

He had no intention of telling her why. In fact, he'd have to be more selective in his topics of conversation. He kept forgetting her naïveté. Just because she liked to fuck non-stop didn't mean she was worldly. "Actually, the decorator found the bed in Beijing. It's supposedly from the emperor's apartments in the Forbidden City. If you like, we could go see the royal residences someday. It's a pretty impressive layout."

"Thank you."

That was too crisp. "For?"

"Lying. I appreciate it."

So she wasn't completely naive. "I'm going to have to see that I lie a little better if it's that obvious," he said with a grin, slipping his slacks and boxers down his hips, lifting up enough to slide them off.

"Please do. Because this is *my* fantasy holiday."

"I prefer thinking of it as my getting-to-know-my-new-ADC-better holiday."

She leaned over and put her finger over his mouth. "Stop. This is *my* fantasy. And put on your robe or we're not going to get into the house."

He quickly slid the black silk robe over his shoulders, closed it, tied the tie. "I'd prefer the house. But once inside, consider me at your disposal."

She slid her dress off her shoulders and down her arms. "I like the sound of that," she said with a smile. "You obliging me."

Dominic Knight hadn't put himself at any woman's disposal since his wife's death. However, with his companion naked, inches away, and, as she implied, impatient, his thoughts weren't on the past. "Inside, not here," he said gruffly. "Put on your robe." Miss Hart's glowing nakedness was bringing his dick back to life. It always amazed him, how it was possible to conceal such abundance.

The "Set Fire to the Rain" ring tone echoed from inside Kate's messenger bag, prompting a visible tenseness in his companion.

Kate didn't move.

He flicked a finger toward the bag. "Answer it."

"They can leave a message."

"It might be your grandmother," he said casually, his gaze in contrast, vigilant. "You should answer it."

"Not now."

The message ping went off.

"I'd check that." Dominic pointed at the bag again. "Andy's been calling a lot."

She gave him a murderous look. "How the hell would you know?"

"You should get a password."

"I *have* a fucking password."

He shrugged. "You should get a better password."

"And you should get some scruples," she snapped.

"I'll think about it." Reaching past her, Dominic grabbed the bag from the seat, pulled out her iPhone, tapped an icon, and glanced at the display. "Andy's wondering how you like Hong Kong?"

"*What?*" She snatched the phone from Dominic's hand, looked at the text, swore, then muttered, "How the hell does he know where I am?"

"I repeat—you should get a better password." His smile was indulgent. "You of all people."

"I'm sorry," she said with cutting sarcasm. "Are you saying this is my fault?"

"All I'm saying," he replied with gentle forbearance, "is

you shouldn't leave yourself open to hacking. You can fix it. Now call him back. Tell him you're busy."

She softly exhaled. "I can't. Andy wants to know about my job at Knight Enterprises, as you probably already know if you read the earlier texts. So I'm not calling him back. I don't have anything to say other than that I'm banging the CEO and I'm not interested in broadcasting that to the world."

Dominic smiled. "You're wounding my ego. It can't be that bad."

"Very humorous," she grumbled, moody and fretful, dropping back against the seat with a sigh. "You're going to fuck up my life in more ways than one."

"We don't have to worry about it right now, do we?"

She gave him a surly look from under her lashes. "Because you have a one-track mind."

"With you I do. I'm leaving a helluva lot of people hanging because of you. So we could debate who's fucking up whom the most." He lightly touched her arm. "But I'd rather do that tomorrow or the next day or the day after that if it's okay with you. Come see my house. You'll like it."

"Just like that. Forget everything. Come in and play?"

He grinned. "It could work."

She sighed, then frowned. "Damn you," she sourly murmured.

"You don't want to get in that line," he said quietly. "It's fucking long."

"So you're troublesome to lots of people, not just me."

"I'm afraid so. Which is why I find your company so

irresistible. You make me forget all that—everything in fact...except—"

"Fucking."

He dipped his head, his blue-eyed gaze surprisingly open. "That answer rings all the bells, Miss Hart. You get the giant stuffed panda."

"As if I could say no," she said so softly, he had to strain to hear her.

But he heard. "Would you like me to carry you in?"

"Like this?" She flicked a finger down her nakedness.

He smiled. "That way or any way. We're alone here."

"What about food? You don't cook. And I certainly don't."

He laughed. Only Miss Hart would be concerned about food. "The kitchen is in a separate building."

"So we're not alone."

"It's some distance from the house. And I promise we'll be alone. You won't see a soul."

"Does the food get cold?"

"You're seriously bruising my ego, Miss Hart. I'm here to fuck you and you're talking about food."

"Just curious."

"A tunnel runs between the kitchen and the house, the food is delivered in warming ovens, an electronic lift carries it upstairs; we pick it up absent human contact."

"Like Marie Antoinette's playhouse," she said, smiling at the memory of the lush film. "I loved that movie."

"Very much like that, yes. There's nothing new under the sun."

A playful glance. "When it comes to sex."

He smiled. "Particularly when to comes to sex. Would you like a menu?"

"For?"

"Ah, finally, I have your attention. I have both kinds of menus, Miss Hart. Which would you prefer first?"

"Need you ask?"

"I would have said no until recently." An infinitesimal lift of his brow.

She leaned over, stretched, and licked a path up his throat. "Show me this antique bed."

At Miss Hart's express order, he tossed the strap of her bag over his shoulder, lifted her onto his lap, opened the door, and smoothly exited the car.

"You're strong," she murmured, her arms around his neck as he crossed the cobblestone drive. "All that virility and power. I like that."

"You're soft and delicate," he said, smiling. "The perfect match." Nudging the unlatched door open with his foot, he stepped into a scented foyer, perfumed by an enormous vase of white lilies set on a black lacquer table.

Light from an open courtyard illuminated the space, the illusion of some mythical Xanadu stunning. "It's like a storybook house," Kate whispered, the interior the equivalent of every romanticized Chinese palace she'd ever seen in books or movies. The furniture was colorful, including some in a bizarre interpretation of European rococo, the carpets were muted, the walls embellished with gilded panels hung with silk scroll landscape paintings and the occasional gold-framed weeping face of Jesus.

"The decorator was faithful to the original owner's

eccentric tastes. She found some old diaries. He wanted a hideaway. I couldn't agree more."

"I'm not going to ask why."

"It's not necessarily about anything disreputable." *Although there were times.* "Mostly, I like the privacy. My life is filled with people wanting things from me. Here, I can be alone."

"Oh dear," she said in playful despair. "I'm intruding."

He grinned. "I might be able to make room in my schedule, Miss Hart. If you ask me nicely."

"Would you please fuck me, Mr. Knight? I promise not to say a word if you'd prefer."

He laughed. "I must have died and gone to heaven."

"Or paradise."

"Sounds even better, Miss Hart. Let me take you there."

He carried her through two of the jewel-like rooms filled with precious objects and came to a stop at a closed door. "Shut your eyes," he said softly.

The blue flame in his gaze, the deep resonance of his voice, set her heart racing. She took a small breath, shut her eyes, and as Dominic moved into the room, she inhaled a cloud of sweet fragrance.

She heard him suck in his breath and opened her eyes.

"I think Leo did this for you." His voice was amused. "He must have cleaned out every flower shop in the city."

"But to very nice effect. We'll have to thank him. Fucking in this room will definitely go into my book of memories." The bedroom had been transformed into a magnificent flowery bower, the profusion of blossoms an entirely white, enchanting backdrop to the brilliant color in the room. Had a decorator helped Leo with the flowers? Kate wondered. How many more people knew of her sexual holiday with Dominic Knight?

"It's a little over the top, but Leo meant well."

"It was sweet of him, really."

"What do you think of the bed?"

The four-poster bed set on an ornamental platform was huge: scarlet lacquer, resplendently filigreed, hung with sheer, metallic gold tissue silk tied back with red braided, tasseled cords. The bedspread was a brilliant emerald green silk, embroidered with red dragons, white peonies, and hummingbirds.

"The decorator re-created a watercolor sketch of Mr. Mendosa's bedroom from 1799."

"It's dazzling—like a beautiful stage set. I'm not sure I dare lie on that embroidered quilt. A team of seamstresses must have worked a year on it."

"Close. Eight months. But everything's usable." He dropped her on her feet, tossed her bag on a chair, and waved toward the bed. "Please, make yourself comfortable."

"I'd love to text a picture to Nana," Kate said, moving toward the outrageously theatrical bed. "But she'd ask questions."

"I agree, it wouldn't be wise. You don't want to be personally linked with me." He smiled. "In terms of your reputation. Other than that, I'm interested in any and all personal links with you."

She smiled back. "I *have* noticed."

"Good, because I've been doing my best to keep you interested," he drawled. "Careful with those stairs." He indicated a three-step platform in mother-of-pearl offering access to the bed. "I'll be right with you." Turning away, he disposed of his robe in two economical movements— untying it and shrugging it off his shoulders—then walked a few steps to a long, low dresser with two banks of drawers, embossed brass fittings decorating the corners. Pulling several drawers open, he surveyed the contents, returned to one of the drawers, and lifted out a white lace bra with a front closing and blue ribbons woven through the laced-trimmed cups.

He turned back to the bed, the bra draped over one finger. "This looks girly. Do you like it?"

"Is Leo a magician?" She'd last seen the bra in Dominic's dressing room.

"Just competent. Do you like it?"

She was sitting cross-legged in the center of the bed, dwarfed by the dimensions and the soaring canopy. "The important question is do you? You were the one who wanted to buy all that stuff."

He smiled. "That must be why I find you so appealing. You don't quibble."

"You find me appealing because I'm available. And I have my reasons for being available." She pointed at his cock. "Him."

His dick responded with exaggerated speed to Miss Hart's bluntness, spiking upward in an explosive surge.

"Now *that* I'd like to have in my phone album," Kate whispered. She could see the blood swelling the faint network of distended veins on his massive erection as he approached her. "Care to share?"

"Not with the world. Sorry."

She playfully pouted. "Selfish."

"I know the feeling. I almost took a picture of you this morning at breakfast. I could have jerked off to that twenty-four/seven."

"Have I mentioned how I adore your flattery, no matter how vulgar?" she said, a teasing light in her eyes.

"You adore my dick even more," he observed. "So get your pretty little ass over here." He was standing at the side of the bed, the heat in his eyes scorching, his erection twitching against his stomach. "Now." He watched her slide across the bed with a singular vigilance, like a hunter sighting its prey.

When she reached the side of the bed, Kate leaned back on her hands, drew in a small breath, and looked up into Dominic's enigmatic gaze. "Don't make me wait. Please. I hate that."

Grasping her ankles, he swung her legs over the side of the bed. "I can make you do anything I want," he said smoothly, drawing her into a seated position.

"*Maybe* you can." Although her body was already beginning to hum and pulse and shamelessly moisten at the soft menace in his threat.

"I'm pretty sure I can. You're getting wet just thinking about what I might do to you, wondering what I might do. Not quite sure what's in store for you." He gently touched her nipple, which had swelled as he'd spoken.

Her eyes shut and she softly moaned.

"You like your nipples touched, don't you?" He gently squeezed the tip, the bruises more livid than they had been this morning. "You don't even mind if it hurts a little, do you? Answer me." Cool, soft as silk, a man allowed anything.

Her lashes abruptly lifted, a familiar heat in her green gaze. "I don't have to answer you."

Dropping the bra on the bed, Dominic slid his palms up the insides of her thighs, stopped midway, and pushed.

She struggled against the pressure, lost, and the way cleared, her thighs opened wide, Dominic slid his middle finger up her wet slit. "Maybe this is your answer," he murmured, skimming the pad of his finger down her slick tissue, grazing her clit as he drew back his hand. "Am I right?" He rubbed her bottom lip with the moist tip of his finger. "You never need lube. You're always ready for sex. Aren't you? Answer or I'll take my dick where the women are more accommodating." He took a step back as though to underscore his intent.

"Don't go."

His gaze was cool, unruffled. "Will you do what I tell you, not argue about every goddamn thing?"

She hesitated.

"You have to decide how much you want this," he said softly, closing his fist around his stiff, upright erection, sweeping his hand downward.

She gasped as the rampant crown swelled larger and the color darkened from red to purple.

"Yes or no, Miss Hart?" His hand rose and fell again.

She drew in a shaky breath, exhaled, nodded.

"I didn't hear you."

"Yes."

He smiled, let his hand drop to his side. "Good. Now my rules. Your pussy is for me alone. Should you want to masturbate, you have to check with me first. I have a better vibrator for you, so you might like to try it. But whether I allow you to use it will be my decision, not yours. And these are mine"—he briefly cupped her breasts, let his hands drop—"to do with what I want. Do you understand?" He lifted her chin with the tips of his fingers.

She was turning liquid inside, melting with shame and desire. She nodded.

"Speak."

"I understand."

"Next—if I tell you to wear a bra, you will. If I tell you to take that bra off, you will. If I tell you to serve these"—a flick of his fingers over the swell of her breasts—"up for my pleasure, you'll hold them and lift them high. Is that clear?"

"Yes, yes." She was beginning to squirm.

"And if you do as you're told, I'll screw the hell out of you because that's what you want, isn't it?" He could see the fury in her eyes, but he forced her to answer. "That's what you came here for, right?"

Silence, incandescent with rage.

He waited because she was flushed and trembling and he had what she wanted—a hard dick.

"Yes," she finally whispered.

"Thank you," he said with a saintly smile. "Now, there are no exceptions to my rules. You must learn obedience. You're much too independent." He placed his strong hands on her hips, stilled her faint squirming. "You can't come yet. And you might want to give me a safe word. If you don't overuse it, I'll respect it. But I'm going to fuck you any way I want today, so be warned."

Damn him, he was going to talk her into an orgasm. "Don't you dare do this to me," she hissed. "I want *you* inside me. Not this bullshit."

"You have no idea what I dare. I'm not Andy or Michael. Not even close. So you'll have to deal with whatever I choose to do to you." The blue of his eyes was stone-cold.

Her carnal agitation gave way to apprehension; she felt a shiver run up her spine. What had she gotten herself into? This isolated house, this man who was looking at her with such indifference, as though they'd not spent the night together, as though he'd not given her pleasure a thousand different ways, as if he were a stranger.

"I know everything about you," he said as though she'd asked. "When your period starts, how you like to masturbate, why you eat your fries with mayonnaise instead of ketchup, how you read lying down on your stomach. Your favorite childhood book, TV program, candy bar. What little I don't know, I'm going to discover in the next six days. Now raise your arms."

She shook her head. "Don't touch me—I mean, please don't touch me," she quickly added, remembering the last time she'd said that to him. "Please—I shouldn't have come here, gotten involved with—"

He saw the fear and apprehension in her eyes and knew he had gone too far. "Me, I know. I'm sorry. I've frightened you." Bending, he gently brushed her lips with his. "I have to treat you more gently," he said, his breath warm on her mouth. "I keep forgetting you're new to all this." He stood up, smiled faintly. "Just tell me no when you don't like something. I won't do it."

"I should leave," she said. But her voice was unsteady, because temptation was only inches away, smiling at her, and she wanted him still, without logic or reason. "It's intimidating. Being all alone here."

"Would you like me to call in some of the staff?"

"Jeez, no!"

"They could stay outside the door then or down the hall, I could key in the kitchen on your phone—whatever you want. Just don't go," he said quietly. "I want you to stay." Taking her hand in his, he lifted it to his mouth and kissed her fingertips one by one, turning her palm at the last and pressing it lightly to his mouth. "I promise not to frighten you."

She shouldn't be so easily comforted; she should have more sense. "How do you know about Andy and Michael?" she asked, because she wasn't going to leave, not really.

"Max finds out everything." Dominic gave her a heart-breakingly beautiful smile. "But I don't care about your... friends if you don't care about them."

"I don't care. I never did. They were just friends with benefits. It wasn't like this with you—where I can hardly breathe for wanting you, where I can't stop wanting you every minute, every second. I've never craved anything in my whole life as badly." She glanced down, mortified at her shameless desire. But she wanted him on his terms, on any terms. She looked up. "So add me to your trophy case with all the others."

"That's very kind of you," he said, feeling strangely gratified. "I don't have a trophy case, but if I had one, you'd be the pride and joy of my collection."

Her familiar smile reappeared. "I like when you're charming."

"I like you anytime." He held out the bra, because talk of other women for any length of time was never good. "I'd like you even more if you put this on. You'd make me very happy."

She grinned. "As long as it's not a one-sided happiness."

He looked amused. "I understand that's a given with you, Miss Hart. Three for you, one for me, four for you, one for me. Is that about right?"

"You're such a dear," she said with a playful flutter of her lashes. "Show me what you can do."

He laughed. "Is this a teaching moment or a test of my stamina?"

"Both."

"Then we both win."

"We are compatible, aren't we?" she teased.

"We have our moments." Finding a woman you were compatible with rather than one that was simply available—a novel concept. Miss Hart was opening new horizons for him. He helped her lift her arms to slide through the bra straps and after gently fitting each breast into the lacy cups, he snapped the front closure. The lace barely covered a quarter of her lavish breasts, the silk fabric straining under its load, the straps nicely adjusted by Mrs. Hawthorne to showcase the spherical beauty of the pale, fleshy mounds. "Very pretty," he murmured, brushing his fingers over her nipples, compressed under the top rim of the white lace. "Can you feel that?"

She smiled at him. "A little."

Her response was so perfectly attuned to his agenda, he wondered for a flashing moment whether she'd arrived on his doorstep in answer to his prayers. Pragmatic to the core, however, he decided that Miss Hart's highly charged libido was more likely the reason for their accord.

Sliding his index fingers under her nipples just enough to ease them above the snug rim of lace, he tenderly stroked the tips into taut, hard buds while she softly purred and moaned and gently rocked back and forth on the dragons and peonies.

"Wait," he whispered, releasing her nipples. "I'll be right back."

"No, no, no." A pouty lament, her hand on his arm to stop him.

Bending down, he sucked on her pouty bottom lip, slid two fingers up her sleek welcoming heat, and, gently massaging, opened his mouth enough to say in a warm hum against her lip, "You have to wait because I said so."

She lifted her hips into his fingers and exhaled a little groan he recognized as acceptance. Then with a last little nibble on her lip, he withdrew his fingers and stood upright.

She uttered a despairing little groan as he strode away.

"No complaints, Katherine," he said quietly, personalizing his intrinsic authority. "That's an order."

He smiled at the instant silence, stopped at the dresser, jerked open a drawer, picked up a small box, upended the contents into his palm, and returned to the bed. "See, that didn't take long. We'll have you climaxing in no time. How does that sound?" A pause, silence. "Answer me. Remember the rules? Do you want to come?"

Her reply was very soft, barely audible; her eyes were shut, her thighs clenched tightly, the flush pinking her skin indication of her breathless desire.

"I can't hear you, Katherine. If I can't hear you, I can't let you come."

"Yes, yes, yes, yes, *yes!*" Emphatic, her green eyes blazing.

"See, you can obey me if you want something badly enough. How much do you want to come?"

"Fuck it," she snapped. "I don't want to anymore."

He grabbed her arm, pushed his other hand between her legs, slid three fingers inside her, and watched her shudder as the violent sensations jolted her body. "Still undecided," he murmured, stretching her slick passage with his fingers, then softly caressing the swollen tissue of her G-spot, pausing a short time later just before her orgasm, waiting until she marginally calmed before renewing his deft massage. Exercising his delicate manipulative skills, he smoothly amplified the rhythm of stimulation and restraint until she was trembling uncontrollably. "I think that answers our question about whether you want to come or not," he said mildly, withdrawing his fingers, releasing her arm.

She was wet, quivering, convulsed with an unbearable hunger, desperate to feel him inside her, her longing so intense she was whimpering.

He rubbed her nipple between his thumb and wet forefinger, a casual act of possession. "One more thing, Katherine, and then you can come."

She would have done anything to come, said anything. "Anything you want," she said in a pleading voice and heard him take a deep breath.

"Just this for now," he said, slowly exhaling. "Afterward, I'll screw you till you tell me to stop. Or maybe I won't stop. Maybe I'll just keep going no matter what you say." She almost came right then and she would have, but he grabbed her chin in a brutal grip and growled, "Not yet."

The shock of it stopped her; she felt his fingers slide away from her face.

"You're doing well, Katherine. It won't be much longer. Look, I want to show you something." He kissed her cheek. "Open your eyes."

Sheer force of will brought her eyes open.

"Do you like these?" A rhetorical question.

He held what looked like two small clip earrings. Teardrop pearls were suspended from tiny diamond starbursts. But in place of the usual spring was a small turnbuckle with diamond studs on both ends. "If it starts to hurt let me know. You should be fine though. These are supposed to be painless," Dominic said, dropping one clip on the bed, and framing Kate's nipple with the other clip.

She flinched.

"It can't hurt yet. Tell me when it does and I'll stop tightening." A few moments later, before she responded, he saw that the pressure was sufficient to hold the nipple clip in place. He stopped tightening and repeated the procedure with the second clip. "No pain? If there is, tell me and I'll adjust them. Hey," he whispered, glancing up when she didn't reply. "Katherine, look at me. Are we good?"

Overwhelmed by feverish sensation, the throbbing inside her jolting her senses with every pulse beat, her breasts swollen, her nipples the orgasmic trigger spurring her toward orgasm, she wasn't capable of fully opening her eyes. Her lashes barely lifted. She nodded.

This was sexual opulence on a grand scale: her full breasts overflowing the insubstantial white lace bra; her nipples elongated under the pressure of diamond vises; her wet pussy ravenous for cock. For his cock. He dragged in a breath of restraint, beat back his renegade impulses, and spoke very softly because Miss Hart was very near to climax. "I'm going to lift you off the bed, Katherine. You have to stand. I want to show you your new jewelry in the mirror." He watched the pearl teardrops vibrate as he picked her up and set her on her feet; his erection took note as well. Placing his hand under her arm, he guided his new playmate, trembling faintly and not entirely aware, to the cheval glass in the corner.

"You have to open your eyes, Katherine." He flicked both pearls with a brush of his hand.

She jerked, gasped.

"If you look, I'll put my dick inside you."

The magic words. Her eyes opened.

She looked and a fierce rush of pleasure streaked down from her nipples to her saturated, throbbing core, then rolled back up again with such intensity, she buckled under the shock.

Dominic caught her, held her upright, hooked a gilded bamboo chair with his foot, and hauled it close. Gently seating her, he stood behind her, bent low to kiss her shoulder.

"Keep your eyes on the mirror," he murmured. "You must. Did you hear me?"

"Dominic, please," she whispered.

"Soon, Katherine. You know it's always better when you wait." Reaching around her, he lightly flicked the pearls, and as she sucked in her breath at the fierce stimulation, he warned, "You're not allowed to come yet. If you do, I won't fuck you. Do you understand?"

A shuddering gasp. She nodded.

"We have to work on your restraint issues, Katherine. Soon, you'll find it easier to control your urges. I'm going to suck on the tips of your nipples now. You have to resist coming. Say, yes, I understand."

"Yes, I understand," she breathed, gripping the arms of the chair tightly, her spine rigid.

Moving around to the front of the chair, he spread her thighs, knelt between them, unhooked the front closure on the bra, and watched her breasts burst from their bindings with a quiver. "Is that more comfortable?"

She wanted to scream and swear, punch him black and blue, but she wanted him to fuck her a thousand times more. So she said, "Yes," because she was dying to have him inside her, now, ten minutes ago, yesterday and the day before. For that irresistible, fathomless, unrivaled pleasure she'd do and say whatever he wanted.

"Unclasp your fingers so I can take off this bra."

She instantly obeyed.

"How docile you've become," he said gently, tossing aside the bra. "I'm pleased. You'll be rewarded soon. But not until I give you permission. You must learn better control.

Now put your hands in your lap and sit up straight." His fingers closed over the diamond clips and he lifted slightly.

She whimpered and stretched her spine.

"There." He dropped his hands. "Now you're sitting up properly. That didn't hurt, did it?"

The streaking thrill had gone straight down to her stomach, curled through her clit with such force she was left panting. She shook her head.

"I didn't hear you."

"No," she whispered, quivering.

"Do you feel like coming when I pull on your nipples?"

His voice was soft as a caress. Would he let her come? "Yes," she answered. "Very much."

"Even if I were to bite your nipples? Would that make you come?"

She could almost feel his teeth on her flesh, her body aching for his touch. "Yes, even then," she said on a suffocated breath.

"You obviously want to come." He gently circled her aureole with the tip of his finger.

"Yes, yes." Frantic, desperate, so wet with longing she could feel the tiny trickle slide from her body.

"I'm afraid you're not quite obedient enough to reward yet. You must stop squirming and"—he sighed softly—"you're ruining that chair."

Every muscle in her body was tense; she didn't know if she could control her orgasm. "Dominic, I *need* to come!"

He leaned forward, looked into her hot, lustful eyes. His sudden smile was beautiful and pitiless. "What makes you think that matters to me?"

Her shoulders sagged. "How long?" Her voice was ragged, her eyes smarting with tears.

"It's up to you. Patience, Katherine." Bending his head, he lightly licked the swollen tip of her nipple compressed under the diamond turnbuckle, then slowly sucked the sensitive, bruised flesh until it stood out prominently, gradually increasing the pressure.

She whimpered. "I want to come."

He lifted his head. "Not yet." He tightened the nipple clamp a half turn.

She gasped at the raw intensity, began to shake, fought against her swelling climax.

Dominic watched her heroic effort to stem her orgasm, anticipated with pleasure schooling the volatile passions of the insatiable Miss Hart. "One more nipple," he murmured, lowering his head. "And then we'll see whether you deserve to come."

She moaned as his mouth closed around her nipple, made a small little helpless sound as he sucked hard enough to coax the tender tip into a hard, stiff peak. "May I come now?" she gasped, her breasts heavy and swollen, her nipples throbbing, her body desperate for release.

He raised his head, ran his fingers over the swell of her breasts, flicked the pearls with his fingertips. "In ten minutes."

Her eyes snapped open. "I'll do it myself!"

He grabbed her hands, held them against her thighs, looked at her steadily and calmly. "Ten minutes, Katherine, or you won't come at all."

She uttered a little despairing cry. "You can't mean it!" The throbbing between her legs was a deep, raw ache.

"Of course I mean it." He smiled thinly. "Now put your hands on your legs. Do it, Katherine. You don't seem to be willing to learn. Are you telling me you don't want to come?"

She quickly obeyed.

"Now don't move," he murmured, gently touching her inner thighs, spreading them wider with his fingers. He carefully parted the soft folds of her moist sex. His fingers closed over her swollen, throbbing clit.

Her back arched, she moaned, pushed against his fingers.

"Do. Not. Move." He emphasized each word with a sharp tap on her clit.

She stifled the expletive that rose to her lips, so close to climaxing, her nerve endings were tingling.

"Very good," he said quietly. "You're learning." He slid his fingers over her hard, tiny nub, slowly, deliberately, softly, giving her what she liked.

She could feel the warmth pulsing inside her, the increasing pressure spreading outward. She didn't dare move, but she whimpered in delight, tightened her muscles against her coming climax.

Dominic abruptly withdrew his fingers, closed her legs, rolled back on his heels.

She cried out, sobbed in frustration.

"It's all about control, Katherine. You'll thank me when you finally come."

When her breathing eased and her body calmed, Dominic leisurely unfolded from his seat on the floor, rose to his knees, and opened her legs again.

The second he slid his finger inside her, she felt the

first tiny spasms ripple through her, hard dizzying pleasure instantly magnify into a flame-hot glow.

"Jesus, Katherine." He slammed her legs together. "Have you no fucking control at all?"

She could hardly breathe, the pressure inside her so intense she could have wept in frustration. "Let me come!" she wailed.

"Hopefully, you can still tell time," he snapped. "A minute left. Watch the fucking clock."

She stared at his massive erection, straining upward, flat against his stomach. "Do I get that then," she said, trembling with lust and anger. "Or will you have some other lesson for me?"

"I said ten minutes. That's what I meant. And yes, you'll get this." He flicked a glance downward.

"Maybe I won't want it."

"You haven't been paying attention, Katherine," he said softly. "It doesn't matter what you want." Smoothly rising to his feet, he pulled over a red silk-covered bench similar to one in Mr. Mendosa's watercolor, and shoved it in front of Kate. "Bend over that and hold on tight. I'm going to fuck you in twenty seconds. You have my permission to climax now."

She quickly followed instructions because even resentful and vowing revenge, he had what she desperately needed. Standing up, she bent forward, clutched the sides of the small bench, and waited, flushed and trembling for her reward.

Casually surveying her plump pink bottom, Dominic shoved the chair aside, moved up behind the unresisting Miss Hart, guided his erection to her pink, dewy cleft, and placed his hands lightly on her hips. "Move back a little," he ordered. "A little more," he commanded because he could; she'd do anything he asked right now. "There, that's good. Ready?"

She came before he'd completely penetrated her— instantly, noisily, without restraint and at some length, in a staggering number of violent spasms that jolted her and pleased him, lit up the pleasure centers of their brains and continued to play out as he held himself rooted deep inside her until every quivering trace of her orgasmic frenzy died away.

Then leaning forward, he whispered against her ear, "See, it *is* better if you wait."

She softly groaned, a low, blissful pleasure sound— answer in part to his comment, in part sumptuous response to his erection shifting inside her as he moved.

"You want more? Is that what you're saying? Or if you want me to stop, I'll stop."

"Don't stop." A frantic whisper.

"So you *do* want more."

"Yes."

His voice was a low growl, hers a frenzied, suffocated breath.

"You don't have a fucking choice anyway."

"I don't care," she confessed, dizzy with longing.

"It wouldn't matter if you did." His thighs forced hers farther apart, his grip on her hips hardened, and driven by a mindless obsession, arrogance, a perfunctory view of legalities and past promises, he growled, "Because you're mine for six more days."

She began shaking.

"You'll like what I'm going to do to you," he said more softly, making sure the edge was gone from his voice. "I promise." And lifting her bottom a fraction to ease his downstroke, he set out to deliver on that promise, slowly penetrating her tight, always hospitable body, moving gently, in and out, *all* the way in and out until she was liquid, yielding, until the sensitive flesh-to-flesh friction was silken and smooth, until she was matching his rhythm with her usual feverish impatience, breathing hard, gasping at the extremity of each deep, plunging thrust. Urging him on.

He obliged her, slowly, masterfully, using all his virtuoso skills to bring her to another screaming orgasm. Then one more. And yet another in which he joined her.

He liked that she was greedy for sensation, immoderate in her desires. He even liked her eagerness. It gave him the opportunity to teach her restraint. But she also gave him pleasure in other ways. Sweeping her hair aside, he bent and gently kissed the nape of her neck. "I'm going to keep doing this, make you come over and over again." For selfish reasons or no reason, because she made him feel something deep down—in his spine, his gut, in the tips of his fingers where his nerve endings shimmered—a delight in living he hadn't felt for a long time.

"Katherine, look in the mirror." Her grabbed a fistful of curls and gently tugged. "Look," he whispered. "See how the pearls swing from your nipples when my dick hits bottom in your pussy? There—like that."

She whimpered at the riveting impact so soon after climax, shut her eyes against the spiking tremors, then sighed as renewed bliss washed over her in monstrous waves.

"You have to look." He stopped moving inside her. "Or I won't let you come again."

The brusque warning dispersed the warm afterglow, but four orgasms and a largely sleepless night induced a certain lethargy. Her eyelids rose by slow degrees.

He saw the effort it took for her to obey, debated how much more he could expect from his playmate, whether he was pressing her too hard. A short debate, a quick decision. "There, see? Jeweled, sparkling nipples. You must be trying to attract my attention tricked out like that." Gripping her hips more firmly, he slid back in with compelling strength until he was fully submerged and she was chock-full and trembling. "How much more can you take?" An ambiguous, perhaps meaningless question in his current mood.

Her eyes met his piercing gaze in the mirror. She forced herself to speak because he was waiting and she was still desperate for him. "You decide."

He smiled at her. "You're becoming a model student, Katherine. I'll allow you another orgasm." He shifted into a languorous, methodical, perfectly positioned rhythm of thrust and withdrawal that never failed to press female orgasmic buttons, nor did it now. Soon Kate was frantically panting, riding his cock with single-minded purpose, her erratic breathing familiar prelude to another orgasm. "I'm going to make you come over and over again the entire time you're here," he said in a demonstrably settled tone of voice, holding himself motionless at the very depth of his downstroke for a moment to heighten the frenzy. "You don't mind, do you?" His platitude was as smooth as his slow withdrawal.

She gazed at his reflection as if she'd come back from the other side of the world—breathless, dazed—but she whispered, "I don't mind," because she'd heard him even on the other side of the world.

She met his next gliding, measured thrust with perfect precision, as if they were lifelong dance partners, as if it was as natural as breathing. Until the prodigal limit was reached, there was nowhere else to go and he pushed that explosive fraction deeper. The sexual equivalent of free-basing crack melted their brains, the world disappeared, bliss crystallized in diamond splinters.

Dominic dragged himself up from the depths of delirium first because he'd had more practice. But what he said next was neither habitual nor customary—and in any other circumstances, beyond comprehension. "I might stop giving you your birth control pills. See what happens—like a game of Russian roulette. Do you think that would add another level of excitement to our fucking?"

She went still under his hands, her eyes flared wide.

"Relax. You have to learn to relax, Katherine. I'll take care of you no matter how the game plays out. Did you think I wouldn't? And instead of these pearls"—he reached down to prod one with his finger—"dangling from your nipples, your breasts will drip milk for a baby. What do you think?"

What did she think? It was impossible! Inconceivable! But her body wantonly opened in welcome, as if reason had become a marginal issue to irrepressible lust.

"I think I'd like it," he murmured, driven by some red-hot,

sexed-up irrational impulse. "A body like yours was made for babies. Interested?"

Since he was moving in her with the kind of undulating rhythm that inflamed and bewitched, overwhelmed intellect with fiery sensation, propelled her frenzied nerve endings ever closer to orgasm—*and* since she understood that she couldn't climax without his approval, her immediate answer was never in doubt. "Whatever you want," she breathed.

With her climax hovering on the brink, Dominic knew how she'd answer—still, such unchecked largesse was intoxicating. Almost as intoxicating as the image of Miss Hart nursing his baby.

He went absolutely still for a split second, an error message flashing wildly in his brain. Another second passed before he resumed breathing, then another before he concluded that the conversation about procreation at lunch was to blame for his bizarre thoughts. Or the illusion suggested by the dangling pearls. Or perhaps it was only that Miss Hart unclothed triggered images of voluptuous fertility.

None of which mattered with his sanity fully restored. This holiday was about sex and games of mastery and submission, power and control. Nothing else. Miss Hart hadn't lost her focus; she was swinging her bottom back and forth, being proactive in her quest for orgasm, her breathing erratic like it was just prior to orgasm. *So get with the program.* Talk her over the edge.

"You have a lot of cum running down your legs, Katherine," Dominic said gently, smoothly matching her rhythm, conscious of her fast-approaching orgasm with the first small tremors fluttering up his dick. "If we're going to get you pregnant, it might be better if you were lying down. Or I could just keep fucking you. That way we'd be sure to make a baby before too—"

She sobbed in a sharp little outcry and climaxed in a rapid-fire series of hard convulsions that spiked through Dominic's brain like a dynamite charge, stole his breath away, ignited an instant, simultaneous ejaculatory explosion.

And left them both gasping for breath.

But Miss Hart was still slippery wet around him, fully available, delivering herself up to him with her bottom raised high. He felt invincible. As if he could fuck forever, as if his cock was made of rock, impervious to all but the lure of Miss Hart's lush, lubricated pussy and his militant lust.

As he proceeded to test his theory of invincibility, he didn't hear Kate's safe word after his next orgasm or the next. But her frantic, high-pitched, "No, no, no!" finally broke through the hardcore death-by-screwing strategy he was pursuing. "A few seconds more," he gasped, grabbing her around the waist to hold her up as her arms gave way. A grunt, a jerk, a half dozen violent, shuddering thrusts later and he stopped moving. And a second after that, he swept her up into his arms, kissed her parted lips, inhaled her breathless sob, and murmured on a labored breath, "Poor baby—I didn't…hear you."

Carrying her over to the bed, he gently deposited her on the silk coverlet, loosened the nipple clips, softly kissed each pink crest, tossed the clips on the bedside table. Pushing his damp hair away from his face, he dropped into a sprawl beside her. Her eyes were shut, she was motionless, her breathing unsteady. "I'm sorry. That was too much." He touched her fingertips. "You have to say no louder when I'm that buzzed. We'll have to practice."

She heard the smile in his voice and whispered, "Fuck you."

He laughed. "At least you can still talk. I thought I might have to call in a doctor."

The scary thought jolted her awake. "No doctors," she hissed, coming up on one elbow, lasering him with her gaze. "That better be in my contract."

"Whatever you want," he said, smiling up at her. "I'm in a generous mood."

A withering glance. "I wonder why?"

Half rising in a ripple of hard, toned muscle, he leaned over and kissed her—light brushing kisses on her temple, cheek, the hollow behind her ear. "I'm really sorry," he whispered into her silky curls. "Don't be mad."

"I should be after all your damned orders, but"—she sighed and dropped back on the bed—"how could I be? I've never come—like that . . . so wildly, and so many times."

He leaned back on his elbows, thinking it shouldn't matter whether she'd come like that a thousand times before. "How many times *have* you come before?" Shocked that he'd asked, he debated countering his question with some bland levity. But didn't.

"Never like that—never, never. Other than masturbating, I came—maybe twice before I met you. Although, I'm not sure if they were real orgasms."

If you're not sure, they weren't real. The thought warmed him in a strange and reckless way.

"Although now that I know how fabulous it feels," she said with a soft sigh, "I probably didn't climax with—well... anyway—it didn't feel like it does when I climax with you."

"I see," he said politely, his pulse rate spiking. But a heartbeat later, he cautioned himself about overreacting. It didn't matter when and if she'd come before. Seriously. Case closed. He ran his finger up her inner thigh, purposefully redirecting his thoughts. Told her they could dine on *The Glory Girl* if she wished or at home—it didn't matter.

When he received no reply, he looked up and saw she was sleeping.

So he covered her and quietly left the room.

SEVENTEEN

Quickly washing up, Dominic put on the white terry cloth robe hanging from the hook on the bathroom door and retired to his study. His first call was to his captain. He arranged to have *The Glory Girl* outfitted for a sail tonight with the stipulation that the plans were provisional. Danny Flynn, an Australian ex-surfer with blond dreadlocks who could sail anything with canvas, said, "If you show up, you show up. Don't worry about it. It won't interfere with my drinking."

Dominic laughed. "Good to know we won't be cutting into your entertainment."

"Bringing a lady are you? Leo gave me a heads-up. Just in case, he said."

"He's always a step ahead of me."

"You pay us enough, he should be." Both men had served together in the Australian commandos and had entered Dominic's employ the same time as Max.

"We can order dinner from Lung King Heen if we come on board," Dominic said. "I'll let you know."

"Good fucking, man. I hear she's fine."

"Miss Hart has to be treated with respect," Dominic warned.

"Don't get your knickers in a twist," Danny cheerfully

replied. "Leo already threatened me. I'll treat her like the bloody queen. Cheers."

Dominic's second call was to Max.

"Sorry to call on your off time," Dominic said, "but I need some information. Who takes care of our grants at MIT?"

"Bill Vandevore."

"Have him e-mail me the grant amounts, departments, projects, and the names of the participants by tomorrow morning."

"For? As if I don't know."

"Then don't ask."

Max sighed. "I'll see that Bill gets back to you. I was just about to call you about something."

"That tone of voice sounds like Liv needs something."

"The Philharmonic charity event was supposed to be at the chief executive's house tomorrow but his wife had a heart attack a few hours ago. I told Liv I'd ask you if we could transfer the affair to your place."

Dominic groaned.

"It's Liv's pet charity or I wouldn't ask." The Hong Kong Philharmonic Orchestra had been part of the ex-pat community since 1895 and was now officially under government sponsorship and unofficially a prestigious charity for the moneyed class in Hong Kong no matter their origins.

"Yeah, I know." An almost imperceptible pause, then Dominic said, "Send the guest list to Leo and tell him what you need. What time do I have to be there?"

"Six."

"What?"

"It's cocktails, seven to nine, but you're the host and some people always come early. The principessa for one, especially when she hears it's at your house. Her husband just signed an oil tanker deal with China for 2.5 billion, so Liv wants a big check from Antonia. We're counting on you."

"I'm not fucking her, Max, if that's what you're saying."

"Everything but, then."

"Jesus."

"Look, she should be good for a hundred grand at least, and it's not as though you haven't fucked her plenty of times before."

"I happen to be busy right now fucking someone else."

"Then you'll have to be really diplomatic. Either to Antonia or Miss Hart. That's up to you."

"Thanks for the advice," Dominic grumbled. "And if I catch your eye at the damned party, you'd better get your ass over and pry Antonia off me. Got it?"

"I'll have Liv invite Lieutenant Penzance from the embassy. I hear he's in demand with the ladies."

"Now you're thinking. I won't be there a minute before six. Miss Hart will be my companion."

"Careful."

"I intend to be. She'll be introduced as a business associate—which she is, at least temporarily. But you owe me big-time for this. I'd prefer not interrupting one of my better holidays."

"I understand. Thanks."

"She's really remarkable, Max. Out of the ordinary."

It wasn't like Dominic to speak so plainly, especially about the women in his life. He was generally reticent about the women he entertained or who entertained him. "I thought so when I met her," Max replied. "I'm glad you're pleased."

"I'm more than pleased. Anyway, thanks for finding Katherine. I mean it sincerely."

Max told his wife afterward that he felt as though someone had punched him in the gut when he heard Dominic speak about Katherine Hart with such unreserved emotion. Dominic didn't expose his feelings. He always kept everything personal locked up inside. On the other hand, Dominic didn't do permanent and that's what women always wanted. "Although, I doubt she'll be in Hong Kong long," Max added sardonically, standing in the doorway of his wife's small office where he'd come to give her the good news. "You know Dominic."

Olivia smiled. "She must be spectacularly better than his other playmates if he's escorting her to a public function." Olivia was fully conscious of Dominic's attractions. Money, youth, and good looks were a rare combination. "She's the usual gold-digger though, I expect."

"She's not." Walking in, Max dropped into a chair near his wife's desk.

"You can't mean it." Having trusted her husband to get results, Olivia had been scrolling through the e-mail list of participants that had to be notified of the party's venue change. She turned in her chair. "Every woman Dominic knows is after his money."

"She really isn't. You forget, I vetted her. She's a small-town girl. Midwest. Focused on her IT skill set, not interested in money. Dominic had told her she could write her own ticket when it came to her contract, but she asked for only a modest fee. And after she saved Dominic twenty million in Singapore, she turned down his bonus offer."

"Good Lord." Olivia's brows arched high. "A saint?"

"No, but different from us. Exemplary small-town upbringing. Not at all like you, darling." Olivia was a slender, blond aristocrat from a diplomatic family, with a refined beauty bred through six centuries of wealthy male forebears who'd married beautiful women because they could. "But you'll like her. Katherine Hart is open, natural, whip smart, and fully aware of Dominic's track record with women. She told me she did her research before the interview. I'm sure she did."

"I see. Then she won't be surprised when he sends her on her way."

"Probably not. She's sensible."

"And beautiful no doubt. You forgot that. Always a requirement for Dominic."

"She's pretty rather than stunning. She's not an every-hair-in-place-put-together kind of glamorous like all of Dominic's"—he shrugged—"pick your label."

"Paid escorts?"

Max shrugged again. "Dominic likes temporary arrangements."

Liv smiled. "I've noticed, everyone's noticed. By the way, speaking of paid escorts, Antonia is sure to appear once she understands the event is at Dominic's."

"I've already told him he's to be nice to her. You want a sizable donation."

"Thank you, darling. You're a dear."

"But you have to invite Lieutenant Penzance to lure Antonia away from Dominic. I have orders to drag her off him if she's too persistent. He's apparently concerned about Miss Hart's feelings."

"Her *feelings*?"

"You *should* look surprised." Max grinned. "Personally, I'm looking forward to a Philharmonic charity event for the first time in my life. Watching Dominic deal with both Antonia and Miss Hart will be worth the price of admission."

Olivia held her husband's gaze for a moment, her eyes alight. "Do you think this unusual young lady has breached Dominic's protective defenses? Insinuated herself past that cool indifference?"

"Ask me next week."

She grimaced. "That means no."

"Not necessarily. Dominic's not the same with her. I actually mean wait until next week. He's scheduled to fly out on Tuesday."

"Without you, I hope. Your holiday isn't up yet."

"Dominic's going on to London without me. I'll meet him in Paris later. We'll see if Miss Hart goes with him or goes home." He nodded at her computer. "You can hit send on your e-mail list now. Then e-mail Leo a detailed inventory of what's needed for the party; he'll take care of the rest."

"It's very sweet of Dominic to agree on such short notice."

"He always comes through." Max grinned, thinking of Dominic's grudging assent. "Even when he'd rather not. So if you'll go out of your way to be pleasant to Miss Hart, I know he'll appreciate it. Dominic's strangely protective of her."

"You said she's young."

"Just out of college."

Olivia's gaze narrowed faintly. "And she's keeping him interested?"

"Who knows why? She's bright as all get-out. Definitely a change for him."

"IT you said. That *is* different. Not sleek and finished like the others."

"Greta's dressing her."

Olivia sat back in her chair, her hand to her breast in a small gesture of surprise. "Julia's designer."

"Yes, Julia's designer."

"My heavens." She dropped her hand; her blue eyes sparkled. "I can hardly wait to meet this fantastic woman."

Kate slept through the dinner hour. Dominic canceled their sail on *The Glory Girl* with a bland explanation.

"You have to treat the sweet young things with more respect," Danny teased. "It's solitaire and whiskey for you tonight, my man. If you ever need any advice on handling the newbies, just ask."

"As if. The only sweet young thing you know is your sister."

"Want me to ask her what women like who don't charge by the hour?"

Dominic laughed. "Fuck off."

"Seriously, if the lady wants a sail—we're here anytime. Day or night. Leo says you like her."

"You say that like it's strange."

"Hey, man—who you talkin' to? It is strange, okay?"

Max and his friends had come on board after Julia's death. They'd seen only one Dominic Knight.

"But nice strange."

Danny could hear the smile in Dominic's voice. "There you go. Life's good. Take pictures for your photo album."

Dominic chuckled. "I'll call you if Katherine wants to go out on the water."

"You know my number. Cheers."

Dominic went into the bedroom every half hour, checking to see that nothing was wrong, that Katherine was still breathing, that he hadn't harmed her in some way. But she was always sleeping peacefully, curled up and cocooned in green silk with red dragons. He finally brought in his laptop rather than continually come and go, pulled up a comfortable chair near the bed, and worked on his e-mail.

He started getting hungry by eight and went to his study to order dinner.

"Just send me two sandwiches now. I'll call you when we're ready for dinner. No, nothing elaborate. Not tonight. Something simple. You know what I like. And if you'll set the table and put out the food, I'd appreciate it. I'll give you a ten-minute heads-up. Thanks, Deshi."

He'd eaten his sandwiches, spent another hour on his laptop, and had just gotten up to check on Kate again when the phone in Kate's messenger bag started ringing.

He made a dash for the chair where the bag had been

dropped, managed to pull out the phone, and was just about to shut it off when it stopped ringing and a text popped up. *Hey, babe. Remember me? The guy who makes you smile?*

Dominic's temper spiked, every muscle in his body tensed. *What did the asshole mean—makes you smile?* A heartbeat later he quickly locked away his anger because Kate was looking at him with faint bewilderment. "Your phone." He tossed it on the chair. "I didn't catch it in time. Sorry it woke you."

"What time is it?" She pushed her tousled curls off her forehead.

"A little after nine."

Eyes wide. "It can't be."

"It's not a problem. We don't have to go anywhere. You were tired." He smiled. "My fault. I kept you up all night and this afternoon was"—another quick smile—"fatiguing."

She smiled back. "Is that what you call it?"

"Call it anything you like." A dip of his handsome head, another gorgeous smile. "It was grand. Would you like a bath—a shower—some food?"

She grinned. "No band tonight?"

"Any night, Katherine. Just say the word."

"How sweet, but I'm starved."

"Good. Me too. I had two sandwiches sent up but"—a small shrug. "So anytime you're ready..."

He made a heads-up call to the kitchen while Kate quickly washed up in the bathroom, then he found her another robe—a magnificent padded silk bathrobe in azure silk, embroidered with pale yellow iris, wrapped her in it, and carried her into the dining room.

"I'm never going to leave if you keep being this nice to me," she teased as he stood in the doorway, surveying the flower-filled room, the table set for two, the lit candles, the chilling champagne.

He looked down at her and smiled. "That's the idea. Now stand here for a minute." He set her on her feet near the door. "I'm going to move your chair closer to mine. You're too far away at the other end of the table."

"Your floors are heated," she said, as he walked back. She wiggled her toes. "Nice."

He smiled. "It's all about comfort, babe." He took a small breath because she looked so sweet wiggling her toes that he wanted to lick her all over like candy. But he'd promised himself he wasn't going to touch Miss Hart tonight. She needed some downtime and he had plans for tomorrow. He took her hand. "Come on," he said gruffly, not used to self-denial. "Let's eat."

"Now you're mad at me."

"Hell no." A practiced smile, a playful wink. "I just get grumpy when I'm hungry."

After escorting her to a chair, he sat to her right at the head of the table. "Now any requests other than what Deshi made for us?"

His simple meal included caviar on petals of potato salad, onion soup, coconut prawns, oven-roasted chicken with baby carrots, grilled Japanese Kagoshima beef with asparagus, cream puffs with strawberries, and a poached cherry tiramisu.

"Everything looks wonderful, but—oh never mind…"

"Ask. They should be able to get you anything you want."

"I haven't had milk for a couple days." She smiled. "Midwest, what can I say?"

"Any special kind of milk?" *Don't even think it,* he warned himself, resisting the reflex jolt to his dick.

"Really, I have a choice?"

He smiled. "Yes, really."

"Chocolate milk, then."

He came to his feet. "I'll be right back." He gestured at the food. "Please, help yourself."

He could have raised his hand and someone would have appeared from behind the carved teakwood screen, but he didn't want to spook Miss Hart, so he walked down the hall and opened the door into the butler's pantry. His butler, Mr. Smith, of indeterminate age and certifiable efficiency, and two of his many houseboys stood to attention. "I appreciate the discretion, Smith. We haven't heard a sound from anyone. Miss Hart prefers her privacy, as I mentioned earlier. I'm here because she'd like some chocolate milk. Can we do that?" He saw Smith swallow hard. "Problem?"

"I'm sure we'll manage something, sir."

"Do what you can. Perhaps we should bring in a supply from somewhere tomorrow." Cow's milk wasn't a staple in Asia. "Apologize to Deshi. It's not something he could have anticipated. Buzz me when you have some. I'll come get it." He smiled. "Thank you all." He turned back just short of the door. "Don't forget the package from Leo. He said he'd have it delivered by midnight. I need it at breakfast."

As soon as Dominic left, the butler picked up the phone and put the kitchen staff in an uproar.

Dominic walked back into the dining room. "The kitchen is going to see what they can do. But we'll have some chocolate milk brought up tomorrow if they don't have any on-site. Ah...you're trying the coconut prawns. My favorite, although these are all"—he waved his hand at the large array of food—"personal favorites. I didn't want to wake you. Tomorrow, you order. In fact, order what you want for breakfast once we're finished."

They ate, they talked, they drank champagne, they luxuriated in a warm, quiet contentment nurtured by soft candlelight, perfumed air, the sweet aftermath of an afternoon of unalloyed pleasure and their own special brand of magic.

It was like a lush, romantic movie come to life, Kate thought.

Even Dominic recognized something was in the air. But he attributed the atmosphere to more pragmatic particulars: a sleepless night of mind-blowing sex, a long *busy* day of the same, a bottle or two of champagne, Leo's *excess* of flowers—and of course the hot little puss beside him whom he'd jump if he could. But none of that was about romance, it was about fucking.

Kate's chocolate milk arrived forty minutes later because it had taken that long for one of the staff to drive into the city and back. After she emptied the glass, it took all of Dominic's self-control not to lean over and lick the small chocolate slick from her upper lip—the bewitching smear more erotic than the most blatant striptease. Correction: what was even more erotic was when she slid her tongue slowly over her upper lip and lapped up the chocolate residue.

At which point, he silently groaned, wrestled his libido to the ground, and told himself that abstinence built character.

She needed a rest. He wasn't a brute.

Accordingly, after dinner, he bathed Kate with the discipline of a eunuch, made excuses to her about being tired, carried her to bed, tucked her in, and held up the remote control. "TV while I take a quick shower?"

She was half asleep. "Some news. I'm losing track of the world." She smiled. "Not that I'm complaining. You're supercharming. I'm sorry you're tired."

"I'll be fine by morning." He found Sky News, set the remote near her hand. "Five minutes, I'll be back."

It was the fastest shower he'd ever taken, but then he'd never had Miss Hart waiting in his bed. Minutes later, he walked back in, wiping his wet hair with a towel, and came to a sudden stop. He really had been too hard on her. She was fast asleep.

Turning off the TV, he climbed into bed, gathered her into his arms, and gave himself points for being virtuous.

Kate sighed, snuggled closer to Dominic in insistent small nudges, and as his arms tightened around her, her breathing slowed again, deepened into sleep.

Dominic gently kissed the top of her head, listened to her breathing, felt her soft warmth against his skin, and lay still in the dark, asking himself questions he'd never asked before.

About the high rush of happiness, swift and frail. About flirting with hope. About chances. About the wild surging in his blood he'd never felt before.

All because of a slip of a woman with red curls and bright green eyes.

EIGHTEEN

Dominic woke early, slowly eased away from Kate, and, taking care not to wake her, slid off the bed. Walking into his dressing room, he put on a pair of gray sweats and exited the room by the hall door.

Entering his study a few minutes later, he sat at his desk, hit the space bar, and watched his computer come to life. Another few clicks of the keyboard and there it was: all the MIT grants. He scrolled through Bill Vandevore's e-mail looking for a name...looking...looking...looking—bingo. He picked up the phone, unconcerned with the time stateside. His employees were paid well enough to answer his calls day or night.

It was a brief call, Bill Vandevore understood what was required of him without a lengthy explanation. "I don't need Andy eliminated from the project," Dominic said. "Just see that he's sent to Greenland on the core drilling team. Increase his fellowship by forty thousand. That should sweeten the assignment."

"Yes, sir, Mr. Knight."

"Discreetly."

"That goes without saying, sir."

"I appreciate your understanding."

"My pleasure, sir." Bill Vandevore was in charge of a very large budget with little oversight. It was a dream job.

He might have even agreed to send his mother to Green-land if Dominic had asked because Knight Enterprises paid him enough to keep her there in five-star comfort. "Is there anything else I can do for you?" he asked, underlining the name he'd written down.

"Not at the moment." There was still Michael, but he hadn't been calling so he was currently safe from Dominic's displeasure. "You'll deal with this promptly?"

"Today, sir."

"Excellent."

Dominic leaned back in his chair after he hung up the phone and felt his pulse rate slow. He softly exhaled, satis-fied the issue had been resolved. Then he sat up, deleted Bill Vandevore's e-mail from his account, from the cache, double-checked his password was in place, and shut down his computer. Picking up the house phone, he spoke to Deshi and Smith, delivered several brisk directives, thanked them, replaced the receiver in the cradle, and smiled.

It should be a very nice day.

When he returned to the bedroom, Kate was walking out of the bathroom, naked and brushing her hair with Dominic's hairbrush. "This isn't really working," she said, holding up the short-bristled brush.

Now that's the way he liked to start his day, Miss Hart smiling at him, her voluptuous body on full display. "Yours must be here somewhere. Leo sent over everything."

She shrugged. "It's a short-term fix. Are we going to eat soon?" Climbing back into bed, she grabbed the remote and flicked on the TV.

Miss Hart's casual domesticity shouldn't have surprised

him; she didn't stand on ceremony. She never would have considered finding some lacy nightgown, or putting on makeup for him like so many women. Her hair was unruly; she didn't feel the need to flirt or seduce. She only wanted to know when they were going to eat breakfast. This morning scene made him want to smile—it was so ordinary. "We forgot to order last night, so I hope I got you something you like. They're bringing up our breakfast now." He walked to the dresser. "What do you want to play today?"

She glanced away from the TV screen, gave him a blank look. Then his question registered belatedly and she grinned. "Why ask me, Svengali?"

He grinned back. "Definitely a user-friendly answer."

"Depends on who's using whom. I figure I'm using your really big dick for my own personal pleasure, so we're about even. Is that too blunt?" she said with fake, wide-eyed innocence.

"I'll let you know if I'm ever in the mood for niceties," he drawled and went back to opening drawers.

"What do you think of this?" he asked a moment later, holding up a sheer, black bra. "I seem to be on some bizarre baby psychic wave. I don't know whether to blame my mother for bringing up the subject or you for your big tits. Although I must not be the only one who plays this game if Mrs. Hawthorne is selling these little numbers."

Kate turned from the TV news. "Is that a nursing bra? She sells *nursing* bras?"

"Along with several other play themes. I'll show you the schoolgirl white cotton bra and panties later and the harem outfit."

"I didn't see those."

"You tried on only a few, Mrs. Hawthorne said. You were being difficult. Shocking, I know," he said with a grin. "So yes or no?" He lifted the bra a fraction higher.

She smiled. "What do they usually say?"

A trifling shrug. "I don't usually ask."

"So I'm special."

"In every conceivable way, Katherine. So, what'll it be?"

She slowly, ostentatiously stretched, gave him a flirty look. "Will I like it?"

"You will," he said, controlling the impulse to fuck her on the spot after that cock-teasing stretch.

"Will it be as good as yesterday?" she purred.

He liked that she was prodigal in play. "Better. I have a new toy for you."

"Now there's incentive," she said, sweetly.

"You'll be able to come whenever you want with the toy. How's that for incentive?"

She clicked off the TV and jumped from the bed, her breasts still jiggling from her leap as she walked toward him.

She pointed as his erection surged under his sweats. "I think he likes me."

He smiled. "Every minute of every day. But we're going to have breakfast first. You have to wait for your new toy. Hold out your arms."

She blew him a kiss, then lifted her arms.

A few minutes later, they were at the breakfast table. The flowers had been changed; various shades of yellow glowed in the morning light.

"I suppose the bedroom flowers will be different when we return."

"I don't know. We'll see."

She grinned. "Have you no control over your staff?"

"Not much," he lied. "Coffee first? I see chocolate milk in that pitcher."

"Coffee, please. I love when you serve me."

"As do I when you serve me," he said, glancing at her, willful intent in his gaze.

Defenseless against his pointed look, as willing as he was willful, she softly groaned. "Oh, God, don't start," she whispered as a flutter of arousal shimmered deep inside her. "I have to eat first."

He smiled. "Don't you always. Fortunately my ego is resilient. Those are yours." He pointed to three domed plates.

Two quick calming breaths and she lifted the first silver cover. An omelet.

"It has lobster in it. I hope you eat shellfish. Open the other one."

Having been distracted by the food, she lifted the second cover with more composure. A beautifully displayed petite bacon sandwich cut in small triangles lay on a bed of creamy slaw.

"Did I do well? One last one," he said, gesturing at the third covered plate.

Kate lifted the lid. Three truffles were set inside a diamond tennis bracelet.

"Thank you for yesterday," he said quietly.

"It's too much." She picked up the bracelet. "This is too much." Each stone was at least a carat.

"It's not nearly enough," he replied casually. "Now eat. I know you're hungry."

"I'll argue later."

He grinned. "I like when you argue."

"Because it always ends with sex."

"That must be why." He lifted his coffee cup. "To a pleasant day."

He had salmon just as he'd had the day before, an omelet with some kind of sausage and peppers, fried potatoes, a fruit plate like hers, a bowl of spicy noodles, and some buns stuffed with a meat mixture. Kate ate a bite of each when he offered it to her. "Diversify your tastes," he said, coaxing her to try each item. "It's a big world out there."

"I like this cozy one." She surveyed the small room that opened on the courtyard, the morning light wintery and pale, the scent of roses drifting on the air. "I like when we're alone."

"Speaking of alone, that reminds me," he said, pulling her birth control pod from his sweats' pocket and setting it on the table. "Should I give you one or not? Do we want to add to this small company? Should we discuss it?"

"There's nothing to discuss." Pithy and direct.

He paused for a moment, then, ignoring her comment, said, "Why don't we decide later. Take off your robe now." An infinitesimal lift of his brow. "If you don't mind."

"And if I do mind?"

A fraction of a second. "Take it off anyway."

A small, chafing glance, a snappish note in her voice. "You're lucky I'm willing to play your games."

"Very willing I'd say."

She flushed under his insolent gaze. "I want one of those pills later," she said, determined to put some limits on what she would allow him.

"I heard you the first time."

"I know what you're doing and you can just stop this ultimate control shit."

"Make me," he said softly.

"It's not a game, Dominic."

"Everything's a game, babe. Business, life, fucking." He smiled. "But any game with you is extraspecial. And yes, I *am* lucky, very lucky that you like to play. Now would you please take off your robe? I'd be very grateful."

"I should say no." But her body was already responding to the deep, rich cadence of his voice, to the vivid heat in his eyes, to the soft, insistent command, to the high-testosterone signals of latent male power.

"Please don't." It was a warning, no matter how softly uttered.

A shiver of arousal went through her at the threat in Dominic's voice. She fidgeted restlessly against the instant, cruel desire, the wild, subversive need, the willingness to be corrupted by his capacity for mastery. "It's unnerving," she whispered, gripping her chair arms as though to resist. "Wanting you this much. Craving you. Losing my reason because of you."

"There's nothing wrong with wanting pleasure," he murmured.

She took a deep breath. "Even if it takes over your life?"

"Even then," he said gently, glancing at her white knuckles. "Do you need help with your robe?"

He knew, he always did. She shook her head and began untying the belt. Dominic had found her another quilted silk robe this morning, celadon green, warm. *For winter,* he'd said, wrapping it around her shoulders. It fit perfectly, like the other one; she hadn't asked why. She told herself she should ask, she shouldn't so easily fall under his spell. But she didn't do either. Instead, she freed the belt, slipped the robe from her shoulders, and sat before him in only the sheer black silk bra.

"I don't know, Katherine," he murmured softly. "When you look like that—your ripe tits ready for nursing like you're already knocked up—I'm not really sure I feel like giving you your birth control pill." The nursing bra left a portion of her breasts exposed. Her turgid nipples and rosy aureoles were framed in sheer black silk, her breasts lifted high under the taut straps, the brandishing display inspiring rash behavior in a man who'd always viewed himself as an arch pragmatist. "If you were nursing my baby, you'd have to share those tits with me." Dominic's voice was low, his gaze audacious, his cock rock hard and aching. "We'd have to put that in writing." He crooked one finger. "Come here." He pointed at a spot beside his chair. "We'll discuss your birth control." Perhaps Katherine was right. Perhaps this was the ultimate control. He could possess her in the most primal, selfish way, make her pregnant, maybe even ignore the practicalities of his life and hers and keep her. Make sure that he got his share of those tits.

She didn't move, her body listening to him with a schizophrenic tension, an unreliable wildness panting yes, yes, yes to all he wanted while her mind was screaming no!

"You always hesitate, Katherine. I don't understand," he sardonically murmured. "We both know you want to fuck. You can't get enough. Are you tired of fucking me? Is that it?"

Every soft-spoken word jolted through her, every deliberate insolence was a controlled threat that aroused, inflamed, tantalized—made her think of what it felt like to fuck him, how he felt deep inside her, how he made her feel when she climaxed. She looked up, met his gaze. "No, I'm not tired of fucking you."

He smiled. "I'm pleased to hear it. I could do you twenty-four/seven if you'd let me."

A very small smile in return. "Sorry."

"That's what I thought." He tapped the plastic pod. "But we really should discuss this. Personally, I'm in some crazy baby zone. Come closer and convince me I'm wrong." It wasn't all about sex, but what it was about eluded him. Perhaps it was buried too deep under the emotional debris of his life.

She came to her feet, drew in a small, shaky breath, urgent desire swelling inside her with a kind of primitive ferocity. Good judgment was flying out the window. "What if I'm in the same crazy zone?"

"That could be dangerous," he murmured, turning his chair as she drew near. "One of us should be sane."

She moved between his legs, leaned in, took his face between her hands, and kissed him with tantalizing deference, offering herself to him. "You're older," she said against his lips. "You be the sane one."

"Maybe we need a referee." He pulled her tight against his thighs as she stood upright, ignoring the devil-to-pay impasse, the danger, willing to take the risk. "Because I'm flipping out and thinking baby. Especially with your tits this close."

"This close?" she whispered, bending.

His mouth closed around her nipple and they both felt the rush, the indescribable, spiking rush that always took them by surprise. The amazing pleasure that was new each time, staggering, electrifying.

Baffling, he thought. *Lethal.*

Awesome, she thought, and pushed against his mouth.

He sucked her until she was frantic, until he wasn't far behind, until they were both breathing hard and he was wondering, sofa or chair? Would he actually make it to either one with his orgasm pushing him hard?

She might have said something, although if she had, she had no recollection.

He wasn't sure whether he heard it or thought it, but he suddenly spit out her nipple, sat back, and grabbed the plastic pod from the table. Snapping the lid up with his thumb, he took out a pill and, with his heart ricocheting off his ribs, muttered, "Open up."

When she did, he shoved the pill into her mouth, handed her his coffee cup. "Drink, swallow, or I won't fuck you."

She drank instantly, so grateful for his intervention, tears sprang to her eyes.

"Hey, hey, don't cry." Taking the cup from her, he set it

down, pulled her onto his lap, and held her close. "I won't let that happen again. It was my fault, not yours."

"Not all of it," she whispered, looking up, fear and desperation still glowing in her eyes. "I'm helpless to stop myself."

"We both are." He wiped away a single tear sliding down her cheek. "But I'm older," he said with a smile. "It's up to me to be the sane one. Right?"

"Okay."

He laughed softly. "So if the crisis is big enough, you'll fall in line."

But she didn't smile. She said gravely, "We can't let that happen again."

"It won't." But he wondered what the hell he'd do tomorrow if the craziness didn't go away. He thought about sending her home. Thought about *not* fucking her tomorrow, then immediately nipped that particular train of thought in the bud.

He told himself he'd been frantic because he'd been waiting all night.

He told himself he wasn't used to waiting for anything.

Then she whispered, "Please, Dominic." She touched the knot on his sweats. "If it's all right with you, I mean if you're not too freaked out."

"Never with you, baby." And speculation gave way to a more familiar lust.

He opened the knot for her, lifted her enough to drag his sweats down his hips, adjusted the sweetest houseguest he'd ever had on the head of his dick, and uttered a low animal sound as she slowly consumed him.

Once she was resting on his thighs and thoroughly impaled, her impatience momentarily assuaged with her drug of choice buried deep within her, she whispered, "I'm sorry, but I need you twenty-four/seven too."

He felt his cock swell inside her, felt the flame-hot surge slide up his spine, felt his adrenaline kick up a notch and explode in his brain. "We'll take care of that," he said on a forced breath, needing to answer her. "I promise."

"It's frightening to be this obsessed," she whispered, briefly resting her forehead against his before sitting back with a sigh.

"And insatiable," he said with a smile.

And overwhelmed with affection. Deeply felt, terrifying to them both.

"We should be more sensible," Kate said.

"I agree."

They'd both always considered their level-headed intellects their greatest assets.

"Irrational desire is—"

"Irrational," he finished. "We'll deal with it."

"You make it sound easy when I'm panic-stricken or maybe sad, no, mostly sad."

He felt every nerve prickle. He went quiet. Then he blinked and said, "Don't be sad. It's not a death sentence. We'll figure something out. Okay?"

She nodded because her throat had closed up.

He touched her cheek with the pad of his finger. "You're lovely, this is lovely, you make me happy. No more tears. Only good times for you and me. Now pay attention," he said with a small smile, changing the subject in the way he knew best. "Do you feel that?" He moved his hips so he touched all her soft, moist flesh, carefully, slowly, lazily, as if he had all the time in the world, as if they had all the time in the world when they both knew they didn't. "How about this?" He flexed his hips upward. "Better now?"

She shivered with delight, whimpered, moving her hips restlessly, asking for more.

She came the first time in under two minutes. No surprise. What was a surprise was the fact that he came with her the second time because he couldn't wait. He was like a kid fucking for the first time, his heart pounding, his blood surging, ready to explode in seconds.

Her high thin scream was like getting a personal best at the Olympics, like winning a gold medal. Her happiness washed over him in a warm, white glow, illuminated him from inside, offered him a momentary glimpse into a world he'd never known.

Lying quiescent in his arms, her head resting on his shoulder, her body momentarily sated, her unquenchable need for him temporarily quenched, she was wildly happy, foolishly lovesick. He was too perfect, she wanted him too much, it was madness.

All too soon, the orgasmic splendor dimmed and the real world returned with a vengeance, reminding Dominic of who he was, who she was, and why they were here. Abruptly lifting Kate from his lap, Dominic set her on her feet, handed her a cloth napkin from the table, took one for himself, used it, pulled his sweats up, tied a quick slipknot. Then he rose, picked up her robe, helped her on with it, grabbed her birth control from the table, and slid it into her robe pocket. "You'd better take care of this," he said brusquely. "I'm not operating with a full deck on this issue."

He needed time to bring his life back to normal, to let the crazy die down. To return to the fun and games instead of this bullshit earnestness. It was the last thing he wanted; major emotional upheavals he could do without. A goddamn relationship with a woman wasn't in the cards. He knew better. He knew how much misery it could bring if things went wrong.

He dipped his head so their eyes were level. "Are you okay with that?"

She nodded, unnerved by his sudden coolness.

He held out his hand. "Come see your new toy."

She quickly took his hand, wanting to please him, erase his cool, clipped tone. She'd never wanted to please a man before; it was unnerving. On the other hand, she was addicted to his touch, to the pleasure he offered, to the brand-new world of carnal desire he'd revealed to her. And her insatiable appetite for the incomparable Dominic Knight, for the sweet, wild joy of fucking him, took precedence over any unnerving doubts.

When they entered the bedroom moments later, Kate stopped wide-eyed. "How large a staff do you have here?" The flowers were all new, masses of purple iris, dramatic contrast to the brilliant colors in the room. The bed was pristinely made, piles of fresh white towels had been placed on a table at the foot of the bed, their clothes from yesterday removed.

"I'm not sure." He glanced down at her. "Would you like me to ask?"

She sniffed. "Very funny, Mr. Plutocrat."

He shrugged. "It's adequate, that's all I know. Leo does the hiring."

"Are they all ninjas? You never see a soul."

"I didn't think you wanted people around. If you do, just say the word."

"How accommodating you are."

"That's the idea, Katherine." He smiled for the first time since his arctic freeze. "Adjust, adapt"—his brows flickered, humor warmed his gaze—"oblige you in all things."

"So you're done being grumpy?"

He looked surprised. "Was I grumpy?"

"Yes, you scared me."

"Sorry," he said, as though he didn't quite understand but was willing to accommodate her.

"Thank you." She drew in a small, shaky breath, her eyes huge, liquid. "Because when you're unhappy, I'm unhappy."

"Jesus, don't cry anymore," he whispered. Lifting her in his arms, he bent low and kissed her softly, then not so softly, his kiss deepening, taking what he wanted, plundering, pillaging, devouring her open-mouthed and impassioned.

Giddy with happiness, she clung to him and kissed him back, hard, hard, hard—her world sunshine bright again because she could tell he wanted her as much as she wanted him.

When he finally raised his mouth, he said, "I'm sorry if I made you unhappy. I don't want you unhappy. Tell me if you are and I'll fix it somehow." His blue gaze was very close, touched with concern, his voice the kind you'd use to coax a kitten in from the cold. "There's nothing I can't fix. Okay?"

She nodded.

He blew out a breath. "Good." He scanned the room as though seeing it for the first time, preoccupied with how best to keep Katherine happy. A novel position for him here at the Garden House, where generally only his pleasure mattered, where he'd only brought women who were disposable. Where he'd never brought a woman who mattered to him. The word *mattered* made the hair on the back of his neck stand up. But he ignored the sensation, shook it away. He had better things to do. "Now, I'm just asking," he said gently, carrying her to the bed. "If you don't want to play, that's fine with me. We'll do something else. Do you like cribbage, chess, baccarat? Or we could watch some movies."

A little tic of surprise. "You have a theater here?"

"A small one. Would you like to see a movie?"

She shook her head.

He seated her on the bed as if she were made of glass, kissed her cheek, then drew up a cushioned chair and sat. "This is a new experience for me," he said with a small smile, sliding into a lounging pose as if he had all the time in the world. "You tell me what you want to do and we'll do it."

"You're sure you're not mad at me anymore?" God, he was gorgeous sprawled on the chair, half undressed, his sweats low on his hips, his broad shoulders resting back against the black-and-white silk upholstery.

"I never was mad at you." He ran his hands over his hair in a small restive gesture. "I was mad at myself. I don't like to lose control like that. I don't like to make mistakes. Especially life-altering ones like that."

"Oh, good—then it wasn't something I did."

He smiled. "Not directly."

"So I really can ask for anything?"

"I told you before I have vast resources at my command and now at yours," he added with a dip of his head. "Surprise me."

"Show me my new toy."

He laughed out loud, amused at his misguided notions. He should have known that money meant nothing to Katherine. "You are so fucking adorable," he said. "You make the world all blue skies and sunshine."

"Back at you," she said with a buoyant grin. "For five more days if you're keeping track."

They both knew better; they both knew it was only play—the future untouchable. They also knew these few days were the cherry on the sundae of life and worth savoring.

Shoving himself out of the chair, Dominic came to his feet, a wide grin radiating his happiness. "I have something else to make you smile. Don't move. I'll be back in five seconds."

Playfully goading, Kate sang out, "One-one thousand, two-one thousand, three-one thousand, four-one thousand, five—"

Dominic slapped a small, shagreen-covered box into her lap and grinned.

"You're fast. I'm impressed."

"You should be." He nodded. "Open it. It's something you'll like."

"You know that, do you?"

"I do."

"Because?"

He knew how to answer that question and that squinty-eyed look. "Because I know what you like."

She smiled. "You are *so* smooth. I'm in awe."

"Let me show you some new awesome wonders, Miss Hart," he said softly, his smile lush with promise. "Open it."

She did, then looked up at him.

"For you own personal use. Want me to show you?"

"Now that I have this I won't need you anymore."

"I'm more versatile, babe. You need me. But you'll enjoy this too." He took the dildo from the nest of white velvet and tossed the box aside. "Are you warm enough?"

"Incredibly warm. In fact, I'm getting hot."

He laughed. "Why do I even ask? I hardly have to do anything and you're primed to go."

"It's not me, it's you. You're drop-dead beautiful and I like your face, too."

He chuckled. "Thanks, I think. But I know what you mean. I'm going with kismet or karma or that long shot that turned into a win for us because this thing we got going—this fucking craving—is crazy. Good crazy. But definitely not business as usual."

"I wouldn't know about business as usual."

A direct hit, typical Miss Hart. "Good thing I'm here

then," he said, soft as silk. "Because I can show you. Take off your robe and bra."

"Why don't you?"

He hesitated for a fraction of a second, then smiled. "My pleasure." Opening his fingers, he let go of the leather strap he was holding and Katherine's new toy dropped to the bed. Reaching out, he untied her robe, pulled out the birth control pills from her robe pocket, and set them on the bedside table. "We don't want those going through the laundry. Sit up a little, there—that's it." Sliding her robe down her arms, he pulled it from under her, unclasped her bra, and cast both items away.

"Someone has to pick those up." She saw that small startle reflex that never failed to disarm her—his shield against the world, slipping for a second, the trappings of power briefly faltering.

Then he rolled his eyes, turned, picked up both items from the carpet, and swung around, holding them out. "Any place special you want them?" he drawled.

"Besides up your ass?"

"Or yours?"

It felt like a slap, a hot, sexy slap in just the right spot. "Sorry, should I say, sorry? I should, shouldn't I?"

"Damn right you should."

"Or," she purred.

"Or I'll see that you learn better manners."

A small heated glance. "How would you do that—*exactly*?"

He laughed. "You're one horny babe, Katherine."

"Is that good or bad?"

"Both. Although I'll probably end up screwing myself to death. At least my sister will be happy. She gets all my money."

"*We* might be happy in the interim."

"True." A lift of his dark brows. "So is this a death match?"

"I'd prefer not, if you don't mind. Just make me happy. You know how to do that."

Happy. Such a strange word in relation to raw, profligate sex. Unique to Miss Hart and honest-to-God true. A thought he locked away the second it surfaced. "Let's start with your new toy," he said casually, picking up the dildo, focusing his attention on more relevant issues. "Take note, the straps are deerskin for softness and warmth on the skin, the dildo is stainless steel for hygienic reasons, the size hopefully adequate to satisfy you." He winked. "You may thank me later in your own personal way."

"Maybe I won't want to when I can climax with"—she nodded—"that."

"I'm not worried," he said with an impudent grin and held out his hand. "Come. Stand up." After helping her down from the bed, he knelt before her, nudged her thighs. "Spread your legs a little."

Her body instantly recognized his tone of voice and sent out arousal signals to each and every sexual receptor, putting them on high alert and drenching her sex.

He looked up, smiled. "Really? I only have to touch you?"

"Consider it a compliment."

He looked amused. "I'm not sure I can take all the credit."

"I don't know about..." Her words ended in a low breathy moan as he slowly inserted the stainless-steel dildo into her dewy cleft.

"Now that sounds like a complimentary moan," he murmured. "Hold your legs together." She didn't move. Sliding his hand between her legs, he gave the dildo a nudge to gain her attention. "Listen to me. Put your legs together."

With her brain focused on the high-pressure incitement, the shuddering, seething frenzy touched off by Dominic's nudge, it took her a moment or two to respond.

"There's a good girl," he softly praised when she finally managed to comply. "Now hold still for a minute." Sliding the leather belt through the front strap, he touched her hip. "Turn around," he said. *"Pay attention."* A curt command that raised her eyelids; she turned. He slid the belt through the back strap, smoothly slid it between her buttock cheeks, and buckled the belt around her waist in back. He began adjusting the Velcro cinches so the dildo would be firmly lodged and anchored fast.

Her eyes went shut at the first soft jerk of the cinch and, clenching her thighs, she softly moaned. When Dominic tightened the second cinch, she gasped. She was fully gorged now with unyielding metal, the pressure on her clit staggering, shocking her nervous system with continuous waves of delirium. "Oh God, oh God, oh God," she panted, the raw assault on her clit merciless.

"Come, walk for me," he said softly, grasping her hips,

slowly turning her, then rising to his feet. "And you're not allowed to come until I give you permission."

"I can't do it." She shook her head, eyes shut and panting, waves of arousal coursing through her, so close to coming she was teetering on the edge.

"You have to, Katherine, or I'll take the damn thing out, throw it away, and you won't come at all," he said sternly. "There, you see, you can do it if you try." He watched her take a small step toward him, waited for her to stop shaking. "Now another step, you're doing well. Now another."

She climaxed with a stifled sob, and her knees gave way.

He caught her, his hands at her waist. "What am I going to do with you?" he softly scolded, holding her trembling body, her orgasm still flooding through her. "You can't seem to control yourself. Look at me," he said with a sudden sharpness.

She struggled to obey; she was still panting, quivering.

He dipped his head, looked into her heated gaze. "Since you can't control yourself, why don't we see how many *times* you can come? I'll give you a minute to rest between climaxes." He glanced at the bedside clock.

Her eyes flared wide. "That's impossible!"

"Forty seconds."

"Dominic, no!"

"Thirty-five."

She gave a cry of protest.

"You really must learn to obey," he whispered, sliding his hand down her belly, forcing a fingertip past the dildo to touch her throbbing clit. Massaging it lightly.

She groaned as the shock waves surged through her

body, whimpered as he stroked her swollen nub, heard him say, "Two seconds, one—"

He twisted his fingers in the belt around her waist, gripped it firmly, and pulled. The dildo drove into her throbbing, pulsing body, hot, delicious pleasure exploded and she instantly climaxed again.

The minute of rest passed with astonishing speed.

She couldn't possibly, she couldn't. Then half dazed, she felt Dominic's hands on her body, on her breasts, her nipples, her thighs, lightly caressing, making her skin tingle, her body ache. He moved the dildo more gently that time, pressed it softly against her G-spot, held it there. And with a sob, she came.

She was utterly helpless to resist, gentle or rough, slow or fast, he deliberately brought her to orgasm over and over again. Until she was sheened with perspiration, the dildo deliciously hot inside her, her G-spot and clitoris violently throbbing, and she was softly keening in continuous, greedy need.

She was gasping for air when he finally picked her up, carried her to the chair he'd vacated, and gently deposited her on the soft cushions. "Rest a minute. I'll wait for you." Pulling up another chair, he sat opposite her and watched the wild frenzy dissipate, watched her slowly return to the world. "Very impressive, Katherine. You might have set a new record. You obviously like your new toy."

The cool insolence brought her eyes open and she met his amused blue gaze.

"How would you score it on a scale of one to ten?" he asked.

"A twenty."

He smiled. "How nice for you. So I did well."

"Don't you always. You're damn near perfect and you know it. Do you want me to say you're good? After so many women you must know that, but if you'd like me to thank you I will. The orgasms were fucking great."

A small dip of his lashes. "Are you testy about something, Katherine? Tell me and I'll remedy it."

I adore you even when you're a bastard. Remedy that. I adore you even when you're making me do something I don't want to do because you know I'll like it in the end. Remedy that. "No, I'm fine," she said with a polite smile.

He leaned forward, held her gaze. "Are you sure? You can tell me anything."

I think I love you or everything about you, which may or may not be love but close enough to be scary. You'll forget me an hour after I'm gone and I'll remember you for the rest of my life. Other than that—"I'm good, really. But thanks for asking."

"Would you rather do something else?"

She rocked gently, smiled. "Not just yet."

He laughed softly. "Take your time."

She lifted her hand slightly as Dominic's erection swelled under his sweats. "But he's waiting."

Dominic ran his fingers over the visible bulge. "He can wait. But whenever you feel like moving, maybe you could come over and help him out." He pointed to her mouth, then his conspicuous hard-on.

"You'd like that?"

"I would."

"Must I?"

That tantalizing little purr that meant she was playing. "Of course," he said mildly. "Why are you here if not to please me?"

"And please myself."

"If I allow it, Katherine. Whether you have another orgasm is my decision, not yours." His voice dropped in volume, a coolness invaded his eyes. "You understand that, don't you?" A pause while he waited for her answer. "Answer or you'll regret it."

"I understand."

"There now, that wasn't so hard." He spread his legs and pointed. "On your knees, Katherine. I want to make use of your mouth."

That soft-spoken order streaked through her body, her nipples tightened into hard points, her arousal instantly stoked by his quiet demand.

"Your nipples always betray you," Dominic murmured. "Don't even think about coming. If you come without my permission, you'll be punished."

There was something in his voice that brought her head up.

His fingers were steepled under his chin, his gaze chill. "Are you afraid you'll be punished, Katherine?"

She tried not to tremble. "Should I be?"

"You should." He held her gaze, then tipped his steepled fingers downward. "Don't keep us waiting."

She flushed, her stomach quivered, everything tightened in her core. She was consumed with need. Desperate again, as if submission alone could arouse her.

Ordered not to come, she moved gingerly with her swollen clit jammed against the dildo, careful not to jar anything as she rose from the chair and moved to where Dominic sat. He helped lower her to her knees, then spread his legs, slipped a fingertip under her chin, and lifted her face to him.

She felt her clitoris harden under his cool gaze, stifled her moan.

He smiled faintly. "You're learning." Reaching out his other hand, he slid a small riding crop from under some magazines on a nearby table. "If you need help remembering who gives orders here"—he slid the crop over her shoulder, up her throat, then set it on the chair arm—"I'll remind you. Now untie my sweats and take it out." Soft, curt, a small stricture to his voice.

She fumbled with the knot, nervous after his warning, anxious to please.

"Jesus, Katherine," Dominic said irritably, the beast inside barely leashed. "Stop. I'll untie it. It's a damn slipknot. There. Do you think you can manage now?"

"Fuck you and fuck your orders." Overlooking the dildo in her anger, she sat back on her heels, gasped, and quickly came up on her knees.

His hands were on her throat in a millisecond, his thumbs pushing her chin up so she saw the cold fury in his eyes. "No, Katherine," he said through his teeth. "Fuck you." Dragging her head forward, he pried her mouth open with his fingers, and forced his cock into her mouth. "If you bite me, I'll whip you. Don't think I won't."

Her mouth relaxed; she'd been about to do just that.

"Smart girl. Now do a good job and I'll let you come a

few times. Screw with me and I'll see that you don't come for a year."

Her mouth full of cock, she glanced up in shock.

"I can, Katherine; I can do anything I want with you. Make sure you swallow. That's an order."

She shouldn't be aroused by his brute malevolence; it was grotesque, shameless. But even as Dominic held her head in a hard, unyielding grip, guided the rhythm, forced the depth of her descent whether she choked or not, coercing her without compunction, she couldn't help herself. She responded to him beyond conscious control, her body recognizing his voice, his touch, his capacity for pleasure; he made her wild, lustful, frantic. Reason had nothing to do with one second of her response to his demands, nor did it control the rush of her heart or the flush on her cheek. He was her self-contradictory craziness and bliss. He was the only man she'd ever wanted, perhaps the only man she'd ever want.

The dildo stabbed sensationally deep inside her each time she leaned forward to draw his rigid length into her mouth. Her clit swelled against the stainless steel, intensifying the fierce delirium, her powerlessness against the solid, inexorable thrust of the dildo was perversely exciting, radical, intense. Awareness of the world was muted, the mysteries of the universe dismissed for the magic swelling inside her. Her sex was creamy wet, the pearly fluid seeping out around the dildo, her desire at fever pitch, her nerves skittish, panic beating at her brain. What if she couldn't curtail her climax? *A year! He couldn't mean it! He couldn't do it— could he?*

"Don't you dare come," he whispered on a suffocated breath, so near to orgasm the top of his head was beginning to lift off. And a tremulous second later, his pressing orgasmic urgency inexorably erupted, his climax burst in hot chutes of semen, jetted, spurted, filling her mouth faster than she could swallow, the overflow seeping through her lips, trickling down her chin.

After a last jerk and a muffled grunt, he finally released her head, leaned back, shut his eyes, and softly exhaled. His chest was still heaving when he felt his erection begin to pulse. First staggered, then unnerved, he promptly opened his eyes and sat up. Christ. Since when was he ready to come a second after an orgasm? He knew the answer: she was kneeling between his legs.

On the other hand, the part below his head was doing just fine and he had five more days to enjoy her.

Sliding his fingers down Kate's cheek as she knelt trembling before him, he said softly, "You're almost there, aren't you. You've been very patient. I appreciate it." He reached down, gripped the belt. "Ready?"

A fraction of a second, then his query registered. "Yes, please," she whispered, quivering, hardly daring to draw a deep breath for fear she might climax, her need for orgasm like mainlining a drug. The more she had the more she wanted.

Jesus, he was going to have to fuck that sweet, eager young thing sooner rather than later. But at the moment: he flexed his fingers and gently lifted the belt.

She instantly came with a tiny, feverish groan, eyes shut and breathless. He gently lifted again and another climax, sharper, more intense immediately washed over the first. She screamed, a wild, startled cry, and clutched his thighs to support herself as her knees gave way, as the tempestuous, high-pressure orgasmic convulsions ravished her body.

What Dominic did next was an arbitrary lapse of judgment, or a deliberate depravity. Or a calculated attempt to distance himself from unwanted emotion. Or perhaps it was nothing more than a thoughtless impulse in this house that occasionally hosted hard-core entertainments.

Dominic jerked hard on the belt.

Katherine shrieked at the violent spasm exploding through her overwrought nervous system, viciously ripping through her core, ravaging her glutted senses. Then she went pale as a ghost and began shuddering.

Oh fuck. What the hell had he done? Had he lost all sense of proportion? Had he turned into some goddamn monster? This was Katherine, for Christ's sake. Calling himself every kind of evil fiend, Dominic instantly unclasped the belt, cautiously eased out the dildo, and flung it away. Gently lifting Kate up into his arms, he tenderly settled her on his lap and drew her against his chest with exacting care. "Jesus, I must be out of my mind," he said, rough, breathless. "I'm so goddamn sorry." He kissed her hair, her cheek, the curve of her ear. "I shouldn't be messing with someone like you." Stretching back, he grabbed a towel from the bed, wiped her mouth, her chin. "I'm such a bastard." He rubbed his chin in her hair, gently stroked her forearm. "If you want, I'll get down on my knees and apologize. Just say the word."

"Word," she croaked.

He glanced at her, a faint smile playing over his lips. "If I'm going to grovel, you have to open your eyes."

She lifted her chin fractionally, opened her eyes.

The same potent green he'd noticed the first time he'd met her. Potent, irresistible, detrimental to the orderly life he'd constructed after Julia's death. But *irresistible*. "Do we need a doctor?" he asked softly.

"No." She was shocked, but not hurt. Not that she was about to let him off the hook. She'd never seen a completely penitent Dominic. "That apology on your knees will suffice," she said, smiling.

He grimaced.

A pointed look, an infinitesimal lift of her brow. "Didn't you mean it?" She had to admit it was a nice little power trip, pointing out to Dominic that he had a conscience.

A small sigh. "Of course I meant it." Lifting her off his lap, he shifted her to one side on the chair, pulled up his sweats, knotted the tie, and said bluntly, "You realize I've never done this before."

"Oh goody." Bright-eyed and teasing.

His expression in contrast was disgruntled, a rudiment of a frown canted his brows as he rose to his feet. "Just so you know, this is a one-time deal."

"I should hope so." A wider smile, blatant mischief in her eyes.

"Stop," he grumbled, "or you'll get a spanking instead of an apology."

"Are you kidding me? Thanks to you I almost OD'd on orgasms."

He winced. "You're right. That was reprehensible of

me." Dropping to one knee, he met her gaze, the blue of his eyes stark with remorse. "I'm sorry I hurt you. It was shameful and despicable. You deserve not only my apology but compensation for my stupidity. I mean it." A sudden boyish smile, open and warm. "How's that? Did I do well?"

"Very well, thank you." Kate smiled back. "And I'm not hurt, so don't worry. You didn't have to toss that dildo. It's perfectly fine."

"No it's not fine," he said, coming to his feet. "It's gone and it's going to stay gone. It wasn't a good idea."

"I liked it"—she gently arched her back in a languorous stretch—"in moderation. So if I were to ask real nicely, might I have it back later?"

He bit on his lower lip. A small pause. "No," he finally said. "I can't trust myself. We'll find something else to entertain you."

"Meaning?"

"Meaning, you're taking a rest right now. You were hardly breathing a few minutes ago. Now don't move, I'll be right back."

When he returned, he brought her a robe, put it on her, then arranged her on his lap, wrapped his arms around her, and said, "How about a movie for a change? I think I have that *Marie Antoinette* movie you like."

"You don't have to watch it just for me. It's not really a guy movie."

"I don't mind."

"You're just being nice cuz you feel guilty. I wasn't hurt, just overwhelmed." She looked up and smiled. "You do that to me."

"Then I'd better stop doing it. We'll try vanilla sex for a while."

"Maybe I don't *want* vanilla sex," she protested. "Why would I want vanilla sex when you make me feel so outrageously good, so incredibly wonderful, so well—insatiable with the other kind of stuff."

He smiled. "Stuff?"

"You know."

"I do. You mean sex toys and domination? You can say it."

"I can say it. I just don't want to."

He laughed out loud, then dropped a kiss on her nose. "You *are* adorable, no question."

"Just because I'm adorable doesn't mean I'm going to settle for vanilla sex," she said with a small scowl.

"We'll see." His expression was grave. "I don't want to accidentally hurt you. I might go off on some rampage again. You're not used to that."

"We'll compromise."

His lashes drifted downward. "We'll talk about it."

"That doesn't sound like we'll talk, that sounds like a no."

"So, how about that movie?"

"God, you won't even argue with me you feel so guilty."

"So, how about that movie?" he repeated, coming to his feet with Kate in his arms.

"Do I have a choice?"

"Sure you do." He grinned. "We can watch any movie you want."

"Oh, hell," she muttered, aware she wasn't going to win this particular argument. "Do you have popcorn?"

"We'll find out."

A wide-eyed look of wonder. "You mean you don't eat popcorn when you watch a movie?"

How not to explain that the majority of his movie-watching was of the adult entertainment variety with his various female playmates? And no one ever saw the end of a movie. "Sometimes I do," he lied. "Butter or no butter for you?"

"Need you ask?"

He laughed. "Lots of butter, right?"

"I wouldn't mind some grated cheddar on top, too."

"Then that's what you'll have," he said, pleased that they'd moved past issues of sex or no sex to popcorn. "Here, sit for a minute. I'll call the kitchen."

The small theater was outfitted with navy velvet chaises rather than chairs, the walls and ceiling were crimson-velvet-covered acoustical panels, and a large screen was spread across an entire wall. A small, well-stocked bar took up half the back wall, the overhead lighting blue and yellow hand-blown glass depicting abstract flower shapes. Clearly the work of an artist.

After seating Kate, Dominic stood beside her. "Soda, mineral water, a drink?"

"I always have a Coke with ice. What about you?"

Usually lots of whiskey. "Me, too—Coke." When he came back with their Cokes a few minutes later, he gestured at the door. "I'll get the popcorn."

Smith greeted Dominic with a smile as he entered the butler's pantry. "Good morning, sir. The film just arrived. They finally found a copy in Kowloon."

"Thank you for going to the trouble. Miss Hart likes this particular movie." Dominic glanced at the tray on the counter.

"One bowl of plain butter popcorn, sir, one butter and cheddar. The chef added some spiced nuts, a few cookies, and sweets. He thought the young lady might enjoy the sweets."

"I'm sure she will. Chocolates?"

"The truffles you ordered, sir."

"Excellent. Tell Liang I need a car brought round at five thirty."

"There's a great deal of bustle up at the house."

"No doubt. Have you heard how the chief executive's wife is doing?"

"She's come through so far, sir. Everyone is hopeful."

"Good news. I'm assuming flowers were sent?"

"Yesterday, sir."

"Good, good. It does make one appreciate one's health."

"Indeed, sir."

Dominic picked up the tray, dipped his head in farewell, and walked through the door held open by a houseboy.

"The master is in good spirits," Smith observed as the door closed on Dominic. "Unusually fine spirits."

The houseboy grinned. "He likes the lady. She's not like the others."

Smith sniffed. "The others were only distractions. Miss Hart is keeping him company."

"The house staff bets not for long though."

"We won't have any such talk," Smith said crisply. "And no one will be betting. Mr. Knight deserves some pleasant companionship no matter the duration. He's been alone too long."

The houseboy respectfully nodded. But he wasn't old like Smith; he'd already bet twenty Hong Kong dollars on three days.

When Dominic returned to the theater, he placed the tray next to the chaise, set up the DVD, slid behind Kate, drew her back against his chest, and flicked on Sofia Coppola's *Marie Antoinette*. He half watched the movie, more interested in the lady seated between his legs, a bowl of popcorn in her lap, her attention focused on the screen as though she hadn't seen the film before.

He handed her the tray from time to time so she could select a cookie or candy, he ate some himself, which he rarely did, and he even enjoyed what he saw of the movie, which surprised him. Perhaps unrequited love and star-crossed lovers struck some enigmatic sensibility or perhaps just holding Miss Hart in his arms made any movie enjoyable. Strangely, the thought didn't disturb him. In fact, the simple pleasures, a movie, popcorn, a beautiful young woman in his arms enthralled by this love story, the kind of homespun companionship they were sharing was peaceful, ordinary, and for him, exceptional. It made him think of fields of daisies and colorful rainbows, he thought and smiled to himself.

After the movie, they dressed in jeans and sweaters and went out into the walled garden. The vine-covered walls protected them from the wind, the gradient of the sun widespread enough to warm the air. Feeling that Kate was comfortable enough to meet one of the houseboys, Dominic had high tea brought out, along with a chessboard. After serving Kate tea, Dominic pointed at the tiered caddy that held three plates of traditional sandwiches and pastries: cucumber sandwiches on white bread, potted shrimp on dark bread, cheese and tomato on rye, scones with clotted cream and strawberry jam, shortbread, colorful petit fours, lemon tarts, poppy seed cake. "And champagne if you like," he added, with a nod at the bottle of Krug '96 in a silver ice bucket on a stand by the table.

She did, as did he.

They spoke of innocuous subjects while they ate.

Dominic mentioned his sister and named off her children when Kate asked.

"I'm surprised you remember them all," she said. "Middle names too."

"Melanie has a thing for names. They're all pretty nice names, actually."

"Do you see them often?"

"Quite a lot. They live in the Bay area, not too far from me. My sister and I were always close, best friends. We still are. In fact, I learned how to get along with women from her," he said with a smile.

"And you learned well," Kate teased. "You can anticipate."

"I don't know about that," he said modestly and changed the subject. "What was it like growing up without siblings?"

Kate grinned. "I was the adored only child. First with my parents, then after they died, with my grandparents. I had unconditional love pretty much all around."

A dark shadow flickered briefly in his eyes, before the

mask slipped back into place. Dominic raised his glass. "Lucky you," he said.

She immediately felt guilty for being so unfeeling. "I'm sorry. That was rude of me."

"God, no." He leaned back in his chair and studied her as if she were a specimen under glass, something rare. "More power to you and your family. It's nice to know unconditional love isn't just an empty phrase."

She wanted to say, *I'll give you unconditional love*, but knew how ludicrous it would sound with their five-day ticking timeline. Not to mention the very wide gulf between a handsome billionaire with tons of women dogging his heels and, well—someone like her. "I didn't always get my way," she said, in an effort to mitigate her faux pas. "I was grounded more than once when I was older."

He lifted his brows. "For?"

She was able to make Dominic laugh then and made a conscious effort to entertain him with small-town stories. She had plenty of them. Nana was a born storyteller and Gramps hadn't been any slouch either. His canoe outfitting business was about schmoozing too, not just sending people off into the Boundary Waters with good equipment and good maps.

"Gramps died suddenly when I was twenty. A heart attack. Although he'd been sprayed by Agent Orange so many times when he was in Vietnam, he always said he was living on borrowed time. His death hit Nana and me pretty hard. You're lucky that both"—she stopped. "Sorry. I forgot. Tell me about Melanie. She's older right?"

He grinned. "Quick save, babe. Yeah, Melanie's almost

six years older. She more or less raised me. She's grounded in a remarkable way. Some people roll with the punches when life's shitty, buckle down, and get on with getting on. Then there're people like me who fight the indifference and neglect as though I'm some fucking Don Quixote on a bike." He smiled faintly. "I was trouble from a young age. Anyway, Melanie was my guardian angel, she made everything hunky-dory when it wasn't." He looked down for a moment, then blew out a breath. "We're going to have to change the subject or I'm going to start drinking seriously."

"Did you like the movie?"

"I liked that you liked the movie. It was fun."

For a long moment they looked at each other, a kind of crackling reminder that the fun would soon be over, shimmering like lightning in the air. Then they both started talking at once.

"You first," he said softly.

"I was just going to say, the casting for Count Fersen was well done. He was the perfect hero, self-sacrificing and all that." Her voice trailed off because Dominic was staring at her like he was memorizing her face.

"I agree. That was nice," he said as her cheeks flushed. "Although self-sacrifice is probably a lost art now."

Another restless silence, the undercurrent of change palpable. They both knew their time together was finite, each moment precious.

"If you're finished eating," Dominic said suddenly, pushing to his feet. "I'll clear up the dishes. No, sit, I'll do it."

She watched him carry the dishes to the wheeled cart the houseboy had used to deliver the food, doing her own memorizing against the future when she'd only have that to remember him by. She was overcome by a poignant sense of loss, and when he leaned over and gently kissed her cheek in passing as he returned to the table, her pulse rate skyrocketed and her belly clenched. He had only to touch her and she was weak with longing. How would she survive without him?

He smiled at her as he took his seat and reached for the chessboard that had been delivered with the food. He needed a distraction, something to focus his mind away from the wild, milling confusion. "Do you play?" He started placing the pieces on the board. "If you don't, I'll show you."

"I play a little."

"Black or white?"

"White."

He glanced up and grinned. "Naturally."

She was good, and two evenly matched games later, he told her so.

"You sound surprised," she said.

He was leaning back in his chair, drinking from a fresh bottle of champagne, feeling calmer, less dislocated. "You play better than *a little*, that's all I meant. It's a compliment."

"From a man who apparently doesn't often lose at chess. Or did you let me win?" They'd both won a game.

"Hell, no. I always play to win."

"I've noticed that once or twice," she drolly noted, the battlefield of chess having tranquilized her agitation as well.

He smiled. "You can always hold your own, babe. Like this game. Who taught you? You're tough to beat."

"My grandpa. He was a sniper in Vietnam. Long-term strategy kept him alive, he always said. Chess was the same he told me: know your opponents, plan ahead, wait for the kill. I beat him the first time when I was eleven. We celebrated with blueberry pie and ice cream."

A lucent warmth lit his gaze. "Now there's a picture. I would have liked to have seen you at eleven."

"No, you wouldn't have. I was a skinny tomboy with a butch haircut."

"Nana didn't mind your butch cut?"

"They both mostly let me do what I wanted."

He laughed. "So they're to blame for your obstinacy."

"Who's to blame for yours?"

"Fuck if I know. Probably fighting for my life in my dysfunctional family."

"Was it really bad?"

He shrugged. "Nah, lots of people had it worse. Melanie and I had each other."

"I feel for you. Nana and Gramps were everything a kid could want."

"Your parents? Do you remember much?" A soft query; he knew some of the answer, but not all.

"Not much. I was only four when they died. I remember my parents working at home, in long stretches like I often do, sometimes all night, so their nerves probably weren't the calmest. They were computer geeks like me. I'd wake up at night when they'd be screaming at each other—I suppose they didn't want to fight in front of me. It wasn't often, but a kid remembers that. It's scary. Otherwise they were supergood to me, played with me, read to me, had tea parties with me and my toys." She shrugged. "Anyway, a little childhood angst. What can I say?"

He'd read about her parents in the brief. Both young hot-shot software programmers, her mother graduated from Berkeley, where she'd met the father, who was from a prominent Bay family who'd disowned him when he'd married a woman they saw as from the raw hinterlands and unacceptable, which was why Katherine used her mother's surname. Her parents' car had gone over a cliff on Highway 1 north of San Francisco; according to the police report alcohol was involved.

"So don't scream at me," Kate said. "I don't like it." She smiled. "Not that I don't do my share of arguing, but I don't as a rule scream. Some Freudian shit I've never looked at too closely. I figure ignorance is bliss. And like you, there're lots of people who have had much tougher lives than me. I have no complaints other than my slight paranoia with screaming."

He held up his hand. "Promise. No screaming." As for any more of his family memories, no way he was going there. "Ready for one more game? Then we have to bathe and dress for a cocktail party. Don't scowl. I didn't tell you before because I didn't want you pouting all day. We just have to stay for two hours."

She groaned. "Why do I have to go?"

"Because I'd miss you if you didn't."

"No, really, why do I have to go?"

"Really, cross my heart, I'd miss you. Some charity event Max's wife helped organize had to shift venues when the hostess had a heart attack. I just found out about it yesterday. I tried to get out of it, couldn't, and there you are—my companion at a boring cocktail party to raise funds for the

Hong Kong Philharmonic. You can meet the president of Hong Kong if you're interested."

She groaned louder this time.

"My exact reaction. Max ignored me."

"You're sure it's okay with Max's wife if I show up?"

"Why wouldn't it be?"

She shrugged. "Because I'm your current fuckee."

"You're also a contractor for Knight Enterprises. And Olivia couldn't care less. If I like you, she'll like you. End of story. Don't argue."

A doleful grimace. "Do I get a reward for this miserable assignment?"

"The minute the two hours are up." He didn't have to ask what she meant.

"So we're talking nine oh one?"

"Or as soon as I can chase you upstairs. We can stay at my house if you like. My mother's gone."

"I don't care. You decide."

"We can decide later." He liked the isolation here. But it didn't matter enough to dispute the point should Katherine prefer the house. "Would you like someone to come in and do your hair and makeup?"

She slammed him with a look. "Do I need it?"

"God, no. I was just being polite. Some women—don't glare at me—I meant women in the generic sense. I've never had anyone *ever* come in to do makeup and hair, here or anywhere."

"Greta," she reminded him with a narrowed glance.

"They were her clothes. Who better than she to help you."

"Because I needed help?"

"No, because I needed her to convince you to wear them."

She sighed. "A part of me still thinks I should have refused."

"No, you shouldn't have. You look gorgeous in all her things. It pleases me."

"So I must please you?" The small familiar rebellion in her voice, her intrinsic need for autonomy in a constant struggle with her sexuality.

"You never have to do anything you don't want to do," he replied softly. "You know that."

She studied a chess piece briefly, then looked up and met his gaze squarely. "I like to please you." She smiled. "You're my dangerous unknown, my high-risk rush, my obsession. And best of all, I always get rewarded."

"We both do. You constantly delight me in every possible way." He was silent for a moment, feeling as though he'd said too much. "So one more game? Loser has to bathe the winner?"

This game he deliberately lost.

NINETEEN

His tub was an oversize claw-foot model placed on an oriental carpet in the center of an alcove adjacent to the bathroom. The arrangement, long an aristocratic practice, allowed servants to bathe their masters, a circumstance not unlike that taking place at the Garden House. Not that anyone would characterize Dominic Knight as hired help, but he was definitely helpful in this instance for his own selfish reasons.

Needless to say, the bath took longer than usual because ultimately Dominic joined Kate, one thing led to another, and by the time they climbed out of the tub, the carpet was soaked. Dominic placated Kate with conciliatory remarks about his well-paid staff who didn't mind in the least if there was a little water on the floor as he led her into the bedroom and shut the door behind them.

"Don't think I didn't notice you're out of sight, out of mind ploy," she muttered, giving him a disapproving look. "I could have wiped up the floor."

"No you couldn't have wiped up the floor. I wouldn't let you. Don't start, okay? It's a stupid fight."

"Sorry."

"Thank you," he said curtly. "Oh God, now what did I do?"

Her eyes were suddenly wet with tears. "Nothing. Really, you didn't do anything." Then her tears spilled over.

"Jesus, don't cry," he whispered, pulling her against his body, holding her close. "I'm sorry. I shouldn't snap at you."

"I shouldn't argue all the time." Her voice was muffled against his chest.

"I don't mind, really. I'll try to be better." If anyone in Knight Enterprises had heard Dominic's response, they would have thought their CEO had finally gone over the edge into some neurotic psychosis due to overwork. *I'll try to be better.* Mea culpas weren't his style. Although if anyone had had the nerve to point it out to him, he would have brushed them off. She was unhappy, he would have said. Why wouldn't I soothe her?

"I'll try to be better too."

Kate's words were barely audible, although her little hiccupping delivery was revealing.

Lightly cupping her chin, Dominic lifted her face, lowered his head, and gently licked away her tears. "Baby, don't cry. Maybe we can make it less than two hours at the party?" His voice was low, husky. "Would that help?"

"Maybe," she said on another hiccuppy little breath, not even sure why she was crying, her nerves shaky, her body in wistful overload, her emotions caught up in a riptide of frightening, tumultuous change. Because she was stupidly falling in love with a man who wouldn't remember her name in a month...or probably a week.

He kissed her then, not deeply, just an affectionate, tender nuzzle.

And suddenly, a part of her was scared, knowing time wasn't on her side. "Do we have to go? I know we do." She tried to smile. "Sorry, I'm losing it for some reason."

"Hey, count me in. It's the last thing I want to do." He kissed the tip of her nose. "Better times in a couple hours—right?"

She chewed on her lip, nodded.

Moments mattered in life; they zipped by too fast, or you were looking the other way when you should have been paying attention. Either way you missed them. Dominic had learned that the hard way. So vague misgivings aside, he wouldn't look back on this moment with regret. Taking Kate by the hand, he drew her to a chair, sat down with her on his lap, his blue gaze half shuttered by his lashes. He took a small breath before he spoke. "I don't want to fuck this up." He saw the sudden wariness in her face, so he chose his words carefully. "There's something I'd like to tell you. I've been thinking about me, us"—he sighed—"my fucking calendar. I have to leave Hong Kong soon."

Her heart stopped beating; it's absolutely true what they say. Fear can make your heart stand still.

"I've pushed everything aside for five days. I can't do that for any length of time. So I thought"—he paused, sure of what he wanted, not completely sure about his approach—"and this is just a proposal..." Her silence, the stubborn tilt of her chin, caused him to pick his words as if he were negotiating a cease-fire after a ten-year war. "I understand you don't want to work for me. I wish you would—you know that—but if you'd rather not, at least come with me when I leave Hong Kong." Her mouth was starting to tighten. "Hey, don't get hot till you hear me out. You set the guidelines, the rules, the game plan. Time, place, how often I can touch you. See, I really mean it. I'll agree to whatever you want. I want you with me. On your terms. You're in the driver's seat on this one, babe." A man of action, he didn't question his motivation, nor her willingness—only her stubborn streak. And he'd manage that, too, like he managed everything else in his life.

Her heart started beating again. She was being offered any version of paradise she wished to draft. An exceptional, extraordinary paradise with a man who in only a few short days had become essential to her happiness. To her continuing and future happiness. One starring Dominic Knight if she wished.

As the silenced lengthened, he dipped his head, held her gaze. "Say something."

She could feel her heart pounding. "I'd like to think about it," she whispered. "If life didn't get in the way, I'd unequivocally answer yes. But"—she dragged in a small breath, seriously overwhelmed by the sheer magnitude of the man and his life, not entirely sure she could stand up to the tidal wave of power, not sure she even wanted to when she loved him so much—"I don't know about—"

"Nana?"

"For one, yeah." She bit her lip; he hadn't mentioned love once. But maybe that was asking too much. "And I left a few job offers hanging."

All manageable. "Understood." Dominic had lost only once in his life and if he'd been with Julia that day, he would have saved her. Other than that, he'd always won. He was confident of ultimate success. Why wouldn't he be? A woman had never said no to him. "Take your time. Think about it. We'll talk later." His smile was boyish, open, and warm. "Now, would you like help dressing?"

"From you?" Her tone was deliberately teasing, preferring to move on to something less fraught with angst and unlikely romantic fantasies.

"Who else?" An amiable, wholly immodest response from a man who could do anything.

She grinned. "How much time do we have?"

"Not that much time. But I can zip, buckle, whatever."

"I'm definitely interested in the whatever," she said playfully.

He glanced at the clock, frowned slightly. "Later, I promise. A car will be out front soon. Here, you sit and I'll find you something to wear."

A moment later, he lifted a gray wool dress off a hanger, tossed it on the bed, rummaged through the bureau drawers, and pulled out a bra and panties. "Something conservative to go with a conservative dress. Since you're a business associate, you should look the part."

"Is that what I am?" Sliding her hands under her breasts, she raised them into lush mounds. "Are you sure?"

He gave her a pointed look. "I'm sure for the next few hours because if you fuck with me, you'll be sleeping alone."

She dropped her hands. "Jeez, don't get surly."

"You don't want to see me surly," he murmured and crooked his fingers. "Let's get this show on the road. Seriously, babe, if I could fuck you now, I would. People are waiting, that's all." His voice went soft. "And I want you with me."

Such simple words but divinely beautiful in her ears, capable of persuading her to be anything he wanted her to be. She rose from the chair.

He hooked the sensible white cotton bra, she put on the white cotton panties, he slid the sheath dress over her head, zipped it up, adjusted the small black satin cap sleeves on her shoulders, pulled the black-satin-lined scooped neckline up a fraction of an inch to cover the strip of white bra that showed, and handed her a black satin belt. "Choose some shoes," he said, turning to the closet. "I'll get dressed."

After slipping on plain black pumps, she clasped the jet-studded belt buckle and surveyed herself in an ebony-and-gold-framed cheval glass. "This bra still shows," she grumbled, tugging the neckline higher.

Dominic shot her a look as he buttoned his shirt. "Don't bend over like that and it won't show."

"I should wear a black bra."

He smiled. "I like the contrast, that hint of plain white cotton is real sexy."

"For you and everyone else."

"Just don't bend over, Katherine." He held her gaze as he reached for his trousers. "Understand?"

A ruinous tremor stirred inside her, a flush rose on her cheeks at the stark authority in his voice. She inhaled sharply as hot desire ignited, burst into flame; she struggled to suppress it.

"I expect you to behave tonight, so keep that hot body of yours in check. Got it?" He shoved his shirt into his trousers with a few swift thrusts, pulled up his zipper. "Damn it, Katherine, I need an answer."

His gaze was as uncompromising as his voice. "Yes, yes, I understand." She took a breath, felt the ripples slow, regained her emotional footing once again.

"Good." He buckled his belt. "I'll introduce you to Olivia when we get to the house. You already know Max. They'll see that you meet whomever you wish to meet. I'm keeping my distance so your reputation won't be compromised. That's about it." He slid a smoke-gray-and-carnelian-checked tie under his collar and smoothly tied it. "Any questions?"

"No, but I need a better tone of voice or I'm not moving from here."

He swung around from the bureau mirror, dazzled her with a smile, and said, silken soft, "Please accept my apology. I'd really like you to come with me. I want to show you off."

She unclasped her arms, which had been folded across her chest. "That's better."

"You look stunning, Katherine." He slipped his arms into a black suit coat, shrugged his shoulders to adjust the fit, buttoned one button, then held out his hands. "Come here, babe. I'm the lucky guy with the best-looking girl at the party."

She'd pulled her hair up with a diamond-studded clip, leaving a few wild tendrils to escape. A touch of dark eye shadow and splash of brilliant red lipstick dramatized the paleness of her skin.

"You clean up rather well yourself," she said, keeping it casual rather than offering him her undying love.

"So we're good now?" He cupped her hands in his. "No tantrums?"

"Don't look at me. I'm Miss Mellow."

"I wish *I* were. I'd like nothing better than to rip off

that dress and fuck you all night." He groaned. "Unfortunately..." He gave his head a shake. "Okay, I can do this."
He released her hands and crooked his arm. "May I escort
you to two hours of hell, Miss Hart? I promise to make it up
to you."

"In that case, Mr. Knight," Kate said with a sweet smile,
"I'd be delighted."

Max and Olivia were at the house to greet them when they
arrived. After Kate and Olivia were introduced, Olivia gave
them a tour through the various reception rooms that had
been readied for the occasion. The staff was still busy with
last-minute arrangements: setting out food trays, adding a
few more vases of flowers, stocking the two bars that had
been set up—all under Leo's cool orchestration. Dominic
thanked Leo for his Herculean effort in such a short time
frame, praised the gala splendor of the rooms, and said he
hoped they could hustle everyone out the door by nine, to
which Leo responded with an eye roll.

And Dominic groaned.

"You only have to smile for two hours, Dominic, and it's
over," Olivia said lightly.

He sighed. "I'll do my best, Liv."

Kate glanced at him, her eyebrows going up delicately.
"It's a good cause. I'm sure two hours will go by quickly."

Dominic's sharp look gave way to a grin. "My conscience,"
he said drolly.

Olivia smiled. "Then how nice that you brought Katherine along, Dominic. The Philharmonic is grateful. Shall
we?" She waved toward the entrance hall.

Moments later the small party was standing near the door, waiting for their guests to arrive—the ladies with a glass of champagne in hand, the men with whiskeys. "You have my permission to escape after two hours, Dominic, whether guests are still here or not," Olivia said with a gracious smile. "And thank you again for stepping into the breach at such short notice."

"My pleasure, Liv. Now tell me, who needs convincing to take out their checkbooks?"

As Olivia began to run through a list of people, Dominic nodded from time to time, commented on one or two, asking for particulars, emptied his glass, and casually held it out for a waitperson to take from him without shifting his attention from Olivia. "I think I have it. A hundred grand from the two ambassadors and the principessa, fifty from Ng, Chen, Tsui, Dan Lee, Malcolm, the Dunhams, Schultz, and ten from all the rest. You're going to take in a haul tonight, Liv."

"That's the idea."

"I hope this won't be too boring for you, Katherine." His voice softened, his gaze for her alone. "If it is," he said, suddenly speaking in a conversational tone as though he'd not just made her blush, "go upstairs and make yourself comfortable. You can't be expected to talk to all these strangers. I'd prefer not talking to them, but"—a shrug, a quick grin for Olivia—"I'm happy to help you out, Liv." He took Kate's hand. "Promise you'll leave if it gets tedious. But not for too long. I'll go into withdrawal."

Her blush deepened. "I promise," she said, a slight tremor in her reply. "Don't worry."

"Hey." He dipped his head, held her gaze. "Are you all right?"

She dragged in a breath, smiled tightly. "I hadn't thought about all the people—looking and staring. Until now that we're actually here."

"How about a breath of fresh air? If you'll excuse us," he said without looking at either Max or Liv. "Come," he said softly, beginning to move away, drawing Kate with him. "We'll check out the stars from the terrace."

"Well, well, well," Liv said on a slow exhalation as the couple walked away hand in hand. "Katherine's definitely more than a playmate, considerably more. *I'll go into withdrawal. Really?* There's no doubt in my mind that she'll be leaving with Dominic on Tuesday. And Antonia's going to be really pissed when she sees that shocking display of affection. I'd better see that Penzance does his duty to crown and country because Dominic might very well be rude. He can be."

"You think?" Max had seen him tear competitors to shreds with a few razor-sharp remarks. "Although he did promise to be nice enough to Antonia to get your donation."

"I'm not sure he's capable of such guile tonight. He's like a changed man. He was never like that even with Julia ... protective and solicitous, guarding that young girl against the cold, cruel world. Do you think that's her appeal? Her naïveté?"

"I doubt it. Miss Hart is pretty no-nonsense and assertive."

"I didn't see that."

"She can be."

"Just like he can be a huge prick but he's not with her.

I don't know, Max. I think we're seeing something astonishing. I wouldn't be surprised if he's in love with her. She certainly is with him."

"No!"

"For heaven's sake, Max. You men never get over the terror of that word."

"I beg your pardon."

"I don't mean you don't love me, darling. I just mean Dominic is going to call his feelings everything and anything but love. And his little Katherine will try to disguise her feelings because, as you say, she's not stupid. Dominic would bolt." She uttered a little trill of laughter. "What fun it will be . . . watching them tonight."

"Or watching Dominic fend off Antonia in order not to anger Katherine."

"Plus we'll be taking in a few million for a good cause." Olivia threw her arms open wide in playful drama. "Won't it be grand!"

Dominic had taken off his suit coat and wrapped it around Kate's shoulders before they walked outside. Holding her close, her back to his chest, his arms around her, they stood in the lee of the wall, the sparkling lights of Hong Kong laid out before them in a radiant panorama.

"I didn't think about all the people staring. I thought it was enough to stay away from you," he said, his chin resting lightly on her head. "I don't know what I was thinking. Any little bit of gossip always stokes them."

"Don't worry." She didn't want to be ungracious or difficult. "I'll manage just fine. I'll ignore the stares and mingle."

"I don't want you to mingle. Jesus," he grumbled, "that's the last thing I want you to do. Every man here is going to hit on you." His arms tightened around her. "Stay by me, we'll deal with the gossip."

"That's stupid and you know it. For you, for me, for your Philharmonic friends, who will be delighted to spread salacious rumors."

"Fuck."

"Is that a promise?" she teased.

"It's a goddamn guarantee. In two hours. Oh, shit."

"I felt that." She rubbed against his rising erection. "Ummm...nice. I remember him well."

"I'm going to see that you don't forget him. Damn, I wish I could have refused this reception."

"You couldn't, it's important. Thank you for bringing me."

"As if I wouldn't." He spoke as if it were the most natural thing in the world for him to bring his current playmate to a public function. When he never had. Nor more than he ever questioned his actions. "I warn you, though, if I see anyone looking down your dress, I'm going to punch him out."

"Don't you dare. It's your fault I'm wearing this bra. Not only is it white, but it's cut too high...so if I move even a little the wrong way it shows."

"Then don't move the wrong way," he said gruffly, "or I'll spank you when this party's over."

"In that case..."

He groaned. "I haven't felt like I was sixteen since, Christ—even when I was sixteen, ready to fuck every second, ready to fuck you every second." He blew out a disgruntled breath. "It's going to be a long two hours."

But once they returned to the reception rooms, time passed swiftly, the crowd descending as predicted by Max earlier than seven, the noise levels escalating as the liquor flowed. The rich, powerful, beautifully dressed and bejeweled people milling through the enfilade of magnificent rooms, air kissing each other, exchanging gossip only those in the small incestuous world of moneyed Hong Kong were privy to, taking our their checkbooks in response to either Liv's or Dominic's smiles, doing their duty to the cultural universe.

Kate deliberately stayed in the background, or at least tried to. But dressed as she was, beautiful as she was, men converged on her like bees to honey. She looked up from time to time from one inconsequential conversation or another, saw Dominic watching her, and, if possible, discreetly met his gaze.

It wasn't always possible. She'd see him frown and her body would begin to heat up, as though his authority reached across the room, imposing its will, expecting compliance. She'd quickly look away, force herself to ignore the tumult warming her senses, concentrate on whoever was talking. She could have left; Dominic had offered her that option. But she didn't—jealous perhaps of all the women besieging him, filled with doubt and suspicion whenever he smiled at one of them. Then he'd catch her eye and grin and everything was beautiful again.

Like him.

He was, literally, the handsomest man in the room.

The women surrounding him all wrote checks or had

their escorts write checks while Dominic charmed and flattered them with hugs and kisses, a light arm around their shoulders, a whispered comment in their ears—before politely moving on. He was truly masterful, Kate thought, faced with the stark reality of Dominic Knight's seductive charm. Each discarded female was left with a smile on her face.

Something to file away in her mental database.

Well into the second hour, Liv hove into view carrying a fresh drink for both of them, shooed away Kate's admirers, and handed over a gin and tonic. "Dominic follows you with his eyes when you walk around the room," she said with a smile. "I find it quite lovely."

"Hardly," Kate shrugged faintly. "He's just a control freak."

"Heavens, no. Not in public like this. Beyond the superficialities, he's indifferent to women." She smiled. "Present company excluded."

"He doesn't look too indifferent right now," Kate murmured, eyeing the crowd of women vying for his favors.

"Nonsense, my dear. He's always polite but totally disengaged. It's habit, of course. There have been so many." Liv's pale hair swung on her shoulders as she glanced at Dominic, and her diamond earrings caught the light. "Although you can see why. He's outrageously good looking."

Olivia spoke in an offhand way, Kate decided, as a friend, not an admirer. "I agree, he's definitely dazzling."

"You're good for him you know." Olivia half lifted her glass in Dominic's direction. "I haven't seen him smile like this for"—she shrugged—"since Julia's death."

Kate was momentarily speechless.

Olivia seemed not to notice Kate's lack of response; perhaps she'd had more than one gin and tonic. "Julia challenged Dominic to think about more than just himself. Made him better for it. She was deeply committed to her charities and causes and she adored adventure sport as much as Dominic. They holidayed in the most dangerous locations. They climbed Everest together—he actually met her on that trip. She was unstoppable. That's why it was so crushing for him when she died so unexpectedly."

"A traffic accident, wasn't it?" Kate found her voice because she desperately wanted to hear more, why he loved his wife, how much he loved her; she wanted to know everything about him. And until tonight she'd had no one to ask. Dominic had offered her a temporary place in his life, but that didn't mean he was going to bare his soul to her after only a few days. He was the most private person she knew.

"A completely unnecessary traffic accident. Julia wasn't even in a car. She was standing in line at Starbucks when an elderly man stepped on his accelerator instead of his brake, drove through the front window, and ran over Julia and two other people."

"How awful."

"Dominic fell apart. He withdrew from the world, spent a year sailing from one port to another. In fact, Max met him in Cape Town, where Dominic was having a mast repaired. It was all quite sad."

Kate couldn't visualize Dominic incapacitated. He was so powerful, commanding, assured. "He must have loved her very much," Kate said, a painful anguish settling in the pit of her stomach.

"They were inseparable. It was a beautiful marriage; they were partners." Olivia smiled. "I don't suppose you've seen any pictures of her. Oh dear, forgive me. How rude of me. As if you want to talk about Dominic's wife when he's so enthralled with you."

"No, I'd like to know. He doesn't talk about his life. Not that I know him very well." She blushed furiously. "I mean I've only known him for a few days."

"He adores you. Don't blush. I think it's sweet. And to be perfectly honest, it's wonderful seeing him smile again."

"I have seen pictures. His wife was very beautiful."

"Julia was almost as tall as Dominic. They made a stunning couple." Olivia slapped her hand over her mouth. "Stop me. I've said enough."

"No, really, you're the only one I can ask."

"Dominic doesn't talk, does he? Julia complained about that. His childhood was very unhappy apparently. Max said you've met his mother, so I don't have to tell you much more."

"I didn't get the impression he's close to his father either."

Olivia snorted. "The understatement of the millennium. Dominic despises his father. He won't stay in the same room with him. Max said they walked into a private club in London not too long ago where the elder Knight was having dinner. Dominic made a scene. He told the steward that either his father goes or he would. It was a simple decision for the club steward. Dominic has so much more money than his father. And his father isn't a poor man."

She paused and shot a quick glance toward Dominic before turning back to Kate. "What I'm about to say is probably the result of one too many gin and tonics, but I was wondering if you're aware of Dominic's, well—there's no other word for it—vices."

Kate's cheeks flamed bright red.

"I see you are."

"I researched Knight Enterprises before my interview. It's standard operating procedure. I found a video. He's since had it taken down."

"I just didn't want you to be surprised. And men will be men. I'm no prude."

"I found it a little shocking at first." Kate kept it simple, but she could feel her face heat up again.

Fortunately Olivia's attention had been drawn away. She swung back and smiled. "See Dominic over there, see that woman clinging to his arm? You might want to go and save him. The principessa thinks she has special rights to Dominic because they were friends once."

"Friends?"

Olivia shrugged. "Whatever Dominic calls them."

"Maybe she does have special rights." Dominic had been surrounded by women all evening and he hadn't seemed unhappy.

"No, she doesn't," Olivia said firmly. "In fact, Dominic told Max to save him from Antonia if necessary. She can be difficult. But I don't see Max. He must be in another room. Would you like to intervene or should I?"

"Are you sure?" Kate quickly glanced toward the group of people, the woman hanging on Dominic's arm movie star glitzy. And he didn't look like he was fighting her off. "I don't want to embarrass anyone."

"Well, first, you can't embarrass Dominic. Second, Antonia doesn't know what the word means. She stole her current husband from under his wife's nose at Cannes two years ago, without so much as a blush. And third, if you ask me, Dominic looks as though he's trying his best to ignore Antonia, her silicone-enhanced breasts jammed into his arm notwithstanding." A faint lift of her pale brows, a flare of her aristocratic nostrils, a teasing smile. "So either you or I have to ride to the rescue."

Dominic glanced up as Kate approached, although he continued listening to an older man who was the center of attention in the small cluster of guests. Save for Antonia; her adoring gaze was fixed on Dominic.

There was no question why Dominic had been interested in the principessa, Kate decided. She was flawless, from the top of her glistening black, carefully tousled hair, past her dark-kohled eyes and full-lipped pouty mouth, down her tall, shapely body to her long, sleek legs and perfectly manicured toes that were slipped into expensive Louboutin heels. Only a few inches shorter than Dominic in her spike heels, she was glamorous with a capital *G*.

Kate stopped at Dominic's elbow not currently in Antonia's grip. "I'm sorry to interrupt you, Mr. Knight, but there's an attack on your Romanian server. I was just notified. It's urgent."

Antonia glared at her.

Dominic's gaze narrowed. "Impossible. We took care of it."

Kate tried to assume a modest, demure expression. "A

renewed attack isn't unusual, Mr. Knight," she said with a small deferential dip of her head. "I wouldn't bother you, sir, but you're the only one with the password."

He debated arguing with Katherine, didn't relish the possibility Antonia would step in, particularly with the president of Hong Kong watching. "I seem to have no choice, Miss Hart," he said brusquely, knowing he was breaking protocol by walking away from the president of Hong Kong while he was speaking.

"I'm afraid not, sir, unless you'd care to give me the password."

"That probably wouldn't be wise." He turned to the older man. "My apologies, Mr. President. Apparently I have a crisis on my hands." Unwinding Antonia's arm, he nodded to the group at large. "If you'll excuse me." Then he turned and strode away.

"What the hell are you doing?" he growled as they walked away.

"Olivia sent me."

"Why?"

"She said you needed rescuing."

"Her timing could have been better," he muttered. "I was speaking with the president of Hong Kong. People don't as a rule walk away from him when he's talking."

"Sorry, she didn't mention it. She only said you'd asked to be saved from Antonia."

He sighed. "True. Oh, what the hell—a crisis is a crisis. The president might even have believed you. So, Katherine"—he flashed a bad-boy smile—"now that you've saved me, what do you have in mind?"

"Not much with people staring at us."

"Not us—you. All the men want to get in your pants," he muttered. "I almost came over to you a dozen times and dragged some guy away."

She turned scarlet. "Thank God you didn't."

"You were too friendly."

"I was not!"

"If you say so." But she could tell he didn't mean it. Taking her elbow in the cup of his hand, he propelled her out of the room and moved them briskly down the corridor, nodding at the few knots of guests they passed, smiling at a woman who started to approach. "Call me tomorrow, Isabelle," he said, not stopping. "I'm dealing with a business crisis right now."

"She didn't believe you." The woman's glare was still zapping Kate's brain.

"Ask me if I care."

"A little discretion wouldn't hurt," Kate muttered, trying to shake off his grip. "People are staring."

His grip tightened. "Sorry."

Kate snorted. "You don't even know what the word means."

"Sure I do. It means I heard you." Then he laughed. "Come on, baby, smile for me. These were the longest two hours of my life." He stopped at his office door, opened it, waved her in.

"I thought we were going back to the Garden House."

He grinned. "I figure you owe me a favor first for letting all those guys look down your dress."

"For heaven's sake, Dominic, this isn't the"—she glanced

over his shoulder and winced. "Some guy just gave you the thumbs-up."

"Don't worry about it." Pushing her into the room, he shut the door, locked it, and kicked off his shoes.

She scowled at him. "I'm not in the mood."

"I am if you don't mind." He flicked his finger in a quick up-and-down motion. "Take off your dress."

"You always say *if you don't mind* before you do exactly what you want. But I'm not doing this now—not with all the people walking by outside."

"We could be working on that bogus attack for all they know. Just don't scream when you come," he said, looking up from untying his tie and smiling faintly.

"Jesus, Dominic, be reasonable."

"I have been for two long fucking hours. Now take it off or I will." He slipped off his suit coat, tossed it on the floor. "I've been watching you talk to all those men, smile at all those men who want to fuck you. It pissed me off. Jack MacKenzie in particular, damned lecher."

"I was smiling at everyone. So were you. It's just courtesy."

"How about you show me some of your courtesy?" He pulled off his tie, let it drop from his fingers. "Let's see that boarding school underwear. Then take it off." He unbuttoned the top button on his shirt.

She looked at him with distaste. "I'm sorry. Were those orders?"

"They were." His shirt unbuttoned, he threw it on his pile of clothing.

"And you're the boss?"

His smile was wicked. "In every possible way, Katherine." He quickly disposed of his socks. "I thought we both understood that. And after two hours of ass-kissing and watching you flirt, I'm a little grouchy, so it would be best if you cooperated."

"And if I don't?"

He went motionless, his fly half unzipped. Then he smiled and went back to unzipping. "We'll have to play it by ear, although I doubt you want that dress ripped to shreds."

"Jesus, Dominic, you're in a mood."

He looked up, about to step out of his trousers. "I am. Sorry." He grinned. "Or whatever meaningless apology you prefer."

"Well, that's bluntly honest."

"You might think about being honest too. You always like to fuck. I don't see the problem."

"The problem is the house full of guests. Or someone could walk by the windows for God's sake," she said with a jerk of her hand toward the bank of French doors.

"I'll shut the curtains."

She watched him stride away, naked and beautiful, all ripped muscle and casual ruthlessness. He wasn't used to asking, or braking hard when an obstacle got in his way; he just reached out and took what he wanted. But it wasn't as though she was averse to fucking him.

"There. You're safe now," he said, walking back.

She stared at his beautifully formed erection flat against his stomach. It was large and intimidating, immodest, arresting. She began to quiver inside. "I suppose if you must have your way," she said, in one last grating poke at his authority, wondering if every other woman he knew responded to him with the same inexplicable longing. Wondering if her monstrous sexual need was her fault or his or no one's fault—just some transcendent mystery. "Ask me nicely," she said though, because she wanted to be more than one of the crowd. She always had.

"Please, darling. I'd be extremely grateful, if that helps," he gently added.

"I'm not sure it does." But she was like an alcoholic needing that next drink, and unbuckling the jet buckle at her waist, she held out the belt and slipped out of her shoes.

"In any case, I thank you for indulging me," Dominic said, taking the belt from her and dropping it. "Turn around. I'll unzip you."

Kate sighed, in surrender and rebuke. "Remind me never to come to a cocktail party with you."

"Remind me never to bring you to one." He stopped her turn with a hand on her hip, reached for the zipper. "It was hell watching you talking to all those men."

"That works out then, because I didn't like you talking to all those women."

"Asking them for money," he coolly pointed out. "There's a difference."

"I'm sure they were more than willing to oblige you in hopes you might reward them for their generosity."

"But I didn't," he said. "I turned them down. You're the only one I want." He slid the satin sleeves down her arms, eased the dress down her hips, and let it slip to the floor while her heart swelled with happiness that he wanted her and the queue of breathless women all were left behind. "There now," he whispered, picking her up by her waist, kicking the dress aside, and turning her to face him. "After an evening of bullshit, I finally have *my* reward."

"So tell me," she murmured, a modern Circe, practicing her arts, "does my plain white cotton underwear intrigue you?"

"It has a certain virtuous charm. Apparently Mrs. Hawthorne supplies props for every illicit and perverse fetish." He smiled. "I believe this is where I ask you how old you are?"

"Old enough," Kate purred.

He shook his head. "Not the right answer. I try to avoid sex that has legal repercussions."

"If I were seventeen, I'd still want to fuck you."

"But you wouldn't because I'm not stupid."

She sighed theatrically. "Very well. I'm twenty-two."

He laughed. "And available."

"And really hot for you after years in a convent school. Oh, you liked that one I see." She pointed at his surging dick.

The convent school comment triggered high school memories, but it was the hot babe standing in front of him that added inches to his dick. "We like everything about you, Katherine." He smiled. "Who would have thought cotton underwear was such a turn-on."

"It doesn't take much for you."

"Or you. Come here." He flicked his index finger. "Let's see if you're wet."

She moved closer and on reaching him, stopped, looked up, and smiled. "I'm always wet when you're around. Maybe it's your shampoo."

"Or maybe you just like to fuck all the time," he said, smiling back.

"I hope that's not a problem."

"It isn't, so long as it's only me you're fucking."

"A shame we've moved out of the Middle Ages," she sardonically noted.

"But I still outweigh you by a hundred pounds," he said, soft as silk. "So maybe the century doesn't matter." Taking hold of her arm in a deliberate act of constraint, he leaned over, slid his hand between her legs, and gently rubbed her sex through the damp cotton knit fabric. "You're really wet, Katherine. And you said you weren't interested in having sex. Too many people, you said, too indiscreet you said." He looked up, his gaze mocking. "Did you change your mind?"

"Don't look so smug. You make me horny, that's all."

"Or do you suppose all those men looking down your dress tonight made you horny?" Sliding his finger under her panties, he delicately stroked her slick cleft before standing upright and licking his fingertip. "That's definitely horny, babe. Ready for fucking." He brushed her nipples with his palms, a casual gesture of possession, lightly pinched the rising crests as they swelled against the soft knit fabric. "Maybe all those men looking at my tits made you wet?"

She shivered at his touch. "No one was looking."

"Liar."

"Well, I didn't ask them to."

He smiled tightly, his gaze cooled. "Are you sure?"

"Dominic, stop it. It was nothing. Cocktail conversation. The most banal chitchat."

"Tell me what Jack MacKenzie chatted about."

She flushed.

"That lurid—my, my."

"It was his idea of flirting."

"Did he ask you to come see his yacht in his usual obscene way?"

She blushed again.

"He thinks women like that. Did you flirt back?" The tone was threatening.

"No!"

"But he must have been hopeful. You chatted with him a long time."

"Jesus, were you timing him?"

"I was timing everyone, darling." He'd resented every man who'd spoken to her. He'd wanted to lock her away, keep her for himself alone, possess her in the most elemental way. An unthinkable concept. Until tonight.

"Okay, I'm done. That's way over the line."

He looked amused. "No sex, then?"

"No, damn it!"

With a proper balance of insolence and regret, he said, "If you're not interested in sex, maybe you could just go down on me."

"I'm sorry, I'm not one of your by-the-hour girlfriends. Jack yourself."

"But I don't want to."

"Good. Then we can leave."

"You're not dressed."

"I'll get dressed."

"You'd have to reach your dress first."

"Seriously, you can't be jealous of those men?"

"No, I just want to fuck you and you're giving me grief a hundred different ways."

She scowled at him. "Ask me about getting grief."

He almost smiled at her before he caught himself. "No one's ever complained before."

"Then it's time someone did."

He slowly exhaled, moved a few steps to the sofa, dropped on it like a rock, slid into a lounging pose, looked up at her from under the dark fringe of his lashes. "We seem to be at an impasse."

"Because you can't have your way."

"Or you yours. I might as well jack off. Throw me my shirt, will you?"

"Are you really?"

"Damn right." He held out his hand. "My shirt, please."

Walking over to the pile of his clothes, she bent, picked up the shirt, and brought it over to him.

"Thank you." Taking the shirt from her, he dropped it on his legs, circled his erection with his closed fist, and proceeded to slowly jack off. His eyes half closed, his right hand moving up and down in an easy rhythm, his left hand idly stroking his heavy testicles, his massive prick rose higher and higher.

She might not have existed; he was in another place behind his lowered eyelids, absorbed in the full blast of hot sensation, a half smile on his face.

Suddenly her breath was lodged in her throat, her gaze trained on each spiking expansion, each turgid swell of his huge erection. Clenching her thighs to contain the combustible frenzy within, the high-pressure jolts to her senses, her mind went white and empty save for the unclouded vision of Dominic's gigantic dick.

She squirmed at his next strong downstroke, felt the warm liquid ooze into her panties, was astonished to hear her soft, breathy moan, the sound so explicitly carnal she was appalled.

He heard it, knew the sound. His lashes lifted marginally. "Ask for it," he whispered, his fingers smoothly sliding downward.

"Please, Dominic."

"Please what?" His voice was hushed, his breathing raspy, his fingers deft, professional, up and down, up and down.

"Please give it to me," she said on a suffocated breath, every sexual nerve fueled and frantic, the hotspur throbbing inside her echoing in her ears.

"Go down on me."

"Afterward, please."

"*No, now.* And get rid of those," he said with a lift of his chin.

She hastily unhooked her bra, shoved a thumb under the waistband of her panties, wiggled her hips.

He whispered, "There's a good girl," and moved so she could reach him more easily. Smiling as she kneeled without looking at him, he quietly ordered, "You don't have to swallow. I'm going to come in you. Did you hear?" She was breathing hard, her gaze unfocused, her hot little sex controlling her brain as usual. Her appetite for fucking was really amazing.

He blamed the long two hours of watching her with

other men for spurring his hair-trigger urgency because she'd no more than lowered her head over his dick and filled her mouth full when he abruptly shoved her away. As she toppled backward, he dived after her, crushed her into the carpet, and plunged none too gently inside her.

She squealed.

He grunted.

And a moment later they both felt the same revelatory, unblemished wonder.

It was like reaching home after an endless journey.

Or finding safe haven from a storm.

Or perhaps finding love for those with an open mind.

Once ensconced in his own special paradise, Dominic's ransacking assault gave way to more rational impulses and he turned his attention to pleasing the woman in his arms. He kissed her gently, moved in her with delicacy and finesse, supplied her with multiple orgasms before indulging himself.

Pleasing her because it pleased him.

Several hot and heavy orgasms later, her eyes at half mast, her voice husky, Kate whispered, "You're worth every minute of trouble." They were back on the couch, the firelight flickering over their sweating bodies.

"Ummm," he said agreeably, concentrating on the exact depth of penetration before she made that hot little gasp.

Like that.

She didn't talk for some time, intent on the successive waves of heated ecstasy rolling through her body. Dominic wasn't interested in talking at all. Then utterly bewitched, nirvana within her grasp, she forgot what was expected of her and said, on a soft, breathy exhalation, "I love you," and knew she'd made a mistake even before he put his hand over her mouth, silencing her.

Bending his head, Dominic replaced his hand with his mouth, kissed her softly, passionately, his pulse racing, wanting to give her something when he couldn't give her that. And after the chaos stilled, he offered her a new kind of pleasure. A particular specialty of his that required a patient dick, good thigh muscles, and both his hands.

Very soon, Kate was panting again.

And life returned to normal.

A knock on the door momentarily arrested Dominic's rhythm. A fraction of a second, no more, then he dismissed the interruption and resumed his activity.

"Nick." Max's voice outside the door was a hissed stage whisper.

"Go away!" Dominic shouted. "Sorry," he murmured as Kate flinched, then returned his attention to her rapidly peaking orgasm, intent on sharing the moment.

When his phone rang a few moments later, Dominic was semi-collapsed on top of Kate, his weight largely resting on his forearms, but not entirely—his climax hurricane-force powerful, his breathing still labored.

He ignored the "Bring It on Home" ring tone.

Two minutes later, when Sam Cooke's voice again interrupted the heavy breathing in the room, Kate weakly murmured, "You should answer that."

Dominic shook his head, his damp hair a cool flicker across Kate's shoulder.

The third time his cell rang, he swore, mustered enough

energy to move, pull the phone out of his suit coat lying on the floor, and glance at the display. "Oh Jesus." Dropping a kiss on Kate's forehead, he eased out of her warm body and with a long-suffering sigh, pushed himself up off the couch. "I have to take this," he muttered. Walking over to the fireplace, he pushed answer and, staring into the flames, put the phone to his ear.

"Just wanted to let you know who you're pissing off," Max grumbled.

"I'll apologize tomorrow." Dominic spoke softly, preferring Kate not hear. She worried about things she shouldn't.

"The president took your side, believed the business bullshit, but Antonia's husband wasn't in the mood to be placated when his wife took offense."

"Don't worry about it. Tell Liv I'll make up Antonia's donation plus another couple mil. Are we good now?"

"Except for that meeting tomorrow. In your current don't-give-a-damn mood I didn't want you to forget."

"I already did. Reschedule for Monday."

"Eight major players are flying in for Christ's sake."

"I'm aware of that. Reschedule."

"Jesus, Nick. Ricci for one is going to be seriously pissed. You know how touchy he is."

"I'm aware of Ricci's temper. Last time. Reschedule. Monday at three. We'll be on *The Glory Girl* till then." He hit end, not in the mood for more advice. He did what he did because he could. He didn't want to think about why now, why her? Or dissect every nuance to hell and back with Max or anyone. Right now, he just didn't want these feelings to end.

Turning from the fire, he said, "How about a boat ride, baby? We'll get away from all this crap. A little peace and quiet, just us. Sound good?"

Kate looked up as he approached the couch, smiled. "Wherever you are sounds good to me."

He bent down and kissed her. "That's what I like to hear," he whispered, his breath warm on her lips. Standing upright, he said, "Let me make a few calls and we're out of here."

TWENTY

The next three days were heaven, or its equivalent in secular terms, bliss palpable, sensation off the charts.

They were alone on the ocean or as alone as one could be on a ninety-three-foot vessel with a crew of ten and a full staff in the kitchen. But they rarely saw anyone, the sailors practically ghosts, Danny sharing a drink with them the first evening and then largely keeping out of sight. Dominic's chef and sous chef supplied them with food on their erratic schedule without complaint. And when Kate and Dominic weren't in Dominic's stateroom screwing, they were wrapped in warm jackets and each other's arms, lying in a hammock on the highest deck.

The stars at night filled the sky, seemed close enough to touch, dazzled, shimmered, amazed, made one conscious of the puniness of man.

The transience of human activity.

The great beauty of the world.

Dominic's favorite song, "Bring It on Home," was usually playing softly in the background, the words casually fitting, sweetly appropriate, not the "I'm your slave" part, Kate realistically noted, but all the rest.

"See, I'm not the only man who wants to give a woman money and jewels," he whispered, humming along with the song, kissing her softly. "Or the only man who wants a woman like I want you."

"Or the only man who can do *other things* too," she said, miming the line from the song, arching up to kiss him again.

A slow-motion kiss that took the place of the million things she wanted to say to him and couldn't because he didn't want to hear them. About pragmatism and the sad ache of regret. About love and longing, about the shadow of fear that was so strong it was making her ears buzz. About the rising panic of losing him.

When she relaxed back into his arms once again, he gave her an odd look because her kiss had been different, baffling. Leaving him off balance. "Just so we're clear," he said, his gaze sharp, even in the dark. "As long as I'm the only man doing them to you, we're good."

"We're good. Tell me why you like that song?"

The world that he hadn't known had tipped, righted itself. The shark in him went back to sleep. He ignored that brief shift in his world. "Dunno. I just always have. It hits something somewhere. All the layers of white noise vanish, the jagged edges smooth."

She smiled. "You're a romantic."

"Yeah, right. How about it's just nice?"

"Nice like me?" she whispered, her smile close, sweet, tempting.

"Not quite that nice, baby," he said softly, leaning over to brush a kiss down her nose. "Nothing's that good."

It was Sunday night, 3:38 glowing bright green on the bedside clock, when Kate suddenly woke. The fact that

Dominic was gone must have wakened her. Anywhere else but in the middle of the ocean, she would have panicked, her unease about losing him having intensified as their holiday came to a close. She hadn't been able to make up her mind whether to stay or go. Dominic had been patient, not pressing her to make a decision. But life without him would be unbearable. Living with him as difficult. A dilemma with no clear answer. How much of herself would she have to give up? How important was her emotional and professional independence? Was a handful of days enough to know someone? Particularly someone like Dominic, who closed himself off from the world?

Confused, filled with doubt, she'd become increasingly clingy and weepy—like some lovesick fool.

Which in itself might be an answer.

Putting on a robe, she left the stateroom and, following the sound of a guitar, moved down the passageway.

Dominic was sitting with Danny high on the bow, both men dressed in jeans and T-shirts, as though the weather was balmy when it wasn't, both men playing guitars, several empty beer bottles on the deck at their feet. *The Glory Girl* had dropped anchor in a cove at sunset, the air was still, the ocean like glass.

Dominic looked up, saw Kate standing in the doorway at the stern, and stopped playing. He smiled and called out, "Would you like to come up?"

She didn't answer.

"I'll come down then. How about that?"

She nodded.

Rising, he handed his guitar to Danny. "Later," he said.

"Drink one for me." He walked across the deck, leaped down the steps to the deck below, and strolled across to Kate. "Hi, baby, couldn't sleep? Maybe I can help you out."

He was supersweet that night, like he'd been since they'd left Hong Kong, indulging her every whim, satisfying her desires with ravishment and delight, offering her pleasure with both tenderness and soul-stirring passion, exerting all his masterful sexual skills and talents to assuage her insatiable lust.

And his.

With morning, however, their holiday came to an end.

A bittersweet, melancholy time for Kate with the future uncertain.

His plans in place, Dominic viewed the day with delight, the beginning, as it were, of something uncommonly good. He was taking her with him. Period.

After *The Glory Girl* docked at noon, they were driven to Dominic's home on the Peak and once lunch was over, they went upstairs to dress for the meeting that had been rescheduled the night of the charity event. Dominic insisted Kate accompany him.

"You can sit out of the way. I just want to know you're there." He smiled at her. "I'm going nuts, as you know, so humor me. Do you want me to find you something to wear?" She hadn't followed him into his dressing room but was standing in the doorway.

"I shouldn't come, I'll be in the way."

"Not in the least. It's a big room. You can sit over by the windows. Or beside me if you wish," he added, smiling at her over his shoulder as he flipped through her clothes that had been hung in the wall of wardrobes. "I'd be pleased to have you sit beside me. How about this?" He held up an ivory wool suit with a short military-style jacket belted in green lizard, a slim skirt, and a pale green silk shell.

"Is that new?"

"I have no idea."

She still hadn't moved, other than the faint wrinkling of her brows. "Did you order more clothes for me?"

He smiled. "I might have. Look, I'd wrap you in sables if I could. Although fur is still PC in most places outside the States, so if you're interested, give me the word. "

"Are you trying to change the subject?"

"Desperately. This is my least favorite fight."

"Then you shouldn't keep ignoring me," she grumbled.

"I apologize," he said, moving toward her. "It's just fun to dress you. You look good in everything"—his voice softened—"or nothing. Come on, babe, give me a smile, put this on, and let's get this meeting over with. We've got better things to do."

She sighed. But she was deep in love, only content when he was near. "Will it take long?"

"I'll see that it doesn't. An hour at the most. Tomorrow we leave Hong Kong. You're coming with me. Don't give me any shit. You are. We can argue on the plane. But I need your game plan. You can key it in on my laptop at the meeting. Be demanding, then I won't feel guilty about abducting you."

"Is that what you're doing?" Maybe that's what she'd wanted all along; the decision taken out of her hands.

He ran his hand through his thick hair. "More or less. I figure if you can't make up your mind, I'll do it for you."

A flashing grin. "Decision-making is one of my major skill sets. Now do you want help or not?"

Not, she decided, considering the time and her inability to resist him.

But she liked the quiet domesticity, the sense of togetherness; she liked watching him. He was businesslike in his dressing like he was with everything else, his movements swift and sure, his ability to transform himself from casual jeans into the full trappings of CEO power in a few short minutes impressive.

Turning to her, he raised his brows. She was still in her jeans and sweater, although she was barefoot now. "We're going to have to get you a maid. I won't always be around to dress you. What the hell have you been doing?"

"Watching you."

"You've seen it all before, haven't you?" he said with male practicality that overlooked total infatuation and desperate longing.

"I just like being with you."

"Okay, that I understand. Try and get away, babe," He smiled. "And that's a total threat. I'm keeping you within touching distance. Now and always." He held out his hand. "Give me that suit. I'll help you."

Before the meeting began, Dominic escorted Kate to a red leather sofa near the window, opened his laptop, keyed in his password, brought up his e-mail, and said, "Write down all my directions, everything you want, everything you want me to do. I'll leave the provisions as my header so I'll see them every time I check my e-mail." He smiled. "Someone like me. I'm going to have to be reminded. I haven't had rules for a long time. Not that I'm complaining," he said quickly as she opened her mouth to speak. "Really, it's no worries. I'm in a hundred percent."

When the other executives arrived shortly after, he introduced Kate as an ace forensic accountant, explained that she'd been instrumental in recovering twenty million that had been stolen from him, that she was sitting in as an observer today.

She watched him as he proceeded to expound on the merits of his business investment in a company that would be mining rare earths in Greenland. He detailed the progress of their sample drill sites, qualified the state of the market for rare earths with definitive historical and projected trend line charts, explained that the investment would likely generate enormous profits for those buying in at the beginning.

He dominated the room. He was larger, younger, stronger, more handsome—but then he was all that with most everyone. In a group like the one around the table, she couldn't say he was more expensively dressed, but he was certainly more beautifully dressed, his dark, double-breasted, Savile Row suit tailored to perfection. He was lounging back in his chair—assured, commanding—one hand resting on the table, his strong wrist and vintage Cartier aviator watch visible below his crisp white shirt cuff.

She quickly looked away because all she could think about was how much she wanted him.

When he finished his presentation, he opened the discussion to questions, his answers succinct and technologically astute. He was civil to the witless, courteous to the venal, and was in the process of offering everyone a tour of the drill sites when Kate gasped.

He and everyone else looked at her.

"Excuse me," she murmured and, dropping her gaze, refocused on the picture on her laptop screen, her sudden paleness matching the ivory wool of her suit.

But Dominic had seen the tears in her eyes when she'd looked up. Quickly shoving his hand into his suit coat pocket, he pulled out his cell phone, glanced at the display. "Sorry, gentlemen, I have to take this call." He nodded at Max. "Max will reschedule the meeting." He scanned the men at the table, smiled tightly. "It's the Pentagon, gentlemen. I can't keep them waiting."

The moment the door closed on eight irate billionaires, Dominic dropped his phone, surged to his feet, closed the distance between himself and Kate, and spun the laptop around.

"Fuck." He dragged in air through his teeth, exhaled in a great rasp, kept his voice deliberately mild when he spoke. "It has nothing to do with you, with us. Nothing at all."

"I wish I hadn't looked," she whispered. An e-mail alert had come through while she was composing her idiotic list of demands and a window had popped up.

And there it suddenly was: another glossy beauty like the principessa spread-eagle on the red lacquer bed in the bedroom of the Garden House—nude, blindfolded, intricately tied in some bizarre rope pattern, clearly aroused; two other splendidly naked women were stroking her body, one with a feather fan, the other with the trailing ends of a silk braided whip. The e-mail read: "Thought you might like to see the Christmas pictures."

Pictures—plural—several more had been taken in what Kate recognized—by the floor—as Dominic's tai chi studio. Clearly the room had other uses; various apparatus were featured in the photos. All with women bound to them.

"I hadn't met you then. I'm sorry you saw those." He slowly exhaled. "That's over now. I mean it. It was a distraction, nothing more—utterly meaningless." He wanted to grab her, crush her to him, tell her he was wrong then and she was now. But he knew better. He stopped himself by clenching his fingers so hard, his nails drew blood. "I'll change my e-mail address so they can't reach me. Break off any contact. Jesus, don't cry. Please."

She wouldn't look at him. "I'm not crying," she said, hiccuppy and defensive, tears running down her cheeks.

Max stuck his head into the room, started to speak.

"Out," Dominic barked.

"I need a minute, Nick." Max's voice was as abrasive as Dominic's.

"Jesus Christ," Dominic spat. "Can't you see I'm busy?"

"It's important, Nick. Kate, would you mind?"

She kept her head down. "Go," she hissed.

"Don't leave," Dominic whispered.

She looked up then, her eyes chips of green ice. "Where the hell would I go?"

He felt an instant calm; he had time. "I'll be right back. And turn that damned thing off." He started to touch her, jerked his hand back. "Don't go anywhere."

*   *   *

"Let's take this somewhere else," Dominic muttered as he entered the adjacent anteroom, glancing at the two wide-eyed secretaries who were new since he was here last. New or not, they'd heard whatever his angry colleagues had said.

A few moments later, the two men were in an office with a view of the harbor, the door shut.

"Say what you have to say," Dominic rapped out, wiping his palms with his handkerchief. "Make it brief."

"You're the company, Nick. It doesn't run without you. You don't delegate or deputize anything major, there's no board of directors. Knight Enterprises is your baby. And you just jeopardized a thirty-billion-dollar deal for a piece of ass...don't scowl. You would have called it the same thing two weeks ago."

"But it's not two weeks ago, this is different, so fucking different that I don't care about thirty billion." *He wanted to say how dare you question me? But Max was more than an employee, he was a friend.* So Dominic got a grip on his temper, unclenched his jaw, and kept his voice level. "Katherine makes me happy, Max, and I'd given up on the feeling. I know that sounds trite, but maybe you'd understand if I said she has the power to heal. As for taking off time, I've done that before. Climbing, skiing, sailing, trekking in the jungle. Almost dying in the jungles of Borneo. I was in the hospital for two weeks that time." He glanced at his lacerated palms, crumpled the handkerchief, shoved it in his coat pocket.

"But you were still focused, Nick, on the phone right up

until they wheeled you into surgery. And right after. Roscoe said you were even running things from your yacht that year you were sailing around the world. Not like now. Call it what you will"—Max wasn't buying the hearts and flowers bullshit after having watched Dominic with women the last five years—"but you're acting like some horny kid, willing to throw away everything for"—he lifted his chin in the direction of the conference room—"her."

"Her name's Katherine," Dominic said in quiet rebuff.

"I'm just saying. Think about it."

"I will, thank you. We lost Ricci, I assume. Anyone else?"

"I'm not sure. You're lucky this is such a lucrative deal. Maybe none of them will punt away a chance at billions."

Dominic smiled. "Good. Then it might not be such an expensive piece of ass after all. Now if you'll excuse me, I have some apologizing to do. A helluva lot of apologizing. Give me a week at least before you reschedule. Katherine is agitated"—he grimaced—"and with good reason. I'm going to need a few days to calm her down."

TWENTY-ONE

An unmistakable pall lay over the evening, even though Dominic had abjectly apologized, Kate had politely accepted his apology, and they'd dined in the turret room on An's very best efforts. Seven courses, an appropriate wine for each course, two chocolate desserts for Kate, and nothing but charming conversation from Dominic.

She'd taken off her suit coat and shoes, he his suit coat and tie, and his shirt was open at the neck, the sleeves rolled up. But a tension hummed beneath the casualness of the scene and the well-mannered conversation.

After dinner as they shared a priceless Napoleonic brandy, Dominic showed her the model of his rocket and offered her the short course in rocketry if she was interested.

She was. Because she liked to see him so animated and engaged, she liked to watch him, his fine mouth, the electric blue of his eyes, his long, slender hands as he ran through the stages of liftoff, his broad-shouldered body as he leaned forward in his chair translating physics into simple terms.

Without a speck of pride she loved him even if he was the most shameless, amoral person in the world. Even if he'd only bring her grief. And she wanted him to touch her so much, she felt faint with longing.

"You're tired," he said suddenly, sitting back, smiling at her. "I get carried away. You should have stopped me."

"I like to hear you talk." She didn't mean for it to come out a whisper. Her face flushed.

He understood. "May I touch you?" He'd never asked that of a woman before, he'd never had to. When she didn't answer, he said, "Forgive me, I shouldn't have asked."

"I want more than just—sex...I want to know your thoughts, your feelings, how you—"

"I know. You can have whatever you want. Ask me and I'll tell you."

"Can you give up all...that—the women, the—"

"Yes, of course. I said I would. It's not a problem."

She held out her hand, her eyes wet with unshed tears. "Hold me."

He was out of his chair in a flash, she was in his arms a second later, and a second after that, he kissed her gently, in apology and gratitude.

In joy.

But much later that night, after they'd made love, after Kate had fallen asleep, gratified and content, Dominic lay awake—restless, something tight and urgent nudging the back of his brain, stealing his sleep.

He finally left the bed, walked next door to his study, and stood at the window, silhouetted against the glow of the city, his powerfully built gladiator's body, tense, coiled for battle. The full moon was like a tangerine-colored mirror in the sky, the brightly lit city laid out at his feet, the silence so complete the vague premonition that had been hovering at the back of his mind like some prophetic bird of prey broke cover.

Bleak and black and terrifying.

He wasn't surprised. Or not very surprised. Perhaps he'd always known the question lay ahead.

Could he share his life?

Had he ever?

Even with Julia, he'd never let her into all the hidden rooms, the dark corners of his soul. Her death had come too soon; he'd never quite reached that deluded point before he'd been plunged back into the vast, anonymous world.

A world that wasn't tepid or gray or equivocal. It was black or white, yes or no, win or lose. It was the only world he'd ever known.

And now he faced a different future—perhaps even children and real Christmases and acceptable emotions—nothing too raw or barbed or insulting. This brave new world had arrived after seven days or eight depending how he counted the virginal hours and dislocating shock waves.

And now he found himself close to panic, feeling as though he had a target on his back and someone was about to pull the trigger.

He took a deep breath, exhaled, took another.

Then he abruptly turned from the window, quietly walked back into the bedroom, picked up his cell phone from the bedside table, entered his dressing room, and threw on some clothes.

Dominic wasn't in the bedroom when Kate woke in the morning. She was relieved. She had a letter to write and needed privacy. Sitting down at a small writing table set in front of one of the windows, she pulled out a sheet of monogrammed paper from a red leather tray, picked up an expensive pen from a red leather canister, and began to pour out her heart to a man who might not even have a heart. Or if he did, it was numbed by cold indifference. Or perhaps placed with loving care in his wife's coffin. And what was left behind was an unblinking enigma of a man, ruthless, without borderlines, slippery as mist, beautiful, passionate, remote. And totally and irredeemably lovable.

It took her some time to decide on a salutation. Personal? Impersonal? Oozing her life's blood? She finally settled on something short and sweet and true.

Dear Dominic,

First, I want you to know that I love you. Right or wrong, deep down I do.

But I can't stay.

If I did, you'd take over my life—even if you didn't mean to. Or, more likely, because you did mean to. I can't lose myself completely—my will, my wits, my reason—because of you. Because of how you make me feel.

It's wonderful, beautiful, a hothouse fantasy come to life.

But in the end, it's madness.

And exhausting, fighting back all the time over every trivial thing. I'd die a little each day if I stayed. I wouldn't be the woman you want. And ultimately, you'd leave me anyway because that's what you do. How's that for cowardly? I wish I were braver.

We both knew it was complicated. But you don't give away anything; you're mysterious and unattainable, and selfishly, I want more.

So as much as I adore you, I'm not the one to melt your frozen heart.

She just signed her name because she'd already handed over her heart on the page. Sliding the letter into a monogrammed envelope, she sealed it, put it into her messenger bag, and went downstairs to find Dominic. She'd wait to give it to him. She wanted a last breakfast with him... so she could fill her memory bank against her melancholy future. She didn't kid herself that leaving him wouldn't break her heart.

Leo met her in the entrance to the breakfast room. "Good morning, Miss Hart."

"I'm looking for Dominic." She scanned the set table. "He hasn't been down for breakfast? Is he in his office?" The awkward pause should have been a clue, but she was so intent on her own revelation that she didn't immediately take notice.

"Dominic left Hong Kong early this morning, Miss Hart. He said you were welcome to stay here as long as you wish."

She suddenly felt faint; her rib cage was pressing all the air out of her lungs. "Is he...coming...back?"

"He didn't say, miss. Please"—Leo quickly pulled up a chair—"sit for a moment."

She sat, took a deep breath, looked up. Leo's face was expressionless, his gaze studiously blank, the perfect emissary. "When did Dominic leave?" She wished she hadn't sounded so plaintive.

"Shortly after three. He left a plane at your disposal when and if you chose to go back to the States. May I get you something to drink?" She was ashen. "Or some breakfast?"

"Thank you, no. I'll just sit for a moment."

He tactfully withdrew.

It all made sense now, Kate thought sadly. Dominic had been incredibly tender last night, gentle, considerate, obliging her in all things, offering her pleasure in such full measure, she felt as though she was lit from within, glowing with lust and love. He'd never once said, "No, or wait, or not just yet." He'd given her everything she wanted, needed. Until she'd finally panted, "No, no more...I can't."

And all the time he'd been making love, he'd been leaving her.

Max's phone call came through as Dominic's plane was taxiing into Qatar for refueling.

"You made the right decision, Nick."

"I don't want to talk about it," Dominic said curtly. "I'm in a fucking lousy mood."

"Are we still on for Paris next week?"

"Of course. Reschedule yesterday's meeting for next week in the Paris office. I'll be staying at the apartment in Paris for the foreseeable future. See that Liv gets a check for the Philharmonic. That's it." Dominic ended the call, held up his empty glass, waited impatiently for the steward to refill it, and once it was returned, drank down half the whiskey in one long swallow. Then he leaned his head back on the seat, shut his eyes, swore, and instantly opened them again.

She was always there, in his brain, on his retinas, the taste of her on his tongue. He had no expectation of sleep in the coming weeks; if he shut his eyes, she was smiling at him, tempting him, making him reckless, making him heedless of everything that mattered in his life. He'd been willing to jeopardize his company, or at least a good part of it, because of her. He'd almost gone off the deep end because of her. Missed meetings, pissed off people, hadn't looked at his e-mail in three days. Apologized more times than he'd ever apologized in his life. Fuck it.

He wasn't meant to have a normal life.

He didn't know what normal was.

But denials and disclaimers aside, he took out his phone a hundred times between Hong Kong and Paris, pulled up two photos and stared at them, thinking each time he should stop punishing himself and delete them. But he never did.

He'd taken a photo from the doorway of his bedroom before he left, wanting a memory of Katherine in his house, his bed.

The second photo was a zoomed-in close-up, the detail so good he wanted to touch her each time he looked at it.

Jesus Christ, life was complicated.

And fucking miserable.

Within the hour, Kate came back downstairs, carrying her overnight bag, and handed Leo the letter she'd written. "Please see that Dominic gets this. I think there's a cab outside for me." She left Hong Kong soon after, having paid an outrageous price for a nonstop ticket to New York, which was the closest she could get to Boston on short notice. But she wouldn't have flown on Dominic's plane if the apocalypse was imminent and his plane was the last one on earth after the shock of his leaving without so much as a goodbye. Or even a handshake. That forced her to smile, the thought of parting with a handshake after days of practically nonstop sex.

And he'd been good for something other than sex too—the salary he'd paid her was enough to keep her in comfort for a year. She'd earned it; she had no compunction taking it. But she deliberately left everything else behind, the clothes, the jewels, the matching shoes in every color of the rainbow, the lingerie, the sex toys he must buy in bulk.

It wasn't as though she hadn't always known what kind of man he was. She'd gone in eyes wide open. He was never going to hand her his heart; she wasn't sure he had one. And why should he commit to a woman when he could have any woman he wanted?

It would be convenient if she could hate him for leaving her before she could leave him. It would be even more useful if she didn't love him. But then, life wasn't perfect; it sucked you in or threw a curve or stacked the deck when you were naively admiring its perfection. Or in her case, ignoring reality with a man who could make you forget the entire world when he was making love to you.

She fought back tears constantly on her journey home. Dominic was always in her thoughts, her memory, her pitifully beating heart. He was a constant presence, an unflagging fantasy, a forlorn desire. One could be practical about whether or not a relationship would work, but that didn't mean your decision made you happy. Or even slightly happy. Or even in the same planet as happy.

She tried to read on the long flight, watched movies without seeing them, finally resorted to drinking. She arrived at Logan Airport in Boston on a commuter flight from New York twenty-six hours later, weary in body and spirit and more than slightly inebriated.

Which may have accounted for her explosive burst of tears when she found the pile of Hermès luggage in the middle of her living room floor. She wasn't sobbing because someone had broken into her home, nor was she lamenting the fact that privacy no longer existed. What made her collapse in tearful prostration was the note that had been left on top of the luggage. The heavy white stock bore the initials *DGK* center top in a dark blue modern font, the message written in a broad, heavy scrawl in matching dark blue ink.

Wear these sometime and think of me—of us.
Fondly,
Dominic

She finally stopped crying when she ran out of tears.

The next day, she even managed to smile the tiniest bit when she dragged her laptop onto her bed, booted it up, and checked her e-mail.

Dominic had responded to her letter, even though he shouldn't have. Even though he'd tried to talk himself out of answering her for the better part of the night. He didn't mention the part where she'd said she couldn't lose her wits and reason completely, or the part about how wonderful it

had been. Or the part about the madness. He didn't mention any of that because she was the clusterfuck in his head,
his burning temptation, his road to ruin and he understood.

He kept it simple:

> I like the part where you adore me, but that part
> about my frozen heart. Ouch. FYI as you can see
> above I've changed my personal e-mail address and
> my personal cell phone number. In case you ever
> want to call or write me.
>
> Miss you,
> Dominic

Then she acted like a mature, rational adult, opened the
bottle of Krug '96 that had been set on top of the luggage
pile in her living room *and* that she'd had the good sense
to refrigerate despite her monumental grief, and drank it
down for her breakfast at two o'clock.

Nana said, "You've been drinking," when she called her.

"I'm celebrating being back home."

"Did you enjoy yourself?" Nana had just received notice
by personal messenger of an anonymous gift of two million dollars for the local school. A well-dressed older man
had arrived in a limo two hours ago, introduced himself
as an attorney from a private educational foundation, and
informed Nana—over her coffee and homemade oatmeal
cookies that he had politely accepted when it was clear
that he would have rather gotten back into his limo and
returned to the Duluth airport—that the foundation was
donating the substantial sum to their tiny school...for con-

fidential reasons. Which was often the case with private foundations, he blandly explained. And she, Mrs. Roy Hart, had been designated administrator of the funds.

Since Nana hadn't been born yesterday or even the day before, and no one had ever bestowed such a magnificent sum on their backwater area school, she surmised that either things had gone really well in Hong Kong or they'd gone badly and the gift was in the way of reparations.

"I did enjoy myself. It was a good experience," Kate said, her voice neutral, or marginally neutral considering the bottle of champagne.

Not exactly a definitive answer. "No regrets, sweetie?"

"Not a single one."

"Why don't you come home for a few days," Nana suggested. "Rest a little after your busy two weeks abroad? I'll bring you breakfast in bed."

It took a fraction of a second for Kate to reply, her amorous breakfasts in bed with Dominic on *The Glory Girl* still vivid in her memory. "Maybe I will in a week or so," she said a shade too brightly. "I have to see about getting a job. I don't have to. I was really well paid, but sitting around doesn't appeal to me."

Poor baby, something was wrong. "I miss you, sweetie. So come as soon as you can. By the way," Nana said, hoping to lighten Kate's mood, "your pictures were a big hit at the bridge club. Steam was coming out of Jan Vogel's ears. You did good."

Kate laughed, liked that she could still laugh. Found it life-affirming that she could still laugh. And in homage to all those self-help articles in women's magazines that appear with great regularity because she wasn't the only woman scarred by love, she sat up a little straighter, which took an extra second or so after a bottle of champagne, lifted her chin, and said under her breath, *Fuck you, Dominic Knight!*

"I didn't hear you, dear."

"I just said I'll be home in a couple weeks, Nana. As soon as I check out my job offers. You know there are six companies that want me."

"You deserve all your success. You worked hard for it. Now remember to give me a little warning and I'll have hot caramel rolls waiting for you when you walk in the door."

"Umm...tempting." Kate blew out a breath, the thought of Nana's caramel rolls making her mouth water. "But I better look for a job first. Soon, Nana. I'll be there soon."

"I'm always here if you need something, sweetie. Just give me a call anytime, if you want to talk or you're at loose ends or bored."

"Will do. Thanks, Nana."

Kate put away her phone a moment later, lay back on her pillow, and felt her restlessness lessen, the tumult in her brain mellow out. Nana was her rock, her source of unconditional love, a best friend, a shoulder to cry on. The most tolerant person she knew—besides Gramps. He'd always said he'd killed so many people and so many people had tried to kill him that he never sweated the small stuff.

Everything was small if you were still alive.

Which clearly put Dominic into perspective, she decided. She'd enjoyed his company, the two weeks had been beyond fabulous. But it was over; her life would go on very nicely without him—thank you very much.

She even half believed it.

She believed it enough to e-mail him back.

Thanks for the number. It's good to be home. Miss you too.

How totally adult was that?

Casual, supercasual.

She did a quick fist pump, threw back her covers, and, leaping out of bed, debated what food she wanted delivered. She didn't have to worry about Dominic scowling if she ate nothing but junk food.

It was a cardinal act of liberation, she decided sometime later, lying among the debris of fast food wrappers and boxes scattered on her bed, stuffed with nonnutritious, highly processed, additive-clogged food.

She was moving on with her life.

Can't wait to find out what's next for
Kate and Dominic?

See the next page for a preview of

ALL HE NEEDS,

the next installment in the All or Nothing Trilogy.

ONE

Dominic stood outside Nana's door, waiting for someone to answer his knock. It was cold in northern Minnesota. He should have considered the weather before he left Morocco; he was dressed in jeans, a short-sleeved T-shirt, and sandals. The car he rented at the Duluth airport had been warm, so he hadn't noticed until he was standing in the wind on this porch overlooking a lake that was still covered with ice.

The door suddenly opened.

"I'm not giving the money back if that's why you're here," the elderly woman snapped.

Dominic smiled, thought of Kate, knew where she'd learned to be outspoken. "Obviously you know who I am."

"You hide that private foundation real well. It took me more than twenty hours to sift through all the shadow companies before I found your name on a document." She smiled. "Love the Web. Opens up the whole world even to people who live in the sticks." She opened the door wider. "Come on in. You must be here for a reason and"—she glanced at his sandaled feet—"you're not dressed for the weather."

"It was warm when I got on the plane."

"What are you, a three-year-old kid?" she said over her shoulder, leading him down a hallway.

"I had a lot on my mind, Mrs. Hart."

"Call me Nana. Everyone does. At least you have an excuse. I suppose what you had on your mind was Katie."

"Call me Dominic and yes, she's been on my mind."

"I have a cousin named Dominic. It's a pretty common name up here. Have a seat." She waved him to a chair in a living room that hadn't changed since the eighties. A hodgepodge of upholstered furniture, nothing matching, framed photos everywhere: mostly Katherine—with her trike, bike, motorcycle—his brows went up at that—high school graduation, the prom—he scowled at the good-looking kid standing beside her—two recent ones with her smiling on campus; one or two of Nana, one of a man in uniform he assumed was Roy Hart, Gramps to Katherine, several that might be Katherine's mother; the resemblance was strong.

"I was wondering if I'd see you," Nana said, sitting down opposite Dominic in a matching Barcalounger. "Thanks, by the way, for the money. I've already told you I'm not giving it back if that's why you're here. With all the cuts in public education, the district needs the money. I didn't mention it to Katie either. There was no reason to tell her. She's not here, if that's why you came, and I'm not telling you where she is."

He knew where she was. That wasn't why he was here. "I was wondering how she's doing."

"How do you think she's doing? A young handsome man like you with bags of money. You'd turn any young girl's head. Leave her alone. You're out of her league."

"No, I'm not."

"Then you choose to be."

Silence. Then he said, "I'm not sure about that."

"Too long a pause, my boy. My baby girl needs some-one who doesn't have to think about loving her."

Dominic visibly flinched at the word *love*.

"There, you see. You can't do it."

"I'd like to try."

"Then tell her."

"She won't talk to me."

"Smart girl," Nana said, her gray perm stirring with her brisk nod. "She was unhappy for quite a while. She's bet-ter now if you really want to know. If you want to help her, you'll leave her alone. She'll get over you. You're not the only good-looking man in the world."

He was pleased to hear Kate was fine; he was dis-pleased to hear she was fine without him. But just talking about her made him happy, so he smiled and said, "She's been doing well in her new business, I hear."

Nana scowled. "Don't try and charm me. I'm an old lady. I've seen it all."

"I'd like to talk about her if you don't mind."

Blunt, honest, a quiet humility in his gaze. "Would you like a drink? You look a little peaked."

"It was a long flight."

"Come downstairs, I'll give you a little pick-me-up. My husband, Roy, made my still years ago when he came back from Nam. He needed something to take his mind off—well, you know what went on over there. He showed me everything I know about making vodka and mine's damn good if I do say so myself."

"No problems with law enforcement?" Dominic followed

her down the stairs to the basement. She was thin and spry at seventy-five, taking the stairs with a little spring in her step.

"I know the sheriff, and his father and grandfather for that matter, and they know me. I give 'em a few bottles now and then. Everything's copacetic. Sit over there at that table. I'll get us a drink. Blueberry okay with you?"

He almost smiled, remembering his mother's face when he'd brought up Nana's hobby at lunch that day in Hong Kong. "Blueberry would be just fine," he politely replied.

Two drinks later, after Dominic had asked Nana about Roy, about Kate as a child, about small-town living, which was like an alien universe to him, after he'd heard about the new roof on the gym thanks to his gift and the eight teachers they'd been able to hire back with five-year contracts, Nana set her glass down, speared him with her gaze, and said, "You must have set Katie up in business."

"Not personally. Six times removed. I've been able to send a few clients her way, but her success is her own. I have nothing to do with it."

"She liked the flowers you sent when she opened her office. Purple irises, I heard. Three or four baskets."

It took him a fraction of a second to answer, the room in the Garden House suddenly too vivid, rocking his world. "I'm glad she liked them."

"She's making lots of money."

"That's the idea."

"Why doesn't she know you've done this for her? It's clear as day."

"You raised her not to be cynical. She's remarkably

innocent despite her intellectual accomplishments. It's one of her great charms."

"Hmpf. From an arch cynic."

"I didn't have the advantage of her upbringing. She was fortunate."

"So you're saying money doesn't buy happiness."

"Pretty much."

"And you're wondering if she can fill that void for you."

"I don't know. She's just on my mind a lot. I thought I'd come and see how she was doing, that's all. I should go. I've taken up enough of your time." He came to his feet.

"I won't ask you to promise me you won't pester her because I can see that you will. But she's like her grandpa. You mess with her, she fights back."

He smiled faintly. "I'm aware of that."

"You mess with her and *I'll* make trouble for you. Roy came back from Nam a little bit crazy and some of it rubbed off. Just so you know."

"I have no intention of hurting her."

Nana softly exhaled. "I don't envy you. You don't know what you want."

His smile was sweetly boyish. "I'm trying to figure it out." He pointed at the bottle on the table. "If you ever want to go into business, let me know. Your vodka is first class. I'm always looking for new investments."

She smiled. "You trying to buy your way to my grand-daughter?"

He laughed. "I'm not so foolish. Katherine didn't care about money. I'm assuming she learned that from you."

Nana met his gaze. "Life's about almost everything *but*

money. I'm not saying you don't need enough to keep a roof over your head, but after that"—she shrugged—"it's about the people you love. That's what makes life worth living. Sorry about the lecture. I'm an old schoolteacher. It's in the blood."

"I don't mind. And let me know what more you need for the school. I mean it. My educational foundation is one of my pet projects. Let me give you my cell phone number."

"I already have it."

Dominic's brows shot up.

"Where do you think my baby girl learned to love computers? There's no privacy left in the world. I don't have to tell you that."

Dominic laughed. "In that case, give me a call if you need something."

"Or if I hear something from Katie?"

Kate would have recognized that small startle reflex. "I'd like that," Dominic said a moment later. "I like to know how she's doing. Thanks for the drinks and conversation."

Nana stood on the porch and watched the wealthy young man walk through the snow in his sandals, get into his rental car, and drive away.

She'd never met anyone so alone, she thought.

ABOUT THE AUTHOR

C. C. Gibbs is the pen name of *New York Times* bestselling author Susan Johnson. She lives in the Midwest and at times in Northern California, is married with three children, and considers the life of a writer the best of all possible worlds. Bringing characters to life allows her imagination full rein, while the creative process offers fascinating glimpses into the machinery of the mind. And last but not least, researching anything, but particularly a book like ALL HE WANTS— thank you Google—is great fun!

Love a great erotic romance?
Don't miss these titles from Grand Central Publishing!

Taken
by Kelli Maine

Slow Surrender
by Cecilia Tan

Haven of Obedience
by Marina Anderson

Bound to Please
by Lilli Feisty